Confess*i*ons

of a

Call Center Gal

a novel

Giffin Press
giffinpress.info
ISBN 978-0615484280
Printed in the United States of America

Confessions

of a

Call Center Gal

a novel

Lisa Lim

for Bella and Mia

One

How on earth did I wind up stuck here in Pocatello, Idaho, a town where every other vehicle is a Ford pickup truck and the wind blows faster than said trucks?

Just yesterday, I spotted a turnip truck bumping along a dirt road and was reminded of the country bumpkin saying, "I didn't just fall off the turnip truck."

But here in Pocatello, my response to that would be, "Or did you? In fact, I'm pretty sure I *saw* you roll off one."

But I digress.

I say again, how did I end up here?

Where do I even begin? Let me pause, rewind and paint a picture. It was the best of times, and it was the worst of times. I was a recent college grad, starry-eyed and optimistic, ready to take on the world of print media.

Instead, I'd watched the fate of print media crumble right before my very eyes. Newspapers, magazines and journals suffered casualties. The *Chicago Tribune* had filed for bankruptcy protection.

I'd applied at every print media outlet within a thousand mile radius, even the obscure ones like the *Coon Valley Times*, *Ozaukee Press* and *Sheboygan Suns*.

Alas, I'd never heard back.

Or worse, I'd receive some version of this lame reject letter:

Dear Applicant, (*Pssh! They didn't even bother personalizing it*)

Although we were impressed with your background and experience, we have decided to pursue other applicants who more closely reflect the requirements for the position (*You are not good enough for us*). We wish you well in your employment search (REJECT! *stamped on my forehead*).

Literally hundreds of these hate mail missives had taunted me. I had found myself spiraling into self doubt and began questioning my choices, my career path. My life had become stagnant, and I was on the verge of depleting all my savings.

It was in this jaded and broke time in my life that Karsynn, my BFF from the University of Wisconsin, had called me again. I checked the caller ID and sighed. I didn't want to answer, but I knew she'd just keep on calling and calling until she got an answer to the question she'd asked yesterday and the day before. And the day before that.

"Hey Kars," I said, picking up on the fourth ring.

"Wassup!" she boomed.

"Nothing," I replied listlessly, cradling the phone on my neck while I moped around the house.

The dreaded question came right away. "Got a job?"

"Nope," I grunted. "No job . . . you?"

"Hell no!" she scoffed. "Um, haven't you been watching the news? Unemployment is at ten percent! Nobody's hiring, so don't take it personally. I'm not."

I heaved out an explosive sigh. "This really sucks."

"I know. Heck, the way things are going now, I'll end up jobless and single for the rest of my life, mooching off my mom, living in her basement."

"And you'll turn into one of those crazy cat ladies who hoard a gazillion strays."

"Uh-huh. One day you'll read about me in the news— Karsynn Alayna Higginbotham, found dead in basement, body half eaten by rats."

"Nope," I said and pointed out, "With all your stray cats, there wouldn't be any rats."

"True, true." She barely contained a snicker. "I'd be the best Crazy Cat Lady in town. I'm slowly accumulating more cats."

"You are?"

"Yep!" A tone of smugness squeezed into her voice. "But not real cats though, just fake ones from my Crazy Cat Lady board game."

"Um . . ." I paused for a beat . . . "They *make* such a thing?"

"Yes and it's a riot!" She squealed with delight. "The whole goal of the game is to collect more cats than your competitors."

"Well, d'oh!"

"Hah! You mock me, but I swear you'd love it, too. The squares on the board say things like *Find a stray cat at the grocery store*—add one cat. And there are wild cards, but guess what? They're called wild cats!"

"Karsynn," I said mildly, "you sound a little too excited about this board game. Are you bored?"

"Bored outta my freakin' mind," she groaned in affirmation. "I have no job, no money, no friends . . ."

"You've got me," I soothed.

"You know what?" she said after a pregnant pause. "I was just thinking . . . why don't you come out here and see me? You could use a mini vacation!"

I almost dropped my phone.

Pocatello wasn't exactly my idea of a vacation spot. In fact, it wasn't even on my radar.

"C'mon," she pleaded, "come visit me. It'll be fun. I can show you around Spudsville, and we can hang out and watch TV, just like old times."

Kars and I had been roommates in college, and on many dateless nights, we found ourselves holed up in our lava lamp lit dorm room, happily watching the tube. And we never fought over the remote because we watched all of the same shows.

All of them.

That is a bond that we share 'til today. Even though we're miles apart, we still watch the same TV shows . . . and gaze at the same moon, of course.

"So what do you say, Maddy?" Karsynn prodded, summoning me from my thoughts.

"Well," I hesitated, "why don't you come visit me in Chicago?"

"I'm broke," she whined.

"I'm broke, too."

"Well, I'm broke-r," she retorted.

After briefly mulling it over, I folded. "Oh, okay. I'll come out and see you."

"Yes! You could sound a little more excited, you know. Don't you miss me?"

I smiled in spite of myself, missing her already. "I do."

The very next day, I'd packed up my bags, loaded up my relic of a Subaru and clunked it clear across the country to her hometown of Pocatello, Idaho.

And I haven't left because I've scored a job interview!

Holy Crappity Cripes! Believe it or not, there are jobs in this Godforsaken place.

Karsynn's mom, Janis, works at a call center for Lightning Speed Communications. It's a DSL *and* cell phone provider, which gives it a double-edged sword, and when Janis had informed us that her company was hiring, our jaws literally dropped.

Eventually, I managed, "But Miss Higginbotham, with the economy like this, most companies are cutting back. And they're certainly not hiring."

Janis patted my knee in a motherly fashion. "Well, sugar, no matter how bad the economy is, and no matter how broke folks are, they will always feel like they *need* their cell phones and their high speed internet access. Even janitors have cell phones. Heck, I even have one, and I'm broke. Anyway, they're hiring customer service reps. Pay starts at twelve dollars per hour, and you can apply on their website. And don't forget to put me down as a referral so I'll get my five hundred bucks."

Fast forward to present—Lightning Speed Communications is where I shall have my first job interview.

And that is why I'm *still* stuck here in The Valley of Potatoes.

Tweedle dee, tweedle dum, I'm twiddling my thumbs, eyeing the life-sized poster on the wall, emblazoned with a mustard yellow lightning rod, which I presume to be the company's logo.

The caption reads: *Lightning Speed Communications, Because Speed Matters.*

Leaning back against the club chair, I anxiously await my name to be called.

Last night, Karsynn and I burned the midnight oil prepping for this interview by googling sample interview Questions and Answers, and I'm feeling pretty confident because I know exactly what they'll ask me:

1) *What are your strengths?*

I'll give an answer that mentions these essential key words: team player, excellent communication skills, multitasker, learn on the fly, dedicated and motivated.

2) *What are your weaknesses?*

Easy. I'll give some lame lie about how I'm such a perfectionist, that I *must* always go back and double check my work to make sure everything looks perfect. I know—*lame*.

But then Kars and I decided that the both of us can't give the same answer. So we came up with a solution. Karsynn's answer will run somewhere along these lines:

"Well, I used to have a problem saying 'no' to people. Now, however, I prioritize my days, thus allowing my excellent time management skills dictate when I can truly say 'yes' or 'no'."

Isn't that brilliant?

Easy peasy. Kars and I are going to nail this interview.

Abruptly, a stout, squat man sporting a military buzz cut emerges from the conference room.

He glances down at his note pad. "Miss Madison Lee?"

That's me, that's me! My heart pounds and my stomach lurches.

Karsynn shrieks, "That's you, that's you!"

Leaping to my feet, I smooth down the wrinkles on my skirt and step forward. "Hi, I'm Maddy." I thrust my hand forward and eyeball him.

"Victor Petraeus," he replies in a stern and detached manner.

"Nice to meet you, Victor." I pump his hand heartily.

Hah! Let there be *no* mistake that I give weak, wet-fish handshakes. Research has revealed that a firm handshake is the key to an interview's success, as it sets the tone for the rest of the interview. That and constant eye contact are essential, hence, the eyeballing.

Awkwardly, he extracts his hand from my deathly grip and gestures. "Right this way, Miss Lee."

So far so good.

I walk into the conference room and hear the door click shut behind me. After a brief and polite banter about things I can't remember, he whips out a thick binder and gets right down to business. "Okay, Miss Lee, let's get started." He clears his throat. "Describe a situation in which you had to think and act quickly. How did you handle the situation and what was the outcome?"

What the HELL? What happened to strengths and weaknesses?

I blink. Several times.

My whole body reverberates in shock as I try to maintain eye contact, but fail miserably.

A long uncomfortable silence ensues.

{{{{{{{{Crickets Chirping}}}}}}}}

I draw a blank, barely able to form a coherent thought. Feeling numb, disconnected, and at a complete loss, I find myself on the verge of hyperventilating.

Just keep breathing, Maddy, I coach myself. In. Out. In. Out. *Come on Maddy, think. Think.*

After racking my brain, I say, "There was this one time—"

Victor nods and gives me a tentative smile.

Encouraged, I continue, "Well, I was babysitting my grandma's poodle, Fifi, when all of a sudden Fifi went into a violent seizure. She was frothing at the mouth and thrashing wildly all over the place." After a brief pause, I add, "It was really traumatizing."

Victor's expression is unreadable and he's madly scribbling away in his binder.

I venture, "Immediately, I dialed 911 and when the operator explained, in no uncertain terms, that they don't respond to animal emergencies, I did not panic. I remained calm and asked if she could kindly give me the phone number to the nearest EV."

Victor looks up from his binder and gives me a blank stare.

"Um, that's short for Emergency Vet . . . err, just in case you were wondering."

He motions for me to continue.

"And so I called the clinic, got directions, threw Fifi into my car and drove like a mad woman to the EV," I gab, hearing the hysteria in my own voice.

Catching myself, I quickly backpedal. "But, I should point out that I *did* drive responsibly. *Yesireee* I did. No reckless driving or speeding on my part. When I said I drove like a mad woman, it was merely a figure of speech." I let out a shrill laugh.

In reality, it was pedal to the metal. I floored the gas all the way to the EV while Fifi lay comatose in the back seat.

Victor doesn't laugh. His eyes are hard as he stares at me deadpan.

The seconds tick by. Oh God! I'm completely losing it.

Taking a deep breath, I press on, "Once we arrived at the EV, Fifi was immediately whisked off and put on some anti-seizure medication."

Victor is still mute and madly scribbling in his binder. "And what was the outcome?" he asks without looking up.

"Well, they were able to stabilize Fifi for an hour, in time for my grandma to arrive. But-but," I break off, bite my inner lip and swallow hard.

"But what?" he asks in a cold voice.

"Fifi . . . um, she eventually died that same night," I mutter softly, ridiculously close to tears.

Victor stops writing and looks up. "I'm sorry for yours and your grandmother's loss."

I nod meaningfully at him. Alas, he has a heart.

Alas not!

Snapping back into business mode, he attacks me with a rapid-fire barrage of outlandish questions:

"Give me an example of a time when you had to deal with a difficult co-worker or fellow student on a project. How did you handle the situation? What were the outcomes?"

"Tell me about a time when you had to persuade someone to see your point of view. What tactics did you use? What were the outcomes? What did you learn?"

"Describe a time when you were assigned a task but were provided little direction on how to complete the task. What steps did you take to complete the task? What was the outcome?"

My brain is aching.

No, scratch that. My brain is *hemorrhaging* as I try to come up with answers that make sense. But Victor doesn't stop and the questions keep whizzing at me like poisoned arrows.

Feeling woozy, I place a clammy hand to my forehead to quell the throbbing ache.

I struggle and fumble through it all while Victor just keeps on writing everything down in his stupid binder.

My scrambled brain is screaming, "Enough!"

One hour later—though it feels more like eons later to me—the appalling interrogation is finally over.

Phew. I sag with relief.

"We'll call you in about a week after your background check goes through," he informs me in a brisk voice.

I nod with my head hunched down.

Defeated, battered and bruised, I wobble out of the war zone, my jelloid legs barely holding me up.

Kars is in my face all at once. "How'd it go?"

Frazzled to bits and a complete basket case at this point, I say dazedly, "I think I bombed it."

"Gak!" she blurts in a panic. "I think I'm next."

That very second, the door creaks open and General Petraeus' square head pops out. "Miss Karsynn Higginbotham?"

I shoot her a look of doom and she shoots me back a look of gloom as she's marched into Guantanamo Bay.

Two

I don't mean to toot my own horn, but TOOT!!! TOOT!!! We got the jobs! And Lord only knows how. Either Karsynn and I had aced our interviews, or Lightning Communications is just really desperate. Whatever the case, I'm not complaining.

Kars fiddles with her iPod and soon ABBA's *Dancing Queen* is blaring from the speakers. Bouncing up and down, we pound our jubilant fists in the air and break into our signature celebratory dance. It involves a shimmy, a jiggle, a wiggle, and a smack on the tush.

Today, we celebrate and tomorrow we start our first day of a six-week long training. I know. *Six weeks!*

Apparently, there's a *lot* to learn.

Kars and I have no sense of direction. Although we arrive at the call center fifteen minutes early, it takes us an eternity to locate the training room. We flounce around like two headless chickens, dodging through hallways, trying to orient ourselves, and half an hour later, we find it!

Wheezing and panting, we creep into class. As I cut across the floor, this dreamy looking guy catches my eye.

He's smolderingly gorgeous. He's so incredibly hot that clouds seem to part, and he radiates from within like Helios the Sun God. I guess Greek mythology serves a purpose after all. I even hear a choir of angels singing. And a string quartet playing, with several harps strumming fluidly in the background.

Miraculously, despite the fact that I'm lost in my own ancient Grecian musical odyssey, and in my own thoughts of the Sun God, I somehow manage to make my way to the back of the classroom, straight into the empty seat right next to *him*. Score!

Kars plops down next to me, oblivious to his beauty. She only fancies men with all the B's—big, butch, burly, buffed, and with bulging biceps a.k.a. beefcakes extraordinaire.

I prefer my men lean and tall, with sculpted features. Kars calls them pretty boys, but I beg to differ. They're just more evolved and look less like apes.

"Class," a petite, pasty blond guy calls our attention. "I think everyone is here now. I'll be passing out this sheet of paper. Please write your name down so I know you're present. My name is Glenn Bland and I'll be your trainer for the next six weeks."

I have no idea what transpires after that as all my energy is focused on that piece of paper. I watch it pass from hand to hand, and finally into the hands of the Greek God.

After jotting down his name, he turns to me. "Here," he says, arm outstretched.

"Thanks." I reach for the sheet of paper.

For a brief second, our eyes lock and I feel myself going weak in the knees.

Swoon. He's even better looking up close.

He has gorgeous green eyes, as green as the Chicago River on St. Patrick's Day. Before writing down my name, I scan the paper for his . . . Mika Harkett.

Hmm, sounds foreign. I wonder where he's from.

Kars nudges me. "Pay attention. Be a sponge. Soak it in."

She's right. I don't want to be thrown into shark infested waters only to flail away and drown. I need to learn how to swim now. Right now, as a matter of fact.

So for the first hour, I listen intently to Glenn, hanging raptly onto his every word as he drones about T1 and T3 lines, optical carriers—OC12, OC3, routers, networks, internet protocols, error messages, covering every mundane detail under the sun.

I find myself yawning appallingly, trying hard to cover my gaping mouth. Glenn's voice is soothing; hush and velvety, like a lullaby. By the second hour, I'm dozing off and Kars is leaning against me, miles away in snooze land. Her mouth hangs open and drool seeps out, sopping my hair.

Gently, I extricate myself from the drool monster and rub my temples. Oh God. How the hell am I supposed to survive through six grueling weeks of this mind numbing crap?

Then out of nowhere, Glenn clears his throat. "Now if you'll get together in groups of four, we're going to do some fun exercises to wake you guys up."

I jolt Kars awake from her siesta. She yawns and stretches out like a Siamese cat. "What's going on?" she asks groggily.

"Groups, we need to get into groups."

Mika turns to me. "Can we join you guys?"

"Sure!" I flash him a bright smile.

Our team huddles in a circle, and I notice the *other* girl for the first time. She's a gorgeous, willowy, blond überbabe, oozing the sex appeal of a Victoria's Secret model.

Wait. I think they're called Victoria's Secret *Angels*.

We make our introductions.

Kars just grunts her name and I say coolly, "I'm Maddy."

"Mika," he says with a casual nod.

And in a girly, high-pitched ring, the Victoria's Secret Angel chimes, "My name iz Ingeborg."

Whoa! She sings like a nightingale, but what a name!

Meanwhile, Kars is making a highly unsuccessful attempt to suppress a snort. I studiously ignore her, trying my best to be gracious to our newfound friends.

I decide to make some small talk. "So, Mika, where are you from?"

"Belgium," he replies with a faint accent.

Kars pipes in with her big mouth, "Hey, you guys make the best chocolates ever!" She pauses for a beat and then adds, "Or is it waffles?" Suddenly she has an epiphany and answers her own dim witted, asinine question, "Oh, I know! You guys make the best Belgian chocolate waffles!"

I make an apologetic grimace.

God. Kars can be so embarrassing at times.

I turn to the überbabe. "Where are you from, Ingeborg?"

"I'm from Pazardzhik, vhich iz in zouthvest Bulgaria," she singsongs sweetly.

Instinctively, I shoot Kars-the-loose-cannon a quelling look.

Uh-oh. I can see the wheels whirring about in her head, but before I can intercept, Kars blurts, "Bulgur wheat!"

Ingeborg squints and shoots Kars a peculiar look.

Thankfully, Glenn stops by our group and briskly hands out four sheets of paper. "Guys, I want you all to work together and figure out these brain teasers."

After taking a minute to study it, I glance at my teammates. "Okay, first one—Hamlet Words. Anybody?"

Karsynn yawns and bats her eyelids like she's not remotely interested. I'm pretty sure she knows the answer but she just can't be bothered. I, on the other hand, have a man I want to impress. I need to bowl Mika over with my wit and intelligence.

I jerk my head at Ingeborg, but she looks lost in space.

Mika shrugs. "Sorry, I don't know the answer either."

"Okay then, how about . . . a play on words?" I eye my teammates, trying to gauge their responses.

They nod approvingly, and so I jot down the answer.

I move on to the next teaser. "Second one. *Hmm,* there's just nothing there."

I get two blank stares and another big yawn from Kars.

"Let's see, how about . . . a blank slate? Or *tabula rasa?*" I suggest.

Ingeborg gives me a puzzled look, as if I had just been speaking ancient Sanskrit. "Vhat did you say? Did you speakity Spanish?"

"*Tabula rasa?*" I repeat. "No, it's Latin for 'blank slate'."

Ingeborg shakes her head. "Szorry, I don't gezt it."

"It's the concept of a young mind that hasn't yet been affected by experience," I find myself explaining.

"Yep, learned that in my psych class," Karsynn quips with a scholarly nod. "The whole nurture versus nature thingamajig."

"Kars," I say in a teasing voice. "Why thank you for gracing us with your presence."

She ignores my jab and tilts her chin at Ingeborg. "Do you want to hear more about this whole *tabula rasa* theory?"

"No!" I say a little too quickly. "Let's get back to the exercise, shall we?" I coax, giving her a tight-lipped smile. If I allow Kars to go on with her psychobabble, we'll never see the light of day.

Kars had been a Psych major in college, which is pretty ironic since she's quite possibly the nuttiest girl I know. Her nickname back then was 'psycho-bitch,' which she naively accepted as a compliment.

She'd thought it was due to her 'mad skills' in psychoanalyzing. But really, she'd got that nickname because she freely doled out her psych advice to anyone who'd listen. And as her BFF and roommate, I was *forced* to listen.

Seriously, I couldn't wait for Kars to get her Psych diploma so I could call her a *certified* lunatic.

I steer Karsynn back to the task at hand, and in ten minutes, we're done! All around us, the other teams are still hard at work.

"Maddy, you're pretty good at this," Mika remarks.

I flip my hand in a *oh-think-nothing-of-it* gesture, but inside, I'm basking in his praise.

Twenty minutes later, Glenn goes over all the answers with the class, and our team slays the competition.

For the grand prize, we are each awarded a Kit Kat bar.

Mika takes a bite out of his candy bar and I catch him watching me with an unreadable expression on his face.

I look away.

After class, Kars confronts me. "All right, Miss Flirty Pants, what's going on with you and Mr. Belgium?"

"Nothing," I say innocently.

Kars is too perceptive. "Maddy! Don't play dumb with me."

My face twists into a Cheshire cat grin. I find myself bubbling and fizzing with joy.

Just then I spot Mika and Ingeborg holding hands as they make their way across the parking lot. They look intimate. He whispers something in her ear and she laughs, nuzzling against his chest.

POP! The bubbles burst and the smile drains from my face.

"I guess Mr. Belgium is taken," Kars states the obvious.

I stare forlornly at the beautiful couple. "Guess so. Anyway, who am I kidding? I can never compete with Ingeborg. She's so *organic-ly* and *rustic-ly* beautiful. Like a willowy model strolling barefoot through a field of wildflowers. Me? I'm just plain ol' boring Maddy."

"You're cute!" she bleats. "You are. You look like a pretty Dutch milkmaid. In clogs. Milking a cow in a red barn."

"Thanks Kars," I say with a trace of sarcasm. "I feel so much better now knowing that I look like a dowdy milkmaid."

She thumps my back. "Just kidding. Actually, you look a little like *whatsherface*, that chickadee from *500 Days of Summer*."

"I wish . . ." I sigh wistfully.

My gaze follows the couple and I catch Mika planting a quick kiss on Ingeborg's bee-stung lips. "She's a knockout. Heck, she even puts Gisele Bündchen to shame."

"Well at least you have a prettier name than her. Jeez Louise, Ingeborg? What the hell were her parents thinking? They were naming their *daughter* for Pete's sake, not an *android*. C'mon, what'd they name her brother? Cyborg?"

"It's probably a pretty name in Europe . . . just lost in translation here."

Suddenly, Karsynn lowers her voice and her demeanor turns dark and sinister. "Bwah ha ha ha. My name is Igor Draganov, descendant of Ingeborg Draganov and I VILL *BREAK* YOU!" she intones in a heavy Russian accent.

Like mean schoolgirls, we explode into a fit of giggles.

Karsynn drapes her arm around my shoulder. "You know, I've always wanted to say that."

We set off down the pavement, tripping merrily over tiny cracks on the sidewalk. *Ah* . . . thank goodness for best friends.

The next several weeks of training seem to fly by. Kars, Mika, Ingeborg and I continue to sit in the same row, and the four of us have developed an easygoing, relaxed sort of comradeship.

In spite of myself, Ingeborg has quickly grown on me. She can be a tad whiny at times, but I can't begrudge her. She's sugar and spice, and everything nice, with an extra heavy dose of naiveté.

I've come to understand why Mika is completely smitten by her. Because I surely am.

And Mika has been a huge help. He picks up all the training material in a snap, aces the troubleshooting exercises and blitzes through the exams.

As for me, I barely scrape through. I hate exams.

I hate the pressure of cramming everything in, and having to spit it all out at a moment's notice. So sitting next to Mika has come in handy. Whenever something is too 'technical,' all I have to do is turn to Mika, and he graciously obliges.

I've learned that Mika is *still* in college. After high school, he'd took some time off to go backpacking around South East Asia and Europe. And he's now in his junior year at Idaho State U, pursuing an undergrad degree in civil and environmental engineering.

He's a green-eyed stud with a green heart.

Every day that I'm in class, I'm keenly aware of his presence, my heart having a tendency to leap whenever I watch him at odd moments of the day. Like right now.

Abruptly, I'm jolted out of my reverie when I hear someone in class calling his name.

Dammit. I'm falling hard for this guy.

But there's no harm in just *looking*. Right?

Sometime later, my eyes gravitate back; I find myself studying his killer cheekbones. I'm being extra discreet, when suddenly he looks up and catches my eye.

Flustered, I focus all my attention on Glenn.

I need to put a *kibosh* on this. I must stop obsessing over this man. *Pssh!* Who needs men?

They're just extra baggage, merely placed here on earth to help women procreate.

"I am a woman of substance," I chant in my head.

After class, Mika disarms me with his sexy, boyish grin. "See ya, Maddy."

"Bye!" I say with feigned indifference, but inside my heart is lurching into somersaults. Team China Olympic acrobatic flips.

Sigh. I certainly don't need a man, but I'd be much happier if I had one. Especially one like Mika.

On the last week of training, Glenn the bland trainer drops the stinkin' S bomb on us. "Class, now as part of your job, you will have to *sell*." And just in case we aren't paying attention, he reiterates, "*Sales* is part of your job. I cannot overstate this enough. Don't just take what I'm saying with a grain of salt, take it with the whole shaker!" he bellows frenetically, causing his entire fragile frame to quiver.

You can hear the low groans and moans sweeping through the class, an infinite tide of dissent the size of a tsunami wave.

Glenn has just given way to infamy.

Unperturbed, he forges on, raising his voice ten decibels so as to be heard over the mounting uproar. "Now, before you offer a product or service, you *must* always use the TSR script. It stands for Telemarketing Sales Rule." Glenn pauses for effect. "The TSR script is a FTC regulation. Essentially, you are asking the caller's permission to sell to them." He stops and surveys the room. "Any questions?"

No one gives him eye contact.

There is a unanimous shaking of heads. My incensed classmates resemble an ugly mob that's gearing up to crucify Glenn.

Tank, an ex UFC fighter, lets out a guttural, ominous growl. Siaosi, the five-hundred pound Samoan slash Sumo wrestler, sits very still with a hungry stare on his face, as though he'd like to roast Glenn on a spit. It's just my trite observation, but I'm pretty sure I'm spot on.

Glenn, feeling the heat and hate vibes emanating from the class, clasps his hands together in prayer. "Class, settle down and pay attention. Listen, this is the TSR script that you are required to say in the course of every call: *If I see a product or a service that may be beneficial to you, is it okay if I mention it later on?* If the caller says NO, then do NOT attempt to sell. But if the caller says YES, then it is your green light to pitch your sales offer and SELL, SELL, SELL!" His chest heaves and his eyes assume a sort of feral look.

There's something unnerving and unsettling about Glenn as I watch the wildness, the madness in his eyes . . . almost like he's possessed. Sweet, docile Glenn has morphed into someone I hardly even recognize. It's as if aliens have invaded his mind, body and soul.

This, I think cynically, trying to still my rising panic, is *not* good. Sales is not my *forte*. It makes me feel uneasy and queasy, grimy and greasy, like I'm coated with 'Car Salesman Slime.'

Over the next several agonizing hours, I learn all about the rainbow of products offered by Lightning Speed. Products that enhance our callers' lives (*Riiiight, Surrrre*), help them save time and money, and make their lives that much better.

Narrowing my eyes at Glenn, I remain skeptical.

It all sounds rosy posy, but it stinks to high heavens.

Um, wasn't this whole economic collapse caused in part by greedy businesses? By banks and credit card companies that gave out loans, mortgages and credit to folks who could not afford it?

Sell to help enhance the customers' lives?

Pssh! More like sell to enhance the deep pockets of the CEOs, the big fat cats and their shareholders. All they care about are BIG dollar signs to line their already stuffed pockets. They don't give a rat's ass about the customers.

You can sugarcoat sales just like you can dress up baloney and call it prosciutto. But you know what? It's *still* baloney.

I grit my teeth, as Glenn is far from finished with his sales lecture. Next on his agenda is 'bundling'.

Lightning Speed Communications has a binding contract with Skylight Network, a satellite TV company, and somehow we have to convince our callers to include their Skylight services on their DSL and cell phone bills. And, we have to promote (*force it down their throats*) Skylight Network if the callers are not subscribers.

Profiling plays a big role in this sales farce. We're expected to do some digging around; if the caller is a DSL subscriber and his cell phone is serviced through our competitor, then we must push him *our* cell phone service.

"Anyone have any questions or concerns?" Glenn asks with slight apprehension.

Karsynn's hand flies up in the air.

He darts her a nervous glance. "Yes, Karsynn?"

"Um, why do we have to sell? Shouldn't that be the job of the marketing department? We are customer *service* agents; we are NOT *sales* agents," she huffs and crosses her arms.

"Yeaaaahhh! Um-hmmmm!" Everyone echoes her sentiments.

Glenn responds like a preprogrammed robot, "Selling is still part of your job."

Tentatively, I raise my hand. "I'm sorry, Glenn, but if a ninety-year-old grandma has no idea how to use a computer and has no desire to, then I'm not going to push our DSL service on her. I just don't think it's right."

Glenn looks at me plaintively. "If you don't pitch a sale, you'll be marked down on the call in the event you're monitored; and if you consistently fail your monitors, that can lead to termination. Understood?"

I sink back and stew, burning with frustration.

I can't believe the security of my job is already hanging in the balance, my future here entirely dependent on how much I can sell. Pretty skewed terms if you ask me.

I'll do it. But I wish I could actually *see* the callers so I could do a *wink* *wink* *nudge* *nudge* and say, "This is all a ruse, DON'T DO IT! If you don't have the funds to purchase a product or service, or if you don't *need* it, don't get suckered in. Caveat emptor! Let the buyer beware!"

Meanwhile, Glenn is gripping the edge of the desk with such force that his knuckles have turned white. "Look, I am not the bad guy here." He breathes out a weary sigh. "And neither is Lightning Speed Communications. This is reality. In the business world, it is all about sales. I don't make the rules, that's just how it is."

My expression softens. *Aw,* Glenn almost seems like a normal person now. Then gradually, his voice grows so eerily soft that I almost have to strain my ears to listen.

Uh oh, not again!

Glenn's beady eyes fixate on us and his pupils dilate, swirling around and around in circles, like an evil Svengali. He chants in a hypnotic voice, "Always remember, service equals sales . . . the sale *begins* when the customer says 'no'."

Overcome by fatigue and boredom, I momentarily lapse into a sort of hypnotic state as I stare at Glenn's crazed yet magnetic eyes, entranced by his cult leader-like voice.

Something stronger inside me takes over. Shaking my head, I snap myself out of the trance.

Hah! I answer to no Svengali, and I refuse to be brainwashed.

Despite Glenn's efforts to blur the lines of distinction between service and sales, it is simply not working.

I remain silent and skeptical.

Service equals sales?

What the hell is he talking about?

Service equals service. *Period.*

And when the customer says 'No', he or she means 'No'. I'm sorry but 'No' does NOT mean 'Yes'!

Glenn is beginning to sound a bit like a rapist.

The rapist pauses for a long minute, appearing to be deep in thought. Eventually, he says, "Now class, think of it this way—people will always buy whatever it is that they *want* to buy. All you need to do is make them *want* to buy it; that's salesmanship in a nutshell. Make them want it badly enough.

Make them desire it. Make them crave it. And you do this by selling the features, and by making it *sexy*. Sell them the *feeling* that they'll get from buying that product or service, and always remember to make it *sexy!*"

Glenn gives a crisp nod of satisfaction. "Now, do you get it?"

That was bullshit. Well, it was pretty amusing, temporarily brow wrinkling, but bullshit nonetheless.

Sell the feeling? Make it sexy???

It's not like we're selling Marc Jacob purses, Balenciaga bags or Louboutin shoes here. We're a DSL slash phone company!

Glenn's eyes shift across the room. "Do you get it?" he repeats.

Silence ensues.

I grudgingly acknowledge the sharp undercurrents of truth to what he's saying. Of course I get it. I may not *like* it, but I get it.

But there is no time to sulk or mull, nor bemoan the fact that we're forced to sell. Before we know it, we're in 'nesting.'

'Nesting' is a period when we're all thrown on the phones, but our trainer is tucked safely by our sides, ready for our beck and call. And we have other more knowledgeable agents known as 'team-leads' to hold our hands and guide us through this whole intimidating process.

This is what 'nesting' is like: I answer the phone, sometimes nervously, others, with fake confidence. The caller asks me a question. I have no idea what he is talking about and/or I don't know the answer. I yell for help.

Here's my scenario:

Me: Thanks for calling Lightning Speed (my voice quivers). My name is . . . (what the heck is my name again?) err . . . Maddy, how can I help you?
Caller: I need help with blah, blah, blah.
Me: Um, yes . . . I can assist you with that. But um, do you mind holding while I . . . err, do some research?
Caller: Of course I mind, but go ahead.

Then I frantically wave a checkered flag until Glenn or a team lead comes to my rescue. That's nesting in a nutshell. We're just dazed, lost and confused the whole time, crying HELLLLP!

Everything made sense in class, but on the phone, I suddenly feel like a fish out of water. I haven't the faintest clue what I'm doing. My troubleshooting consists of taking tentative shots in the dark.

Thank God for Glenn and the team leads, they're our saviors.

But I quickly discover that they're *not* the biggest life savers.

As it turns out, the biggest life saver is not a person, but an inconspicuous, yet highly significant button on the phone—the 'Not Ready' button.

This discovery was huge and all-encompassing, parallel to stumbling upon the Holy Grail. I owe it my youth, I owe it my sanity, and without it, I'm certain I would've aged tenfold.

When I'm in 'Not Ready,' it means a call cannot come through, because hey—I'm *not ready* to take one!

How fab! It's meant for completing technical tickets, and for emergencies (*I think*); but most of us just end up staying in 'Not Ready' to take a breather from taking call after call, after call, after call. The 'Not Ready' button is revered as a Godsend, and is hailed amongst us as mankind's greatest invention, the pinnacle of human achievement, even better than sliced bread.

During my 'nesting' period, I keep a diary and here it is, unveiled in all its nightmarish gory.

Maddy's Nesting Dairy:
Number of calls taken = 488
Number of pills popped = 2 bottles (Tylenol Extra Strength)
Number of times I felt like shoving my head in the oven = 1000

Day 1 of nesting – I *hate, hate, hate* being on the phones. Feel utterly hopeless and confused. Sometimes instead of pushing the Hold button, I accidentally jab the Release key right next to it. I blame my fat fingers. Also, I stay in 'Not Ready' a lot. It is my haven. By the end of the day, I feel like going home and SHOVING MY HEAD IN THE OVEN!

Day 2 of nesting – Good news: I did not shove my head in the oven. Bad news: I'm still alive, back in this garish call center, being repeatedly abused over the phone.

Day 3 of nesting – Things are improving. Occasionally I feel lost, but I'm learning to use my 'resources,' a.k.a. the knowledge base. Transferring calls to other departments, or worse, conferencing calls with a third party is all a blurry mystery to me. Still using 'Not Ready.' If it's there, why not use it, right?

Day 4 of nesting – Feel more comfortable on the phone and with the phone buttons now. The calls are going smoothly. My ultra-secret weapon: bullshitting. I make certain I sound 100% sure that I know what I'm doing, even when I haven't the foggiest idea, because once the callers sense I'm unsure, they pounce on me like a pack of wolves and question every single thing I tell them. But now that I'm on BS mode, everything is just fine and dandy. Well, all except for the fact that an 8 hour shift is equivalent to 8 hours of callers bashing me nonstop.

Don't feel the urge to jab 'Not Ready' as much now; am becoming slightly more competent.

Day 5 of Nesting – Hey, this is a piece of cake! Don't need to resort to BS as much, but I whip it out when desperate measures call for it. Suddenly, things are starting to *click*. I actually *know* what I'm doing. 'Not Ready' is only used when I feel I deserve a much needed break. Hmm. Perhaps I'll go home and bake myself some chocolate chip cookies in the oven.

On the very last day of nesting, I'm like a bird, ready to sprout my wings, leave my nest and soar. After logging on to my phone, I whack the calls, one by one, out of the ball park!

I skip the 'selling' part, since I'm not held accountable for my sales quotas, at least not *yet*.

But I'm pumped! I feel a thrill, a rush of adrenalin like I'm flying a plane solo for the very first time. I am Amelia Earhart. Let's hope I don't crash this plane. Bring 'em on!

Beep!

"Thanks for calling Lightning Speed Communications, this is Maddy. What can I do for you today?"

"*Habla español ?*"

"Hola *señor!* Um, como estas. Sorry . . . no," I say in my broken, hacked up Spanish. "I . . . err . . . no habla espanol. Uno momento por favor." Then I promptly transfer the call to the Spanish queue.

It's pathetic really, since I took Spanish in high school, but other than that, I can only say random Spanish words like *burro* (donkey), *mijo* (my son), *vamanos* (let's go), *papi chulo* (hot daddy), *chica* (girl), *quien es tu papi* (who's your daddy?) and *la princesa* (the princess).

Oh, and I can count to ten—*uno, dos, tres, cuatro, cinco . .* .

Okay, I guess I can only count to five.

I am completely incapable of carrying on a conversation in Spanish. Fortunately, that's what the Spanish queue is for and they get paid more than I do because they're bilingual.

So, TRANSFER call.

Beep!

"Thanks for calling Lightning Speed Communications, this is Maddy. How can I help?"

"G'day. Me name is Poida Woite. And I need some help with me password."

How awesome! An Aussie from Down Under!

I peer at his name on my computer screen: Peter White.

"I can help Mr. White, but first—"

"Poida," he interjects kindly. "Just call me Poida."

"Okay, Peter," I say amiably. "I'll just need to ask you a couple of questions for verification." And once that is out of the way, I tackle the task at hand. "Now you mentioned earlier on that you needed help with your password?"

"Aye mate," he huffs in affirmation, like pirate Captain Jack Sparrow. "I'd like to change it to Inicondi88."

"Now, Peter, let's make sure that I've got this right. Is the first letter *I* like *igloo?*"

"Norrr, *I* as in *int,*" he corrects.

Int??? What the heck is int????

"Um, you mean *I* as in *India?*" I persist.

"Nyet! *I* as in *ipple,*" he says, agitation creeping into his voice.

Pause.

Now I'm even more confused. What the hell is an ipple?

"De fruit!" His voice rises with frustration. "*Ipple* de fruit! *I* for the first letter of the ilphibet!"

"Ohhhhhh." I stifle a laugh. *"A as in Apple.* Yes. Gotcha! So you want your password to be Anaconda88?" I confirm.

"Ibso-bloody-lutely!" he exclaims with a mixture of relief and exasperation.

My mouth twitches at the corners.

I reckon that they don't speak English in Down Under; they speak Strine.

Peter chuckles heartily. "Bloody hell, Sheila, I was beginning to think ye were a muppet. Ye dun't know i dunny from i bottom dollar. More is the pity, the great Ozzie vernacular is fizzing ind only i galoot like ye ne'er tire of diddling me, mekin me seem silly as i two bob watch."

O-*kay*, I didn't understand nearly half of what he was saying. Something about a puppet, I gather.

"Puppet?" I ask perplexed. "Did you just call me a puppet?"

"Muppet." He emits a throaty laugh. "Muppet means *idiot.*"

An idiot? Who is the idiot here? At least I can pronounce the letter A. I'm sorry but 'A' is *not* pronounced 'I'.

Crikey! After that call, I have this sudden urge to throw some shrimp on the barbie. Perhaps I'll even adopt a dingo and name him Mitch. On second thought, I'll name him Poida.

Beep!

"Thanks for calling Lightning Speed Communications. This is Maddy, what can I do for you today?"

"Halo. My name is Klaus Klum and I am locked out of my account," says the caller in a heavy German accent.

Guten Tag. He hails from Doytchland!

And I'm half-wondering if he is related to Heidi Klum.

Aside from *kinder, dachshund, ausfahrt, du arschgefickter hurensohn, fahrvergnügen* and *ich bring dich um*, the only other German word I know, I'd learned from Heidi on *Project Runway.*

Oh, I can't wait to flex my German skills. I've been waiting to say that word since the day I learned it on the Bravo channel.

Now is my chance. Patiently, I bide my time.

Before the call ends, Mr. Klum bellows, "Dahnk-uh shoon."

"You're welcome," I say graciously. This upcoming moment is pivotal. "Thanks for calling and *Aufiderzein.*"

I said it! What a momentous occasion!

Next time, I'll kick it up a notch and say, "YOU'RE OUT! *Aufiderzein.*"

Maybe I'll get a Russian, and we can discuss Pushkin and Matryoshka dolls.

I'm proud to say that I have *quite* the collection of Russian nesting dolls, which incidentally, are all made in China.

Hey, this job really isn't so bad after all. Although I'm sitting at a tiny desk in a crappy, cramped up cubicle in a windowless call center located in Pocatello, Idaho . . . I feel so globalized. I am connected to the world.

Three

The Lightning Five conference room is an explosion of pink confetti; balloons emblazoned with words like 'Congratulations!' and 'WOW!' decorate every space.

Our graduation day is feeling like a slightly overplayed event, think prom night, circa 1980.

Spread out before us is a Costco sheet cake, doughnuts from Daylight Donuts, and a whole smorgasbord of food and drinks. An imposing podium is set up in the front, and thirty five brass trophies are proudly displayed on a makeshift table.

"They sure rolled out the red carpet for us," Kars remarks, while slicing a fat piece of cake.

I fill up my paper cup with some virgin punch. "Not bad at all. Although I wish they would've told us this was a fancy soiree. I would've glammed up."

"Oh, Mika!" Ingeborg gushes with childish delight. "You have that vary nice Italian suit. You could have vorn it today, yah? And I could've vorn my zequined dress. Babe! Ve vud have looked vanderful." She does a little princess twirl.

Mika smiles at Ingeborg indulgently as she pirouettes, spinning around and around, like a ballerina in a musical box.

Karsynn inclines her head toward me and whispers, "What is Ingeborg smoking, and who is her dealer?"

I shrug. "She's making me dizzy."

Glenn clears his throat. "May I please have everyone's attention?" He is standing behind the podium, beaming at us like a proud parent. "I just want you guys to know that I am so proud of you; I feel honored for having had the opportunity to be your trainer for the past six weeks. You guys are a fabulous group, and I've truly enjoyed getting to know you," he says earnestly, almost choking up in the process.

Kars harrumphs. "What on God's green earth is he even talking about? He doesn't *know* me; he doesn't even know my favorite ice cream flavor."

"Mint chocolate chip," I say without missing a beat.

Glenn concludes his speech, "Before I hand out these trophies, I have a little surprise for you guys. Now for those of you who don't know, I used to be a professional ballroom dancer. And today, I will be performing a special stunt for you."

There is a stir of interest through the crowd as Glenn struts like a peacock to an open area and assumes a dancer's stance.

Other than the sound of him cracking his knuckles, the room is hushed. Everyone is silently waiting in anticipation.

Without further ado, Glenn breaks into a fast paced, zipping jive, showcasing his flair and fancy choreography, drawing cheers and laughter from the crowd. And then out of nowhere—BAM!

He executes two dramatic back flips. One after another!

We're a little stunned at first, but soon the whole room breaks into rapturous applause.

"Holy mackerel!" I gasp. "His form and landing was sharp and clean! It was perfect. As effortless as Plushenko's quad-triple-double toe loop combination."

Kars gives a short hiccupping laugh. "I wouldn't go *that* far; he's more of a Johnny Weir. But this is better than anything I've seen on *Dancing with the Stars*."

Glenn is in his element, taking a bow, preening and posing, clearly enjoying the limelight.

Presuming this whole shindig is over with, I head for the punch bowl only to stop myself in my tracks. Glenn is fervently waving his arms in the air, motioning for Mika to join him in the front.

Looking surprised, although not very pleased, Mika shakes his head. "No, Glenn. I don't want to do it."

Glenn's voice rings loud and persuasive. "C'mon on down here, Mika!"

Mika refuses to budge.

With an instinct for entertaining a crowd that rivals the likes of Letterman and Leno, Glenn turns to his audience for support.

"Class, since I've gotten to know Mika, I've learned that he, too, shares a passion for dancing. When Mika had lived in Belgium, he was the founder of a street break-dancing group called the B-Force. So once again, c'mon down here Mika and show us what you've got!"

Mika shuffles his feet, clearly uncomfortable with the attention. Suddenly, Ingeborg pumps her fist in the air and chants, "Mi-ka! Mi-ka! Mi-ka! Mi-ka!" And pretty soon, everyone is rallying and chanting for him, including *moi*.

Mika gives a half embarrassed smile and remains glued to the spot; but I can see his resolve slowly wavering. Resigning himself, he squares his shoulders and jogs to the front of the room.

He begins warming up with some simple three-step footwork. Seconds later, he drops to the ground and pops out the familiar coffee grinder move. A smile touches my lips; he's visibly more relaxed now. Then while doing a side step, he blazes into a suicidal back head flip, followed by a front head flip.

WHOA! That's two headsprings with no hands!

He should be in the Cirque du Soleil.

A roaring applause breaks out, even mightier and louder than Glenn's reception. I even hear a couple hoots and wolf whistles from the crowd.

"He did that trick so effortlessly," I mutter, audibly floored.

The crowd wants more. They rally and egg him on, "WOOT!!! WOOT!!! Mi-ka! Mi-ka! Mi-ka!"

Graciously, he obliges. Dropping to the ground, he whips out a dizzying windmill move. His lean, muscular legs rotate and spin around in rapid motions. I swear I even feel a breeze. Who needs an electric fan when you have Mika?

Next, he combines more power moves using his strong elbows and strapping forearms to propel him through the air like a boomerang. After more fluid flares and turtle crunches, he rolls back and freezes with a one-handed handstand.

A thunderous applause fills the entire room. He has brought the house down! Apparently, our dear friend, Mika, has a knack for showmanship.

My mouth is slightly agape. "Wow. He's incredible! As light as a leaf, as hard as concrete, yet as flexible as a rubber band."

Kars nods energetically. "Gotta give Belgium boy props!"

Without breaking out in a drop of sweat, Mika jogs back to a chorus of rowdy applause, slightly impeded by slaps on his back, high fives and knuckle bumps as he passes by our cheering classmates.

We cluster around our newfound celebrity friend, shielding him from the estrogen filled skanks who flock around him like country hens in heat, jostling for his attention.

Ingeborg flings herself at him. "Dat vas so avesome babe."

He smiles and gently disentangles himself, keenly aware of all the snooping eyes on him.

Kars delivers a solid punch to his arm. "Holy crap, Mika! We didn't know you had moves like that!"

"You founded the B-Force, eh?" I smile with frank amusement.

Somewhat pink around the ears, he laughs. "That's why I didn't mention it; you girls are already giving me a hard time."

Glenn returns to the podium and announces, "Class, listen up. If any of you are interested in ballroom dancing, please know that I give private lessons at my studio downtown. And my partner, Bruno, gives break-dancing lessons. So if you're interested, just shoot me an email and I'll provide you with the details, okay?"

Nice plug, I think to myself.

"And now," Glenn continues, "it is finally time for me to hand out these trophies that are so well deserved of *all* of you. I want you to know that you are *all* winners today."

One by one, Glenn calls out our names and we claim our mini trophies. They're shiny brass balls haphazardly affixed to cheap plastic sticks. And for the *pièce de résistance,* the brass balls are burnished with the company's lightning rod logo.

I accept my trophy, hold it up to Kars and manage an uneven smile. "Um, I sure do feel like a winner."

After all that shenanigans, we're allowed to 'party' for an hour in the conference room and then report back to class.

Our fates will be decreed today.

Kars, Mika, Ingeborg and I mingle in a corner, still tight knit and clique-ish after six grueling weeks of training. We are the Band of Brothers in this torrential battle field, looking out for one another in the trenches.

"I hope ve vill all be on de same team," says Ingeborg, wide-eyed with optimism.

"Me too. If we're lucky enough, we'll end up with a nice supervisor like Dawson. From what I hear, he's super easy going."

A shadow of a frown touches Karsynn's forehead. "I hope we don't end up on Hillary Hildegard's team. She's a witch! The micromanaging queen." Kars drops her voice a decibel. "My mom says people call her the Not Ready Nazi. Her team has the lowest Not Ready time in call center history, and if she ever catches you in Not Ready, you're in deep shitz."

I shudder involuntarily. "Please don't let me be on *her* team."

"Don't worry, ladies. We'll be fine wherever we go," says Mika in a voice as cool as a cucumber. He remains poised while the rest of us have completely lost it. He has a talent for remaining calm and collected in the most chaotic situations. "Who knows? Maybe Hillary is not as bad as they say," he proffers.

At that, Kars emits a loud, exaggerated snort.

But I certainly hope Mika is right.

To distract ourselves, we head for the food table and pile up on the goodies that are quickly disappearing.

I stack up on the tortilla chips and scoop myself a hefty portion of guacamole dip, happily indulging myself. After inhaling everything on my plate, I swiftly head back for seconds. Chips and dip in hand, I whirl around only to find Mika smiling at me with mild amusement.

Self consciously, I slide a chip in my mouth, crunch on it, and catch the falling crumbs.

Mika seems to sense my mounting discomfort. "I like girls with healthy appetites," he says simply.

I glance over at Ingeborg. She's munching on a celery stick. Nothing else is on her plate.

Great. Now I feel like a ginormous pudding.

I can even feel my ass expanding.

Humph . . . Mika may like girls with healthy appetites, but he certainly doesn't *date* 'em.

The training class has never been this quiet. Like sitting ducks, we await our fates.

Glenn fixes me with a steady look. "Maddy . . ."

My stomach is in knots. *Please let me be on Dawson's team.*

"You'll be on Hillary Hildegard's team."

A sharp pain twists in my gut. Noooooooooooooo. I bury my head in my hands and make a muffled cry of despair.

"Ingeborg," Glenn bellows. "Hillary's team as well."

She squeaks with terror and turns sheet white.

"Karsynn." Glenn pauses for a beat and looks straight at her.

Her eyes are clamped shut, almost like she's dreading what's coming her way.

Glenn lays it on her gently. "Hillary's team."

Kars bashes her head against the desk.

Unperturbed, Glenn continues roll calling more names, poor unfortunate souls, all doomed for Hillary the Not Ready Nazi's labor camp.

Sometime later, the tide begins to shift when we hear Glenn say, "Mika, you'll be on Dawson Darling's team."

Mika shrugs with a casual expression of indifference.

Kars glares at him resentfully. "You lucky duck! You get your freedom while the rest of us take the train to the Gulag!"

Mika shoots her a feeble smile and apologizes with his eyes.

When Glenn is finished roll calling, he distributes printouts of our schedules. As it turns out, most of us will be working a crappy shift from noon 'til 8:30 pm, right smack in the middle of the day. I won't have time to do anything in the morning, afternoon *or* evening for that matter.

The best shifts by far are: 8:30 am to 4 pm—so I still have the whole evening left to enjoy, or 3:30 pm 'til midnight—so I can have the whole morning to myself. But since I am the low man on the totem pole, I am stuck with a shift where my whole day is wasted at work. Bummer!

Before dismissing us from our final day of training, Glenn shepherds us to our cubicles. They don't look like much, but what more can you expect from a cubicle? It's a six-by-six foot partition without a view.

And although Kars and I are on the same team, a row of cubes separate us, like the Red Sea. Ingeborg's desk is just two cubes away from mine, so we can still holler at each other.

We're curious to see where Mika's cubicle is, so we traipse over to his desk. Standing by his cube, I scan the floor for mine. "You're quite a distance from us Mika," I point out. "I'd say you're about eight rows across."

Ingeborg pulls a face, slightly miffed that she and Mika won't be joined at the hip.

Mika gives a playful grin. "Ladies, don't worry. I'll come over and visit."

Glenn rounds us up like sheep one final time. "All right guys, so you'll report to your supervisors on Monday. You may bring in pictures and plants to decorate your cubes if you wish." He pauses and glances around, as if trying to memorize all our faces. "And although you're no longer in training, please don't be a stranger. My office is right next to the exit stairwell on the north side, so feel free to stop by and pay me a visit anytime, okay?"

We nod and murmur our goodbyes.

Glenn glances furtively at his watch. "Oops, it's time. Must dash. I have a meeting with HR."

As he prances away, I overhear some snippets of conversation, something about how the shit hit the fan after word got around that Glenn executed a back flip *and* encouraged Mika to perform a stunt on company property. I guess if Mika had gotten injured, the company would have been liable, and so Glenn had violated some sort of code in the Employee Handbook.

Poor Glenn . . . I hope he's not in any hot water.

Four

"Hurricane Katrina has struck again!" Karsynn surveys the pile of clothes strewn across her room.

My suitcase is empty but my stuff is everywhere and the room is in utter chaos. To be honest, Karsynn's room was pretty much a pigsty even before I moved in, but I did sort of take it to a new level today.

Looking helplessly around, I cry, "I have nothing to wear."

Karsynn seizes me by the shoulders. "Look, it's just work—at a *call center*, remember? We don't have to dress up since we don't meet any clients. Plus, my mom says some lady comes into work dressed in her pajamas for Christ's sake. So your skinny jeans and grandma top are fine."

"Grandma?" I glance down at my blousy, ethereal Leifsdottir top; it's laced with ruffles, gathered with ruching, and stitched with tiny, iridescent rosettes. "This is vintage inspired," I cry in an injured voice.

"Po-*tay*-toh, Po-*tah*-toe," she tuts. "You say vintage, I say granny."

Eyeing Karsynn's camouflaged pants, red bandana and mossy green top, I bite my tongue and let that comment slide. I am not taking fashion advice from someone who dresses like Rambo—First Blood Rambo, not the new Rambo.

I change the subject. "This isn't about work, it's about Mika. Remember? Before I'd left work on Friday, he said he needed to talk to me about something. Privately. So we're meeting for lunch in the cafeteria today."

Karsynn looks askance. "You mean I'm not invited? Not even Ingeborg?"

"Nope." I grin impishly.

She strikes a thoughtful pose. "Hmm. I wonder what he wants to talk to you about."

"I've been wondering that myself all weekend," I say offhandedly, trying to still my fluttering emotions.

Kars eyes me suspiciously. "You're hoping he's got the hots for you, eh?"

"Me? No! Yes! Oh, I don't know." My voice falters.

"I *know* you've got the hawts for him." Karsynn snickers and falls head-first into a pile of clothes.

"I do, but he's going out with Ingeborg. And I *love* Ingeborg. I would never do anything to jeopardize our friendship. Plus, it's strictly platonic between me and Mika."

"Platonic, Plutonic. Po-*tay*-toh, Po-*tah*-toe." Kars rolls her eyes. "It's all semantics to me."

Studiously ignoring her, I reach for a black scrunchie, and in two swift motions, my hair is up in a neat ponytail.

"Jesus-Mary-Mother-of-Joseph, take the hideous thing off right now," she orders fiercely. "Scrunchies are so nineties! You've got gorgeous, glossy hair. I'd sell my firstborn to have hair like yours. Besides, if you leave it down for a change, Belgium boy may notice."

"Whatever," I say dismissively. But I do take off the scrunchie and run a brush through my hair a couple of times.

Kars swings her feet out of bed and paces the floor. Scanning our checklist, she says, "You got your cinnamon scented candle?"

I peer inside my bag. "One cinnamon scented candle—check!"

"Photos?"

"Got 'em!" I hold up my favorite snapshots.

Our cubicles will be our home away from home, so we plan on decorating and personalizing our cardboard partitions.

Kars taps a large box. "One basil garden—check!"

My eyes widen. "You're bringing your Aerogarden to work?"

The Aerogarden is a hydroponic device that uses some sort of NASA space age technology. Well, at least that's what Karsynn tells me.

She hoists the large box into her arms. "Yeah, why not? I love the smell of basil. Plus, it'll help me snag a man."

I stare at Kars, bemused.

She pads to the door. "Oh yeah, didn't you know? In Italy, sweet basil is thought to attract husbands to their wives."

I raise my eyes to the ceiling. "We're in *Idaho*—not Italy."

"There could be Italian men working there," she quips airily.

Shaking my head, I prop the door open. "After you."

Kars and her indoor garden trot out.

"Is that everything?"

Her head pops out of the burgeoning greenery. "Yes, ma'am."

"Let's boogie!" I slam the door shut behind me.

As soon as Kars and I troop into work, we spy Hillary the Not Ready Nazi at her desk, sitting ramrod straight with her back to us. We take this opportunity to check out our new boss.

Hillary is staring at her monitor, and appears to be reviewing an excel spreadsheet of some sort.

Abruptly, she attacks her keyboard with brute force, pounding it into oblivion. TAP! TAP! TAP! TAP! TAP!

I stiffen. She looks so intimidating, and already my fear for her is all consuming. Kars and I remain firmly glued to the spot, transfixed by her muscular fingers that are hammering away at the keys.

My gaze shifts to the Madonna biceps that decorate her arms.

Gulps. I'm pretty sure she pumps iron.

Sensing our presence, Hillary swivels round.

My heart stops and my eyes widen in horror. Egad! She is a grisly ogre living amongst us. I find myself blatantly staring at her hatchet nose. It looks like a nose job gone wrong, almost like it's collapsing inwards.

She's even got a slight moustache.

Or as they call it these days—a nose neighbor, a crumb catcher, a trash stash, or a tea strainer.

With an expression of mild petulance, Hillary raises a tufted unibrow that's mushrooming out of control. "And you are?"

"Um, I'm Maddy," I manage feebly.

"And I'm Karsynn, reporting for duty," she pipes in chirpily.

"And we're on your team," we say in unison. Then we eye each other, struggling to keep a straight face.

Hillary doesn't look the least bit amused. She rises ceremoniously to her feet. Fully erect, she towers over us. Oh God. She must be over eight feet tall.

Kars and I cower in the corner as the giant looms over us.

Hillary immediately fires out her commands, "Make sure you come into work at least fifteen minutes early so you have time to boot up your computer and log in to all of your apps. I *expect* you to be on the phones taking calls at twelve sharp! That is when your shift starts and that is precisely when I *expect* you take calls! And I *expect* you to be ready to take calls at ALL times, so don't even *think* of touching the Not Ready key," she says acidly. "And I *expect* you to obey my orders, so don't even think of questioning me. If I say 'Jump', you say 'How High!' "

Each time Hillary spits the word *'expect,'* her saliva sprays onto our cheeks. Gosh. Her mouth is an industrial humidifier, vaporizing the air around us. I need some Vicks Vapor-rub.

"Understood?" she roars, striking fear into our hearts.

We bob our heads up and down.

Her lips curl into a sadistic smile and I quickly plaster a smile on my face, stretching it as tightly as a bungee cord that's about ready to snap.

Hillary's nostrils flare with annoyance. "You are dismissed!" She swivels back to face her monitor.

Kars and I exchange a look of alarm, wearing identical raised eyebrows. After collecting ourselves, we slink back to our cells.

Jeez. We haven't even started our shifts, and already she's made us feel like convicted felons facing death row.

Ingeborg, already seated in Cell Block D, waves at us and demurely slides on her headset. On anyone else, it looks like a plain metal band. On Ingeborg, it sparkles and shimmers like a diamond encrusted tiara. But tiara or not, once that headset is on, you're chained to your desk.

"What's her problem?" mutters Kars. "Heck, it's not even noon yet. We've got five minutes before we have to start taking calls."

"Well, I guess we better hurry then," I say, scrambling over to Cell Block A. Hurriedly, I chuck my bag onto the desk and fire up my computer. But I soon realize that 'fire up' is the wrong word.

I grit my teeth as my computer chugs and spits at a leisurely pace. By the time I'm logged in, I can already hear Ingeborg taking her first call.

"Thank you for calling Lightning Zpeed Communications, my name iz Ingeborg, vot can I help you vit today?" she twitters like a canary.

I *love* Ingeborg's accent! It puts a smile on my face.

Hillary the Giant Not Ready Nazi stands up from her watch post and fixes her steely gray eyes on me. She raises her tufted unibrow, making her meaning quite clear.

Humph. I wasn't aware that this is a *no-smile* zone.

Hillary the Giant's height gives her the added advantage of enabling her to spy over us. Hmm. I wonder why she's so mean. Maybe kids had picked on her and called her names like Andre the Giant, The Jolly Green Giant and Tall Chief.

Poor Hillary. I'll try to be nice to her.

Instantly, I wipe the smile off my face and load up my apps. I plunk the cinnamon scented candle on my desk and stick a sepia-toned photograph on my cubicle wall. It's a picture of me and my dad, taken on a muggy July afternoon at the Navy Pier. His hair is tousled from the wind and his eyes are crinkled from squinting in the afternoon sun. I vividly remember all the details of that summery day. We had sat on a weathered bench by the pier, and he'd held my little hand in his big hand. Together, we'd feasted on our Häagen-Daz waffle cones and my dad was smiling at the camera with an ice-cream moustache.

My dad had passed away from lung cancer eight years ago.

Losing him was devastating. I'd lost my dad and my best friend all in one day. He's the realest thing I've ever had, and he left the biggest gap in my life when he'd left.

I gaze at the photograph with affection, smiling back at him. Taking a deep breath, I slide on my headset.

Okay, now I'm ready to take a call.

Beep!

"Thanks for calling Lightning Speed Communications. This is Maddy, how can I help?

"Because your FUCKING lines are down, it has cost my business over FIVE HUNDRED THOUSAND DOLLARS IN FUCKING DAMAGES!" blasts the caller.

Sheesh, someone has a potty mouth.

"Sir, I apologize for any inconvenience and I'll be glad to look into this matter for you. But could you kindly refrain from using such foul language with me," I say all primly and properly.

"FIX MY FUCKIN PROBLEM FIRST AND THEN WE'LL SEE YOUNG LADY!"

"Oh-kay, sir," I say in a constricted voice. "First off, let me ask you a few questions to authenticate you."

The verification process is excruciatingly painful as he is less than cooperative; it's literally like getting a root canal without anesthesia.

By some miraculous fluke, I manage to get him authenticated.

"Sir, do you mind if I place you on hold for a few minutes while I do some research?"

"YES! I DO FUCKIN MIND BEING ON HOLD. BUT GO THE FUCK AHEAD! YOU FUCKIN IGNORAMUS NIMROD."

Welcome to the world of Customer Service.

Now that the A-hole is on hold, I check the intranet site to see if there are any known issues.

I scroll down the list and *Bingo!*

There is an outage in Arizona, due to severe thunderstorms late last night that damaged some of our OC3 lines.

And that happens to be where this moron is calling from.

Next, I check his account details. Hmm, I notice he's on our Consumer Package. Uh-oh, this does not bode well for him.

With the Consumer Package, we do *not* guarantee coverage twenty-four/seven. We only guarantee coverage at all times for Business Packages because business clients are designated special lines that aren't affected by bad weather.

Well, not *quite* as much.

And since this caller is calling about a business account, he should technically be on the Business Package.

Exhaling sharply, I brace myself and hop back on the phone with the tyrant. "Thanks for holding, sir. I'm so sorry but we have a known issue in Arizona, where the lines are in fact down. Our technicians are working hard to fix it," I say reassuringly.

He goes ballistic. "I NEED THIS FIXED NOW! WHY AM I PAYING FOR SOMETHING THAT I CAN'T EVEN FUCKIN' USE?"

"Um, actually, sir, you're on the Consumer Package and you're paying . . ." I rifle through my stack of papers and locate the page that lists all the fees. "Let's see here, Consumer Package—you're paying $24.95 per month. Now if you run a business, then you're *supposed* to be on the Business Package which costs $249.99 per month," I inform him in a brisk and professional tone.

"WHY THE FUCK WOULD I PAY $250 WHEN I CAN GET IT FOR $25 A MONTH?" he snarls mockingly. "GO ON, TELL ME BITCH! WHY DON'T-CHA FUCKIN ENLIGHTEN ME?"

"Well, sir," I say ever so sweetly. "If you *had* been on the Business Package, your DSL service would be up and running right now; and it would have saved you (drum roll please and a pause for effect) FIVE HUNDRED THOUSAND DOLLARS."

Heated pause. I can hear him fuming on the line.

"FUCK YOUUUUUU!" *Click.*

He hung up. Well good riddance! Didn't his momma ever teach him good manners?

If his tone was marked by gentility rather than hostility, my empathy for him would have been unequivocal. I'm always on the customer's side, and to be quite frank, his frustrations weren't without merit. But since his *modus operandi* was to attack me, I operated thusly in defense mode. 'Tis the nature of the game.

Before I know it, my phone goes *Beep!*

Here I go again. "Thanks for calling Lightning Speed . . ."

Call after call after call comes through and thankfully none of them are as bad as the first one. After taking about fifty calls in a row, it's 2 p.m. and I'm scheduled for a fifteen minute break. Apparently, there's some labor law requiring call centers to grant fifteen minute breaks to their workers every two hours.

Uncle Sam *did* get something right.

This is what my schedule looks like:

12–2 p.m.: On the phones
2–2:15 p.m.: Break (Hells Yeah!)
2:15–4:15 p.m.: On the phones (*Moan*)
4:15–4:45 p.m.: Lunch (cue Harlem Gospel choir belting out Hallelujah chorus)
4:45–6:45 p.m.: On the phones (*Groan*)
6:45–7 p.m.: Break (cue choir of Angels singing *Glory, Glory, Glory to God*)
7–8:30 p.m.: On the phones (pop two Tylenol pills)

In a haste, I log off my phone, pop a Tylenol pill and saunter to Karsynn's cubicle. Ingeborg skips over to join us, and then the three of us sashay to the Ladies room.

Together.

I don't know what it is about us girls, but it's like some sort of strange, unspoken ritual, necessitating us to tend to nature's call together.

I walk into a stall and use my elbow to shut the door behind me. Being the germ freak that I am, I tear off some toilet paper and mummify my hand so my fingers don't touch the handle or the lock. Next, I tear off more toilet paper and strategically place it on the toilet seat before carefully setting my bum down.

Karsynn, the self-proclaimed space craft, is already hovering over her toilet. I know this for a fact because she's hovering so high that it sounds like rain drops hitting the pavement.

Since I barely know Ingeborg, I haven't the slightest idea what her toilet technique is.

"So how did your calls go?" Karsynn talks over the sound of her raining pee.

"Mine started off real bad, but then it got better." I raise my voice so as to be heard over the toilets flushing around me.

Kars cries huffily, "Well mine sucked big time!"

"Ugh!" I moan peevishly. "Don't you just hate these motion-sensored toilets?"

Suddenly, without warning or provocation, my toilet flushes.

I leap into the air like my bum's caught on fire. "Hey! I wasn't done yet!" I glare at my toilet reprovingly.

Oh! The nerve of it! Now I'm paranoid that some nasty toilet water has sprayed up my bum. Mental note to myself: bring baby wipes next time.

After taking care of business, I amble out of my stall and join Ingeborg and Karsynn at the sink.

Karsynn frets, "I wanted to go into Not Ready, but Hillary the Giant Not Ready Nazi was watching me."

Ingeborg giggles. "I know, she vas vatching me, too."

"I'd be careful if I were you," warns Kars. "I'm pretty sure she wants a piece of you."

Ingeborg shrugs, wide-eyed with innocence. Turning to me, she asks, "Vas ze Giant Not Ready Nazi vatching you, too?"

"Like a hawk," I groan with displeasure. Then it all of a sudden occurs to me, "Um, I think we should refrain from calling her the Giant Not Ready Nazi. I mean, it's a little too obvious, don'tcha think?"

"*Ya think?*" Karsynn raises a sardonic brow.

"Seriously, if she catches on, our heads could be on the chopping block."

Kars nods. "Right. We need to be covert. Let's come up with a code name for her."

"How about Ze Führer?" suggests Ingeborg.

"I like that," I say.

"Me too," echoes Kars. "Hillary the Giant Not Ready Nazi is hereby dubbed The Führer!"

Satisfied with her code name, I'm about to wash my hands at the sink only to discover that the faucets are also motion-sensored.

Grrrrr, this is so frustrating.

I wave my hands under the faucets and nothing happens.

After several attempts of frantic waving, the water gushes out for two seconds and then shuts off. I reach for the soap and guess what? The soap dispensers are also motion-activated.

What a fiasco! Giving my hands a proper wash is turning out to be a painful and time consuming ordeal.

After spending five minutes doing a Hokey Pokey dance with the uncooperative faucets, we finally leave the restroom. I glance at my watch. Crapola. There's only four more minutes left on my break.

Some break.

Happily, we spot Mika at the water cooler.

"Mi-ka!" we call out to our brother.

He turns at our exclamation and Ingeborg trips prettily to his side. "Hey." He smiles at his Bulgarian beauty; she beams at him beatifically. After that adorable exchange, he turns his attention to the American rejects.

"How's the new job go-*ing*?" taunts Kars.

"It's go-*ing*," he replies with a half-smile.

"Oh! Be right back!" I sprint to my cubicle. Hurriedly, I grab my water bottle and dash back.

Time is of essence.

When I arrive at the water cooler, Karsynn and Ingeborg are noticeably absent. Mika is the last man standing.

He shifts his weight from foot to foot. "Ingeborg went to check out Karsynn's Aerogarden. She, um, loves to cook with basil."

"Oh." I fill up my BPA-free bottle with some Mount Olympus spring water.

He clears his throat. "So . . . don't forget to meet me for lunch at the cafeteria."

"I'll be there," I say without meeting his eyes.

Glancing at my watch, I gasp in horror. I have to be back on the phone in T-minus ten seconds. "Later!" I abandon him with a toss of my head and scurry back to my cell.

The cafeteria is packed, but I spot Mika instantly; he's seated at a table, sipping on a Coke. Regular, not diet—my kind of guy.

Our eyes meet across the room and his face breaks into a grin.

Smiling back at him, I approach his table.

I'm surprised to see that he has one plate of food for himself *and* one for me.

"Hi," I say coolly, when I'm within earshot.

"Hi," he says, equally coolly. "I got you some food. It's chicken fajitas with a side of guacamole, and I thought it's something you might like. If you don't like it, you don't have to eat it, all right?"

"No. This is great," I insist. "I love Mexican food. Thanks."

I slip into the chair across from him, lift my plastic fork and throw caution to the wind. "So what do you want to ask me?"

His sits back and rakes his fingers through his hair. "It's sort of a favor."

"What favor?" I press.

After a hesitant pause, he says, "I'd like you to be my tutor."

I sit in a stunned stupor. "Your tutor?" I say, trying hard to conceal my disappointment.

"Yes," he affirms and ventures, "I'm struggling with my ESL class. I've failed it twice already and I'm retaking it for the third time this semester."

"ESL, um . . . what's that?"

"English as a second language. It's a prerequisite course for all international students at the U," he explains. "If you don't want to do it, I'll understand," he quickly adds.

"No, it's not that," I protest. "I'm just a bit surprised. You speak very good English."

"Well, the ESL class focuses on grammar, sentence structure, that sort of thing . . . and I'm not very good at all that."

I make a non-committal *hmmm* sound, fork a mouthful of guacamole, and allow my eyes to dwell on him while I mull it over.

Admittedly, I'm a bit crushed that he only wants me to tutor him. And since I secretly admire Mister Forbidden Fruit, I really shouldn't be spending more time with him.

On the flip side, we're strictly friends and he's such a nice guy that I can't possibly say no. Or can I?

Mika watches me intently.

"What if I said no?" I ask, with a delicate lift of my brow.

"No?" he says with a pained expression.

"Okay, I'll do it." *Sheesh*, I cave in way too easily.

A smile spreads across his face. "Really?"

"Yes. But I'll have you know up front that I have absolutely zero teaching experience."

He brushes off my concerns. "If I didn't think you'd be a good teacher, I wouldn't have asked you."

"I appreciate your vote of confidence, but . . ." I falter and bite my lip. "I'll figure something out."

And so we arrange to meet every Saturday at the university library for some 'tutoring' sessions.

Over our lunch, we talk about random things and I learn that Mika is a U.S. citizen.

While vacationing in New York, his mom had went into labor six weeks prematurely; and thus, he has dual citizenship.

I bite into my fajita. "Dual citizenship? *Ahh*, now it all makes sense to me. I've always wondered if you were working here illegally."

"If they deport me back to Belgium, there'll be one less person to work the potato farms," he says in all seriousness.

I give a little laugh. "Do you want to hear a potato joke?"

"Of course, how can I refuse?"

"It's pretty dumb, so don't say I didn't warn you." I bite back a smile. "Okay, here goes. Why did the potato go to the beach?"

"I don't know." He shrugs. "Why?"

"It wanted to get baked!"

He rewards me with a smile. "I've got one, too. What does a British potato say when it thinks something is fantastic?"

I take a stab at it. "It's smashing?"

"Close. It's *mashing*," he corrects and we crack up.

Spuds rule! Although I'd never tell a potato joke to a native Idahoan for fear of being potato jacked.

Twenty-five minutes go by really fast. When we notice the time, we scarf down the rest of our lard laden Mexican meals and scurry into a lift that obediently pings open.

Perfect timing.

It zips up to the third floor, the door slides open and we step out. I'm just about to round a corner when Mika taps me lightly on my arm.

At once, I feel goose bumps rise.

He gazes steadily into my eyes. "I really appreciate you doing this for me. I forgot to say thank you."

"Sure, no problem," I mutter.

He turns and starts for his cubicle. Abruptly, he stops and does a double take. "You look a little different today."

I toss my hair this way and that way, as if I were starring in a Garnier Fructis commercial.

Mika continues staring at me, and a slow grin breaks over his face. "You're wearing your hair down. It looks . . . nice."

My cheeks feel hot and I'm positive they're crimson.

I tuck a stray hair behind my ear and stare after Mika as he strides off.

Ahh. I'm floating on cloud nine.

A gigantic, poufy cloud shaped like a big, fat, Idaho Russet Potato.

Ping! Sounds the lift and my cloud disperses.

The doors swish open. Kars and Ingeborg spill out of the lift and galumph toward me.

"Where'd you guys go?" I ask.

"We went out back by the duck pond for a cigarette break," Kars wheezes, looking out of breath.

I shoot her an incredulous look. "But you don't smoke."

Kars gives a culpable shrug. "Well Ingeborg smokes and I just started. My mom says all the supervisors, managers and team-leads smoke. So it's a good way for me to do some networking. You know, instead of golfing, I'm smoking to build up my contacts."

I blink, completely perplexed by this.

Kars rests one hand on my shoulder. "*Look*," she says. "It's my plan to get off the bleepin' phones. Everyone in upper management smokes; if I want to become a supervisor or team-lead someday so I can get off the phones, what better way than to light up with the worst of them?"

I shake my head in disbelief. "So you're smoking in order to climb the corporate ladder?"

"Exactly!" says Kars, seemingly proud of herself. "Hey, if you can't beat 'em, join 'em."

I am astounded by her convoluted logic and I am so tempted to smack her silly head. "Kars, that's the dumbest thing I've ever heard. Smoking to get a promotion?"

"Hey, it sure beats sleeping my way to the top," she quips.

"Um, ever heard of this thing called *hard work*?" I ask with a tinge of sarcasm.

"Doesn't work," she scoffs. "Just ask my mom. She's a diligent worker—been that way her entire life, and she's *still* stuck on the phones."

Out of the corner of my eye, I catch Ingeborg glancing at her watch every two seconds. I ask the dreaded question. "Is it time Ingeborg? To get back on the phones?"

She fervently nods her head.

We split up and scamper back to our respective Hell Holes.

Hours later, it's finally time to leave.

I am dog tired, so past the point of exhaustion that I can barely speak. I am so drained by the rigors of this job that my whole body aches. Gosh. It feels as if I've been doing construction work all day, like my body has been flung on the freeway, and run over a hundred times. By Hummers.

Listlessly, I grab my things and drag my feet up. I'm about to bolt when I see Hillary marching to my desk.

Frozen to the spot, I watch her advance on me with a mixture of suspicion and apprehension.

She stops in front of me and crosses her gorilla arms. "Do you want to work overtime?" she demands huffily. "Service levels are atrocious and we need people to stay back and help out."

I blink.

Err . . . does an inmate wish to lengthen her prison sentence?

Smiling kindly at her, I shake my head determinedly and decline the offer. Thanks but *no thanks*.

Five

Thank GAWD it's Friday night.

I'm so drained that the only thing I can muster the strength to do is flip on the TV. *The Vampire Diaries* comes on.

Sheesh! Not another vampire show. After *Twilight* and *True Blood*, I'm all vampired out.

I chuck the remote to Kars and she switches the channel to E!.

Yay! Our beloved *Chelsea Lately* is on. It is hands down the best talk show on TV and Chelsea Handler is a Goddess amongst Goddesses; our Queen Bee.

As you can probably tell, I am a huge fan, and so is Kars.

Watching Chelsea is a blast. She's funny, witty and we learn so much from her. Just by tuning in to her show, we have vastly expanded our vocabulary. For instance, we incorporate words like *shadoobie, coslopus* and *pickachu* into our daily conversations.

In Chelsea Land, *shadoobie* = poo.

Pickachu and *coslopus* = va jay jay.

So it's work appropriate and very versatile.

The other day, Hillary the Giant Not Ready Nazi had walked around with her barn door wide open. Kars had yelled, "The Führer's *pickachu* is peeking out!"

To which I'd replied, "*Holy Shadoobie!* Her *coslopus* is a jungle."

And no one had caught on to a word we were saying.

After *Chelsea Lately*, we tune in to *The Daily Show* with Jon Stewart. Later on, we flip the channel to CBS to catch *The Late, Late Show* with Craig Ferguson. Love that guy and his bizarre humor. Not to mention, I find his Scottish lilt so incredibly wonky and sexy, even though half the time I'm not even sure I understand a word he's saying. But let's face it, Scottish accents are just plain sexy. Slap a Scottish accent on a green ogre and I'll immediately find him irresistible, case in point—Shrek.

I have an odd propensity for anything Scottish. I've always dreamed of living in the Scottish Highlands, speaking nothing but Gaelic, and listening to the sweet, harmonious music of Celtic Thunder.

As much as we love our shows, all we ever do every night is vegetate in front of the tube. We used to have so much more spunk. We'd stay up until two in the morning, chatting about everything and nothing. I kind of miss all that. Since we've started working at the call center, we don't talk anymore. And frankly, after talking on the phones nonstop for eight hours straight, we're just *all talked-out.*

My throat is sore, my voice is hoarse, and the last thing I want to do is chit chat.

Midway through *The Late Late Show,* Kars is snoring loudly on the sofa. I throw an Afghan over her and tuck in the corners. It tends to get chilly down here in Janis' basement.

Stifling a yawn, I call it a night. After all, I have a student to tutor tomorrow.

Early next morning, I find myself wandering aimlessly around Idaho State U. I root around my bag, retrieve the campus map and study it. Okay, I need to locate the Eli M. Oboler Library.

"Are you lost?" a familiar voice pipes in from behind me.

I spin around. "Mika!" I cry joyously.

His face is flushed from the wind and he is smiling at me.

I smile back. "Good thing you found me. I had no clue where I was going."

"Is this your first time on the ISU campus?"

"Uh-huh." I scan the area. "Where did you come from? You appeared out of nowhere."

"You see that brick building over there?" He gestures toward it and I nod, squinting in the sunlight. "That's my dorm."

I am momentarily surprised. "I had no idea you lived in the dorms."

Good. That means he and Ingeborg don't bunk together.

He nudges me playfully. "You ready to be my tutor today?"

"Ready as I'll ever be. Lead the way my friend."

He walks at a brisk pace and I try to match his stride.

"So, which dorm does Ingeborg live in?" I ask casually.

"She lives with her parents; her family moved from Bulgaria about a year ago."

With some hesitation, I ask, "Um . . . so how long have you two been dating?"

"About six months now," he says, walking at a fast clip.

I formulate over a dozen questions in my snoopy head, but before I can broach them, we've arrived at our destination.

Like a true gentleman, Mika holds the door open and I breeze in. We find a quiet spot in the back of the library and he wastes no time. Unzipping his backpack, he retrieves a stack of papers and slides it across the table. "Here you go. That's all of it."

Sifting through the pages, it dawns on me why Mika finds his ESL course so daunting. All his assignments cover the mechanics of grammar and writing: nouns, verbs, pronouns, adjectives, adverbs, prepositions, conjunctions, interjections . . . Zzzzzzzzzzzz.

In order to become a good writer, one *must* be a good reader; they go hand in hand like ketchup and fries, like curry and naan, like macaroni and cheese. It is by reading that the mind absorbs the nuances of the language and how it is used.

My dad was a prolific author of numerous books on modern architecture. To this day, I enjoy reading his work. He could turn a bland subject into a vivacious one by injecting his idiosyncratic humor, double entendres and playful puns.

Needless to say, he'd spurred my interest and fostered my love of writing. He'd made writing seem cool and consequently, I came to enjoy the thrill of crafting a story.

And he'd instilled the importance of reading in me from a very early age. Every weekend, he'd drive me over to the Book Stall on Chestnut Court and there, he'd let me go hare wild. It was such a thrill! I'd grab armfuls of books—Enid Blyton, E.B

White and Nancy Drew when I was younger; and when I was slightly older—Agatha Christie. Detective Hercule Poirot taught me to become a better listener, to pay attention to what people aren't directly saying. Crime novels aside, I'd got hooked on comics, too, especially Betty and Veronica. That had been my one guilty pleasure. I'd loved the entire Riverdale gang: Archie and Jughead, Big Ethel, Reggie, Midge, and even Moose.

My dad had also immersed me in the works of Jane Austen, Emily Brontë and Charlotte Brontë. Oh, how I'd adored *Anne of Green Gables*; and when I'd turned thirteen, he introduced me to my very first teeny bopper romance— *Sweet Valley High,* and I learned that a good storybook trumps any dry textbook.

After flipping through Mika's assignments, I slam the stack of papers on the table with surprising force. "Enough of this!" I balk. Mika looks slightly taken aback, but I've garnered his full attention. "Look, I know your teacher thinks it's important that you learn about verb conjugations and noun declensions, and they *are* important, but . . ." I pause to articulate my thoughts. "When I was a kid and I wanted to learn how to ride a bike, I just hopped right on my BMX and eventually I figured it out. Now what I did *not* do was hunker down and study the mechanics of putting a bike together. By plunging in and riding my bike, I was able to enjoy the wind in my hair, the sun in my face, the scent of freshly cut grass. It was *fun*," I say with exuberance. Getting a bit carried away, I add, "I remember how much I loved zigzagging along the road on my pink BMX, avoiding potholes, popping wheelies." I find myself smiling fondly at the memories.

Anyway, where was I before I so rudely interrupted myself? What was I trying to say?

Oh yes, I need to tie it all in. "So it's the same thing with the English language. The best way to learn and enjoy it is to read something that grips you. It can be a mystery, a sci-fi, a thriller, anything. And once you're hooked, there's no turning back."

Mika leans back and hesitates. "Reading's not really my *thing*, though."

I blanch and pound my fist on the table. "That's because you haven't found the right book," I say with a firmness that surprises me.

The corners of his mouth twitch.

I flash him a perfunctory smile. "What types of shows do you watch on TV?"

He drums his fingers on the table. "The History channel. I dig war movies, documentaries, anything to do with World War II. I just like *facts*."

"What else?"

"*Top Gear*. It's a Brit show about cars." After a beat, he adds, "I also like watching Anthony Bourdain and Andrew Zimmern on the Travel Channel."

"That's a pretty good start." I stand up and grab my things.

He slides his chair back. "Where are you going?"

"*We* are going to the county library."

The very minute we troop into Marshall public library, I'm like a woman on a mission. I head straight for the computer kiosk and after a quick search, I march to the book aisle, scan the shelves for the title, locate the book and thrust it into Mika's hands.

He reads the title out loud. "*A Long Way Gone: Memoirs of a Boy Soldier.*"

I give a scholarly nod. "True story about a young kid engulfed in Sierra Leone's civil war. And it's not too long; only a little over two hundred pages. It's the perfect book for you," I say, trying my best to sell it to him.

"I'm sold."

Next, I drag Mika to the periodicals and step back, giving him some space and time to explore. After perusing the aisles for ten minutes, he has made his selections: two copies of *Motor Trend* and the most recent issue of *AutoSpeed*.

Mission accomplished.

While Mika registers for his library card, I idly browse the aisles. Surreptitiously, I pluck a steamy historical romance from the shelf.

After giving the cover a cursory glance, I flip it over and read the blurb on the back.

Scottish Laird Iain McLean is forced to wed Dundee lass Adamina to settle an ongoing dispute between two clans. Whilst the reunion may have brought peace to the Highlands, Iain finds himself at war with his own emotions. Strong willed and sensual, Adamina battles her fierce attraction for Iain, determined to remain his wife in name only. At the outset, Iain only seeks the pleasure of sharing his bed with Adamina. But he is soon lured into a love so absolute and a passion so deep that he finds himself torn between a woman and his clan, facing duplicity, betrayal and ultimately, redemption.

Well *hello* Laird Iain McLean! *Sizzle.* My whole body tingles with anticipation. I can't wait to snuggle under the covers tonight and read all about the sexy Scottish Laird who ravishes his feisty, fetching, bonnie lass. This book sounds like a delicious romp across the Highlands.

Satisfied with my choice, I sail over to the checkout line.

Oh, snap! The only librarian on duty is still assisting Mika.

I stand behind him and remain as quiet as a church mouse.

Sensing my presence, Mika turns around and notices the book in my hand. "What'cha got there?" he asks casually.

"A book," I say innocently, biting my inner lip.

"What book?" he asks with a flicker of curiosity.

I grip the book tighter. "Just one of the classics . . . *Jane Austen,*" I inform him with an air of Olde English eloquence, and with the prudence of a matronly, spinsterish aunt.

"You're all set!" exclaims the mousy librarian.

Thankfully, Mika returns his attention to the front desk.

My shoulders begin to relax and I sigh with relief.

Phew! Saved by the librarian.

Suddenly, Belgium boy does the unthinkable.

He whips back unexpectedly and pries the book out of my clenched fingers. After a mad skirmish and scuffle, Mika reigns victorious, book in his hand.

"Eeeps!" A shriek escapes my lips and I lurch forward, determined to wrestle the book back for dear life.

Alas, it's too late.

Mika is already reading the title out loud. "Interesting . . . *The Scottish Laird's Virgin Bride.*" His voice is playful yet tormenting, and I catch a faint glimmer of enjoyment on his face.

I fix him with a sharp, chilling stare.

Unfazed by my daggers, Mika studies the cover. The corners of his mouth begin twitching uncontrollably, and I find myself cringing and burning with shame.

Laird Iain McLean, fully decked out in a red kilt and tartan, is pictured frolicking in a celestial forest with a scantily dressed woman, whom I can only presume to be his wife, Adamina.

My face flushes hotter and hotter with utter humiliation.

Impulsively, I snatch the book back, and with as much dignity as I can muster, I check out my smut novel and stalk out of the library without so much as a glance back.

Mika is soon beside me.

But I am so crippled with embarrassment that I can scarcely even look at him. Awkwardly, I pretend to be preoccupied with the contents of my bag. To make matters worse, we had dropped off my car at home and took Mika's car to the library, which means I'll have to ride home with him. Oh, the *agony*.

I slide into Mika's car and remain mute.

Seconds later, the engine roars to life and we're coasting down the freeway in his low rider Impala. The air remains heavy with my silence and Mika mistakes my embarrassment for anger.

His expression softens. "Are you mad at me?"

I smile weakly in return and shake my head.

He shifts gears and looks meaningfully at me. "There's nothing wrong with dirty romance novels." After a beat, he adds, "You'll have to let me know if that's a good one, maybe I'll read it."

I bite the insides of my cheeks to keep from smiling. "You're *not* going to read it."

He grins. "You're right. I probably won't be reading *The Scottish Laird and his Virgin Bride* any time soon."

I laugh, and the more I think about it, Mika's right. There's really nothing wrong with reading trashy romance novels. It's like eating junk food every once in a while, like an In-N-Out burger and fries with a milkshake. I crave it every so often and it hits the spot, no pun intended.

Consuming coming-of-age novels just gets old and stale after a while. Plus 'healthy' literature and serious fiction plays havoc with my mind. Just last month, I had read *The Lovely Bones* and it was so dark and depressing that I almost put a gun to my head and pulled the trigger.

After reading that novel, I just *had* to escape to a happy place; somewhere far away, up in the Scottish Highlands. And thus, I turned to Harlequin.

Some of Harlequin's historical titles are remarkably well written and meticulously researched, and they continually open my eyes to new facets of history. I have learned more history from romance novels than I have from eighteen years of schooling.

Hmm. I realize now that I had overreacted.

I flick Mika a sideways glance. "So, any plans this weekend?"

He keeps his eyes on the road. "I'll be hitting the slopes up at Pebble Creek. We're supposed to be getting a ton of fresh powder tonight. It's going to be epic!"

"You're going skiing?" I ask airily.

He puts on an indignant air. "Um, no. I'm going boarding."

"Oh, *sorrrrry,*" I say with a trace of sarcasm. "I didn't mean to ignite the feud between you riders and skiers."

Mika rewards me with a wry smile. "Skiers? Could you possibly be referring to those wanker two plankers with prissy poles who deck themselves out in neon onesies?"

I smother a giggle. "So, when you're not tearing down the mountain in your plastic tray, your assignment from me this week is to read the book and magazines in your spare time."

"Yes, ma'am," he says, pulling his car into Janis' driveway.

Yes, I still live there with Karsynn.

Mika stalls the engine and turns to face me. "Thanks again, Madison." And for a little while, his gaze lingers.

"Anytime," I say in a stilted voice, inching out of my seat. I step out of the car, slam the door, and fly down the path.

Wrestling with the lock, I throw a glance over my shoulder.

Mika waves at me through the lightly tinted windows.

I wave back.

Six

Beep!

"Thanks for calling Lightning Speed. This is Maddy, how can I help?" I ask on autopilot.

And then the strangest thing happens. The customer actually starts *spelling*.

"M-y n-a-m-e i-s B-e-n W-r-i-g-h-t," he spells. *Spells!!! W-T-F ?!?*

"I w-a-n-t t-o s-p-e-a-k t-o t-h-e C-E-O," he orders, and yes, he is *still* spelling.

Yeah, they all want to speak to our CEO, Siegfried Miles, like Siegfried sits around all day twiddling his thumbs, just waiting to speak to fuming customers. Siegfried has a company to run for Pete's sake.

I give the speller the standard spiel. "I'm sorry, Mr. Wright, our CEO is unavailable to take calls, but you can write a letter and mail it to his office if you'd like."

Not surprisingly, the speller doesn't take this kindly.

He flips out and starts spelling again, this time an octave higher. "N-O! N-O! N-O!"

Oh my God. This guy is such a hoot!

Oddly enough, all this spelling is infectious.

On impulse, I start spelling myself, "Y-E-S Y-E-S Y-E-S."

"M-A-N-A-G-E-R!" he yells and spells.

Uh oh, I guess he isn't amused.

"O-K," I say politely, not wanting to antagonize him further.

Drats! That's too bad. I was enjoying the call and I wanted to spell some more with Mr. Wright. We were just about to get into a spelling spar and he had to go and end it.

What a buzzkill.

Oh well, hopefully I'll get him next time. He sure broke up the monotony of my calls. How refreshing! A speller!

Time to go get The Führer.

I stride over to her cubicle and stand there until she notices me. It doesn't take long.

"Yessssssssssss?" she hisses.

"Um, I have a caller who wants to speak to a manager. And he's very upset."

Hillary shoots me a terse look. "For future reference, I would prefer that you phrase it like this: *I have an escalation, and the caller is irate,*" she snaps. "You work at a call center and I *expect* you to *speak* call center lingo!"

I stare at her, unblinking. She's obviously barking mad.

"So tell me, what's going on now?" Hillary's voice is laced with irritation. "Why is the caller irate?"

I'm quite taken by the Spelling Bee, and I find myself feeling slightly protective over him. "Well, he's actually really nice. But I think he may have some sort of speech impediment. So . . . um, he spells." I cast a lopsided grin.

The Führer says nothing.

And so I carry on explaining, "At first, he wanted to speak to the CEO. I gave him the standard spiel, but he didn't like it and spelled for a manager."

She gnashes her teeth. "Transfer him to me. Extension 4444."

My poor little Spelling Bee. Little does he realize what he is in for. The Führer will chew him up and spit him out like the tobacco she chews.

Sigh. He should have just stuck with me. We could've gone places. I just know that we could've formed a meaningful kinship and spelled the night away.

Reluctantly, I release the Hold button and conference the call.

"Mr. Wright, thank you for holding. I have Hillary on the line now. She's my supervisor and she'll be assisting you from here," I say with a deep sadness in my voice, and drop off the line.

Bye-bye my little Spelling Bee.

Be safe, keep on spelling and buzz, buzz away.

Beep!

"Thanks for calling Lightning Speed Communications, this is Maddy, how can I assist?"

"Hello, I'm just calling for shits and giggles. I've got a complex question for you, since you're supposedly a tech whiz."

"That I am not, but go ahead, what is your complex question, sir?"

"If a tree falls in a forest and no one is around to hear it, does it make a sound?"

I consider this briefly and pose this question to Mr. Jean-Paul Sartre, "Well, sir, if you did not have sexual intercourse with your wife and she's pregnant, did she have an extramarital affair or is she just the Virgin Mary?"

Click!

We're in Janis' basement and as usual, Karsynn and I are glued to the tube, watching the MTV Movie Awards with a mixture of titillation and boredom.

I know. We live pretty sad, pathetic lives.

In my defense, Zac Efron is at the awards show, so really, that should explain everything.

Ian Somerhalder struts on stage to present the next award.

Karsynn swoons. "He is simply bootylicious."

"Quit talking like Beyonce. By the way *bootylicious* and *booh-tay* are not real words."

Karsynn blanches. "For your info, Beyonce is now known as Sasha Fierce. She can sing, act *and* dance. That sista is a triple threat! And by the way," she adds, "booty *is* a real word, it's in the dictionary."

"Which one?" I challenge.

"The urban dictionary," she states matter-of-factly.

"The urban dictionary doesn't count," I counter. "You can't use it in Scrabble."

"Hah! But I'm pretty sure that in Webster's dictionary, booty means pirate treasure or prize. So it *is* a real word," says Kars triumphantly. Then out of nowhere, she lets one rip.

It is mammoth!

Unlike her usual Mount Saint Helen eruptions, this one is a Krakatoan explosion. In fact, it is so massive that the aftershock tremors resonate through the lumpy sofa cushions.

"Your farts stink!" I choke through the fume of flatulence. "It smells like something crawled up your ass and died."

She looks at me with an expression that says she's inordinately pleased with herself. "What? Yours don't stink?"

"Nope! Mine's all air and packs no punch. But yours, yours are silent killers." I shudder. "And I even *felt* it," I add, cringing with disgust.

KAPOW! She swats me with a pillow. "Feel *this!*"

"OW!" I squawk, half laughing. "You really outdid yourself this time; that one tipped the Richter scale. It was a magnitude of 20.0."

While I'm no stranger to breaking wind, Kars actually trumps me in this sport. We're in such a comfort zone that whenever I let one loose, Kars will let one rip and announce smugly, "Mine was better."

I'm always happy to concede.

But tonight's fart episode has got me thinking . . . maybe we're getting a little *too* close for comfort. Maybe we need some space.

Maybe it's time I move out.

Janis and Kars have been nothing but kind and generous, giving me shelter and feeding me for two months. They've offered me unlimited hospitality, making it very clear that I can stay for as long as I want. And the last thing I want to do is overstay my welcome.

"Kars," I say in all-seriousness. "I think it's time. Time for me to get a place of my own."

Her face contorts. "You want to move out?"

I nibble my lips. "Umm-hmm."

Karsynn looks crestfallen. But her state of distress is short lived. "I have an idea!" Her face lights up. "Why don't we move out *together* and get a two bedroom apartment?"

I pause to allow myself to digest this. Now why didn't I think of that? I'll have my own place, I'll still have my best friend *and* I'll save on rent money.

"Sure, why not?" I hear myself saying.

"Yes! My mom will be *so* glad to be finally rid of me."

I fervently shake my head. "Are you kidding me? Kars, your mom will miss you like crazy."

Honestly, Janis and Kars are joined at the hip, and I envy the strong bond they share. When Kars breaks the news to Janis, I just *know* she'll be sad to see her baby go.

Hmm, I wonder if *my* mom even misses me.

I doubt it. She's far too busy with work to even notice I'm gone. My mom is an OBGYN. And if you scramble the letters and use a little imagination, OBGYN sort of resembles G'BYE.

As a kid, that's exactly what I'd called her—the G'BYE doctor; and quite aptly so as she was always bidding me adieu, rushing off to help deliver some stranger's baby.

After we'd lost my dad, things got worse. My mom had completely checked out. I *never* saw her. I'd felt alone, I'd felt raw, I'd felt angry, and I would've surely gone off the deep end had it not been for my dad's parting words. He'd said, "Maddy, my love . . . always stay drunk on writing."

Whenever I was down, whenever I'd miss him, whenever I was upset, whenever I was feeling alone, he told me to pick up a pen and just start writing. Anything. My feelings, my dreams, my hopes, my stories. And so I'd write and write to blot out the tears, to blot out the hurt, to blot out the pain, to blot out the world.

I'd write until my fingers blistered and bled. Eventually, they hardened and calloused. But it was cathartic, helping me heal in more ways than one. And it solidified my aspirations of becoming a writer.

Just like my dad.

But things don't always go as planned. Sometimes life throws you curve balls, and you either learn to swerve them, or hit them like there's no tomorrow.

At this point in my life, I'm just swerving.

I breathe out a heavy sigh. Resigning myself, I reach for my phone and call my mom. It's been over two months since I'd left home, yet it never occurred to me to call her sooner.

One summer, I went away to Young Writers Camp.

Oh, I know. I was a nerd with a capital N, and that camp was nerd proof.

When I'd arrived home, my mom was oblivious to the fact that I had been gone for an entire month. The whole time I'd been away at nerd camp, she'd assumed that school was still in session and that she just *happened* to miss me at home. For a month.

Go figure.

It's not like her head was in the clouds or anything like that; she was simply married to her job. And while her practice had flourished, our relationship wilted.

The only time we'd spent together was in her Audi, since she chauffeured me to school every morning. During those brief moments, I'd chat with her, tell her about my day, ask her about hers . . . just *be* with her.

But all that had changed when I'd turned fourteen. She'd dragged me to the DMV, signed me up for a hardship license, and that was the end of that.

Our time together—*finito*. Our relationship—*kaput-o*.

Although my mom's still around, I feel like I've lost her. It's as if I've lost both my parents. What can I say? I'm an orphan, so to speak. Little orphan Annie.

I press the phone to my ear and after a couple of rings, my mom answers, "Hi, dear!" Before I can get a word in edgewise, she launches off, "Honey, you won't believe this! I'm dating now, he's an Ob-Gyn. Vince works at the UC Medical Center and I've only been seeing him for a month, but I think he's prefect and—"

I cut her off. "Wait. Did you just say he's an Ob-Gyn?" I ask, feeling somewhat disturbed by this. "Mom, please don't tell me you're dating a Vagina Doctor."

"Oh, Madison!" she scoffs. "There's nothing wrong with male Ob-Gyns."

"Err, yeah there is. Mom, any man who chooses a profession that involves shoving his hand down a woman's *pickachu* on a daily basis is seriously a pervo. It's legalized, medical rape!"

"It's called a pap smear," she scolds. "And when was the last time you had one?"

I sigh dramatically. "Mom, I really don't want some stranger scraping my *pikachu*."

"I'll do it," she insists. "Make an appointment with my clinic."

"Mom, *stop*. Let's discuss Vince again. What is he like?"

"*Ahh,* Vince is a wonderful man; a divorcee, no kids. Anyway honey, I'm sorry I've missed you at home these past few weeks. I've just been *so* caught up with work—and with Vince of course," she adds impishly.

See, she doesn't even realize I'm still in The Valley of Potatoes.

"Mom, I'm still in Idaho visiting Kars, remember? And guess what?" I pause for effect. "I've got a job here!"

"Well that's great news honey," she trills with pleasure. "At a newspaper?"

I clear my throat. "No. At a call center."

"Honey, the line is fuzzy. All I got was *call* something." Then she emits a tinkling laugh. "Madison, please don't tell me you're a call girl. I raised you better than that."

"Ha-ha mom. Very funny. No. I am *not* a prostitute. I work at a call center." After a beat, I add, "As a customer service rep."

There is an excruciating pause, a silence bordering on awkward. *Sheesh!* I'm beginning to think she'd be happier if I *were* a call girl. After all, hookers aren't reviled as much as call center reps, even though both professions offer the same service.

Oral service. Sorry, but it begged to be said!

Her voice drips with disappointment. "But Madison, *why?*"

"Well, it's a job, albeit a thankless one. But a job nonetheless, and I needed one. I was tired of sitting around doing nothing. Plus, it's not that bad. Really. I've even learned a lot," I gab, trying to remain upbeat and positive for my sake and *hers.*

She perks up. "So tell me, what have you learned?"

"Patience. You'll be pleased to know that I've learned to control my tongue."

This elicits a sardonic *harrumph* from her. "What about the people who work there? What are they like?"

I decide to give her what she expects to hear. "Well where I sit, to the left of me is a beached whale. Three rows in front of me is another beached whale. Four cubicles across, you'll never guess, another beached whale," I ramble in a monotone.

I've actually gotten to know one of these whales. He's a five hundred pound Samoan, and his nickname happens to be Tiny.

Now don't get me wrong; having curves or being curvaceous is good thing but there is 'curvy' and there is 'coronary,' and Tiny is a walking heart attack.

Here lies the shocker—Tiny acquired that name because he is actually the *smallest* of all his siblings.

Meanwhile, all I can hear is static on the line.

"What did you say again honey?" Her voice crackles.

"Um, nothing . . ."

A beat. Another beat.

"Well, if you're sure about that job, then I guess it's okay," she says disconcertedly. After a pause, she adds, "*Really*, there are plenty of *other* jobs out there you know."

She's obviously out of touch with reality. "Mom no, *not really*. There are *no* jobs out there. And—"

She cuts me off, "Look sweetie, I must dash! Vincent is taking me to the opera tonight, but you take care of yourself. If you need money, let me know and I'll wire you some right away. 'K, love?"

I sigh out loud as she clicks off.

Money will be the last thing I ask of her.

Seven

"KAR-SYNN," I holler with a sense of urgency.

Her head pops out of her cubicle. "What?"

"Get over here," I command. "NOW!"

Kars races to my cube and I seize her by the shoulders. "You will *not* believe this, but I am talking to a Miss Fuck-a-Lot."

She stares at me bug-eyed for several minutes. "You've got to be kidding me!"

"No I'm not, and yes I *am* talking to a Miss Fuck-a-Lot."

"No—you—are—NOT," she says severely.

"Look! Check out her name." I point at my screen.

Kars peers at my monitor and spells the caller's name out loud, "F-A-U-G-H-A-L-A-T-T-E."

"She's French," I explain succinctly. "She says it's pronounced Fuck-a-Lot."

There is an instant palpable hush.

Kars stares at me deadpan.

Seconds later, we explode into a spasm of giggles.

"Hello? Anybody there?" An agitated voice crackles in my ear.

My laughter instantly evaporates. Whoopsie! I forgot Miss Fuck-a-Lot is still on MUTE.

Remorse washes over me. I feel terribly awful for neglecting her.

Shoot! I have no idea what she's been harping about for the past five minutes. As soon as she said her name, I pushed MUTE so she couldn't hear my gales of laughter and screamed for Kars.

"*Merde,* I have to get back to her," I say wistfully. "*Mais c'est chouette, les name est magnifique.*"

Kars tuts, "*Sacré bleu! Zut Alors! Au revoir Mademoiselle Fuck-a-Lot.*" Then she shimmies over to Ingeborg's cubicle.

Keeping half an ear turned to their conversation, I catch some snippets, something about French people having the best names *au contraire,* followed by Karsynn's wild and infectious laughter echoing through the maze of cubicles.

Poor Miss Fuck-a-Lot. Oh, to be cursed with such a name.

After composing myself, I release the MUTE key. "I'm *so* sorry Miss Fuck-a-Lot, but we have a *really* bad connection. You were breaking up there for bit," I say in my most apologetic voice and proceed to give her my full and undivided attention.

Moments later, I'm still assisting Miss Fuck-a-Lot when I hear Hillary the Giant Not Ready Nazi's ear-shattering scream.

Uh oh, her meeting must be over now.

"Karsynn! You've been in NOT READY for over ten minutes. GET BACK ON THE PHONES RIGHT NOW!" The Führer blasts, sending shock waves throughout the entire center.

Karsynn stiffens, collects herself and scuttles like a cockroach to her cubicle.

When we're not slaving away in Hell, we're apartment hunting, which ends up consuming our entire weekend.

Pocatello Plaza is the eighth apartment complex we've looked at so far, and eight is certainly the charm.

"This is the one!" Karsynn cheers while doing a cartwheel in the middle of the living room.

I shake my head, marveling at her boundless energy; she's the Energizer Bunny on speed.

As I pace the floor, going back and forth between the kitchen and living room, one word keeps repeating in my head—Love!

It even features vaulted ceilings! *Ahhh*. A warm and virtuous glow envelops me. I'm standing in the Sistine Chapel. Now all I need is a Michelangelo mural on the ceiling.

Gazing out the lofty bay windows, I gasp with joyful wonder; it bestows upon me a picturesque view of the Rocky Mountains.

I'm sold!

Satisfied with our decision, we sign on the dotted line.

Rent will be $950, plus we'll have to fork over another $900 for the security deposit. Well, that just about wipes out most of my earnings. But, it's worth it. My heart is bursting with joy.

"I feel like a grown-up now," I say jubilantly, as we leave our future pad behind.

Kars flashes a full-wattage grin. "Amen sista. We'll have our very own place."

Moving day arrives before we know it. Mika had offered to help us move, and his offer was snapped up without a moment's hesitation. We need all the muscles around to lift our bulky stuff, and so our Man-with-the-Muscles Mika is on site, with his shirt sleeves rolled up, raring to go.

Kars puts him to work right away. Upon discovering that the elevator is kaput, Kars conveniently places herself in charge, appointing herself Directress of Project Move.

"So." Mika rubs his palms together. "Where is this sofa going?"

"All the way up to the top," says Kars, not trying to hide a smirk.

I smile at him sheepishly. "Sorry, Mika, we're on the top floor so that makes it twelve flights of stairs."

"Hey, it's not a problem for me. But will you be okay, Maddy?"

"Me? Yeah, I'll be fine," I mutter somewhat dubiously, fully aware of the insurmountable task ahead.

Kars wastes no time in cracking her whip. "Maddy! Mika! Ready, Set, HEAVE!"

Mika lifts one end of the sofa while I grasp the other end. Like Sherpa carriers, we begin our ascent of Katmandu.

"Urnnggh," I grunt, using every inch of my body, every ounce of strength to lift and mount the steps.

This sofa, donated to us courtesy of Janis, weighs a ton.

Janis treated herself to a brand spanking new Pottery Barn slip-covered sofa, on the assumption that she'll be rolling in the Benjamins for getting us the jobs.

Apparently, referral money is big money.

While I'm struggling under the weight of the sofa, Mika seems to be doing just fine. He lugs the sofa with ease, while I'm sweating from the sheer exertion, wheezing and panting, trying to keep up. But that's totally fine with me because right this very minute, I have the best aerial view in Pocatello.

Each time Mika flexes his toned forearms, his T-shirt hitches up a few inches. And the sight of his sun bronzed, chiseled body unsettles me. My liquid eyes linger on his washboard abs; beads of sweat accumulate on his pecs, glistening in the afternoon sun.

Phew. I wipe my brow. It's getting hot in here.

I find myself entranced by his taut skin, and the tiny trail of fine hair that leads down, down, down to his . . . *Gulp.*

I'm hiking down the Treasure Trail. *Sexy music playing in the background.* I'm wandering down the Happy Trail.

"To the left," Kars yells like a drill sergeant and I'm thrown off the Happy Trail.

Sweat pouring down my face, I glower at her belligerently. She's taking her job a little *too* seriously, barking out orders with a ruthless ferocity as Mika and I clumsily navigate the sofa up the narrow stairs. Humph. She has zero compassion for her Sherpa carriers.

"Maddy! Move! Keep MOOOVING!" Kars screams in my ear.

In between ragged breaths, I manage to say, "Just in case you've forgotten Kars, I'm Maddy your BFF, (*WHEEZE*) not Maddy the Mule."

Mika's eyes flash with concern. "You want to take a break?"

"Nurrggghh," I grunt, wearing a determined expression, but I seriously doubt I'm fooling anyone. "I'm fine. Let's . . . nurgh . . . keep go-ingggg."

Karsynn booms, "THAT'S RIGHT, KEEP GOING! YOU'VE GOT TEN MORE FLIGHTS OF STAIRS TO GO!"

In retrospect, we could've picked an apartment unit on the first floor. But Kars insisted that we live on the top floor.

I had some initial qualms, but after my eyes were treated to the spectacular view from the top, I knew I just *had* to be up high, scraping the skies.

Now that I'm lugging this bulky sofa up these endless flights of stairs, I think that was quite possibly the *stooooopidest* decision ever.

What the hell were we thinking?

After mountaineering the sofa up to the very peak, we tackle two queen sized mattresses, two box springs, our fifty-inch LCD TV, two headboards, the dining table, the side tables, the lamps, loads and loads of boxes filled with clothes, cooking utensils and all our mindless crap.

By the time we're done carting everything up to Unit 12 B, I'm about ready to pass out.

"I-I think my back is broken." I collapse onto the floor and moan like a dying cat.

Even Mika is slightly out of breath. "You okay, Maddy?"

I whimper, "I think I'm going to *DIE*."

Karsynn surveys the damaged goods (Mika and I) with both hands on her hips. "You two did a great job."

I glare at her with an expression of an axe murderer.

That COW! All she did was scream, "A little to the left, a little to the right."

In a futile attempt to redeem herself, Kars begins handing out bottles of Fiji water. "You two take it easy. I'll be arranging the furniture."

"Go right ahead." I lie lifeless on the floor, while Kars shuffles a coffee table around me.

Mika slides off the kitchen counter. "I'll help you out," he offers and gets right to work.

I refuse to budge. My joints have swelled up so much it looks like I'm suffering from elephantiasis.

And when I move my knees, I hear a "Snap, Crackle, and Pop" sound.

I'll surely need to see a chiropractor after this debacle.

On a positive note, this whole experience has given me a newfound respect for Two Men and a Truck Co. and Starving Students Moving Company.

Fully exhausted after the Big Move, we gather in the kitchen to replenish our fluids.

"Mika, we want to treat you to a nice meal for helping us. Pick a restaurant," I say, crossing my arms.

Mika mimics me. He folds his arms across his chest and leans his sexy, sweaty body against the refrigerator.

"Nah, you girls don't have to buy me dinner. It was nothing."

Kars grumbles, "Just tell us where you want to go eat! We're freakin' starving here."

"In that case, what about IHOP?" he suggests.

"IHOP? You want pancakes for dinner?" I ask, just to be sure and he nods. "Mika," I say mildly, "I love breakfast any time of the day, but we want to treat you to a meal at a *nice* restaurant. Somewhere slightly more upscale. I'm sorry, but the International House of Pancakes is *not* a restaurant. It's a diner. And we can make you pancakes any day."

"Yeah! Now hurry up and pick a nice restaurant." Karsynn begins tapping her foot impatiently.

"How about Red Lobster? Ingeborg's working there tonight, and I have to pick her up after her shift ends."

"Red Lobster it is!" I quickly exclaim, before he has a chance to change his mind.

Mika looks from me to Kars. "Do I have time to go home and take a shower?"

"NO!" we holler in unison.

Red Lobster is an absolute madhouse and the flustered hostess informs us it'll be a forty minute wait. Figures; it's a Saturday night. So we sit and wait like hungry wolves.

I spot Ingeborg at the bar and nudge Mika, gesturing in her direction. But he already sees her.

Gak! My mind has a hard time parsing the sequence of events that follow. Ingeborg is flirting with some old geezer. Now, geriatric geezers can be vaguely attractive, especially if they resemble silver haired foxes the likes of Liam Neeson, Colin Firth, and Clooney. Heck, I'll even lump centenarian Clint Eastwood into that category.

But this particular geezer isn't even a silver haired fox. In fact, he's a hairless Sharpei, and his splotchy paws are mauling the fair Ingeborg.

Sharpei leans forward and whispers something in Ingeborg's ear. Giggling like a schoolgirl, she spills onto his lap.

Then Sharpei morphs into a massage monster, squeezing and kneading her flesh like dough. And sweet Ingeborg seems to be enjoying it in a very uninhibited way.

I stare agog.

Kars is gawking.

Mika's face is ashen.

At once, he springs to his feet and advances on them.

"Uh oh," I groan.

Mika stands rigidly behind Ingeborg and the Sharpei. His jaw is clenched and his fists are balled up.

"Yeah! You go get him, Mika! Deck him! Pummel and pumice him to a pulp! Rearrange his face!" Karsynn riles.

"Karsynn!" I chide. "This isn't funny!"

Mika's face tightens as they continue with their shenanigans.

I can't believe it! Ingeborg and Sharpei are so enamored with each other that they're totally oblivious to Mika.

After an excruciatingly painful minute, he taps Ingeborg on her shoulder. She cranes her neck and nearly jumps out of her skin.

"Busted," blurts Kars.

"She's got Mika," I say, clearly stupefied. "What is she doing with *him*?!?"

Now Mika and Ingeborg appear to be in a heated argument.

I strain my ears to listen, but can barely make out a word.

Seeing his opening, Sharpei scampers off with his tail tucked between his legs.

How cowardly!

Meanwhile, Ingeborg and Mika are still squabbling like a pair of seagulls. Suddenly, Ingeborg spins on her heels and darts into the kitchen, and poor Mika just stands there, looking positively crushed. Eventually, he makes his way back to us.

I shoot him a look of concern, unsure of what to say.

So I say nothing.

But Kars, as usual, can't keep her trap shut. "So, I guess Ingeborg's robbing the grave," she says in a cavalier fashion.

I glare at Kars mutinously. If looks could kill, she'd be dead as a dodo. Releasing a nervous laugh, I turn to Mika. "Oh, pay no attention to her."

His lips fall into a sharp line and he seems preoccupied with his thoughts. The atmosphere is tense to say the least.

"Maddy, table for three," announces the chirpy hostess. I drag my heels across the floor and poise myself for a painful and uncomfortable evening.

Ah, it sure feels good to be home in our new crib. I'm so stuffed I can hardly walk.

I'd ordered the Ultimate Feast and I annihilated my *entrée*.

Oh, and I'd polished everything off Mika's plate as well. Barely a minute into our meal, he had lost his appetite.

But I don't blame him and I'm sure no one of good conscience could. Heck, if I saw some cougar rubbing up all over my man, I'd lose my appetite, too.

Swollen and engorged, I waddle to the sofa and sink into the cushions with a sated sigh. Stifling a yawn, I rest one hand over my belly.

Gosh. I look like I'm in my third trimester. I think I may be having twin food babies.

Kars flops onto the sofa. "I've never seen Mika look so pissed. Did you see him stabbing that lobster with his fork? He looked like he was trying to kill that poor thing and it was already dead."

"I know." I pat my protruding belly. "Good thing I rescued it."

We sit there for a while in silence, letting our food digest.

Kars looks pensive, and I can tell by the look on her face that she's about to go off on one of her psych spiels.

And I'm right.

"I have a theory," Karsynn begins, "about Ingeborg. You know what her problem is?"

I smile indulgently. "No, pray tell, Dr. Higginbotham."

"She suffers from the Electra complex. Yep! Siggy Freud came up with that one. It's the female version of the Oedipus complex. Although I don't think she has 'penis envy' like Freud proposes; I think her dad was probably absent for most of her life, and now she's looking for some old geezer to replace him. You know, to fill that fatherless vacuum in her life."

I raise my eyes to the ceiling. "Kars, both you and I lost our fathers pretty early on in our lives (while I had lost my dad to cancer, Kars had lost hers to the State Penitentiary). So how come we're not out there dating older men?"

She knits her eyebrows together. "How do you know we're not?"

Her words seem loaded with potential meaning. "What are you talking about?"

"Nothing," she says with a mysterious smile.

Languorously, I stretch out my legs. "I'm just going to vegetate here all night."

Kars hops off the sofa. "Okay, I'm heading out."

I jerk my head up. "Huh? Where?"

"Somewhere," she says vaguely.

I eye her with considerable suspicion.

"Speaking of which, I must get ready now." She skips to her room and slams the door.

"You're going out? At this hour?" I holler. "With whom???"

No response.

I plump up the cushions and wait for Kars to emerge from her room. I need to grill her for more details.

But my eyelids feel so heavy . . .

They flitter and flutter like butterflies, and soon drift shut.

I'd had an inkling Kars was seeing someone. Unbeknownst to me, that *someone* works right under the call center roof. Tongues are wagging and rumor is swirling around the center that Kars has hooked up with Bob Seely.

What can I say about Bob? Well, he's a slimy supervisor. Not to mention, he's barrel-chested with Buddha tits, his hairline is rapidly receding, his teeth yellowing, his wardrobe screams for a makeover, and he walks around with permanent sweat stains under his pits. And worst of all, he's married! MARRIED!

My new cubicle neighbor, Truong Nguyen, broke this shocking news to me today. Apparently, Truong had heard it through the grapevine that is now creeping out of control.

And by the way, the girl who *used* to sit by me is gone. WOOT! WOOT!

I think her name was Nina, or was it Mina? Anyway, she was appallingly arrogant, with an ego the size of two continents.

Seriously, that girl lacked a modesty chip in her brain. All day long, she'd brag about how wonderful she was, how wonderful the callers thought she was. Incidentally, she'd been voted employee of the month, for *twelve* consecutive months in a row, and her plaques were displayed on every inch of her cubicle wall.

She really bugged me. I wasn't jealous of her or anything like that; it was her whole *I'm-better-than-thou* attitude that really got under my skin.

I remember a time when she had peered over my cubicle wall and smirked, "Hey, did you get nominated for the Excellent Service and Sales Award last month?"

"No," I gritted curtly.

"Well I did, and I WON. *Again.* Tee-hee-hee," she crowed hysterically.

Give me a freakin' break. Who the hell cares?

So I'd basically ignored her most of the time, which mind you, was quite an arduous task since she encroached upon my space and tried to get in my face every chance she got. And now that the bitch is gone, I welcome Truong with open arms.

"How do I pronounce your name?" I ask my new neighbor. "I want to make sure I say it right."

Truong smiles pleasantly. "It's like the word *trunk,* you know, like tree trunk, but with a 'g' at the end instead. Or, you can just call me Trunk."

My gaze shifts down to his scrawny chicken legs. He looks severely underfed. All skin and bones. A bag of bones.

Calling him Twig would be more suitable than Trunk. So I decide to pass on Trunk and try his real name.

"Okay, *Truong,*" I say, testing the waters. "How's that?"

"You nailed it." He beams and begins unpacking.

Humming a happy tune, he sets a ceramic rooster on his desk and steps back to admire it.

"Oh! You collect roosters!" I exclaim delightedly. "I adore the chic French Country theme. Or are you trying to create a Rustic Barnyard look?"

"No, Maddy. This is not a looster," he tactfully corrects. "This is a cock."

There is a slight pause as I digest this. It becomes apparent to me that Truong can't pronounce the letter 'R'. And a rooster and a cock essentially mean the same thing— they're both male chickens, so he must prefer the word 'cock' for obvious reasons.

"Oh . . ." I trail off. "Well how cute." I cast a lopsided grin.

"Um-hmm," he hums, angling the cock a smidgen to the right.

Since Truong appears absorbed with this task, I reach for my latest issue of *US Weekly*.

"Maddy?" he purrs, as I'm leafing through the pages.

I jerk my head up. "Yeah?"

His eyes glint with mischief. "Would you like to stroke my cock?"

I'm rendered speechless. And when it finally sinks in, I giggle good-naturedly. "Truong, cut it out!"

Truong is what you'd call a flamer, he's very much on the frou-frou side. He dons a Hermès scarf to work every day, year round. Always dapper and debonair, he exudes a sort of Parisian air.

So *really*, it should come as no surprise that Truong collects cocks. And what a collection he has!

My mouth slackens as he whips out rooster after rooster. Soon, his whole desk is cramped with cocks.

Gawping at his colorful collection, I ask, "Truong, weren't you on Dawson's team before?"

He nods in affirmation and continues decorating his cubicle with finesse and flair. I watch, slightly entranced. Every cock is meticulously and aesthetically placed for optimal serenity and balance. Very *feng shui,* if I may add.

"Well, why did they move you here?" I probe, seized by a surge of hope that perhaps they fired that bragasaurus Mina or Nina *whatsherface.*

"My Not Ready time sucks, so I'm sentenced to time in the Not Ready correctional facility."

"*Ahh*, I see." I smile, feeling a sudden kinship with Truong.

I can already tell we're going to become chummy friends.

"Well, Truong, welcome to Gulag camp," I say cheerfully.

He snickers. "Hopefully Hillary doesn't break me."

I give a little laugh. "Let's hope not! What would this center do without the ABC?"

Truong is known in this center as the ABC. And *no*, he is not American Born Chinese. Truong is 100% Vietnamese.

He's called the ABC because he's the first to broadcast any news, gossip, scandal and hearsay. Seriously, Truong is a Perez Hilton in the making.

And today, the latest and juiciest news to hit the wires involves my best friend. I'm completely thrown when Truong gives me the exclusive on Kars and Bob the Married Man.

"It can't be true," I cry in a strangled voice.

Karsynn would never stoop to something this low. She dated plenty of losers in college, but they were never *married.*

"Well, you know what they say." He flicks his scarf. "Where there's smoke, there's fire."

But I still don't believe it. Not until I hear it from the horse's mouth. I need to talk to Kars about this in person— right *now*, as a matter of fact.

Beep!

I guess the inquisition will have to wait.

"Thanks for calling Lightning Speed Communications. This is Maddy, how can I help?" I flip through my new tabloid magazine; it's a much needed distraction from this scandal that Karsynn's purportedly embroiled in.

The caller demands in a distinctly British accent, "Oiiii! AM I CALLING BLOODY INDIA?!?"

"Yes, sir, you're calling India. And I'm a slumdog living in the slums of Mumbai," I inform him blandly. "Happy now?"

"Ecstatic," he says with contempt.

Sheesh! Right this minute, I wish I was actually Indian so I can rant 'And you're a bloody British Imperialist who colonized my country for centuries, exploiting my good people.'

"And I'll bet you're reading some daft tabloid magazine like *People*," spits the hoity-toity, Earl Grey tea drinking bastard.

Bwarhahaha! I'm laughing inside. Yes, I happen to be reading a gossip mag. But it's *not People*, it's *US Weekly.*

Nevertheless, I refuse to dignify his asinine question with an answer. I mean, c'mon already. What does he expect me to say? That I'm reading Hemmingway? Nietzsche? Rushdie? Or Dostoyevsky? Shakespeare perhaps?

D'oh! I can't focus on heavy lit when I have a job to do.

Reading tabloids uses zero brain cells; hence it is very work appropriate.

"Go on. Tell me," he taunts. "You're reading *People* magazine, aren't you?" he repeats snidely.

Disdaining to answer him, I get straight down to business. "Sir, I'll need to ask you a few questions to verify you."

"WHAT?" he barks and goes ape shit on me. "BLOODY NORA! THIS IS BOLLOCKS! SHITE MAN, WHAT MORE DO YOU WANT FROM ME? YOU WANT MY FARKIN BLOOD TYPE??? MY DNA?"

Cor Blimey. Holy London Bridge Is Falling Down. This bloke swears like Gordon Ramsay. In training, I learned the term for what this dick is trying to do. He's trying to 'hook' me by pushing all my red buttons, hoping to get some sort of a reaction out of me.

And, I'm supposed to stay calm by not taking his 'bait.'

This jerk is such a class act that I simply *refuse* to give him the satisfaction of taking his bait. Over my dead body!

Taking a sharp intake of breath, I press on, "No, sir, I do not need your blood type, nor do I need your DNA," I say in a calm and collected manner. "But what I do need is your first and last name."

The fact that I do not take his 'bait' only serves to infuriate him further. He continues hurling obscenities at me.

"FARK MAN! YOU HAVE ALL MY INFORMATION YOU NINCOMPOOP! I PUNCHED IT ALL IN BEFORE I EVEN GOT TO YOU!"

"I apologize, sir, but I never got it. So I will need to verify you again," I say breezily.

"YOU FOCKIN IGNORANT MORONIC TWAT! YOU'RE RUBBISH! RUBBISH! THIS IS A FOCKIN CHARADE AND I'M NOT DEALING WITH THIS FOCKIN SHIT! SOD OFF AND GET ME YOUR SODDING SUPERVISOR!"

"One moment please," I sing-song sweetly.

Sure thing you filthy, foul mouthed bloke! Swearing every two seconds just showcases your limited vocabulary. But I do find it mildly amusing when Brits use the word 'sod.' Although I am fully aware of its intended meaning, it always reminds me of a chunk of lawn.

I jab the HOLD button and saunter to The Führer's lair.

She's not there, and so I wander through the maze of cubicles, trying to track her down. It doesn't take long, since she is Hillary the GIANT Not Ready Nazi after all.

I spot her chatting with another supervisor.

Standing ten feet away, I linger and lurk.

When two supervisors are in the middle of a conversation, you don't interrupt, you just lurk in the background. Just as I'm doing now.

Lurking.

Oh brother! Tuning in to their conversation, I discover it's the same topic I've heard over a gazillion times. Hillary is regaling stories of her glory days, competing in the Beijing Olympics on the U.S. Volleyball team.

Oh God. Here we go again. Hillary continues to brag, brag and brag, while the other supervisor, Stalin, tries unsuccessfully to ingratiate himself into the conversation.

Poor Stalin can't seem to get a word in edgewise.

Ten minutes later, the brag session is finally over and Hillary turns her attention to me. "What's going on?" she asks frostily.

"I've got an escalation."

"What's it about?" she asks with a significant lift of her brow.

Every time I see her caterpillar unibrow, I have the strongest urge to pluck it out. "I tried verifying him, but he won't let me; he's pretty irate and hostile and, um . . . he loves dropping the F bomb."

Hillary seethes with rage. She absolutely loathes it when the callers curse and she hates it even more when they refuse to let us verify them. After all, security is paramount and we have nothing but their best interests at heart. *COUGH.*

Hillary elbows me aside and bulldozes back to her desk while I scurry behind.

Whoa! Look out! Hillary looks totally riled, like a raging bull ready to charge at a flapping red cloth. From my cubicle, I watch the bull in action as she jams on her headset, pounds the keyboard with fervor, glares at the monitor and signals for me to transfer the call.

With the utmost pleasure, I do just that. "Sir, thank you so much for holding. I'm sorry for that long wait, but I do have my supervisor on the line now, her name is Hillary, and she'll take very good care of you from here."

As I release the call, I catch this fiery glint in Hillary's eyes.

It's going to be a slaughter fest.

Yeah! You go get him Hell-raiser Hillary!

Trample him! Go for the kill!

Eat him alive and spit him back across the pond!

In times like these, I'm actually glad Hillary is my supervisor. When it's time to go into battle and engage in enemy warfare, she's a formidable opponent, and someone I'm very thankful is on my side.

Eight

Gasp! The rumors are true.

My head is spinning as I stare at my best friend in disbelief.

"Kars—you *cannot* go out with him," I implore. "He's married for God's sake."

She stares at the ground and takes a drag off her cigarette.

"You're Karsynn for crying out loud. *Kar-synn*. With a K and a Y. You're supposed to fall for guys with names Kayson, River, Leaf or Joaquin. Not—" I break off. "Not Bob the Builder who looks like Joe the freakin' plumber."

She folds her arms across her chest. "Stop talking like Sarah Palin!"

"It was McCain the Maverick," I correct.

"What?" Her voice rises in irritation.

"John McCain was the one who brought up Joe the Plumber."

"It wasn't him," she rebuffs huffily. "It was Palin."

"Oh, who cares! Quit changing the subject. We're discussing Bob now. BOB—Bob the Builder," I say, barely suppressing a snort.

Kars rolls her eyes and takes another drag from her Marlboro Light.

"Besides, you're into the B guys—big, burly, beefcakes with bulging biceps," I remind her. "You can't turn around and date a P guy."

Kars sputters, "What the heck is a P guy?"

"A P guy," I repeat succinctly, "pudgy, porky, paunchy, potato head."

"Bob is not a potato head!"

"Oh yeah he is," I say with gumption and proffer, "and, here's more Ps for you—he's a pig-headed player who's putrid, puerile, pathetic, and makes me want to puke!"

"Well you know what? At least Bob is circumcised," she fires back with a vindictive smirk.

I blink. What the hell is she talking about?

Then the penny finally drops.

"First of all, I am *not* sleeping with Mika. How dare you even insinuate that? And don't you bring Mika into this when I'm not even dating him." After a pause, I add, "And what makes you think that *all* European men aren't cut?"

Karsynn continues blowing cigarette smoke out of her nose.

Humph. Little does she realize how ridiculous she looks when smoke is only coming out through *one* of her nostrils.

"Kars, that was a pretty low blow. You—you home wrecker!"

"Bob doesn't have any kids," she snaps. "So there's no home to wreck!"

My voice drops to a solemn whisper. "The sanctimony of their marriage . . . of their love . . . is . . . *was* their home. And you took that away." I swallow hard.

"Quit being so pious and melodramatic! There was never any love on his part; he told me so! He doesn't love her!"

I cannot believe she's fallen for his line of bull crap. "Kars, if he cheats on his wife, what's to say that he won't cheat on you?" I beseech. "He'll never leave his wife and even if he—"

"He will," she interjects with surprising force and conviction.

Well, she certainly has some Pollyanna notions regarding this whole farce. I smile in an exhausted way. "Okay, let's just say he does. Then what? You will always have trust issues. When Bob is out late and you're at home all alone, you'll always wonder if he's with *another* woman."

A beat of silence ensues.

"He'll change," she says at last.

"Yeah right he'll change," I scoff theatrically. "When pigs fly."

Karsynn chucks her cigarette to the ground and grinds it under her foot. "Well maybe I'm his Angelina."

I guffaw and almost choke on my own saliva. "*Puh-lease*, Bob Seely is no Brad Pitt. And don't you even *go* there."

This topic has always been a hotbed of controversy between us. While my loyalties lie with Team Anniston, Kars has always been a staunch supporter of the Jolie-Pitt camp, and we have never seen eye to eye on this one.

I abhor men who cheat on their wives and despise women who sleep with married men, and now I'm torn because my best friend is one of *those* women.

Even worse, she's in total denial.

In denial + stubborn + date a cheater = doormat.

I want to shake her until she sees sense. If I can help it, I will not allow my best friend to become some scumbag's doormat. Or anyone's doormat, for that matter.

Try as I may, convincing Kars this is all wrong is turning out to be much harder than I had previously thought.

Time to shift gears. Digging in my heels, I plead in a serious, no-nonsense tone, "Kars, please don't violate *women code*."

"Women code?" she huffs haughtily.

"Yes. Women code," I repeat. "And cardinal rule number one of women code—you do not steal another woman's husband!" I say tersely. "Some men behave like farm animals, and women owe it to one another to practice restraint. We must stick together. You know, *Solidarity to the Sisterhood* and all that. We need to look out for one another and abide by women code!"

"I didn't *steal* her husband. Bob loves *me*."

"Well then make sure you head over to Petco," I say wearily.

"The pet store? For what?"

"To buy your new boyfriend a leash."

In one last ditch effort, I say, "Look, Karsynn, aside from the fact that he's married, dating a co-worker is just plain stupid, okay? It's like eating and taking a *shadoobie* at the same place. You just don't *do* that!"

"Quit badgering me! If I want to date Bob, it's my business, *not yours!*" she says sharply.

I flinch and recoil like I've been bitch slapped. Kars has never lashed out at me like that.

"Our lunch is up. We should go back inside now," she mutters in a dismissive tone. "And leave me the hell alone!" Spinning on her heels, she stalks off in a fury.

"Karsynn!" I call out to her retreating back. But she just picks up her pace. For some inexplicable reason, I find myself racing to catch up with her. In no time, I'm hot on her heels and my stride matches hers, but we walk back to our cubicles in dead silence.

I don't know what to say to my best friend anymore.

It has been almost a week now, and we're *still* not speaking. I'm a complete wreck, and it hurts that a snake-in-the-grass like Bob Seely has come between us.

Truong instantly knows something's amiss and tries his best to cheer me up with heap loads of food. His family owns a Japanese restaurant, even though they're Vietnamese (there's more money to be made in Japanese food, he had once explained). And every day, Truong waltzes into work bearing a bounty of sushi rolls—California rolls, Caterpillar rolls, Spider rolls, Spicy Tuna rolls, Maki rolls. A whole smorgasbord of sushi rolls!

Usually, I'm always happy to indulge. But today, I'm feeling out of sorts. Gingerly, Truong slides a paper plate on my desk. It's stacked with Caterpillar rolls and Spider rolls.

Bless his heart. He knows the critter rolls are my favorite.

"Eat something," he cajoles.

"Thanks, Truong," I mutter despondently.

Unfazed by my misery, he says, "I blought something extla for you." He lifts the lid off a Styrofoam container. "Would you like some flied lice?"

Truong still can't pronounce the letter 'r' no matter how hard I coach him. In his defense, he's only lived in the States for five years, and so he still struggles with the language. But it's mainly with the pronunciations; his vocabulary is vast and spectacular.

I shake my head. "No thanks, Truong, I'm not in the mood for some fried parasite. But thanks."

One hour later, Truong and I log off our phones. It so happens that we're scheduled for our breaks at the same time, and we decide to just chill at our cubicles. I don't hang out with Karsynn on my breaks anymore. That's a thing of the past. She's far too busy canoodling with Bob and I'm shocked by her abrasiveness. Cavorting openly with a married man? It just ain't right.

Consequently, our friendship has become strained, and we've been avoiding each other, which is a difficult thing for me to do when we've never gone so much as a day without talking.

Plus, I haven't even seen much of Mika lately, or Ingeborg for that matter. Not after they had their heated spat at the Red Lobster.

Lately, I've been navigating Mika's moods, and his forecast has been stormy, gray and cloudy; his demeanor tells me he wants to be left alone, and so I keep my distance.

Whenever our paths cross, we wave, say Hi, put on a happy facade. Although outwardly friendly, our exchanges are more of a strained politeness.

Ingeborg keeps mostly to herself, Mika is in his own gloomy world, and Kars is hiking the Appalachian Trail, violating *women code*.

But that's okay, because I have Truong. I watch him attack his food with wanton abandon. Sniffing deeply, I am rewarded with the sweet aroma of fried rice.

Ahh, nothing beats fried rice from a restaurant.

No matter how hard I try, I simply cannot duplicate this dish at home. I firmly believe that you need the scorching fire from a gas stove to heat up the wok to insanely high temperatures. One afternoon, after watching Iron Chef Chen Kenichi whip up a dish of fluffy fried rice, I became inspired. I'd puttered around my kitchen trying to mimic it. It was disastrous! Cooking fried rice on my electric stove, in the absence of high heat, was crippling.

My mouth waters at the sight of Truong's fluffy fried rice.

He waves his wooden chopsticks. "Changed your mind?"

Before I can respond, he scoops up a hefty portion of fried rice, plops it onto a plate and sets it on my desk.

"Thanks, Truong," I say gratefully and dive right in.

Mmmmm it pops with flavor and oozes with oomph.

I scarf it down in minutes.

Sighing contentedly, I lean back and my eyes fall on the plate of sushi rolls. I had planned on saving them for later, but the caterpillar rolls beckon me to eat them *now*. My mind conjures up a bizarre image of the sushi rolls. They morph into caterpillars, wriggle their bodies and sing in chorus, "Eat me! Eat me! Eat me!"

I cave in and plunk a roll into my mouth.

"Truong, can I ask you a personal question?" I ask in between chewing.

"Of course," he says at once.

"Have you . . ." I hesitate. "Have you ever slept with an uncircumcised man?"

"Why of course," he says blatantly. "I'm not circumcised myself, you know. I happen to like the turtleneck look. Or, as I like to call it—hot dog on a bun." He shrugs and continues, "I've never understood the weird practice of decapitating one's penis."

I stifle a laugh. "So have you, or have you not?"

"Yes." He shoots me a devilish smirk. "And for your info my dear Maddy, uncut cocks are the best." Then he winks and adds, "There's more to *chew* on."

I gag and almost throw up my roll.

Sparing no details, he continues frenetically, "Yeah, I was with this uncut guy once and he kept yelling '*Bite it! Gnaw it! Chomp it!*' He liked it real rough you know, and with plenty of teeth."

Ugh. I'm feeling slightly nauseous. Scrambling to my feet, I race to the restroom and regurgitate my sushi roll.

God help me. As I'm bent over the accursed toilet, it flushes!

My entire face is drenched in toilet water.

I really want this day to end.

After my last call for the day, Mika magically materializes at my cubicle. I hope this means he's snapped out of his funk.

"Hey," he says, shifting his weight from foot to foot.

All my senses are on full alert. "Hey."

After a pause, he says, "Sorry I've been kind of distant lately."

"You have?" I wrinkle my brows. "Haven't noticed."

A flicker of a smile ignites across his lips, and I realize just how much I've missed him.

"I . . ." he struggles for the words, "I just needed some time to myself. To clear my head, figure things out . . . about Inge."

"Of course." I try to keep my tone neutral.

"So, I know you usually tutor me on the weekends, but I was wondering if you could tutor me today instead."

I hoist my bag over my shoulder. "Like right now?" I ask and he nods. "Okay."

"Okay," he echoes, and we start for the elevator. "Let's hit the library."

I smile inwardly. I finally find a guy I like and all he wants to do is take me to the library.

Ah, *c'est la vie.*

I try to focus. I really do. But every time I look at Mika, a vivid image of an uncut penis pops into my head. Out of sheer curiosity, I had googled an image of an uncircumcised penis.

That image had me reverberating in shock, and I don't believe I've recovered since. It has been irrevocably burned into my retina, and it takes everything inside me to block out that disturbing image—the image of a wrinkled anteater ready to suck up its lunch. Eeeps!!!

We're in the county library, seated on squashy, vinyl covered chairs with worn out padding. And strange as it may seem, our 'tutoring' sessions don't involve much tutoring. More often than not, Mika reads a book and I help edit his papers. I'm convinced that with enough reading, his writing will surely improve.

As I'm correcting one of Mika's ESL assignments, he plunks his book down with a thud. I jerk my head up.

"I'm done!" he says, exceedingly pleased with himself.

"Good!" I say robustly. "I can start you off on the next one."

His face glows with anticipation. "What's it called?"

"*The Pillars of the Earth*. It's historical fiction at its finest, a towering medieval tale, a ripping thriller, a—"

He cuts in, "Is it action packed?"

"Yes." I smile reassuringly. "It is."

"Okay." He flashes a quick grin. "I'll read it."

We head for the shelves to locate the book and I tentatively broach the subject, "So, how are things with Ingeborg?"

"We sort of ended things," he says quietly.

"I'm sorry."

After a pause, he adds, "It was mutual."

"Oh." My eyes linger on him, but his inscrutable expression gives nothing away.

There is a lull in our conversation as we peruse the aisles, tracking the book by the author's last name: 'F', for Follett. First name Ken.

Booyakasha. I find it first.

I pluck the book from the shelf and hand it to him. "Are you feeling okay?"

He shrugs. "I've been better."

Next, we browse the magazines. Mika hovers indecisively over the Cars and Trucks section while I flip through the latest issue of *Cosmo*.

Sometime later, he peers over my shoulder. "What are you reading?"

"Some article about soul mates," I say distractedly.

"You believe in soul mates?" he asks, and his question takes me by surprise.

"I do . . ." I find myself considering this for a bit before continuing, "I think a soul mate can be a friend, a lover, a child. Someone that you connect with, someone that *gets* you, and sometimes even aggravate you."

He searches my eyes. "Do you have a soul mate?"

"My dad," I say simply and return the magazine to the shelf.

His expression grows thoughtful. After an unreadable minute, he says, "Ingeborg and I had a long talk."

I shoot him a sidelong glance, waiting for him to say more.

"I'm fond of her and I care for her, but I think we both realize that we're better off as friends." He presses his lips together as if to stop himself from saying more.

I'm still lamenting the loss of the golden *ex*-couple when Mika catches me off guard. "So, how are things with you and Kars?"

"Not so good," I say quietly. "We're not really speaking to each other."

"I heard about her and Bob."

"Yeah, well who hasn't?" I frown with distaste. "He's *married* you know, and she'll just get her heart broken. Besides, dating someone you work with is just a *bad* idea."

He gives me a peculiar look. "And why is that a bad idea?"

"Because it is like dumping on your own doorstep," I say like it's a given.

His eyes narrow to slits. "I see . . ."

After Mika checks out his reading materials, we traipse out the library and trudge through a foot of slushy, gray snow.

His gaze shifts down to my hands.

Aha! They are *sans* a smut novel.

"Hey." He nudges me in the ribs. "How come you didn't check out a book tonight?"

"I'm not done reading the other one," I say curtly.

His mouth twitches. "Um, you mean *The Scottish Laird and his Virgin Bride?*"

My hand flies up to swat him but he easily evades me.

"Oh, shut up!" I cry, half laughing and punch him in the arm.

In one seamless move, he playfully grips my wrist. I squirm and try to twist out of his iron grip, but he doesn't budge.

He just stares. And stares. The force of his gaze is so intense it nearly knocks me off my feet.

It feels as if I'm crashing against the Pacific surf, and beating against the jagged cliffs.

Holding my ground, I stare back, unsmiling, unblinking.

Gosh. This feels semi-erotic, actually.

After a long minute, Mika eases his grip. Then he drops his gaze and we resume walking.

I clear my throat. "So, do you still want to read the book when I'm done?"

Mika laughs jovially. "No thanks. But I'd read a book about a Belgian Laird and his virgin bride."

"Oh, I doubt there's such a book," I say with a smirk.

He arches an eyebrow. "And why is that?"

"In relationships, especially when it comes time to commit, Belgian men tend to . . . waffle a bit."

His eyebrows knit together in confusion.

I bite the insides of my cheeks to keep from grinning. "Get it? Belgian Waffle!"

A smile tugs at his lips. Suddenly, he springs forward, but I'm much too quick for him this time. I pull away sharply, eluding his grasp and thwarting his ambush. Laughing and shrieking, I break into a run as he chases after me, dashing and splashing through puddles of melted snow.

Nine

Beep!

"Thanks for calling Lightning Speed Communications, this is Maddy, how can I help? I ask impassively.

"I need some help setting up my surveillance cameras," says the caller.

Part of our job in the DSL department entails assigning ports to surveillance cameras so our customers can view live feed from remote computers. After verifying the caller, I dive right into the technicalities. "Sir, what would you like to name Camera One?"

"Bedroom Cam," he huffs, sounding like Deep Throat.

"Okay," I say and type away. "And Camera Two?"

"Bathroom Cam."

"All right . . . and Camera Three?"

"Kitchen Cam," he says hoarsely.

As I'm tapping at the keys, I begin to see a pattern here.

"And Camera Four, sir?"

He is quick to respond, "Laundry Room Cam."

I'm guessing he'll probably say Garage Cam next. That should just about cover every room in the house.

Wow. This guy sure is serious about his home security.

"This is the last one, sir. What you like to name Camera Five?"

"Crotch Cam," he replies coarsely.

Silence. I'm not typing. Um, what? Did he just say crotch cam?

I blink. Yes. I believe he did. The hairs on the back of my neck are standing at attention. *Ai yi yi.* This caller is giving me the heebie jeebies.

I stammer, "Err, sorry, my computer just shut down on me so I'll need to reboot. Do you mind holding for just a few minutes?"

Deep Throat grunts, "Hoh-kay."

With trembling hands, I place him on hold.

Good God. This caller is one sick perv. I wonder if he's using these cameras on unsuspecting women. Maybe he's recording his own wife. Even worse, he could be one of those icky pedophiles.

This is serious. I need to report this.

I march imperiously to The Führer's den and relay everything to her. She listens intently and when I'm done, she immediately takes charge. "Get me his info *now*. I need to run a background check on this guy. *Pronto.*"

My heart races as I dart back to my cube. I scrawl down his name and address on a note pad and scurry back to Hillary's desk. Standing behind her, I can see that she has pulled up the National Sex Offender Registry web site.

"Go ahead," she fires off. "I'm ready."

Galvanized into action, I rattle off the caller's first and last name, followed by his address. Hillary pounds her keyboard with fervor and clicks 'submit.'

We wait.

Seconds later, we're staring into the eyes of a sexual offender, convicted for aggravated sexual abuse of a child and attempted first degree felony. Okay, now I'm really getting the chills.

Hillary stares at me deadpan, and the reality of the situation begins to sink in.

For the both of us.

"Shut down his service. Transfer the call to me; I'll handle it from here," she instructs in a subdued manner.

I'm hightailing it back to my cubicle when I hear Hillary call my name. Halted by her voice, I whirl around.

"Nice work. I'm glad you brought this to my attention. As soon as I'm done with this call, I'm reporting him to the authorities."

I am still in a daze. Did that really just happen? A compliment from The Führer?

Stunned and bewildered, I stumble back to my cubicle and swiftly transfer the call.

Afterward, I slump back in my chair and replay the events. Crapola! I've just caught a predator over the phone! And I *know* Kars will be thrilled to hear all about my successful sting op. She lives for stuff like this; she's a huge Nancy Grace fan.

On impulse, I walk to her cubicle only to stop myself in my tracks. For a split second, I had forgotten that we aren't speaking. And it's a painful reminder. She has put up a wall between us, and it hurts.

It was Frost who had once said, *"Something there is that doesn't love a wall. That sends the frozen-ground-swell under it."*

I am that frozen ground, and my heart swells.

I miss Kars. Tonight, I will break down that wall that divides us. Tonight, I shall channel the strength of President Reagan when he'd commanded, "Mr. Gorbachev, tear down this wall!"

Feeling good about my plan, I hop back on the phone.

What an abysmal and uneventful night. Slouched on the sofa, my eyes stare numbly at the TV screen, watching the credits roll for *Hairspray,* the musical. Prior to that, I watched the entire HSM marathon and the complete third season of *Chuck.*

Gaawwd! My mind is overdosed on cheesy musicals and spy shows. But watching Zac Efron and Zac Levi was well worth it.

Mika bears an uncanny resemblance to both Zacs. He's a cross between Efron and Levi, so I've sort of gotten my Mika fix for tonight.

I glance at the clock. It's 2 a.m. and Kars isn't even home yet. In my guesstimation, she's out on a late night, secret, rendezvous with Bob the Knuckle Headed Builder.

Sigh. I feel so sorry for his wife. Oh, to suffer the betrayal of a wayward spouse. I try to remove myself from the situation, but I can't help but feel a stab of sadness and disappointment.

Disappointment in Kars.

Just the other day, Truong had tried to defend her actions, saying that sometimes things are not so black and white. But I disagree. Some things *are* black and white.

He is a married man; what is so gray about that? How much more black and white can a marriage certificate be?

But then again, who am I to even judge? I, myself, was pining after Mika while he had been dating Ingeborg.

I glance at the clock again. It's getting late.

No use waiting up for Kars when it's highly unlikely she'll be coming home tonight.

Flicking off the lights, I amble groggily to bed.

My talk with Kars will have to wait until tomorrow.

Beep! Beep!

Jarred awake, I'm in a state of complete confusion.

"Thanks for calling Lightning—"

Whhhaa? Wait a minute! I'm not at work.

I glance blearily around. A flood of cherry blossom sunshine pours through the slanted venetian blinds. My eyes take a moment to adjust to the glare.

Okay, I'm definitely not at work. I'm in my bedroom. Thank God! I flop facedown onto my duvet.

Beep! Beep!

Huh? There goes that beeping sound again.

Beep! Beep!

Oh, d'oh! It's the doorbell.

Rubbing my eyes, I tumble out of bed and stagger to the front door. Yes, yes, I'm coming. Hold yer horses will ya?

Throwing open the door, I come face to face with Janis.

"Miss Higginbotham." I stifle a yawn. "Come in. I'm sorry but Karsynn's not here."

Janis glides across the room and sinks gracefully onto the sofa.

After adjusting her skirt, she eyeballs me. "I came to see *you.*"

"Me? Oh, okay." I plop down next to her.

Without preliminaries, Janis forges full speed ahead, "I know Karsynn is seeing that bastard Bob Seely. I've tried talking some sense into her, but she's just so stubborn. And this is not the first time that Bob's crossed the line; he's had lots of affairs at work in the past."

"But why do these girls fall for him?" I scratch my head. "It's not like he's the catch of the century. Nor is he remotely a catch *at all*."

Janis purses her lips. "Do you remember when Bill Clinton was president?"

Of course I do.

"Even back then, Bill wasn't conventionally handsome and yet I had the biggest crush on him." Janis sighs and stares out the window.

I follow her gaze, but I don't see anything unusual except for the magnificent Rocky Mountains staring back at me. What a view!

Janis snaps out of her reverie. "It's a power thing, Maddy. Women are fascinated by men in power. Look at skinny Obama with his Mickey Mouse ears; women still find him sexy."

"But—but Bob Seely is an oversized toad. And he's just some lame supervisor at a call center."

Janis smiles wryly. "Power is power my dear. Some women just find it attractive."

"I just don't understand why Kars is with someone like Bob. He's such a douchelord; even in college, she'd date these jerks who treated her like dirt."

After a pregnant pause, Janis takes a deep breath. "I'm going to share a bit of my past with you. I've kept it hidden from a lot of people, but it may help you understand why Kars is the way she is."

I sit up straighter. Janis has my full attention.

A sullen look clouds her usually cheerful facade. "I may seem carefree now, but I wasn't always this way. I was diagnosed with severe depression and I battled it for sixteen years. My husband at the time—Karsynn's dad—couldn't handle my illness." She averts her eyes. "It was so bad that I flirted with suicide once or twice."

A short gasp escapes my lips.

In a strained voice, she continues, "And so he left us."

"But Kars had told me that her dad's in prison."

Janis manages a half-smile. "Well he left us, and then months later, he was incarcerated. Under California's three strikes law, once you're convicted of a felony three times, that's it—you're in the slammer for at least twenty-five years."

"So he's locked up forever?"

Janis nods gravely. "Karsynn's dad . . . well he wasn't much of a father figure. He wasn't much of anything. In fact, he was a cheater. I caught him having affairs with several women; one of them was my best friend. And he conned my family out of lots of money. But despite all that, Kars loved him; she thought that if she loved him enough, he'd change."

I'm stunned. I'd always assumed Kars had an idyllic childhood; at least that's the impression she had given everyone.

Janis ventures on with a pained expression, "But of course he never changed. And poor Kars had to endure so much. She had this deadbeat dad, coupled with my depression, she now has a warped sense of what love really is. Kars sees love as something she has to work for. She had to work for her dad's love; she had to work for *my* love . . ." Her voice falters and tears rim her eyes.

I reach for a Kleenex and hand it to Janis.

She takes it and wails, "I was such an awful mother, Maddy, so consumed with my own suffering. I was self destructive and Kars was there the whole time, picking up the pieces. And I'd fall over and over again, back into my black hole."

I sit very still and very quiet.

Janis sniffles. "Now Kars thinks she has to stay and be loyal no matter how much she is being hurt. Like she did with her dad . . . like she did with me."

"I never knew that about Kars," I say in a stupor.

"It was bad," Janis admits. "I'm afraid that's why she's drawn to men like that; and it just feeds her insecurities."

Now the pieces of the puzzle begin to fall into place.

For as long as I'd known Kars, she'd always shied away from the good and stable guys. In college, she had constantly dated all the bad boys and the dysfunctional douchebags. Perhaps majoring in psychology was her way of trying to understand *herself*.

Janis continues, "All those years, Kars was always there for me, and she put up with so much. But no matter what I did, no matter how awful I was to live with, she never left me."

"But it all worked out in the end Miss Higginbotham." I wear a tender expression on my face. "You're all better now."

"Yes, I'm better, Maddy. My daughter loved me, and continues to love me in spite of it all and now she thinks that if you truly love someone, you should put up with any kind of abuse."

I remain silent, not really knowing what to say.

"Maddy, I know things have been strained between you two, but Kars needs you," she says in a pleading voice.

"Don't worry, Miss Higginbotham, I'll talk to her. I'll fix things between us."

She squeezes my hand. "Thank you."

I squeeze her hand, too. "And thank you for sharing all that with me."

"Thanks for listening, honey. Kars is a lot like me in many ways; she may put up a tough front, but inside, she's the biggest butterball."

I find myself smiling affectionately, just thinking about Kars. She's rowdy and rambunctious, filled with a wild, uninhibited zeal for life. At times, she can be abrasive but her bark is much louder than her bite.

And there's also another side to Kars, the sweet and lovable side. The Kars that makes me laugh so hard my stomach hurts; the Kars that farts herself awake in the middle of the night.

Janis interrupts my thoughts. "All I want is for the two of you to patch things up."

"We will." I give her my most reassuring smile.

"Before I forget, Kars will be having surgery next week." Janis springs this on me out of nowhere.

Stricken, I blanch. "Surgery? What kind of surgery?"

"Oral surgery. Jaw surgery actually, to correct her overbite."

"You mean her jaw will be sawed in half, and then bolted back together?"

"Yes," Janis says, and I gulp.

Feeling queasy, I head toward the kitchen to fetch a glass of water.

"Would you like something to drink, Miss Higginbotham?"

"No thanks, sweetie." After a tentative pause, she says, "Now I know it sounds pretty bad, but her orthodontist assures me it'll be okay."

"But why? Does Karsynn really *need* to correct her overbite? I mean, she's had it all these years and she's been fine."

"She does." Janis sighs. "It makes it hard for her to chew food properly; and that leads to indigestion, to heartburn."

Hmm. Maybe that's why Kars is always so gassy. Maybe this surgery will make all her farts go away.

Uh oh, Kars will *not* be happy about that.

Janis' brows crease with concern. "Kars will need plenty of care. She'll need to be on an all-liquid diet for six weeks. There'll be lots of pain for her, lots of swelling."

I wince. "Poor Kars."

Janis' expression mirrors mine. "My poor baby. I'll be taking two weeks off work so I can take care of her. She'll be moving back with me temporarily, so I can keep an eye on her around the clock."

I slowly sip my water. "When is her surgery?"

"Monday at 10 a.m."

I gasp, "That's only two days away!"

Janis offers a warm smile. "I know she'll want you to be around; you comfort her. In a good way."

"Don't worry, I'll be there. I'll stop by before and after work, every single day," I promise.

"Good!" says Janis, getting to her feet. "I'd best get going." At the front door, she stops. Spinning around, she confesses, "You know, I did kind of push Kars to see the orthodontist this week. And . . . I *may* have had a tiny hand in convincing her to get this surgery done soon. You see my dear, it's all about *timing*."

I draw a blank. "Timing?"

An evil glint flashes in her eyes. "This . . . this *thing* with Kars and Bob, well let's just say that it won't last much longer."

I blink, still very much perplexed.

An eerie Mona Lisa smile touches her lips. "You see, Kars will never leave Bob. But, what I *can* do is make Bob leave *her*."

There is a stunned silence as I digest this.

"And once that bastard is gone, I plan on getting my baby some help, some therapy," she adds with conviction. "Bye now, sweetie. In the meantime, I'm going to cut the head off that snake." With those parting words, she disappears out the front door.

I stare after her open-mouthed.

That was so Machiavellian. Although in this case, the end *does* justify the means.

Mothers. Never *ever* underestimate the power they have over our lives.

Knock! Knock!

"Enter at your own risk."

Cracking the door ajar, I find Karsynn in the midst of stuffing shirts into a bulging Adidas gym bag.

"What's up?" she asks, without looking up.

Leaning heavily against the doorframe, I mutter, "Nothing."

There is a lull of silence. Casting my eyes downward, I draw tiny swirls on the carpet with my restless foot.

Eventually, Kars jerks her head up. "Really?"

"No," I say truthfully. "I hate that we're not talking."

We eye each other warily. The ball is now in her court.

She makes an exasperated sound. "Look, I've been giving you the cold shoulder because I don't appreciate being second guessed all the time. I'm a grown woman, Maddy; give me some credit here. I *know* what I'm doing."

"I know," I say quietly. "I just don't want to see you get hurt."

After a stretch of silence, she mutters something indistinct.

My eyes crinkle at the corners. "Sorry, um what did you just say?"

"I said I, *too*, hate that we're not talking," she says through gritted teeth.

I smile broadly. "Well good. Glad we're on the same page."

Karsynn summons up a conciliatory smile and hurls a sock at me.

I catch the sock with one hand. "Kars, I still hate the fact that you're seeing that prick." I'm compelled to say more, but I decide to drop it after seeing the look on her face. "Anyway, what I'm trying to say is I've missed you," I say sappily.

"Aww, you have?"

"Of course. Plus, you're about to get your jaw cracked open in two days."

"Don't remind me," she says grimly. After a slight beat, she adds, "These past few weeks have sucked. I've really missed you, too, Mads."

I hold out my arms. "Let's hug it out."

And so we do. We hug it out and call a truce.

Now that we've got that out of the way, I hop on her bed and sit cross-legged, Buddha style. Just like old times.

Kars resumes packing.

Leaning back against her pillows, I reach for the Opi nail polish I spy resting on her side table. "Nice color. Black Cherry Chutney."

She giggles. "Isn't that hot? I was in the mood for some Indian lovin'. And guess what else I've got?" She waves another bottle of Opi. "This one is Curry Up, Don't Be Late."

"Oooohhh, I like that color."

"You can use it anytime."

"And you're welcome to use my Pink-O de Gallo Opi if you'd like," I offer.

"Give me some sexy Latin lovin'." Kars swivels her hips in a disjointed manner. "C'mon, join me and do the *sallllllllllssssssa.*"

Without meaning to, I burst out laughing.

Karsynn has got to be the worst salsa dancer in the cosmic universe. She has as much rhythm, grace and finesse as an elephant stomping to a ballet. But then again, I'm no better.

"Get on your feet and *sallllllllssssssssssa,*" she rolls her tongue.

"Um, can't you see I'm busy?" I say, applying a first coat.

"So, are you nervous about the surgery?"

"A little." She abandons the salsa dancing and bounces on the bed. "Now, do you want to know what the best part is?"

"What?" I carefully apply Black Cherry Chutney on my pinky toenail.

"Losing weight!" she exclaims brightly. "I'll be on this all-liquid diet for the next six weeks since my jaw will be wired shut. *Girrrl*, you'll see me shed some major pounds. The fat will just melt off my body!"

I'm glad Kars is taking this in stride. Although I'm slightly nervous about her impending surgery, I don't share any of my concerns with her. She'll be going to hell and back and I need to keep her spirits up.

"Maybe I'll go on the liquid diet to keep you company," I hear myself saying.

"You're such a doll," she cries with delight. "Maddy, we are going to turn into some skinny bitches!"

Half-laughing, I raise an imaginary wine glass. "Here's to us becoming skinny bitches."

"To skinny bitches!" Karsynn echoes, beaming at me.

Ten

Beep!

"Thanks for calling Lightning Speed Communications, this is Maddy. How can I help?"

"I WANT TO KNOW WHY THE HELL MY PASSWORD IS NOT WORKING. YOUR SITE TELLS ME I'M LOCKED OUT! WHAT THE HELL IS GOING ON?"

"Okay, sir, I can help with that. Let me just verify you first."

"FINE!" He makes a guttural sound of protest.

I flinch and run through the painful process of verifying the beast. Then I pull up the 'Crystal Ball' app which tracks our callers' log in attempts. It's a pretty nifty tool; it gives me the precise date and time that a caller logs in, along with his city, state, country and IP address.

I type the caller's info into my gypsy app and wait.

Seconds later, the Crystal Ball tells me that a mustachioed gigolo will come into my life. Mwahahaha.

Okay, back to business.

Apparently, the caller used the wrong password.

Several times actually.

It is *crystal* clear. The Ball does not lie.

"Sir, according to our records, the incorrect password was entered three times. So that's why your password is suspended. All you need to do is—"

I DID *NOT* ENTER THE WRONG PASSWORD!"

"Well, it's quite possible that someone else could've entered the wrong password. Have you, by chance, shared your log in info with anyone?"

"NO ONE ELSE HAS MY INFO!"

"Have you responded to any phishing attempts? Perhaps you have a virus on your computer."

He barks, "I DO NOT HAVE A VIRUS!"

I'm compelled to say, "Sir, *you* may not have a virus, but your *computer* may." But of course I don't. Instead I say, "Well, if no one else has your info and your computer is clean, then . . ." I pause and continue with some hesitation, "Um, then I'm afraid it was probably *you* that entered the wrong password."

He draws in his breath with a loud hiss. "I said it *wasn't* me. Are you calling me a *liar*?" His tone is threatening.

"Err, no . . ." I say feebly, even though I want to yell, "YES! YOU'RE A LIAR! I HAVE PROOF THAT YOU ENTERED THE INCORRECT PASSWORD THREE TIMES. THE HITS ON OUR SERVER MATCH *YOUR* IP ADDRESS!"

"So, if I did NOT enter the wrong password, then EXPLAIN WHY I AM LOCKED OUT!"

"It's quite possible that your password got corrupted," I bullshit.

"Corrupted?" he guffaws.

"Yes," I inform him in a tone that is so convincing that even I, myself, am convinced. "Corrupted," I repeat, unwavering.

As call center tradition goes, the customer is *always* right. It has been drilled into my fat head. Thus, it is imperative that I bullshit. If all else fails, always blame the tool, but never, *ever* blame the carpenter.

Hah! Too late for me; I've already made the fatal mistake of blaming the crazed carpenter.

"HOW CAN MY PASSWORD BE CORRUPTED?" he erupts once again.

Jeez, take a chill pill dude. It's only a password.

I continue bullshitting my way out of this since he leaves me no other option. "Well, sir, think of it this way—your password is like a car. Your car will not run smoothly forever. There are times when your car will break down and simply refuse to start. Likewise with your password, there are times when your password will become corrupted and refuse to work," I expostulate, surprising myself at my ability to produce fantastic amounts of BS that make perfect sense.

Click!

D'oh! He'll just have to call back to reset his password.

Feeling sorry for his next victim, I promptly log off my phone.

Kars had her jaw surgery this morning and my stomach has been clenched in nerves all day.

I've been worrying myself sick.

I glance at my watch. It's not too late.

Time to go pay my best friend a visit at the hospital.

It's almost 10 p.m. when I arrive at St. Mary's hospital. A nurse at the front desk directs me to Karsynn's room. Although I brace myself for the worst, I am not in the least bit prepared for what I see when I walk in. Poor Kars looks like she had been hit by a UPS truck. Her eyes are shut, and they look puffy and swollen. And her whole face is wrapped up in rolls of bandages.

I bite my inner lip and swallow hard. After composing myself, I step into the room and slip into the chair next to Janis. She's slumped forward in her chair, appearing to be fast asleep.

Although I try not to make a peep, she stirs and sits up.

"Hey sweetie," she whispers groggily.

"Hi. How is she?"

"She's doing all right. They gave her some morphine to help manage the pain."

For a while, we sit in silence, watching Kars in her deep slumber.

Eventually, I ask, "Will Kars have to stay here for a while?"

"No. Just for tonight, she'll be coming home with me tomorrow."

Tomorrow? Kars looks like she should be here for another week. At least. "So soon?" I ask in a strangled voice.

"Yes, dear. Don't worry, she'll be fine. Her bandages will come off tomorrow." Janis manages a tiny smile and adds, "Last night, Kars made me cook up a storm. She said it was her last hurrah before six grueling weeks of soft, bland food." Janis gives a heavy sigh. "That all-liquid diet is gonna be hard on her."

"Oh, before I forget, what sort of liquids can Kars have?"

"Let me check, I wrote it down here somewhere." She roots around in her handbag. "Aha! Here it is!" she exclaims, dredging up a piece of paper. "It's called Ensure; it's some sort of protein shake that's infused with vitamins and minerals."

I make a mental note of that and decide to take my leave. Kars and Janis need their rest. "Well, I'll get going now. But I'll stop by Costco tomorrow and pick up some Ensure."

"Thanks, Maddy. That's very kind of you."

I tread softly to Karsynn's side. Gently, I place a sprig of fresh basil next to her pillow. I had pinched it off her Aerogarden today.

Janis stands up and envelops me in a hug. "Thanks for coming, sweetie. I'll let her know you stopped by."

My arms tighten around her and I blink back the tears.

"Kars will be okay," Janis says softly.

"I'll stop by your place tomorrow," I say in a hushed voice and quietly make my exit.

Lugging ten cases of Ensure to Janis' front doorstep is proving to be a pain. But that's how you save money, by buying in bulk.

And today I've learned that Costco helps you save money in life *and* in death.

While perusing the aisles, I'd walked by some caskets!

Caskets. You heard me right. Costco sells discount caskets.

For some inexplicable reason, I'd stopped by a casket kiosk and browsed the samples. A dark mahogany casket had caught my eye. It was fully pimped out with gold and silver trimmings, and upon closer inspection, I'd discovered the upholstered interior featured an adjustable mattress and silk cushions for neck comfort.

I'd thought to myself, "Now why on earth would I even care? I'd be a corpse." And while flipping through the casket catalog, I happened upon an interesting caption: *Eternal Rest.*

I couldn't stop myself from laughing.

Curiously, I find myself *still* laughing right now, hysterically actually, slightly delirious from fatigue. And by the time I'm done hauling all ten cases of Ensure, I probably *will* need a Costco casket.

Ding! Dong!

Janis flings the door open and gawps when she comes face to face with ten cases of Ensure, stacked to the sky.

"Tah-dah!" I exclaim. My eyes shine with pride at the sight of my miniature Ensure State Building.

For several seconds, Janis gapes at the towering structure.

Then she whips her head and stares at me, and then back at the structure again.

"Kars will need to drink plenty of this stuff. And I got some for myself, too." I shrug. "I figure we won't be needing groceries for a month since I'll be going on this Ensure diet with Kars."

She shoots me a circumspect look. "It's nice that you're being a supportive friend, but this liquid diet is gruesome. Are you sure you can commit?"

"Of course!" I say firmly. I mean, how hard can it be? Whenever I'm hungry, I'll just crack open a can of Ensure.

Janis shakes her head and ushers me into the foyer. "Kars is upstairs in my bedroom watching TV. Go on up, I'll put these away."

Obediently, I start for the stairs.

I'd normally insist on helping Janis, but I'm pressed for time. I have to leave for work in exactly thirty-five minutes.

The door to Janis' bedroom is ajar and I spy Karsynn through the opening, propped up on a La-Z Boy. The TV screen is flickering, but she's staring off into space with a faraway look in her eyes. As I stand there observing her, tears begin to well up.

Her entire face is swollen, and her pearly, alabaster skin is now gaunt and sanguine.

Karsynn angles her head slightly and spots me. Instantly, her eyes come to life. "Hey you," she mutters, and in her attempt to say those two words, her nose starts bleeding uncontrollably.

"Kars!" I cry in alarm. "Don't try to talk!"

Oh God. Blood continues gushing out of her nose. In a panic, I grab several wads of tissue and stuff them into her hands.

I tut and fuss about her. "You need anything else?"

She shakes her head and jams tissue up her nostrils.

"I'll talk. You just listen, okay?"

She nods and fervently points to her iPhone.

I reach for it and hand it to her, and watch as she deftly thumbs in a text. Within seconds, my phone blares with Springsteen crooning *Born in the USA*. Springsteen's hit is set as my ring tone and I blame the call center for this travesty. All the callers have me convinced that I'm born in India. Every time I inform them that I'm in Idaho, and *not* India, they flat out refuse to believe me.

Whipping out my BlackBerry, I read Karsynn's text:

Don't feel sorry for me. I feel sorry for u, having 2 go in 2 work & get on d bleepin' phones.

"Oh, Kars," I gush. "You are one broken jawed trooper."

In response, she gives me two thumbs up. Then she picks up her iPhone and rapidly texts away. Once again, my BlackBerry blares with Springsteen's raspy voice.

My cheeks look like a chipmunk preparing 4 winter.

"No they don't!" I protest, but Kars doesn't appear to be the least bit convinced.

I watch her nimble and dexterous thumbs work in tandem; then I hear The Boss croon for the third time.

It's much, much worse than I had ever imagined :-(

When I glance up, I can see the pain in her eyes. I plant my hands on her trembling shoulders, searching her eyes through the flood of tears.

"You'll be okay," I soothe.

She remains inconsolable. Heaving and choking, tears continue spilling down her swollen cheeks.

"You'll be okay, Kars," I repeat.

Stifling a sob, she nods slightly.

I gather her into my arms, and she hugs me back hard.

Eleven

Ding!

Oh, I have a new email in my Outlook inbox.

Usually, I'm inundated with mindless emails that I can't be bothered to read. But this particular one is a splendid treat. It's an email from our site director Richard 'Just-Call-Me-Dick' Jones. Every time I read his emails, I'm simply appalled by all the spelling errors made by someone in upper management.

C'mon already, you cannot rely on the spell checker. It is not foolproof. And just because you spell a word correctly, it does not mean that it is the correct word.

I skim his email for all the errors.

Cha-Ching! This one is a gold mine.

To: All employees
From: Richard.Jones@lsc.com
Subject: Congratulations Alicia Sparks

Please join me in welcoming Alicia Sparks, who has just excepted the managerial position for the graveyard shift. This is a very impotent position and I'm vary confident that Alicia will succeed in fool filling all the golds we have set fourth. Alicia brings with her a welt of experience. She holes a degree in unclear physics and she has worked in a call center for moor then fifteen years. Further moor, Alicia has held a position as a teem lead for too years. Were very happy two have her on bored.

Dick Jones,
Site Director, Pocatello ID

"Truong, have you read the email from Dick Jones?"

"No," he replies absently.

"Read it!" I say gleefully. "It's littered with spelling errors."

Truong clicks it open. "Let's see, what have we got here . . . um, *unclear* physics? Well, I've never understood physics myself." He snorts. "And why would someone with a degree in nuclear physics want to work in this dump?"

"Who knows?" I shrug. "Hopefully she can spell."

Truong catches another error. "Impotent? D'oh, did he mean *important?*"

"I know." I snigger. "I wonder if it's a Freudian slip."

"Too bad Dick didn't try to spell *public*," he smirks and plugs away at his keyboard. Moments later, Truong jabs his mouse pad with a flourish. "I just sent you an email."

I click it open.

From: Truong.Nguyen@lsc.com
To: Madison.Lee@lsc.com
Subject: mis-spellers

Edumacation is vary impotent four you. Stay in pubic skool.

p/s—I cunt except people who cunt spell. Day rally irrigate me.

pp/s—Two Bee Ore Knot Two Bee, that is the question my fwend.

I roll with laughter. Dick sure out-dicked himself today. I'm sure *nothing* can top that email, but I am in for a pleasant surprise when Outlook alerts me to a new email from none other than Dick Jones. Still exhilarated by Dick's first email, I proceed to read his second one.

From: Richard.Jones@lsc.com

To: All employees
Subject: Clarify Stimulator

We have just launched Clarify Stimulator, which is a fantastic tulle that will help you with you're call handle thymes. So please keep in mine to use the Stimulator, if your not already doing so.

Dick Jones,
Site Director, Pocatello ID

"Truong, check your email. He sent another one!"

Silence as Truong reads. Seconds later, he falls off his chair, convulsing with laughter.

Tsk-tsk. Dear Dick Jones . . .

*Sim*ulator and *Stim*ulator mean two very different things.

The Blue Balls Café is pretty empty today. Truong, Mika and I pick a table by a window overlooking a pond choked with algae.

Truong has the hawts for Mika, and he had been bugging me nonstop to hook him up. So here we are in the cafeteria, the three of us, on a lunch date.

Truong is convinced that Mika is gay. The problem with Truong is he thinks *every* cute guy is gay. Over the past couple months my gaydar has vastly improved, thanks to Truong. But Mika is *not* gay. He is the epitome of straightness.

Truong, of course, begs to differ.

Mika bites into his burger and smiles feebly at Truong, who won't stop making googly-gooey eyes at him. Christ almighty, Truong needs to get a grip on himself.

"Oh, Mika," he purrs. "You're such a *cutie patootie.* Where do men like you come from?"

"I'm from Brussels," says Mika in between chewing.

"Blussels!" Truong echoes. "I just *love* Blussels splouts."

I stare at Truong in blank astonishment. Huh? What can Brussels sprouts the *vegetable* possibly have in common with Brussels the *country*?

Mika appears just as puzzled, but he offers Truong a polite smile. "That's um, healthy."

Truong giggles like a giddy, star-struck tween in the presence of Justin Bieber. "I am a huge fan of splouts; there's a Vietnamese noodle dish called Phở and it is served with bean splouts. Have you tried it?"

Mika takes a sip of his Coke. "I like Asian food, but I've never had Vietnamese before."

Truong gasps, "You haven't? Then you must try Phở noodles! My Aunt Dung's restaurant specializes in Phở. And let me tell you, her place serves *the* best noodles in town. Would you like to go there some time?"

"Sure," says Mika. "What is the name of her restaurant?"

"It is called Phở Hoa," Truong enunciates, suddenly sounding a lot more Vietnamese.

Mika leans back. "Do they mainly serve noodles?"

"Well, they also serve some good lice dishes, but Phở noodles are their specialty. You *must* try it," he insists.

"I will," says Mika. "And how do you say Phở?"

"You say it like this: *fuuuuuuuuuuuh*," fuhs Truong.

"*Phhhhhuuuuuuuuh*," says Mika.

"No," corrects Truong. "It's *fuuuuuuuuuuuuuuuh*."

Humph! When Truong had first introduced me to Phở noodles, I was super adventurous. Most first-timers play it safe and order the beginner's Phở. Not me. Bold and brave, I had dived head first into my Phở initiation, ordering the Phở with all the bells and whistles. It came with beef tendons, beef steak, beef tripe, beef flank, beef balls, the whole shebang! Truong was so proud of me.

The next day, he had gifted me a T-shirt imprinted with the words 'Phở King' and I accepted it with immense reverence. I consider Truong a Phở ambassador, so I embraced the shirt like it was a gift from Kofi Anan, and even fancied myself a Phở aficionada, a connoisseur of sorts.

Now I realize the joke was on me.

"Truong," I say sulkily. "You can have your *fuuuuuuuuuuuuuh*king T-shirt back."

He laughs gregariously. "It's still a cool shirt. No?"

I fix him with a Medusa glare. Unfazed by my paralyzing glare and snake hair, he continues coaching Mika, who still happens to be butchering the Phở word.

Fart. I'm starting to feel like a third wheel.

"Mika," I cut into their annoying speech lesson, "what do you miss most about your country?"

"My family and the food," he says without missing a beat.

Truong gushes, "Oh, what's your favorite food from home?"

Mika's eyes crinkle at the corners. "Belgian trippe sausage."

"Is it a beef or a pork sausage?" I ask with interest.

"It's made from pork and cabbage. Back home, the sausage is made out of the choicest pork from a recently butchered hog."

"Ugh," I groan, feeling slightly squeamish. An image of a pitiful pig pops into my mind. It's fattened up and ready to be slaughtered. Oh, no. I can even hear the distinct high-pitched screech of a pig squealing for its dear life.

"*Ooooooh Miiiiiii-ka*," shrills Truong.

For a split second there, Truong had sounded like a squealing pig.

"Yeah?" says Mika apprehensively.

Truong rests his chin on his dainty wrists. "Have you tried Vietnamese trippe sausage?"

"Can't say that I have."

Eyeing Mika with a come-hither expression, Truong picks up a french fry and points it to his nether region, an area I prefer not to mention. "Ahem . . . well, I've got one right here." He grins wolfishly.

Without meaning to, I burst out laughing. But I quickly clap my hand over my mouth when I catch the look on Mika's face, which has turned several shades of red by now.

"Truong!" I chide. "Get your mind out of the gutter."

Thankfully, Mika quickly recovers. Instead of crimson red, his cheeks are now tinged a light pink and he's smiling, taking it in stride. "Sorry, Truong, I'll have to decline your offer," he says good-naturedly.

Truong pulls a tiny face. "If you ever change your mind . . ."

"Truong! Quit harassing Mika!" I admonish and crack open a can of Ensure. I take a swig. *Mmmmmm*, not bad at all. Tastes like watered down chocolate shake.

Right then, Bob Seely plods into the cafeteria, bursting out of his black cotton T-shirt, which I'm almost positive he'd purchased at Baby Gap.

Truong smirks, "Simon Cowell wants his shirt back."

"*Tsk-tsk*," I tsk. "He thinks he's all that and a bag of chips."

"Bag of chips?" Truong snorts. "More like a sack of potatoes."

I take two successive chugs of my Ensure. Honestly, I have no idea what Kars sees in that Potato Head.

Mika smiles at me with frank amusement. "Is that all you are having today?"

"What?" I jerk my head.

"*That*," he says, pointing to my can of Ensure.

"Oh, this?" I raise my can. "Kars is on an all-liquid diet so I'm on the diet to support her."

Truong rolls his eyes. "Girl, if Kars jumps off a bridge, are you gonna jump off, too?"

"No," I say defiantly. "But I'd be waiting at the bottom of the bridge to catch her. You know, I'm just being a supportive friend." I take another swig to prove my point. "Plus, it's a good way for me to keep fit, lose some weight, detoxify my liver—"

Oopsie! My stomach makes a gurgling noise. And each time I think it will stop, it chugs and churns like a locomotive train.

Zoinks. It even makes a high-pitched whistling sound.

Mika's mouth twitches and Truong erupts with laughter.

"Screw it," I snap and reach for one of Truong's fries.

Something is missing though. I fish out my bottle of powdered cinnamon and dust it all over the plate of fries.

I am gaga over cinnamon, and I *love* cinnamon rolls and Cinnabons, much to the detriment of my burgeoning waistline. And I sprinkle cinnamon on everything. It is truly my wonder spice and I never leave home without my faithful bottle.

Truong and Mika stare at me as if I'm whacko.

"What?" I cry defensively. "It tastes better. Try one," I offer.

Mika politely declines.

Truong grabs a cinnamon fry and sticks it in his mouth.

That's one thing I love about Truong—he'll try anything and is game for everything.

"So?" I look at Truong expectantly.

He twists his lips. "Tastes like a soggy churro stick."

"Cinnamon has a ton of health benefits," I inform him. "It helps reduce inflammation, it lowers your cholesterol, it—"

Truong interjects, "Says who?"

I tilt my chin. "Says Suzanne Somers."

"Hey!" Truong exclaims, waving a french fry at me. "Do you own a Suzanne Somers Thigh Master?"

"Yes," I say indignantly, "as a matter of fact I do."

"You do?" His mouth slackens.

I nod fiercely. Like every woman in the world, I strive for slender thighs. "The Thigh Master is *the* best way to shape and firm your inner thighs with just a few squeezes a day," I intone in my best infomercial voice.

Truong makes a cuckoo sign at me.

Out of the corner of my eye, I catch a glimpse of Bob sitting down next to Nina, or is it Mena? Anyway, she is that annoying bragasaurus who used to sit by me.

"So, they didn't fire that bitch," I say to no one in particular.

Truong instantly knows who I am referring to. "Nina? Nope, she's a KGB agent now! A spy amongst us."

Mika shoots me a quizzical look.

"She works in Quality Assurance," I explain.

Hmm. Perhaps that's why my last few monitors have been less than stellar. That KGB spy is probably monitoring my calls. We have never jelled, and we harbor a mutual dislike for each other, so maybe now it's payback time. At my expense.

All of a sudden, I hear a shrill peal of laughter from the Bob-Nina table. Whirling around, I eye the pair with revulsion. Bob reaches across the table and fondles Nina's blowfish lips; she reciprocates by suckling his sausage fingers.

Ugh! What the hell was that? Bob is a total man-whore. And Nina is a total she-slut.

Consumed with repugnance, I feel a surge of outrage on Kars' behalf *and* on Bob's wife behalf. That *three* timing bastard! For all I know, Bob probably has a harem of women stashed somewhere.

Truong, just as sickened by the sight of Bob and Nina, raises an eyebrow at me. A perfect arch. I raise mine right back.

Meanwhile, Mika is whopping down his cheeseburger, totally oblivious to this whole exchange.

It's been three weeks since Karsynn had her jaw surgery, and I marvel at her tenacity. Eating is still painfully uncomfortable, yet she manages without complaining.

For breakfast today, Kars is having scrambled eggs with basil.

We'd ditched the Ensure diet two weeks post-surgery.

Well . . . I'd ditched the diet much sooner, but Kars doesn't need to know that.

"So," I say cheerfully. "You'll be back to work next week?"

"Uh-huh," Karsynn confirms. "I'm just dying to get out of the house; I never thought I'd be excited about going back to the call center purgatory."

Janis reaches over my shoulder and pours me a fresh cup of coffee. "I still think it's too soon. It's still a bit hard for her to talk, especially for eight hours straight."

"Mom, *please*. I'll be fine," Kars whines and promptly changes the subject. "So what's new at work, Maddy?"

I sip my coffee. "Nothing much, really. Truong is still obsessed with Mika; he flirts with him shamelessly. Oh yeah, and he calls him Mikquisha."

Kars chuckles and bits of basil scrambled egg spray out of her mouth. "And what about you, Maddy? You still in *lurrrve* with Mikquisha?"

I toy with my coffee mug. "Even if I like him, I don't think he likes me in *that* sorta way."

"How do you know if you don't ask him?" she implores.

"Ask him? No, I could never. Besides, if he likes me, surely he would've made a move by now. But no. Nothing so far . . ."

"Hullo? It's transparently obvious he's into you. I've seen the two of you together; you're both so sickeningly cute it makes me want to gag."

I shoot her a look that says, "Yeah right."

Kars forks a mouthful of eggs. "Are you still tutoring him?"

"Uh-huh. Once a week, without fail. You know, I really don't do much except edit his papers and suggest books for him to read. And there's hardly anything for me to edit. All I do is tweak his punctuations. A semi colon here, a comma there. Seriously, I'm just dotting his I's and crossing his T's."

Kars eyes me suspiciously. "Hmm. Then why are you two still meeting up for tutoring sessions?"

"I've mentioned it a couple times." I shrug nonchalantly. "But he insists he still needs my help."

Kars waves her fork in the air. "See! That's a good sign."

"Oh, I don't know." I breathe out a weary sigh. "I just feel like that geeky girl in high school who he only sees as a tutor, not the cute cheerleader he takes to the prom."

Kars rolls her eyes. "Stop it! You're starting to sound like a Taylor Swift song."

We exchange silly grins across the table, then we burst out singing *You Belong to Me*, crooning the best parts. Sometimes, I think Kars and I are distant descendants of the African Zulu tribe. We randomly burst into song, and for some inexplicable reason, we make strange noises with our tongues, like *Ali Li Li Ayi Ayi Ayeee Ayeee*. Just like the Shaka Zulu tribal women.

When we're done singing, clapping and making tribal sounds, the entire kitchen table is covered with bits of scrambled eggs.

Janis wipes the surface with a rag and shoots Kars a parental look. "Honey, you don't need to be singing in your condition."

Kars brushes off her concerns with a wave of her hand. "So, Maddy, how's Ingeborg?"

Gingerly, I pluck a sliver of basil out of my hair. "She's doing good; she's dating this guy on Pablo Escobar's team. Archibald. I think he must be ten times her age!"

She smirks. "With a name like Archibald, I'm not surprised. Is he at least cute?"

"He looks like Sean Connery, minus the teeth."

"What?" she guffaws.

"I know. It's weird. One minute I looked over at his cubicle, he had teeth and the next minute, they were sitting in a glass of water."

Kars slurps her juice through a straw. "Hey, I'd date a James Bond with dentures."

"Well, they're an oddball couple, but they make a good match. After all, Ingeborg could be mistaken for a Bond girl."

"That she could," says Karsynn. After a pregnant pause, she asks, "Who is your favorite double O seven?"

"Pierce Brosnan," I say without hesitation, "although I think Clive Owen would make the ultimate Bond. Maybe even Zachary Levi. What about you?"

"*Psssh!* Connery any day. And I'm *so* glad that you didn't say Daniel Craig."

"Daniel Craig?" I echo. "What's wrong with him?"

"Sean Connery—chest hair. Roger Moore—chest hair. Even your dashing Pierce Brosnan had chest hair. And then WHAMO! Daniel Craig—no chest hair! He's plucked, preened and waxed up like a baby seal."

"Baby seals are cute," I insist. "Now, would you rather go to bed with a woolly mammoth or a baby seal?"

"Woolly mammoth!" she says at once. "He'll keep me warm at night; the slippery baby seal will just slide right off the bed. Plus, I like real men, and real men have hair on their bodies."

"I know." I roll my eyes. "You've said it many times before. You don't like your men to look prettier than you."

"Um-hmmmm, I don't have a penchant for pre-teen girls." She pauses for effect. "Like *you*."

Instinctively, I kick her under the table. "Mika is *all man*."

"Mika may be, but not Zac Efron." She smirks.

"Hey! Don't you be talking smack about my Zac," I cry in an injured voice. "I'll take Zac over Sean Connery any day."

"Not me," says Karsynn. "I'll have to side with Ingeborg on this one and pick Connery."

Burying my nose in my coffee mug, I speculate, "You may be right about Ingeborg. Maybe she really *is* trying to find a replacement for her daddy to fill this fatherless vacuum in her life. Only in her case, it's granddaddy."

"Better an old man's darling than a young man's slave." Kars laughs. "Is he nice? Grandpa Connery?"

"Yeah, he seems like a really sweet guy. He dotes on Ingeborg and she seems genuinely happy. And . . . he's not *married*," I say for good measure.

An awkward pause follows.

I tentatively broach the subject, "So, are you still seeing Bob?"

Another pause ensues. I wait for Kars to fill the silence.

Eventually, she says with a pained expression, "I haven't seen him since my surgery. And he hasn't returned any of my calls."

Janis, who had been washing dishes at the sink, strides over and squeezes Karsynn's shoulders. "You deserve better sweetheart."

I nod, agreeing with Janis. "You do, Kars."

I am compelled to rehash the Bob and Nina incident that I had witnessed in the cafeteria the other day. But somehow, I can't bring myself to. And I don't think I need to. Kars looks suitably chastised and I have a feeling she already *knows* it's over.

Twelve

Today is Karsynn's first day back at work since her surgery Today is Karsynn's first day back at work since her surgery and there is a noticeable buzz about the floor as we breeze into the office. I make a beeline for Truong's cubicle and tap my AP wire on the shoulder.

"Truong! What's going on?"

He whirls around. "I've got ball breaking news! The shit hit the fan," he cries, bubbling with excitement. Then he sees Kars, and his bubbles fizzle somewhat. He darts a nervous glance in her direction and tones it down a notch. "Bob got fired . . . Nina, too. I just saw security escort them out."

"What happened?" demands Kars.

Truong dithers. "Um, are you sure you want to know?"

"Tell me!" she shrieks and I can hear the hysteria in her voice.

"It's not so pretty," he warns. After a sharp intake of breath, he spills the beans, "Bob and Nina were caught boinking in the parking garage. And security caught it all on tape."

All the color drains from Karsynn's face, and her expressions vacillate between shock and sorrow.

Before we can pump Truong for more details, The Führer stands up from her watch post and cracks her whip. "Girls! Get to work!"

Kars skulks off to her cubicle while Truong and I pretend to look busy at our desks.

As I am loading up my apps, it suddenly dawns on me. This means Bob is out of Karsynn's life *forever*. I can't wait to share this fab news with Janis. Her skillfully orchestrated Jaw Surgery Plot had been a success. But this is even better.

Truong whispers, "*Pssssst*. There's more to it."

I furrow my eyebrows. "Huh? What are you talking about?"

He fills me in on all the salacious details. "Apparently, Bobby overstepped his boundaries, and that dipshit was having affairs with *several* women, one of them who just so happens to be Adnan's wife."

I draw a blank. "Who's Adnan?"

"He's the Armenian security guard."

My eyes widen in horror. "Scandalous."

Truong lowers his voice. "Girl, this is beyond scandalous. You don't mess with the Armenians *period*. Adnan and his Armenian army organized a bloodless coup d'état. They planned this whole thing strategically and tactically. You see, Bob is no knucklehead. He knew that there were cameras in the parking garage, and he was so dang sure that he was in a blind spot. But what he didn't know was that Adnan and his boys installed *extra* surveillance cameras."

I gasp, "This is more twisted than a Chuck Palahniuk novel."

Truong giggles devilishly. "The plot thickens! Adnan and his army remained vigilant. As soon as Bob slipped, they were there to capture it all. And the next day, they handed the evidence to Dick Jones."

Abruptly, The Führer stands up, face like thunder. "Madison Lee, Truong Nguyen, GET ON THE PHONES!"

My hands tremble as I scramble for my headset. I'm about to take my first call when I notice a Starbucks caramel frappuccino sitting on my desk. It's topped with whipped cream and drizzled with caramel sauce. The decadent treat sits next to my phone in all its caffeinated glory.

"Truong, is this from you?"

"Uh huh. And I got it with skim milk, too."

I beam at him. "Thanks, Truong! You're the best!"

Hours later, I'm no longer singing Truong's praises. Slumped on a chair in the HR office, I curse Truong and his stupid email for getting me and Kars in this predicament.

Kars is in the hot seat next to me.

"Do you think they'll fire us?" she asks anxiously.

My stomach churns with dread. "I don't know."

It had all started innocently enough with a silly joke email that Truong had forwarded on to me—*Learn to Speak Chinese in 5 minutes* . . . a joke that had been floating around the internet for quite some time now. And *that* email is now printed out and sitting on Linda the HR Manager's desk.

Earlier on, when I'd read that email, I laughed so hard I almost fell off my chair. And I'd thought it was so funny that I forwarded it to Kars. Over my lunch break, I decided to check up on her. Kars has a tendency to bottle up her feelings, and I had wanted to make sure she was okay.

I found her sitting at her desk, looking solemn and subdued.

"You okay?" I asked gently.

A tear had gathered at the edge of her eye, and I stood by Kars, doing the best thing a friend could do—I listened as she poured her heart out.

After Kars had got everything off her chest, she actually started feeling sorry for Bob. "I wonder if he'll be okay; I mean, he's lost his job, his marriage is in shambles," she mused out loud.

Bob was not my concern, Karsynn was. She had hit rock bottom and I'd wanted to lift her spirits and help her forget all about that awful man-whore. That slithering snake in the grass. Then a thought had occurred to me. "Kars, have you checked your email today?"

"No," she replied absently.

My eyes twinkled with mischief. "Pull it up," I instructed.

In hopes of getting a chuckle out of Kars, I read each line out loud, in what I'd hoped was a very convincing Chinese accent. I'd got all the way down to #5: I bumped my knee against a coffee table. Altering my voice and channeling Jackie Chan, I said, *"Ai Bang Maii Nee."*

It worked! Karsynn had keeled over laughing.

And she'd even got in on the action, too. While I'd recited #6: Staying out of sight = Lie Yeeng Low, Kars channeled Chow Yuen Fatt, Jet Li *and* Kung Fu Panda by whipping out the Kung Fu Crane Stance, followed by a drop kick, and finishing off with a Kung Fu Reverse Punch.

I'd laughed so hard my stomach hurt.

Kars looked like a Shaolin Panda monk.

It was all quite harmless fun, and comical really, speaking Chinese while Karsynn whipped out more kung fu moves. Until The Führer had showed up.

Very quietly, she'd stood behind us and cleared her throat.

My back shot up! Ramrod straight!

Kars froze in the midst of a Kung Fu Lotus Stance.

"What were you doing?" Hillary snarled in an eerily low voice.

My blood ran cold, terror ripping through my nerves. I tried to open my mouth and speak, but it had gone bone dry.

"WHAT WERE YOU DOING?" The Führer screamed and I jumped out of my skin. "ANSWER ME!" she roared like a lion.

"Err . . . I was, um . . . speaking Chinese?" I squeaked like an overwrought mouse.

Kars released a nervous laugh. "Um yeah, Mandarin is one of the hardest languages to learn."

Hillary made a vicious sound of protest. "YOU WERE NOT SPEAKING MANDARIN!"

Kars and I blinked.

Hillary seethed. "Is that all you two were doing?"

"I think so." I scratched my head, pretending to be foggy on the exact details.

At this point, Kars had completely lost it. Hugging herself tightly, she rocked back and forth, babbling on like a crazed homeless woman. In the midst of muttering something indistinct, she darted me a *look,* and I instantly realized that it was all a ploy to throw Hillary off the scent.

Sadly, it didn't work.

Hillary snarled and stepped closer. "Let me just see for myself."

I lurched forward. "There is nothing to see," I said in a sudden panic.

Like a raging lunatic, Hillary elbowed me aside and planted herself in front of Karsynn's computer. We shrunk back in a corner as Hillary read the entire email. To add insult to injury, she read each line out loud in a dry monotone, without a Chinese accent, and with no sense of humor whatsoever. It was painful, like hearing Chairman Mao tell a joke.

Then Hillary flew into a blinding rage and launched into this huge tirade about the political *in*correctness of our actions.

"My niece is Chinese! And I don't appreciate you mocking her language," she shrilled.

I stood there, paralyzed.

Hillary threw Kars a vicious glare. "Or her culture!"

Kars muttered, "I was merely celebrating it."

"WHAT?" yelled The Führer.

"N-nothing," Kars stammered. The tremor in her voice was unmistakable.

Hillary continued giving us an earful, and we quickly learned that her sister had adopted a little girl from China. Hence, she took what we had done *very* personally. In fact, Hillary was so incensed by the implication and so fueled with outrage that she marched us straight to the HR office.

Fast forward to present . . . the air is zinged with tension and Linda from Human Resources stares down her hawkish nose through her bifocals, looking like ferret faced Judge Judy.

Linda glances from me to Kars, and then back to me. Pursing her thin lips, she shakes her head reproachfully.

My stomach lurches. I hope we don't get fired.

While we sit and stew in our seats, Linda consults the thick Employee Handbook. Her lips tighten, and there is an increased intensity in the lines around her mouth. The more she studies the handbook, the deeper the lines and creases become. The seconds tick by, the tension crackles and mounts, the silence seems too heavy to bear.

I don't want to lose my job over this. I need to do *something*.

Before Judge Linda has a chance to pass her verdict, I jump in and blurt out, "In our defense, Linda, just because we find a racist joke funny, that doesn't make us racists. And, also, I happen to be half Chinese."

My sudden outburst emboldens Kars to speak. "Yeah, I think it's important to be able to laugh at yourself. That movie *Borat* had me in stitches, but it doesn't make me anti-Semitic. I'm Jewish for crying out loud."

"I know," I pipe in. "I thought the movie *Bruno* was hilarious, but that doesn't make me homophobic."

Karsynn adds fiercely, "Yes. I'm all for the LGBTs!"

Linda shoots us a puzzled look. "BLT sandwiches?"

"No," I rush to explain, "LGBTs means Lesbians, Gays, Bisexuals and Transgenders."

Seriously, I'm a bit surprised that Linda doesn't know the lingo. It should be common parlance for someone who works in HR.

Kars says plaintively, "Yes. So as you can see, Linda, we love everyone. We're cultured and diverse people. We're innocent and this is a simple open and shut case. And, um . . . the prosecution rests their case." She paces up and down the room as if she was a top notch attorney at law.

Linda blinks.

"And that email is not even racist," I add. "Even Truong found it funny, and he's the one who sent it to me."

Linda jams her bifocals up her nose, only to have them slip back down. "Now that's entirely different," she says with a petulant twist of her lips. "Truong is Chinese, so it is entirely okay for a Chinese person to be tickled by a joke about Chinese people. But what you girls did is politically incorrect," she says severely.

Hello. I'm the one who is part Chinese; Truong is Vietnamese, *not* Chinese. But I'm not a narc, so I don't reveal this. Besides, if I get Truong in trouble, I'm sure the sushi rolls and Starbucks fraps will be a thing of the past.

Linda flicks off her bifocals in a dramatic fashion and leans back in her Herman Miller Aeron chair. "Let me give you girls an example. Now myself, being a Caucasian, I would *never ever* call an African American a nigger. However, it's entirely okay for an African American to call himself one."

Kars and I exchange horror filled glances, then we stare at Linda in alarm. "But you—you just said the N word."

"I was merely giving an example," Linda says patiently.

Now it's our turn to glare at Linda disapprovingly. "It doesn't matter," I retort, filled with righteous indignation. "You're white! You're *never ever* allowed to use that word."

"Yeah!" quips Kars judiciously. "Not even in an example. That word is off-limits! It should be entirely erased from your vocabulary. And the fact that you used it—it's *racist*," she hisses impudently.

Linda raises her eyes heavenward.

YAY! Hip Hip Hoooray! We have been exonerated. And, we're off the phones for two hours! Kars and I, *and* Linda from HR, are in Diversity-Sensitivity training. The three of us are sitting in the Lightning 7 conference room, watching sensitivity exercises on the tube.

In the first scene, a Hispanic woman is on the phone and she's talking to some guy named Jesus (she pronounces it *Hey-Soose*). After hanging up, she informs a white guy that Jesus needs some supplies at the work site. Apparently, Jesus can't seem to get the job done without those supplies. To which the white guy replies, "What's the matter with Jesus? (he pronounces it *Geez-Sus*) Jesus can't make tacos and burritos without his supplies, so he's taking an afternoon siesta?"

Oh dear God. This is so racist! I find myself cringing at all the clichéd racist rhetoric; but at the same time, it's like watching an episode of *The Office* with Steve Carell, only in this case, the acting is horrendous and there appears to be a haze tinting the picture reminiscent of B rated movies.

Although I'm trying so hard to suppress my laughter, a loud snort escapes me.

Linda shoots me a quelling look.

"I have Hispanic blood in me. *I swear*," I cry defensively.

And I do. My dad's great grandmother is part Mexican; so since I am part Latina, that makes it okay. I am allowed to be tickled by a racist Mexican joke, at least by Linda's accounts.

Slightly vexed, Linda shakes her head.

In the next scene, a guy is watching his co-worker (a curvy woman) devour a Snickers bar. The woman makes an offhanded comment about how she shouldn't be eating chocolate, since it is so fattening.

To which the guy responds, "As long as your fat stays in the right places, all the men will still be chasing you."

Kars whispers in my ear, "Bob actually said that to me."

"What?" I balk. "He is such a douchelord! A deity among douches!"

Linda glares at us, clearly annoyed. "Sssshhhh."

Clearly, she's taking this training *way* too seriously.

Two hours later, the Diversity-Sensitivity training is over.

Dammit! Now we have to hop back on the phones.

Before we step out, Linda halts us. "Now, if you're working on Christmas, please do *not* wish the callers Merry Christmas; instead, say Happy Holidays, okay?"

"Okay," we say brightly, wide-eyed with innocence.

Linda chides, "Girls, remember! Be mindful! We live in a multicultural country. So you don't want to offend the Jews, the Muslims, the Hindus, the Buddhists—"

"Or the atheists or agnostics," adds Kars with a faint smirk.

"Or them either," agrees Linda in all seriousness.

I smile reassuringly. "Don't worry, we'll be *very* sensitive. We won't offend anybody's religion, race, culture, nationality—"

Kars jumps in, "Language, sexual orientation, disability, size, marital status, beliefs, education, lifestyles, gender or physical appearance."

I nod fervently. "Rest assured, Linda, I shall not discriminate, segregate or abate."

Linda's mouth parts and stays parted. Eventually, she says, "Now girls, you have ten more minutes before you're scheduled to get back on the phones. All right?"

"*All right-y,*" we chime in unison and sashay to the break room.

Kars nudges me. "Maybe we'll see some eye candy."

"Maybe." I smile coyly.

In the break room, I reach inside the freezer for my popsicles and gasp in horror. "Someone's been eating my popsicles! There's only one left! I feel violated!"

Kars harrumphs. "That's why I never store any food in the break room. Too many morons here steal food. Such vermin!"

"So, where exactly *do* you store your food?" I slam the freezer with deliberate force.

"The lactation room," Kars says simply. "It's equipped with a mini fridge slash freezer. Nothing's stored there except for breast milk. And more importantly, no one will steal your food."

I make a mental note of that. "Here," I hand Kars the last popsicle. She takes it and I toss the Dreyer's box into the trash can.

I miss.

The box ricochets off the trash can, skates across the linoleum floor and stops in the middle of the break room.

Right that second, Darren and Carlos strut into the break room. Darren bends down and reaches for the Dreyer's box. Box in hand, he holds it like a ball and shoots it into the trash can like a pro basketball player. NBA, not college level.

Darren Williams is tall and gorgeous, with light olive skin; and he sports a sexy goatee that very few men can pull off—the Orlando Bloom goatee. A faint tache and soul patch combo.

Carlos Martinez is a suave Latino from Venezuela, with the physique and build of a matador.

Kars and I try not to stare. They're too beautiful for words.

Darren acknowledges us with a lift of his cleft chin.

We *kind of* know him. He sits right next to Mika and whenever we pay Mika a visit, we are very aware of Darren's *hawtness.*

"Hey," I grunt with casual indifference.

Kars tilts her chin. "Wassup brotha."

Playing it cool, we swagger out of the break room.

Out of the corner of my eye, I spy Darren and Carlos heading for the foosball table. My eyes gravitate to their solid butts that are nicely shaped by their fitted jeans. I'm so glad that fitted jeans are back in fashion.

That's one of the reasons why I resent baggy jeans—no bum watching. Bum watching is very much like bird watching. It's a lifetime activity that can be enjoyed in many parts of the world, transcending language barriers and cultures.

Kars and I continue staring. It's not every day you get to see such fabulous butts when so many men these days are cursed with assless frog butts.

"That Hot Cocoa is one fine specimen," I say dazedly, tripping over a snag in the carpet.

Kars is in a similar trance. "Hot Cocoa Darren? Nah, I was checking out Carlos, the Hot Tamale."

HR Linda ambles by, peering through her bifocals, waggling her finger at us admonishingly.

Whoopsie! I guess she must've heard us.

Thirteen

Tick Tock, I'm watching the clock. *Yessssssss! Only six* more minutes left, then I'm done for the day! I'm so euphoric that my shift is almost over that I'm humming a happy tune, "Heigh-ho! Heigh-ho! It's home from work I go!"

Ordinarily, I'd jab the Not Ready key five minutes before my shift ends, but not today. I've been written up for excessive Not Ready time, so I have no choice but to stay logged in.

Only three minutes left. Two. One minute left.

My index finger hovers over the Log Out button—

Beep!

"F#@!*&!#@!*!" I release a steady stream of profanity.

"Thanks for calling Lightning Speed Communications. This is Maddy, how can I help?"

"This is a relay call. My name is Amy and I'm a California relay service operator. Have you taken a relay call before?"

I bash my head against the keyboard. "Yes I have," I mutter, struggling to keep the impatience from my voice. I know it's not this operator's fault, nor is it the deaf caller's.

Honestly, I have nothing against the hearing impaired.

The timing is just crap. And relay calls take forever and ever.

Kars perches on my desk. "You ready to roll?"

MUTE. "No, you go on," I say miserably. "I'll be stuck on this call for a while. It's a relay call!" I sob theatrically on her shoulder.

Kars shoots me a sympathetic look.

We had carpooled today, like we do on most days. But it's okay, I won't have Kars suffer alongside me.

She slides off my desk. "Are you sure?"

I nod despondently.

"Okay, ciao!" she tinkles and sashays off. I watch her disappear down the hallway, headed back to our cozy apartment.

"Now," instructs the relay operator, "repeat again what you just said, only this time, say it much, much slower so I'm able to type and keep up with you. Go Ahead."

I slow it down to a snail's pace. Thank—you—for—calling—Lightning—Speed—Communications—This—is—Maddy—how—can—I—help? Go—ahead."

Long pause.

All I hear is the operator's acrylic fingernails clacking away at her keyboard.

Another long pause.

And finally, "My name is Tina Connor and my internet is not working. I can't pull up any sites. Please help. Go ahead," relays the operator.

After spending *way* too much time going through the verification process, I ask, "What—browser—do—you—use? Go—ahead."

More keys tapping. More silence. "The internet. Go ahead," relays the operator noncommittally.

I bury my face in my hands.

Somebody please put a gun to my head and just freakin' BLOW MY BRAINS OUT!

I silently count to ten and grit my teeth. "Do—you—see—a—blue—E—on—your—desktop? Go—ahead." I draw in a ragged breath and resign myself to my abysmal fate.

More pause. More waiting.

And then . . . "What is a desktop? Go ahead," says the operator, suppressing a snort.

Oh yeah, I'm sure she's enjoying this. She thinks this is *such* a lark, but I'm not tickled by this. Not in the least! And why does this caller even *own* a computer? It should be downright illegal!

Deep breath. Find my inner peace. Yoga. Chi Kung.

Think tranquil and serene thoughts.

Think Japanese botanical garden.

Think pristine koi pond.

Ohm . . . Ohm . . . Ohm . . .

After my meditative hiatus, I press on, "When—you—boot—up—your—computer—the—very—first—screen—that—comes—up—is—your—desktop—Do—you—see—a—blue—E—on—it?—Go—ahead!"

Sheesh. I simply *cannot* wait for this call to end, but getting this caller off the line is like trying to pass an Act of Congress.

Fifty minutes go by and I fail to see the light at the end of the tunnel. Not even a flicker.

One hour and thirty-seven minutes later (*oh yeah, I've been keeping track*), the call finally comes to an end.

Feeling completely drained, I grab my bag and drag my feet to leave. Spinning around, I spot Mika lounging at an empty cubicle. He's reading a book, and his forehead is slightly creased from rapt concentration. I bite my lip. He looks so endearing, it hurts.

Glancing up, he catches my eye and smiles.

I tilt my head to the side. "You waited for me?"

"Uh-huh," he says, like he's proud of the fact.

My heart skips a beat. "Oh."

Surreptitiously, he stows the book away. "Kars called my cell and said you might need a ride home."

"You didn't have to wait for me; that call took forever. But, um . . . thanks, though, for waiting."

"No problem," he shucks. "So, you want to go grab a bite?"

"Sure!" I hoist my bag over my shoulder. "Let's go!"

As we stroll out into the frosty night, there's a noticeable spring in my step. I'm quite positive I look like the cat that just ate the canary topped with whipped cream. And this is not even a real date! Kars you sneaky little devil. I owe you one!

Ever the chivalrous one, Mika opens the door to his low rider Impala and I slide in. The first time I'd been in Mika's car, I was pleasantly surprised. It may look like a fishing boat, but it rides like an airplane.

We speed off and I feel buoyant, like I'm floating on a hot air balloon. Every time we go over speed bumps, it feels like we're bouncing on clouds.

I steal a glance at him. "What year is this baby of yours?"

"Nineteen sixty-four," he says, beaming like a proud daddy.

"It's older than my rust bucket. Mine's an eighty-four."

He gives a respectful nod to my relic of a Subaru.

Feeling rather restless, I start rubbing my arms.

"You cold?" he asks at once.

"I'm fine," I mutter, but he cranks up the heat anyway.

"You feel like pizza tonight?"

"Pizza sounds good," I say with an easy smile.

"Cool." He fishes out an iPod from his coat pocket. "I know of a good pizza place." Expertly, he plugs in his iPod and seconds later, my ears are treated to a brand of music unlike anything I'd ever heard. It sounds like Indian hip hop music.

But instead of Bollywood, this is Bolly*hood*.

"Who's this?" I ask.

"Panjabi Hit Squad; this track is from Desi Beats," he says in a highly animated voice. "It's bhangra music."

This particular song has a slight R&B feel to it, and every so often a female's velvety vocals blend in with the catchy beats.

He darts me a glance. "So, what do you think of bhangra?"

Listening raptly, I say, "I think if Mary J. Blige were to cut an Indian record, this is what it would sound like."

This elicits a smile from Mika. "What about you? What do you listen to?"

"I tune in to NPR most of the time. As for music, it's a hodgepodge, but Jack Johnson is probably my favorite."

When I listen to Johnson's drifting chords, the strum of his ukulele and his laidback acoustics, I'm magically transported to a paradisal beach in the Maldives where coconut trees sway lazily in the wind, and I inhale the salty island breeze.

Needless to say, it's nothing like the Panjabi Hit Squad. But bhangra is pretty catchy. Sinking back into the worn out leather seat, I chill to the music for the rest of the ride.

Papa's Pizzeria is empty for a Friday night. Tiny tables and chairs are crammed into a minuscule space.

Holy Ravioli! This place is a dive. It's a hole in the wall. In fact, it's so small that it's a hole *in* the hole in the wall.

A rat hole, to be precise.

Mika instantly reads my mind. "Don't worry, Maddy. This is the town's best kept secret. They make *the* best pizzas."

At the register, Mika turns to me. "So, should we get a whole pizza or just individual slices?"

"A whole one!"

"A whole pizza it is," he declares. "What kind?"

"Is ham and pineapple okay with you?"

He nods his assent. "Drink?"

"7 Up with lots of ice."

"My treat," he insists and shoos me off.

I pick a dimly lit booth, remove my coat and slide in.

My ears perk up when I overhear Mika conversing with an elderly man behind the register—in French!

Minutes later, Mika strides over and carefully sets our drinks on the table. "Our pizza should be ready in about ten minutes."

"Sweet," I say airily and remove the plastic lid from my cup.

He shrugs off his navy bomber jacket. "You hungry?"

I spoon an ice cube into my mouth. "Ravenous!"

"Good!" he exclaims and scoots into the booth. "You won't be disappointed. The owner of this pizzeria, Giuseppe, he's Italian; his family immigrated to France twelve years ago and they just moved to Pocatello last year. Giuseppe was just telling me that he finally got his green card today."

I crunch on an ice cube. "I heard you speaking to him in French. Is that what most Belgians speak?"

He pokes a straw through the plastic lid. "Well in the north, the Flemish or the Flanders speak Dutch. And in the south, the Walloons speak French. In Brussels, they speak both languages." He takes a sip of his Coke. "Near the German border, some speak German; and most of the younger crowd can speak English." Half-smiling, he adds, "Some people make fun of us; they say we can speak three languages, but none of them intelligibly." He laughs. "Of course I don't agree with that."

"So are you Flemish or are you a Walloonian?" I ask cheekily.

I can't help it, but every time I hear that word, an unpleasant image of a chesty cough comes to mind. An image of phlegm. Flemish phlegm, to be precise.

And Walloon? Is that a wandering tribe of baboons?

Mika chuckles heartily. "I'm a Wallonie."

"Oh. *Parlez-vous Francais?*"

"*Oui.* I'm what you'd call a Francophone."

I rest my chin on my hands. "Say something in French."

Just then, our pizza arrives at the table.

"*Jambon et ananas pizza,*" he says with a flourish.

"What does that mean?" I ask breathlessly.

"It means ham and pineapple pizza."

I snicker. "Say something else."

"*S'il vous plaît permet de manger.*"

Ah, it all sounds so romantic. In fact, I think anything said in French sounds dreamy, lovely and complimentary. You can say you want to murder someone in French, saw his neck off with a blunt pocket knife and scalp the skin off his head, and it'd still sound romantic . . . like waxing poetic in my ear.

Actually, French *is* considered a Romance language because it is derived from Roman, and deeply rooted in Latin (which was the primary language used by the Romans), so it sounds romantic because it *is* a Romance language after all.

I release a dreamy sigh. "Oooh, what did you just say?"

His mouth twitches. "It means 'please, let's eat'."

"Bon Appétit!" I exclaim, Julia Child-style.

For a while, we eat in companionable silence, sharing in the growing comfort of warm dough and mozzarella cheese filling our empty stomachs.

Mika reaches for another slice. "So, are you going back home for Christmas?"

"No, I'm forced to work."

"Me too," he groans. "By the way, where's home for you?"

"Me? I grew up in Lake Forest. It's near Chicago."

He leans back. "So, is Chicago a lot like Pocatello?"

I laugh. "Pocatello is much smaller than Chicago, by like *two million people.*"

Mika chuckles. "I've never been to Chicago." After a pause, he says ruefully, "I haven't traveled much around the States."

"You mean you've never left Pocatello?" I cry aghast.

"Well, I've been to Boise," he says defensively. "And I've even been to Paris."

I blink. "Paris, France?"

He shakes his head. "Paris, Idaho."

"Mika!" I gasp. "That is not acceptable! You need to get away from here and breathe a different air. Go to Yellowstone and see the bears and bison. Go to Vegas and catch Celine Dion's show! Next time I go home, you're coming with me," I say adamantly.

"Okay," he says, unaware of a stringy piece of mozzarella that's sticking to his bottom lip.

I have this sudden impulse to wipe it away, but I resist.

That would feel too intimate.

"Oh, and by the way," he adds with a wry smile, "of course I've been to Paris, France. Belgium borders France, and Paris is only a hundred and sixty miles from Brussels."

"Well, I've never been." I sigh wistfully. "Someday, I'd love to go to Europe."

Mika reaches for a napkin and wipes his mouth. "Come back home with me sometime."

"For real?" I suck in a surprised breath.

"Of course," he says. "I'd love to show you around."

I find myself grinning stupidly. "You know what I've always wanted to see?"

The corners of his eyes crinkle. "What?"

"The famous Pissing Boy Statue."

He laughs. "You mean the Manneken Pis?"

"Yeah, and isn't he dressed in different costumes each week?"

"Yep." He takes another sip of his soda. "Now why would you want to see the Manneken Pis?"

"Why not?" I huff with offended dignity. "It's one of the most famous landmarks in Brussels."

"It's not fair." He grins. "You guys have the Statue of Liberty and we've got the Pissing Boy Statue."

"Sounds fair to me," I say in a teasing voice. "So, when will you be going back?"

"Well after I graduate, I'm going back for good."

"Oh . . ." I trail off and find myself staring at my cup of soda.

Lifting the cup to my lips, I sip in silence. His words seem to settle like rocks and boulders in my chest.

He breaks the silence. "When will you be going home?"

I give a careless shrug. "Not any time soon."

"You have a slight accent." He wrinkles his brows. "Is that a Chicagoan accent?"

"I do? I didn't realize it. Speaking of accents, people from MinnesoooOooooota and WisConsin have a much stronger one. Trust me, it sounds like a whole different language."

"I know exactly what you mean." He gives an amused half-smile. "Darren's from Wisconsin and whenever he offers me a soda, he calls it 'pop'."

I giggle helplessly. "You mean *pahp*."

Mika continues, "And he calls the water fountain a bubbler. Yesterday, he asked me where the bubbler was, and I thought he was looking for a ground geyser."

"You gotta love Wisconsin accents."

"So . . ." He pauses for a beat. "Do you know Darren?"

I bob my head. "Yeah, he's the guy who sits next to you."

"Well," he hesitates. "Darren's been asking me about you; he wanted to know if you're seeing anyone."

I gulp down my soda. "What'd you tell him?"

He makes a conscious effort to avoid my eyes. "I, err . . . told him that you think dating someone at work is like dumping on your own doorstep."

I choke on my 7 Up.

"You okay?" he asks, his voice laced with concern.

I nod, trying to find my voice. I take another healthy swallow, and this time it goes down the right pipe. Clearing my throat, I say, "So, you really told Darren that?"

"Yes." He searches my eyes and asks a question that fills the room. "Is that how you really feel? About dating a co-worker?"

Before I can respond, Mika quickly adds, "If not, I can easily clear things up with Darren."

I open my mouth and clamp it shut. If I tell Mika that I am not opposed to dating a co-worker, he'll assume that I like Darren.

Arrgh! What I really want to say is that I like him.

You, Mika.

Suddenly, Springsteen croons *Born in the USA* and I'm saved by The Boss. Bolting upright, I reach for my phone. "Wassup!" I answer. "Yeah, I'm with Mika. We're at Papa's Pizzeria." Short pause while I listen. "Uh-huh, sure no problem." I hang up.

"Kars wants me to pick up a pesto pizza."

"How is she doing?"

"Better now that she can eat solid food." I stand up and reach for my bag. "I'll go place that order for her."

Mika pulls out a ten dollar bill. "Here, let me get it."

"No," I protest.

"I want to," he insists. "You've been tutoring me every week; it's the least I can do." He stuffs the ten dollar bill in my hand.

"Okay," I relent. "But on one condition."

"What's that?" he asks with a tilt of his chin.

"If you ever thank me for tutoring you again, I'll make you eat a ten dollar bill."

"Yes, ma'am," he says with a wave of his hand, indicating gracious dismissal of the matter.

As I'm walking toward the register, I'm suddenly halted by Mika's voice.

I throw a glance over my shoulder. "Yeah?"

"Keep the change," he says, not trying to hide a smile.

The doorbell chimes as we duck out of the pizzeria. Walking down the sidewalk at a brisk pace, I elbow Mika playfully. "Hey, can you speak Gaelic?"

His mouth curls slightly at the corners and he shakes his head.

I hug my coat tightly around me. That's too bad. If Mika could speak Gaelic, I'd get down on bended knee right now and say, "I want to marry you and bear your children."

"So . . ." he interrupts my moony fantasies, "are we still on for my tutoring session tomorrow?"

I tuck my frosty fingertips inside my pockets. "I am if you are."

"I sure am. Same place?"

"Well, instead of the library, why don't you come over to my place?" I ask on a whim.

"Your place it is," he says with an easy smile.

Fourteen

What the hell was I thinking? My place is a *mess*.

Despite our best efforts, Kars and I are hopeless at cleaning. Sporadically, we leave our crap lying all around the apartment, and things just end up staying wherever they land. Sometimes I tidy up and other times Kars will, and the only time our messy apartment becomes an issue is when we have guests over.

Like today.

Newspapers, books and bras are strewn everywhere. Yes—*bras*. Our living space is littered with bras. Demi cups, full coverage, wireless, T-shirt bras, strapless, convertibles, racer-backs, multi-ways, shelf bras, built in bras, peepholes, push-ups, front closures, water bras, sports bras (even though neither of us play any sports).

But I can explain. When Karsynn watches TV, she insists on going bra-less. It's her firm belief that the brassiere underwires restrict her blood circulation.

Karsynn's bijongas are rather small—34AA, or poached eggs as she calls them—and she is certain that if she goes braless, her Berthas will start sprouting again. And that's not all. She claims that going braless lowers her breast cancer risk.

When I'd scoffed at that idea, Kars whipped out some medical study and paraded it in my face in mock reproof. So now I am a born again braless believer, and will admit to going braless on occasion, usually in the privacy of my own apartment.

Karsynn shimmies by and performs her magical bra maneuver trick. She reaches under the back of her shirt, unhooks her bra, wriggles down the straps, yanks it out of one sleeve and yells, "*Presto!*" all with one hand.

After performing her Harry Houdini trick, she carefully sets her bra on the arm of the sofa, and that is where it shall stay for months on end, or until it's laundry time.

Hastily, I grab all her bras, including the black Wonder Bra she'd just plunked down and chuck everything into her bedroom.

"Wonder Bra," Karsynn frets, "I love it and I hate it. When I take it off, I *wonder* where my boobs went."

I bubble with laughter. "Let's be thankful that men don't wear Wonder Briefs."

In preparation for Mika's arrival, I morph into the Tasmanian Devil and whirl around, full steam ahead, tearing through the living room, flinging books and several more bras into our bedrooms.

Then I lug out my dependable Dyson and begin industriously vacuuming away. Wheezing, panting and slightly spinning, I'm still in my SpongeBob T-shirt and yoga pants when I hear a rap on the door. Meanwhile, Kars is sulking in front of the TV because I had forced her to put on a bra. "If I get breast cancer, it'll be all *your* fault," she grumbles.

Swinging open the door, I find Mika hovering in the hallway, his long and lean figure filling the space.

"Come on in," I say pleasantly.

He steps in and promptly removes his shoes. He is fully aware of our house rule: shoes off as soon as you enter.

"Yo, Mika!" Kars hollers from the sofa. "Thanks for the pesto pizza! Best pizza I've had in a long, long time."

"Anytime," he says. "As long as Maddy keeps on tutoring me, I'll buy you pizza."

Karsynn gives him two thumbs up and returns her gaze to the telly.

Mika perches on the arm of the sofa. "What are you watching?"

"The US Open," Karsynn mutters. "Nadal versus Federer."

"You play tennis?" he asks, eyes on the tube.

"No," she grunts. "I just like watching Rafa's solid butt fly across the court."

Mika bites back a smile. "Nadal looks unstoppable today."

Kars is in a deep trance. "Male tennis players should wear shorts that are the same length as female tennis players' . . . "

"*Okay.* Let's sit over here, Mika." I steer him in the direction of the kitchen table.

Mika sits precariously on a rickety fold-up chair, and I settle down on the wobbly chair across from him.

I assume my favorite sitting position—Buddha-style.

His gaze travels across the room. "Your place looks great. I haven't seen it since I helped you girls move in."

"Well we've put up more stuff. Just some random things we picked up at IKEA . . . a bunch of Österbymo picture frames and colorful FÅBORG rugs to brighten up the place," I flex my mindless knowledge of IKEA's all-Swedish product names.

His gaze rests on a picture of me and Kars, swimming in our oversized XXL, bright red Bucky Badger sweatshirts.

"I didn't know you and Kars went to the same U."

"Oh, me and Kars go *way* back."

Kars yells, "And the Badgers always beat the Gophers."

Mika shoots me a quizzical look.

"Football. Wisconsin Badgers and the Minnesota Gophers," I explain. "What's your school's mascot?"

"Benny the Bengal, who just so happens to look like Tony the Tiger." He retrieves a stack of papers from his backpack.

I wait for him to slide it over, but he stalls.

"I finished reading *Pillars,* and I took the initiative and got another book," he says, exceedingly pleased with himself.

"Cool! What book?"

He pulls it out of his bag and holds it up for my inspection.

"*Marley and Me,*" I read the title out loud. "*Marley and Me?*" I repeat, this time gasping in surprise. "I thought you only liked reading books on war, history, and all that manly sorta stuff."

"Hey! *Marley and Me* is *manly.* Have you read it?"

"No," I admit. "But I've seen the movie and I was bawling—"

"Wait! Don't tell me! I haven't seen the movie but the book is really good so far." He winks. "Okay, dawg?"

Merrily, I burst into song, "Hot dog, hot dog, hot diggity dog."

He smiles and reminisces, "That dog in the book, Marley, he reminds me of my dog, Lola. She was this lumbering oaf with two left feet, always slipping, sliding, falling on her face. And she had these dopey eyes that sucked you right in."

"*Awww*," I gush, uncrossing my legs and crossing them back again. "Let me guess, was she a Lab?"

"No, she was an Airedale Terrier, and she was the perfect guard dog," he says with pride.

"Huh . . . how?" My eyes pop open in surprise, half-wondering how Goofy had made a great guard dog.

"She'd foam at the mouth so much that strangers mistook her for having rabies, and they were terrified of her." He smiles with satisfaction. After a pause, his expression softens. "Lola was the best dog ever. No dog can ever replace her. Not even close."

"Mika, are you crying?" I ask in a teasing voice.

He brandishes a tough exterior. "Only onions make me cry." Then he turns the tables on me. "Did you have any pets?"

"I wish." I sigh wistfully. "But I'm allergic to dogs, cats, any animal with fur, so I wasn't allowed to have pets." After a slight beat, I say with attempted bravado, "But it's okay, my dad more than made up for it."

Mika's face is alight with interest.

Smiling briefly at the memory, I continue, "When my dad was still around, we went camping a lot in the summer time, and he'd trap plenty of lizards for me."

"Pet lizards?" he exclaims with amusement.

"Sagebrush lizards," I say dreamily. "Somehow, some way, he'd always managed to scavenge up a sagebrush lizard for me. And when he'd drop that lizard into my arms, I'd hold it close to my heart and coddle it like it was my baby, like it was the most precious thing on earth."

"Your dad sounds like a cool guy."

"He was the best!"

Mika stares at me for the longest time, and then he says with some hesitation, "You said your dad *was* the best. Is he not around anymore?"

"No. He'd passed away a few years ago . . ."

"I'm sorry."

I look him flush in the face briefly, and then lower my gaze. "When my dad was diagnosed with lung cancer, he was a fighter. He'd never wanted anyone to feel sorry for him. No matter how sick the chemo had made him, he soldiered on every day. But once his oncologist had deemed his cancer terminal, he accepted it. You know, he was okay with it. Many people don't know this, but lung cancer is one of the most fatal forms of cancer. It has a very poor prognosis and it is very hard to treat." After a sharp intake of breath, I continue unsteadily, "He had stage three lung cancer and died within ten months of his diagnosis."

"It must have been hard for you," Mika says gently.

I twist my fingers together. "I was knocked down."

My dad had been everything to me; he was the raw earth beneath my feet. He was my north, my south, my east and my west; and when he'd passed, I'd found myself lost. My beloved compass could guide me no more.

The look Mika gives me is one of warmth and understanding, with no trace of pity whatsoever. Leveling my gaze with his, I smile at him with misty eyes. "When my dad found out that he only had months to live, he wanted us to have good, happy memories. With his insistence, we hopped into our RV and drove all across the country . . . to Yellowstone, the Grand Tetons, Grand Canyon, the Arches in Moab, all the Utah national parks, the Redwood forest, Yosemite, Sequoia. We camped, we had fun, we ate at all the best restaurants, and he caught me plenty more lizards."

Mika's eyes embrace mine with an unutterable tenderness.

"Okay." I clear my throat. "Let's start this time, for real."

We go back to our usual routine. I edit. Mika reads. And in five minutes, I am done editing. This is getting to be pointless. Stealing a glance at Mika, I find him totally engrossed in his book. Seeing no sense in ending our 'tutoring' session so soon, I reach for the *Tribune* and begin leafing through the pages.

Mika's gaze snaps up in surprise. "I don't see much of that anymore—people reading the papers."

"What can I say? I'm an old fashioned sort of gal."

"Wait!" he exclaims. "You read the *Chicago Tribune*?"

"Uh-huh. I have a subscription. Home delivered, seven days a week for only $2.75 per week. I also subscribe to the

Idaho State Journal. Gotta support the local papers, too, you know."

"But why? When you can read the news online for free."

I leaf briskly to the next page. "Online news sites leave out so many good stories. Stories they deem un-newsworthy." I pull out the travel section. "But newspapers always give me a little bit of everything . . . stories about my backyard, my town, my community. Oh, and I love the comic strips. Plus there's just something about the *feel* of the pages on my fingertips, the smell of fresh ink in the morning."

Kars hollers from the sofa, "I haven't read a newspaper in ten years! I just take out the coupons and give them to my mom."

Mika darts me a playful look. "I know. Newspapers and Bruce Springsteen? I think somebody is stuck in the past."

I am about to broach the subject on Springsteen, that while I may admire his no frills, no pretense approach to his music, I am simply *not* a fan. His music, more specifically his voice, just does not *do* anything for me. He sounds like a severely constipated heavy smoker.

But I get sidetracked when Karsynn taunts, "And Maddy also loves to wear *grand-maww* clothes."

"Vintage!" I cry defiantly. "Haven't you guys ever heard of the term *oldies but goodies?*" I huff with annoyance.

Unperturbed, Karsynn and Mika carry on discussing me as if I were an inanimate object. After enduring several more minutes of their relentless teasing, Karsynn goes back to the telly, Mika goes back to his book, and I go back to my newspaper.

And in the background, I hear Rafael Nadal grunting his way through what I am sure is an epic match.

Fifteen

New hires, a.k.a. newbies or spring chickens, are forced to work the holidays in this call center. Everything here goes by seniority and since I was hired in October, I am basically at the bottom of the cesspool. Which sucks, because I had to work on Thanksgiving and today, I am forced to work on Christmas! The day our Savior was born. It's blasphemous, sacrilegious, heinous and atrocious.

But then again, what am I griping about? I'm not even religious. I'd say I'm more spiritual than religious, and when I say that, people often ask me, "Well what the hell does that mean?"

To me it means that while I believe in God, I don't necessarily subscribe to any religious doctrines or to organized religion. But I digress. Truth of the matter is, I am just peeved that I have to work on a holiday. On the bright side, my best buddies are also working alongside me on this abomination.

"*Psssssssssst.* What you got there, Ingeborg?" I catch a whiff of alcohol as she sashays by holding a Hello Kitty water bottle.

"*Sssshhhhhhh*, don't tell anyone. It iz vodka, not vater," she whispers conspiratorially.

Kars and I raise our Snapple bottles in silent salute, the very ones we filled with some cheap red wine called Fat Bastard.

We bought it at the liquor store for only twelve bucks a pop; and it is seriously *the* best wine you can purchase at that price.

"Cheers! We've got some wine ourselves." Kars clinks her Snapple bottle with mine and we slosh back our wine.

"*Salud,*" says Ingeborg and knocks back her vodka. "It iz nice you zitting by us today Karzynn."

Karsynn so happens to be sitting in the cubicle next to me; Truong has a ton of seniority so that lucky duck has the day off. Nearly all of the cubicles are empty since only a handful of us are working today. The only supervisor in charge is Dawson Darling, and he is a man who lives up to his good name, the antithesis of Hillary the Giant Not Ready Nazi. Suffice it to say, he's super laid back and we love him to death.

Ingeborg takes another swig. "Tee-hee-hee, isn't this vild?"

Kars and I chug down our Fat Bastard in acknowledgement.

"Ingeborg, I just *love* your accent," I say with utmost sincerity. "I'm going to start talking like you tonight."

Ingeborg shrugs. "Go ahead, I am horn-nerd."

Eyeballing Kars, I say in a grave and serious tone, "Kars—vat vud you like to do zoonight?"

"Vat-evahh, Mazziee," she manages between sputters; and for some odd reason, this strikes us as hilarious. We find ourselves hooting hysterically like a pair or hyenas.

It must be the alcohol. It's really not that funny, yet we're still laughing and convulsing so hard, our sides are splitting.

To celebrate Christmas, Karsynn and I had shared three bottles of Fat Bastard right before coming into work, so we're undeniably a little buzzed now. But we didn't drink and drive. Being the responsible citizens that we are, we'd took a cab to work as a Christmas present to ourselves.

Mika appears to be the only sober one around. Striding over, he grins at us with frank amusement. "You girls are hammered; I can smell the alcohol from a mile away."

It doesn't take long for Mika to notice my choice of attire. And when he does, he stands stock still with a deer-in-the-headlights sort of look. "Nice sweater, Maddy," he says in an unnatural and stilted voice. Then he turns to Kars and manages an uneven smile. "Um . . . you, too, Kars."

And the more Mika stares, the more his face contorts. I watch it go through several alarming transformations. Eventually, he turns to me, as if hoping I'd offer some sort of explanation for this colossal calamity.

"It's Ugly Christmas Sweater Day," I announce gaily.

And much to my surprise, tracking down an ugly Christmas sweater had proved to be a challenging task. Goodwill and Salvation Army were completely sold out of them! They've become such a popular fad that they're selling on eBay for fifty bucks a pop. And I refuse to pay more than five dollars for an ugly Christmas sweater.

Luckily for us, Karsynn's grandma Dottie keeps a closet full of ugly Christmas sweaters. Dottie happens to be quintessentially quirky, but I find her absolutely adorable.

Last Sunday, we had dropped by Dottie's condo and found her curled up on the sofa, numbing herself with a bottle of Southern Comfort. And she was snugly swathed in a Snuggie, looking like she was wearing a robe backwards.

The Snuggie is quite possibly the dumbest invention ever, yet at the same time, super ingenious! Hell, I wish I'd invented the Snuggie. It's a commercial hit and I'd be laughing all the way to the bank.

Dottie had been over the moon to see us. And while I'd tactfully avoided any reference to her Snuggie, Kars blurted, "Granny, what's up with that big cape you're wearing? You look like Darth Vader."

And without missing a beat, Dottie said in a deep baritone-d James Earl Jones voice, "Luke, I am your father."

I couldn't believe my ears. Ninety-year-old Dottie was a Stars Wars buff.

Then Kars burbled, "You look like a member of an evil cult."

At that, Dottie became visibly affronted. Apparently, Dottie's a devout Catholic, and she fully resented the 'cult' reference.

I'd shot Kars a quelling look, but she bungled on, "Do you have any ugly Christmas sweaters we can borrow?"

Dottie had placed one hand over her bosom and bristled crossly, "I happen to love my Snuggie. And young lady, if a sweater looked ugly to me, I would *never* buy it."

I immediately jumped in and attempted to defuse the situation. "Dottie, pay no attention to Kars. That Snuggie looks so cute on you. You err . . . look like you're in a church choir. And I'm sure nothing you own is ugly, but would you happen to have any festive holiday sweaters we could borrow?" I beamed beatifically.

"Why of course I do, sugar," Dottie cooed, her ruffled feathers soothed. "Upsy daisy, here I go." She struggled to her feet. "Stay right here, girls. I'll be back in a jiffy."

When Dottie was out of earshot, I raised my chin at Kars and said smugly, "See! That's how it's done!"

And that's how we scored our ugly Christmas sweaters, the ones we're proudly sporting right this very minute.

Still a bit shell-shocked, Mika looks like he has no idea what to make out of our Christmas montage of holiday hideousness.

"Mika, you be the judge. Who has the uglier sweater, me or Kars?" I strike a pretty pose in my garish cable knit sweater that's featuring a Santa of questionable ethnicity.

He's purple!

Hmm, or maybe he is more of a mulberry magenta.

Not to be outdone, Karsynn's sweater actually plays music. If you squeeze Rudolph's nose hard enough, it lights up and plays a garbled tune—*Rudolph the Red Nosed Reindeer,* of course. And it probably sounds garbled from being thrown in the washer one time too many.

To showcase her sweater, Karsynn honks Rudolph's nose a few times for good measure.

Mika doubles over. "I'll have to go with Karsynn's."

It has been almost an hour now, and I have yet to receive a call; that is the beauty of working during the holidays—most people think we're closed! And anyone who does call in on Christmas day is a freakin' Scrooge.

Beep!

Speak of the devil.

"Thanks for calling—" I pause in my semi-drunk state, trying hard to remember what I should be saying. Oh yes! "Lightning Speed Communications. Now how can I help you this Christmas day?" I slur sentimentally.

"I need you to update my billing address," says the caller.

"Oh-kay." I hiccup. "I can help with that. Let me just ask you a few questions to verify you."

After the caller has passed verification, I ask blearily, "Um, what did you say you needed help with again?"

"Updating my address," he says patiently.

"Right," I say fuzzily.

Jeez louise, Maddy. Pace yourself and pull yourself together! You've only had some wine. Although, I think it was the comedian Jo Koy who once said that wine is real classy . . . until you drink a few bottles, then it's just booze.

Right. Focus. Everything is a blur.

I squint, hunting and pecking at my keyboard while he rattles off his new address. Midway through the call, his voice falters and cracks. Seconds later, I hear a muffled sob of despair.

"Um . . . are you okay, sir?" I ask tentatively.

"Sorry to call you today, but-but I just feel so alone. My wife just left me and she took the kids. *Sobs.* And I just lost my job. *Sniffles.* And I know it's only a matter of time before my home's foreclosed on," he wails piteously.

"Oh no," I say empathically. "I'm *so sorry* to hear that."

Then I run out of things to say. Bugger! I have no idea how to comfort him. Meanwhile, he's having a good cry over the phone. An infinite sadness tugs at my heart. I even feel a bit tearful. It hurts to hear a grown man weep.

"Sir, why don't I give you two months of service—for free!" I exclaim in hopes of cheering him up. 'Tis the season of giving, and it is the only thing I can give him right now.

"O-okay," he stammers. "I just really appreciate you being there to take my call."

"Well that's what I am here for. Now you can talk all you want. I am listening," I say with a tenderness that surprises me.

He proceeds to tell me his whole life story.

When the call ends two hours later, I feel so utterly down and depressed. To liven things up, I start giving all my callers two months of free service, and it feels so good to give. I feel a thrill compounded by kindness and generosity, at the thought that I could be helping someone out in some small way, that perhaps I've made a tiny footprint in their lives.

A little bit of kindness goes a long way. Jill Robinson, founder and director of the Animals Asia Foundation, has brought about huge changes in the attitudes toward animal welfare throughout Asia, and her tireless plight all started with rescuing one Moon Bear.

Someday, when I am old and gray, I hope to emulate her and set up my very own charity foundation. I'll name it The Mika and Maddy Harkett foundation, you know, like The Bill and Melinda Gates foundation. I've got to start somewhere, so why not here? Why not now? There is no time like the present.

With the trickle of calls that filter in, most of the customers are pleasant enough, and I repay them with my generosity.

But one of the callers is so darn nasty that I am convinced he is the Grinch that Stole Christmas.

"I WANT MY INTERNET UP AND RUNNING NOW," he explodes, rupturing my eardrums.

"Sir," I slosh, "I am stho sthorry. But the sthevere winter sthorm has cut one nof our lines inth yer area. Unforsthunately, we won'th be able tho get our stcehnicians outh sthere sthill sthomorrow."

"THERE'S NO EXCUSE FOR THIS BULLSHIT! AND DON'T GO TELLING ME IT'S 'COZ IT'S CHRISTMAS. I DON'T CELEBRATE THIS BLASTED DAY SO I COULDN'T CARE LESS."

"Oh," I say in a relaxed and fluid voice, still abuzz from the wine. "Stho what holiday do you selethbrate, sir?"

"NONE OF YOUR GOD DAMN BUSINESS."

"Um, okay. Well, is sthere anything else sthat I can help you with?" I ask blearily. MUTE. *Burp.*

"WELL NOW THAT YOU MENTION IT, THERE IS!"

Great! I've just cracked open a can of worms. I hate that we're forced to ask our callers that asinine question: *Is there anything else?* Even if there is *nothing* else, it forces them to think of something.

The floodgates open, or rather, the Hoover Dam breaks, and The Grinch barrages me with problem after problem, fires off complaint after complaint, and harangues me with rant after rant. Sweet baby Jesus, save his miserable soul!

After spending an hour assisting him with his never ending needs, I've *had* it with his sour attitude. Before The Grinch can launch into another tirade, I kindly cut him off, "Well, if that is everything, thanks for calling and have a Merry Christmas," I say in a jolly ol' fashioned way and promptly disconnect the call.

Whooooopsie! I was supposed to say Happy Holidays.

Oh well, hopefully that call won't get monitored.

And I did *not* give The Grumpy Grinch two months of free service.

Bah-Humbug to him!

Without even taking a breather, I take thirty calls in a row. Now I am starting to feel slightly aggravated.

"Why in the name of the donkeys in Bethlehem are all these people calling us on Christmas?" I groan.

Kars looks just as annoyed. "I know, what the hell? Don't they have better things to do?"

We're both so fed up that we jam our Not Ready keys to stop the flow of calls and saunter to the Ladies room.

Aha! This time I have come prepared.

After locking the door behind me, I rip off a piece of Post-it note and stick it right on the eye of the toilet sensor. There!

Demurely, I set my bum down and wait.

And wait.

Nothing happens.

"HA! I HAVE OUTWITTED YOU!" I shout triumphantly at the toilet bowl. No more nasty water spraying up my bum.

I rise ceremoniously to my feet and peel off the strip of sticky paper. And sure enough, the toilet flushes.

Genius. I am so proud of myself.

Standing in front of the faucet, I am washing my hands with a gratifying smile, feeling incredibly smug.

Kars narrows her eyes at me. "Maddy, I think you should hold off on the Fat Bastard. I just heard you talking to the toilet."

By the time that Kars and I hop back on the bleepin' phones, the calls have died down.

"WOOT! WOOT!" I whoop in a celebratory mood.

A head pops out of the cubicle in front of me.

"Greetings," I announce grandiosely. "Merry Christmas! Feliz navidad! Mele Kaliki Maka!"

An equestrian looking woman glares at me.

"Mele Kaliki Maka is the thing to say, on a bright Hawaiian Christmas Day," I carol gaily. "C'mon, sing with me."

But Horse Lady does not sing back. In fact, her whole face is molded in a permanent scowl.

"I'm Maddy," I say in a gracious manner and extend the olive branch. "And you are?"

"Tori," she says frostily and scrunches up her face, looking like a horse that just ate a lemon.

I offer the sour horse a kind smile. "Tori, nice to meet you," I say merrily. After all, poor Tori looks like a horse that just ate a lemon, so that warrants some kindness on my part.

"Keep your voices down," she says tersely. "You're creating a ruckus in here. You and that other girl." She points at Kars.

"Sorry."

"And I do *not* celebrate Christmas!" she hisses.

"If you don't mind me asking, what do you celebrate Tori?"

"Birthdays!" She flashes her horse teeth, displaying more gum than teeth.

I find myself staring at her mouth, slightly mesmerized by her out of whack tooth-to-gum ratio. "Well doesn't it suck that we're forced to work today?" I say with strained politeness.

Tori shoots me a filthy look. "I volunteered!"

My mouth falls open, forming the capital letter O.

Since it's Christmas, I decide to take the moral high ground and play nice. "Do you have any kids?" I ask amiably. Kids are a safe topic and serve as an excellent conversation warmer.

Tori's face softens a micrometer. "I do. I have a daughter. And she just turned thirteen yesterday."

"Ah, she's a teenager now," I say brightly. "What did you get her for her birthday?"

"I paid for her boob job and nose job," she says this like it's no big deal, like she just bought her daughter a sweater from Old Navy and a scarf from Abercrombie.

My smile wavers slightly. "Oh, how nice."

Now, I have nothing against people getting 'work' done if it makes them feel better about themselves, you know, whatever floats your plastic boat. But I *do* think that thirteen is a little *too* young to be going under the knife.

Karsynn gives me one of her classic Karsynn looks, and I know she's thinking the exact same thing. But I remain placid and civil.

Who knows? Tori may strike me as odd, but in her daughter's eyes, she could very well be Mother of the Year.

Blatantly, Tori fixes her patronizing eyes on me, looking me up and down with an air of spiteful evaluation. Her sharp gaze stops at my chest. Then she turns her critical eye on Karsynn's chest. "You girls have lovely *little* blinkers," she smirks, adding, "and *those* are some of the ugliest sweaters I have ever seen."

Her sarcasm is not lost on me. I am barely a B cup and Kars is a 36AAA. Not to mention, our ugly Christmas sweaters have completely obliterated our barely-there-bijongas. But still, that is no excuse for Tori to be bitchy and disrespectful. Poor Kars is already convinced her bijongas look like poached eggs. I dart Kars a worried glance, and I can tell by the look on her face that she's smarting from the insult.

Tori has been malicious and mean-spirited all night, and she has worn down all my tolerance for her nastiness. And as for our ugly Christmas sweaters, well d'oh! That is the whole point of it.

But I do not deign to tell her so. She just wouldn't get it.

I never set out to provoke Tori, and I was poised to exit the conversation, but that was before her undeserved attack.

Okay, Tori wants to play dirty. *Fine.* I can play dirty, too. I can do passive aggressive. With my lips set in an angry line, I give Tori a taste of her own medicine. Casting a disdainful eye her way, I see that her acrylic sweater is completely covered with pet hair and dander. Aha! Horse Lady must own a horse after all, or at least a dog or a cat. And her bijongas are definitely fake. They resemble gigantic, rock hard cantaloupes, and those dingle bobbers point at me like rocket propelled grenades.

"At least ours are real," I say demurely. "And what we lack in size, we more than make up in sweetness."

"Well that's debatable," sneers Tori.

Karsynn bolts up. "Well if you weren't such a miserable horse, maybe you'd see our sweet side."

Tori's oversized horse nostrils flare up. *Neiiigggh!!!*

Karsynn's claws are out now. *Hissssssss!!!* "And you know what, Tori? We didn't purchase our bijongas, so we'll never suffer from buyer's remorse."

Touché. And *burn.* I believe Kars has just struck a nerve.

Tori looks absolutely stricken. "You-you," she sputters.

"What?" Kars lifts her chin coolly, feigning innocence.

"You girls are nothing but jealous little bitches!" Tori arches her back, overtly displaying her cantaloupes. "And just so you know who you're talking to, I was Miss Idaho 1990."

Karsynn emits a loud, exaggerated snort. "So you were a pageant queen? Well how *lovely*. Perhaps along with your boob implants, you should've gotten a brain implant, too."

Tori huffs and puffs and grabs her things. "You know what? Thankfully for me, my shift ends right now. And I am *so* glad. I simply cannot *stand* to be in the same vicinity as the two of you!"

"Likewise," I say eloquently.

"It's too bad you girls are stuck here on Christmas!" Tori rubs salt into our open wounds, then storms off in a fury, leaving a cloud of horse hair in her wake.

"Bye bye, Seabiscuit! See you at the Kentucky Derby!" Kars hollers after her. "That horse sure poisoned our peaceful night."

The plume of horse hair travels my way. "Ah-ah-CHOoooo!" I sneeze, clearly allergic to it. "Hasn't she heard of a lint remover?"

Kars crosses her arms. "My Christmas wish is for something large and heavy to fall on her airbags and deflate 'em."

"Hear, hear," I grunt in approval, raising my Snapple bottle filled with cheap red wine.

"Amen to that," affirms Ingeborg, lifting her Hello Kitty water bottle filled with vodka.

Seeing my near empty bottle, Ingeborg totters over and tops it off. "Here, have some vadka."

I give a gracious nod at her generosity.

And so begins the bijonga discussion: Real vs. Fake.

Kars muses out loud, "I wouldn't mind getting implants if they'd actually look natural. Heck, I don't want to end up looking like I've got David and Goliath for chesticles."

"No, don't do it!" cries Ingeborg. "You are beautiful just de vay you are. I had a breast veduction; they hurt my back too much."

Waving my bottle in the air, I claim their attention. "All right, here are the cons so far—they look fake and they hurt your back. What about the pros? Other than the obvious of course." I take a swig. "Holy shit!" I gag and hack. "This shit is strong!"

Blargh. This vodka has killed just about every germ in my body. Hell, maybe even a couple of my organs. I'm pretty sure my GI tract is blitzed into oblivion.

"What the hell is this?" I splutter.

"Balkan 176. It iz 176 proof." Ingeborg grins impishly. "It iz a Bulgarian vadka, and it iz dee varld's strongest."

I stare at her for what seems like several minutes. "Ingeborg, I don't think this vodka is meant to be consumed neat."

Ingeborg simply knocks back another belt of her vodka.

"Give me some of that!" Kars orders. "I'll drink it straight."

Obligingly, Ingeborg tops off her bottle. "Dar ya go."

"*Merci mille fois*," Kars tinkles gaily, and for a little while she looks thoughtful as she nurses her potent drink. Suddenly, she bursts, "Oh! I've got it!"

"Got vhat?" slurs Ingeborg.

"Another reason to get airbags—for identification!" Kars cackles derisively. "It's like a fingerprint!"

I shoot her a puzzled look.

Kars explains, "Didn't you guys hear about that murder case in the news? This poor woman was murdered by her ex-husband. He mutilated her face, cut off her fingers and yanked out all her teeth so the cops had no way of identifying her. But guess what? They did!"

"How?" I ask, befuddled yet riveted.

"By the serial number on her boob implants!" Kars practically yells, all hyped up about this CSI-like case.

I take a swig of my turpentine.

Yech. It tastes like shoe polish, but I gulp it down anyway.

"Now that could be a pro, but it could also be a con," I say objectively. "Say your murderer *knew* about this, you know what'll happen? When the cops find your dead body, you'll have no face, no fingers, no teeth *and* no baby feeders!"

"Yikes!" Karsynn's eyes pop open in a horrified sort of way. "That would be awful."

"Zimply terrible," seconds Ingeborg.

For the next several minutes, we lapse into a deep silence and remain poignant. The mood is morbid and macabre to say the least. "Enough about murders and mutilations!" I slap my thigh forcefully. "It's Christmas guys. *Christmas.*"

To lighten the mood, I flick on my radio.

"Yessssss," I cheer as my favorite Christmas song plays on the airwaves. My whole face is animated as I listen to *Baby It's Cold Outside*. I'm being extra cheesy, snapping my fingers like Sinatra, grooving to the tune, swaying to the melody—

Karsynn butts into my reverie, "You do know, don'tcha, that this is a *date rape* song."

"Quit ragging on my song," I cry huffily. "I do *not* need you psychoanalyzing it."

DA *DA* *DA* *DUM* *DA* *DA* *DUM* *DUM* *DUM*

The wavy, synthesizing hum of a digital keyboard emanates from my radio.

"Ack!" shrieks Ingeborg. "*Last Christmas*. I love dis song!"

"We *love* this song, too!" Kars and I squeal with delight.

Last Christmas is Wham!'s best hit ever, although, *Wake Me Up Before You Go-Go* trails closely behind. Kars and I watch a lot of VH-1's *I Love the Eighties*, and we are huge fans of eighties bands with kooky names. Names like A-Ha, Duran Duran, Pet Shop Boys and of course Wham!

We know *all* of the words to this song, and so does Ingeborg. Together, we sway drunkenly, belting out the chorus. Mika saunters over, clutching his sides. Surprisingly, he joins in on the chorus; and soon all four of us are singing and slurring sentimentally off key.

The Gods must be smiling down upon us. There are no calls in queue. Nada.

"Okay everyone." Kars claps her hands. "Time to exchange prezzies!"

This year, all four of us agreed to do a Secret Santa. But it is no secret since we just couldn't keep our mouths shut. Mika is my Secret Santa, I'm Karsynn's Secret Santa, Kars is Ingeborg's Secret Santa. And so, by natural deduction, Ingeborg is Mika's Secret Santa.

"I want to go first." Without wasting any time, Karsynn rips into the wrapping paper. "*Aww,*" she gushes. "A basil seed kit for my Aerogarden."

"Look," I point out, "It touts seven types of basil: Napolitano basil, Italian basil, Thai basil, Globe basil, French basil, Lemon basil and Red Rubin basil."

"Maddy, this is the best gift ever!" Kars hugs me tightly. After we peel apart, she turns to Ingeborg. "You go next."

Kars and I had brainstormed on Ingeborg's gift all weekend, and I'll have to admit, what we came up with is simply brilliant.

And I even chipped in on it, too.

Ingeborg rips open the envelope. "A hundred dollar gift zertivicate to um, Glamour Shots?" She casts us a dubious glance.

Kars rushes to explain, "It is from me *and* Maddy. We think you need to get some professional photos taken so you can hook up with a modeling agency. It can be a start to your portfolio!"

"Ingeborg, you're wasting your beauty here," I admonish. "You should be gracing the covers of magazines."

Self-effacingly, Ingeborg waves off the compliment.

"Now check this out," I barrel on. "Your Glamour Shot session includes a personal consultation with a professional makeup artist *and* hair stylist to help you look your best for your portraits."

Gosh. I really am selling it. Guess I *do* have it in me to sell as long as I believe in what I'm selling.

Karsynn prances about in a happy clamor. "Ingeborg, don't forget us when you're gracing the covers of *Maxim*. You could even be the face of Victoria's Secret," she says with glowing rapture.

"Um, thanks girls." Ingeborg then jerks her head at Mika. "Your zurn now."

"Here I go." He slits open the envelope. "A gift card to iTunes! Thanks Ingeborg." He smiles warmly, and Ingeborg smiles back, equally warmly.

I am pleased to report that their relationship has weathered the transition to friendship pretty seamlessly. Mika has even become friends with Archibald a.k.a. Sean Connery.

"I'm next," I squeal with delight. After all that waiting, I am bursting with anticipation.

Mika leans forward in his chair. "I think you're gonna love it."

Without wasting another second, I tear into the paper with gusto. "Oh. It's a CD. Bruce Springsteen's Greatest Hits," I say in a strangled voice, then catching myself, I quickly paste a smile on my face. "It's awesome!" I add with false cheer.

Mika's green eyes are dancing. "I *knew* you'd love it. You have Springsteen on your ring tone and I assume you already have him on your iPod. But being that you're an old fashioned sort of gal, I thought surely you'd appreciate him on CD."

I amp up the volume of my fake smile. "Thanks!" I say stiffly.

Moments later, after all the wrapping paper had been stuffed into the trash can, I glance up at the display board. *Ah*, I am delighted to see that there are still no calls in queue. And for the rest of the night, not a single call comes through. Snow is falling outside and we are having a whale of a time inside, chatting, chilling, grooving to Christmas tunes, munching on microwave popcorn and guzzling more vodka. And I come to the satisfying realization that Christmas at a call center is not so bad after all.

In fact, I feel so warm and fuzzy inside that I decide tonight is the night that I tell Mika how I feel about him. I have a small hunch that he likes me. Over the past couple weeks, he's been coming over to my place for 'tutoring' sessions, but all we do is read and make goo-goo eyes at each other from across the table. And he usually stays over for hours, until daylight bleeds into moonlight.

My stomach tends to gurgle like clockwork at 7 p.m. sharp, which triggers a knee-jerk reaction from Mika. He'd whip out his iPhone and place our orders—a Hawaiian pizza for him and me, and a Pesto pizza for Kars. And whenever we crave Chinese food, he'd drive over to Panda Express and pick up three large orders of Orange Chicken and Kung Pao Chicken. After our takeout dinners, we'd usually lounge in front of the TV and watch a movie on Netflix.

Last Saturday, we had watched *Burn After Reading*, and I'd noticed for the very first time that Mika has a really strange laugh. It's silent.

Seriously. No sound comes out *at all* when he laughs. Zilch.

His eyes will crinkle, the corners of his mouth will twitch, and his entire chest will quiver, but no sound whatsoever is emitted.

When Kars had caught on to his bizarre laugh, she had to put in her two cents. "Yo, Mika! Are you mute?" she teased, and taunted him with her evil Bwah Ha Ha Ha laugh.

During the funniest parts of the movie, Mika had looked like a fish gasping for air. I've become so fascinated by his silent laugh that I'd always opt for a comedy, just so I can watch him in action.

Luckily, comedies are my favorite form of entertainment. No other emotion quite compares to laughter. Well, except *love* that is . . . which is what I've been feeling of late. Mika has quickly become one of my best friends, and sometimes, it even feels like he is my boyfriend.

So why not tell him how I feel?

While I sit and muse, a slew of radio commercials egg me on. Dodge: Grab Life by the Horns, The Army: Be All That You Can Be, Nike: Just Do It!

Hmm, perhaps it's a sign from up above.

It *must* be.

Like the three wise men who had wisely followed the North Star the night baby Jesus was born, I shall follow these three radio ads tonight. Yes. I shall tell Mika today. On Christmas Day!

Time just flies by when you're having a blast, and before we know it, our shift is over.

Mika, the only sober one around, insists on giving me and Kars a ride home; Ingeborg's new flame, Sean Connery, will be picking her up.

Before leaving the building, I quickly excuse myself and hop into the restroom to freshen up.

When I catch a glimpse of myself in the mirror, I jump back in fright. My face looks like a squashed tomato, my hair is a matted mess, and my eyes are severely bloodshot. I look a sight!

Hastily, I do what I can to salvage my appearance.

I'm savagely trying to subdue my hair when Ingeborg breezes in, looking as fresh as the morning dew. Her eyes are bright and clear, her rose petal skin is glowing, and her silky hair cascades obediently down her shoulders. Seriously, she was drinking like a sailor all night. That girl can hold down her liquor like a true champ. In comparison, I'm a lightweight. A super featherweight. I can barely walk, let alone stand.

Afterward, we burst through the exit doors and step out into the icy, cold night. Tittering and swaying, I throw my head back and gaze at the bright, moonlit sky.

"Oh, look. It's still snowing!" I slur with childish delight. Arms outstretched, I stick my tongue out to catch a falling snowflake, just like in the movies.

Dumb idea. Unsteady with drink, I stagger backward, lose my footing, and skid and slide around the ice.

Mika latches onto my waist in the nick of time, hauling me upright, and keeping a tight grip on my arm. And he doesn't let go.

As we make our way to the parking lot, Ingeborg spots agent 007 by the street-light. "Babe!" she shrieks with joy. Surefooted, she flies down the icy path in six-inch stilettos and flings herself into his arms. Sean Connery nuzzles her with his Santa Claus beard.

"Bye, Ingeborg! Bye, Arch!" we yell, uproariously drunk.

Mika releases me and fumbles in his pocket for his car keys.

I slosh about, attempting to walk without his aid. Unsteadily, I take one step at a time, putting one foot in front of the other.

Gak! I almost face plant.

Mika's strong arms encircle me from behind. Grabbing onto his shoulders for leverage, I brazenly press my body against his.

He shoots me an odd look. "Um, you okay, Maddy?"

"*Mmmmm.*" I squint at him sexily, laying on my womanly charms.

His smile widens with amusement. "C'mon, Madison, let's get you home."

Kars is soon beside us, giggling nonstop. Keeping a firm grip on my arm, Mika wrestles with the lock, yanks the door open and deposits me into the back seat. Kars clambers in after me.

Languidly, I stretch out while Kars arranges herself in a fetal position. Sometime later, we're coasting down the highway and my head is throbbing like a busted subwoofer.

Pressing my forehead against the windowpane, I watch the world outside whiz by. *Ugh.* I'm feeling woozy.

I'm going to do this. I'm going to tell him.

After what seems like an eternity, Mika's car pulls up to our apartment complex. Kars inches out the back seat, mumbles good night and slams the door in my face. F@#%.

Huffily, I crank the door open. Slowly and very steadily, I step out and position myself by the driver's side. Mika rolls down the window. "Hi there," I mutter, my eyes glassy and unfocused.

He pins me with his gaze and I drown in his liquid green eyes.

The vodka emboldens me. "I, err . . . need to um . . . tell you something—" I clap one hand over my mouth.

Aiii Yi Yi! I can feel the bile rising in my throat. Spinning around, I stumble to the nearest shrub and bend over.

Dammit! It's a fancily decorated shrub, strung with hundreds and hundreds of multicolored Christmas lights. They glisten in the night, like twinkling fairies. But it's too late. My stomach heaves and I upchuck all over the festive bush.

"Ugh," I groan, wiping my mouth with the back of my hand.

Reeking of vodka and vomit, I stagger toward my apartment complex. The automatic glass doors swish open and whoosh shut behind me. I squint over my shoulder, blinking in the headlights.

Mika's Impala backs up the driveway, bumping along the icy, snow-filled road. Then it dawns on me. Egad! Mika saw me retching all over the festive shrub.

I swear I'm never drinking vodka again.

Or as Ingeborg calls it—*vadka*. No more *vadka* for me.

That will be my New Year's Resolution.

HICCUP.

Sixteen

The day after Christmas, I'm back at work, suffering from a permanent hangover. The calls have been trickling in; it's been so slow that management was offering VTO—voluntary time off.

As tempting as it was to take VTO, I'd decided to stay.

I'd splurged over Christmas, drinking the Crewlade (those darn J.Crew catalogs reeled me in with their guava colored cardigans) and going a little overboard at Anthropologie, so I need to stay at work to offset the damages made to my Visa.

Plus, why not stay at work when there's *no work* to do, right? It's like getting paid to browse the internet, chit chat and do absolutely nothing.

As I glance around, I see that we're all lumped together by the common bonds of disinterest and ennui. I pull up Outlook and begin banging out a mindless email.

To: Truong.Nguyen@lsc.com,
Karsynn.Higginbotham@lsc.com, Mika.Harkett@lsc.com,
Ingeborg.Draganov@lsc.com
From: Madison.Lee@lsc.com
Subject: Word of the Day

Word of the Day: **ca·pa·cious**
Function: *adjective*

Etymology: Latin *capac, capax* capacious, from Latin *capere*

Meaning: Capable of containing a large quantity; spacious or roomy

— ca·pa·cious·ly *adverb*

— ca·pa·cious·ness *noun*

Example: I need a capacious handbag to haul all of my crap.

And then I click Send.

'Capacious' is a fancy schmancy word I come across all the time. Journalists and famous writers love tossing it around, and I always get such a kick out of it.

Within minutes, I receive a flurry of emails in my Inbox.

To: Truong.Nguyen@lsc.com, Karsynn.Higginbotham@lsc.com, Madison.Lee@lsc.com, Ingeborg.Draganov@lsc.com
From: Mika.Harkett@lsc.com
Subject: RE: Word of the Day

My cubicle is NOT capacious

To: Truong.Nguyen@lsc.com, Ingeborg.Draganov@lsc.com, Madison.Lee@lsc.com, Mika.Harkett@lsc.com
From: Karsynn.Higginbotham@lsc.com
Subject: RE: Word of the Day

Do these pants make my backside look capacious?

To: Madison.Lee@lsc.com, Karsynn.Higginbotham@lsc.com, Mika.Harkett@lsc.com, Ingeborg.Draganov@lsc.com
From: Truong.Nguyen@lsc.com
Subject: RE: Word of the Day

I marvel at the vast capaciousness of Tyra Banks' forehead

Beep!

"Thanks for calling Lightning Speed Communications. This is Maddy. How can I help?"

"My name is Amy Heinz, and I can't connect to the internet."

Her voice is low and raspy, like too much testosterone is pumping through her veins.

"Um, Mister, sorry, err *Miss* Heinz, I can help. But I'll need to verify you first." As we're going through the whole authentication rigmarole, I jab the MUTE key. "Truong!" I cry. "This woman I'm talking to, a Miss Heinz, I swear she's a man."

"Must be a woman smoker."

Releasing the MUTE button, I proceed with troubleshooting. I ask the caller to check if the light on the modem is turned on, still very much unsure if I am speaking to a man or woman.

Perhaps I am speaking to a transgender. And if indeed I am, do I address a transgender as a he or a she? The transgender could be a male who is trying to convert to the female species, and he hasn't *yet* begun hormone therapy. Hence the manly voice.

Or, the transgender could very well be a female converting to a male, who *is* on hormone therapy. Hence the manly voice.

Hmm, something to think about.

I whip out my BlackBerry and text Kars a message:

If you don't quit smoking, you'll end up sounding like a dude or a shemale transgender. xoxo M

Then I turn off my phone and briskly stow it away.

I don't want Hillary breathing down my neck about the 'No Cell Phones on the Floor' policy.

"No," says the caller. "The light on the modem is not on."

"Okay Miss Heinz, now I need you to—"

Truong interrupts. "Err, did you just call her Miss Hind? Like Miss Ass? And are you sure you're not really talking to a dude named Mister Hind?" he implores with a sense of urgency.

Studiously ignoring him, I continue assisting my caller. "Miss Heinz, can you unplug your modem and then plug it back in?"

While she takes care of that task, I push MUTE once again and address Truong's pressing question. "No, not Mister Hind. Her name is Miss Heinz, like the ketchup."

"Oh," he says, clearly disenchanted.

Truong once shared an overtly sexual dream of his. In this fantasy dream, he was marooned on a magical island where it rained nothing but asses all day long. Butts just fell from the sky, nonstop, pouring down on him. He confessed that he never wanted that dream to end.

"Sorry to rain on your parade, Truong. The next time I'm talking to a Mister Ass, Arse, Anus, Buttocks, Backside, Bum, Tush or Hind, I promise I'll let you know, okay?"

He shoots back a winsome smile.

Within minutes, I determine that the modem is faulty and inform Miss Heinz that I'll need to send out a new one. "Ma'am, can you please confirm your mailing address and email address?"

She rattles off her mailing address and I compare it against our records. Everything matches and is up to date. Then the manly voice startles me when he-she says, "My email address is hard-as-a-rock@lightningspeedmail.com."

"Hard-as-a-rock@lightningspeedmail.com?" I repeat *just* to be sure. "That is your email address?"

At this point, Truong is beside himself.

"Yes, that is my email address," Miss Heinz concurs.

I can't help it. This is just too much fun.

"Um, sir . . . *sorry,* ma'am, just to clarify, your email address once again is hard-as-a-rock@lightningspeedmail.com?"

The shemale concurs yet again, "Yes it is!"

"Great!" I exclaim. "We'll shoot you an email with the tracking number once the modem is shipped out."

After the caller disconnects, Truong squeals with delight. "See! I told you she was really a dude."

Several days later, I slug into work, set my things on my desk and glance over at Mika's cubicle. It's still empty.

Mika has caught the flu bug and he has been MIA for the past two days. When we had talked over the phone last night, he sounded terrible. I had insisted that he go see a doctor, but he flat out refused.

I kept pestering him about it and he kept dodging the subject until I was so fed up that I demanded, "Well why not?"

His huffy response to that was, "Why should I see a doctor when I have WebMD?"

He's so stubborn. The type of guy who won't see a doctor unless his femoral artery is gashed, his intestines ruptured, and his skull cracked open, blood spraying out of every orifice.

Even then, I'm not sure if he would.

Beep!

"Thanks for calling Lightning Speed Communications, this is Maddy, how can I be of service today?"

"My name is Doctor Frederic Feingold Wood the Third," comes a dry and pompous voice, "and I am having some major issues with your website."

A doctor cometh knocking on my door. An image of George Clooney pops in my head; he's on the ER set, suited up in scrubs with a stethoscope dangling effortlessly around his neck.

"Well, Mister Wood, I'd be happy to assist you with—"

"You will address me as Doctor Wood," he snaps in a sharp, cutting, almost cruel voice.

"Okay, Doctor Wood," I say apologetically.

Sheesh! Clooney evaporates, only to be replaced by Doctor Evil.

"As I've mentioned earlier on, I am a doctor. Hence, I prefer to be addressed as such. Now, I want *Doctor* to be prefixed to my name on all your records. This is paramount! If it is not already stated so, I suggest you update it right *now*," he demands self-importantly.

"Okay, Mister, um—I mean—*Doctor*," I quickly catch myself.

Whoopsie! I'm so conditioned to use words like *mister* and *sir* that I have to consciously tell myself to use *Doctor*.

Unfortunately, Doctor Evil is not so forgiving. He blows his top at my slip of tongue. "*DOCTOR* Wood!" he screams like a lunatic and I flinch. "Young lady, you are not *listening* to me. That is an absolute pet peeve of mine!" He raises his voice ten octaves. "I did not spend *years* working to get my MD to be called Mister. I shall be addressed as Doctor every day, until the day I die. Even my tombstone shall bear the title bequeathed to me, and that's *Doctor* Frederic Feingold Wood the Third! GET IT? Or is it too difficult of a task for simple-minded people like you?"

I'm stunned into silence. God. What an arrogant, portentous, pompous ass. I would certainly hope that he did not spend eight or nine years in med school solely for the title. Okay. I get it. Doctors save lives and kudos to them for being a great service to the community. I'm even a huge fan of Doctors Without Borders. But c'mon already! Nurses, firemen and cops devote their lives to helping others and saving lives. They may not have spent half their lives in med school, but the jobs they perform on a daily basis are no less valiant, yet they do not demand to be called Nurse Betty or Fireman Johnny. Heck, even Jesus did not demand to be called God.

And while it's certainly no secret that most doctors can't keep their profession a secret for longer than two seconds, this caller actually tops the list of being *the* most narcissistic, self-indulgent egomaniac I have ever come across. I feel sorry for his wife. He probably needs constant praise and adulation on a daily basis to validate who he is.

It sickens me. This caller sickens me, and he's a Doctor. If the only callers I got were stuffy, conceited, ostentatious doctors like this quack here, my whole body would just shrivel up and DIE.

Shouldn't doctors be healing instead of killing?

I have to grind my teeth to refrain from calling him Mister.

But by the end of the call, my resolve wanes. He has been nothing but rude, running his mouth at me in a hostile way, his tone condescending whenever I try to interrupt him with pertinent questions.

Despite my best efforts, he just keeps on inferring that I don't know how to do my job, and that he *knows* what he's doing.

"I know what the hell I'm doing, what do you think I am? Stupid?"

"Err . . ."

"Don't answer that!" he blasts. "You clearly have no idea what you are talking about! You people are fuckin' useless! Good for nothing, towel headed, turban wearing Taliban!"

"Um *Doctor* Wood, I don't live in a Taliban regime that forces me to cover up. And even if I did, women don't wear turbans. I believe the headscarf is called a hijab and the garment is called a burka."

Plus, I highly doubt the Taliban are operating call centers; they're much too busy indoctrinating future terrorists in their madrassas.

"Burka, Buppa, Buca di Beppo, they all sound the same to me!" he scoffs mockingly. "Missy, let me tell you, I know exactly what I'm doing! I graduated summa cum laude from Harvard. But I'll have to say, your website is horrendous! I highly doubt anyone can figure it out."

Well then why the hell are you calling me? Go figure it out yourself if you're so damn smart. I can navigate the site without ANY problems whatsoever and so can my five-year-old niece. So you are obviously very DENSE! Although I shouldn't be surprised given that your last name is Wood. You graduated with Latin honors, but can you even tie your own shoelaces? Why don't you go summa cum laude in your face! You should rightly sue your own alma mater!

"GET ME SOMEBODY ELSE WHO KNOWS WHAT THE HELL THEY'RE DOING," he roars.

"Sure. No problem, I'll get another agent on the line for you."

I decide to amuse myself at his expense. "Thanks for calling *Mister* Wood, and have a nice day *Mister* Wood," I babble happily and transfer him back into the queue.

Humph. That dipshit doctor really needs to shut up and eat some humble pie. What a *vacca foeda!*

That's Latin, by the way, for stupid cow.

Quantum materiae materietur marmota monax si marmota monax materiam possit materiari?

Oh! Was I just speaking Latin again?

Silly me! Sometimes it just sort of slips. Anyway, the literal translation is: How much wood would a woodchuck chuck if a woodchuck could chuck wood?

And finally, *Sona si Latine loqueris:* Honk if you speak Latin. Yes. I learned Latin from car bumper stickers.

Karma's a bitch. I should never have messed with that doctor. As I trudge into work the next day, I can hear Truong hacking from a mile away. Yikes! He is coughing so violently, I'm afraid he'll hack up a lung.

And Tiny is taking rapid, shallow breaths and turning very blue. "Tiny, are you all right?"

He shakes his head and shoots me a look of pure agony.

Glancing over at Ingeborg, I'm immediately taken aback. Her rosy cheeks have lost all vestiges of color. She is pale, gaunt and shadowed with sickness. Christ Almighty! This is a Hot Zone.

Truong emits another whooping cough.

"Are you okay, Truong?" My eyes pop open at his decaying, emaciated frame.

He groans like a dying man, "I think I may have the swine flu. My nephew got it from preschool and he probably spread it to me." *Hack, hack, hack. KEKH!*

"Swine flu? SWINE FLU?" I wheel my chair back. "What the hell are you doing at work contaminating the whole place? You should be quarantined!" I fume.

I absolutely abhor it when sick people drag themselves into work, spreading their germs everywhere, infecting everyone.

"How the hell am I supposed to stay healthy?" I splutter. "You expect me to wear a mask to work?"

HONK. Truong blows his nose into a Kleenex. And then he does the unthinkable! Like a lecherous leper, he holds the tissue up to my face and peels it open in extra slow motion.

Grossness. I'm forced to stare at his gooey, green mucus.

It's his way of saying go *eff* yourself.

And it's very apparent that he's enjoying my discomfort.

"Truong! You're a revolting pig!" I cry in mock disgust, edging myself as far away from him as possible. Squirting out a glob of Purell, I begin savagely sanitizing my entire work space. "Next time you're sick, please stay at home like you're supposed to!" I huff, smearing more anti-bacterial gel over my keyboard.

Work becomes exceedingly more difficult when I'm trying not to breathe the whole time. I swath my nose and my mouth with a tissue every time a cough breaks out. Consequently, my speech is muffled when I converse with my callers.

My gaze shifts down to my hands. I turn them over ruefully, examining the blisters and cracks. Perhaps I was being a little too militant with the hand sanitizer, but I'll be damned if I catch the swine flu. When the flu virus hits me, it hits me as hard as a ton of bricks, putting me out of commission for weeks.

A huge wave of relief washes over me when my shift finally ends. "Bye, Truong! Bye, Tiny! Bye, Ingeborg! I hope you guys feel better." I gather my things and blitz out of the building without so much as a glance back, consumed with fear of being ravaged by the plague that is now sweeping the entire call center.

Listlessly, I turn my key in the lock in slow motion and shuffle into my apartment. I find Karsynn slumped on the sofa, glued to the TV. She'd took the whole day off because today is a pivotal day. It's the season premiere of *Gossip Girl: Season Three* and Kars just *had* to watch it when it aired. And so she'd called in sick even though she's as healthy as a horse and as fit as an ox.

Incidentally, Karsynn *never* gets sick.

I'm convinced her ancestors had ploughed and toiled the barren fields of Ireland in the 1800's, surviving through the potato famine and thus blessing her with stellar genes.

"Hey, Kars," I mutter miserably. "Good thing you ditched work today. A swine flu pandemic has hit that place."

"*Shhh* Chuck and Blair are together at last," she says quietly.

"Did you record it for me?" I ask and she nods in response.

Marching purposefully to the kitchen sink, I fill up a glass of water, rummage through the medicine cabinet and gulp down ten Echinacea pills, followed by ten Vitamin C tablets. That should build up my immune system.

Next, I heat up a can of Campbell's hearty chicken soup. I sit and eat, but my mind is still rattled by the whole swine flu business.

Clasping my hands together, I pray silently:

Dear Heavenly Father,
If you forsake me from the swine flu, I promise I'll be much nicer to doctors and call them Doctor, no matter how arrogant and obnoxious they may be. Amen.

Satisfied with my short appeal to God, I set my dirty dishes in the sink. "Good night, Kars."

She jerks her head up. "You're off to bed? Already?"

"Yep! I need to stay healthy. According to Doctor Oz, sleep is my best defense against the H1N1 virus."

After brushing my teeth and washing my face, I tuck myself in for a restful night of sleep.

Ahhhh, I dream of Mika dressed in nothing but a kilt.

I'm encircled in his strapping arms and he's whispering sweet Gaelic in my ear . . .

Gaol ise gaol i, Gaol ise gaol i,
E o hao-o hao o,
Ro-ho i o hi o,
Hao ri ri o hu o
Gaol ise gaol i, Gaol ise gaol i.

Morning arrives much too soon. My throat feels scratchy, my joints ache and I am running a fever so high that my brain is scalding. With Herculean effort, I drag myself out of bed and stumble into the bathroom.

I inspect my appearance in the mirror only to groan with displeasure at the reflection staring back at me. God. I am one hot mess. I look like shit and feel like shit.

Pssh! I can't go into work like this. No way in hell.

I stagger out of the bathroom and rifle through my purse, in search of my PTO calendar.

PTO stands for Paid Time Off. In short, my vacation time *and* sick time are lumped together in what call center lingo refers to as PTO days. Ultimately, what it all boils down to is this: when I call in sick, I am sacrificing a day of vacation.

Fuck that. All of my vacation for next year has already been prescheduled. Two weeks in the summer, and another week for Thanksgiving. So that leaves me with zero PTO time for sick days. The reality of the situation slowly begins to sink in.

I *have* to go into work. I bury my head in my hands and make a muffled cry of despair, "Noooooooooooo!"

Hours later, looking bedraggled, like something an alley cat just dragged in for supper, I blunder to my cubicle and collapse into my chair with a weary sigh, as though all the strength has been leached from my body.

"Oh, Maddy. *My, my, my,* you look like shit," Truong remarks with a satisfied smirk.

"You just shut yer swine face," I snap.

Summoning up all my energy, I hunch over my keyboard and sluggishly log in to all my apps.

Dammit! What the hell is my password again? They make us change it so many times that I can never keep track.

I type ZacLevi88

Your password is incorrect.

Zac8Zac8Zac8

Your password is incorrect.

Efron888

You are now locked out.

Just great! I breathe in hard through my clogged up nose and cough up a hail storm. *Hack, Hack, Kak, Hack.* CrAcK. OWWWwwww! I think I've just cracked a rib.

Like a cripple, I press one palm over my rib cage and hobble to The Führer's desk. "Hillary?" I croak.

Her eyes flash with irritation. "What?"

"My password is locked. Can you submit a ticket?"

She harrumphs. "I'll get it taken care of in five minutes."

"Thanks," I mutter and let out a whooping cough.

"You're sick, too?" Her tone is angry, almost accusatory.

"Yeah," I grunt. "Isn't everybody?"

"I'm not sick," she points out. "Only weak people get sick."

I muster a feeble smile and limp back to my desk.

Sinking into my chair, I cover my forehead with both hands to quell the throbbing ache and skyrocketing temperature. For the rest of the day, I take calls in that exact catatonic position.

It sure is a good thing that we don't meet clients face to face. Truong is hunkered over his desk, arms sprawled out, taking calls with his head deeply burrowed in his scarf.

Ingeborg is rolled up into a ball, both eyes tightly shut, but I know she's not asleep because her lips are still moving.

Tiny is slumped miserably in his chair, chin resting on his chest, a fuzzy blanket draped over his shoulders. Still, he's shivering and quivering, like he's about to go into labor.

Lord help us, we're a pretty darn pitiful, pathetic lot.

When our shift finally ends, Truong stares at me with his sunken eyes and says in all-seriousness, "Next time you're sick, Maddy, do me a favor and stay at home like you're supposed to."

But Truong is incapable of keeping a straight face for longer than two seconds. He suppresses a loud snort, which triggers an intense hack fest.

Swaying with exhaustion, I choke with laughter, hacking and hiccupping along. Eventually, I manage to stop coughing long enough to say, "And waste a day of vacation? *Hells no!*"

He pats my arm and croaks hoarsely, "C'mon, Maddy, let's go grab some coffee and Cinnabons."

Seventeen

New Year's Eve was another anticlimactic day, and January flew by in a frantic blur, by far the busiest month of the year. We were slammed with call after call, and February couldn't creep in soon enough. And before I could even say, "Look out!" Valentine's Day rears its ugly head.

Someday, I need to do my civic duty and petition for Congress to have Valentine's Day expunged from the calendar. Singles Awareness Day is what they should call it. This dreadful and emotionally damaging day strikes me with fear . . . fear of being alone, fear of discovering that nobody loves me.

Thinking back, I'd used to look forward to Valentine's Day. My dad always had red roses and Godiva chocolates delivered to my classroom. His sweet gesture made all the other kids green with envy. The enclosed hand written card always said: "From your secret admirer," but I recognized my dad's spidery handwriting.

Every morning, on Valentine's Day, I have fond memories of waking up to the sound of his chipper voice singing this beautiful song:

There is beauty all around, when there's love at home;
There is joy in ev'ry sound, when there's love at home,
Peace and plenty here abide, smiling sweet on ev'ry side;
Time doth softly, sweetly glide, when there's love at home.

There was plenty of love in my home. But that was then. Now I'm just a miserable cow on V Day.

As I drag myself into work, I pass by a repulsive bouquet of blood red roses at the front desk, waiting to be picked up by some lucky gal.

I exhale sharply as I pass by one heart shaped balloon after another. Finally, I sink into my seat with a dramatic sigh.

Oh! What's this?

A red gift box is sitting on my desk.

Who could this be from?

I glance furtively around.

Very carefully, I untie the pretty sash and lift the lid open.

Be still my beating heart . . . lying inside is *the* most romantic gift ever. *Gush.* I find myself gazing adoringly at a heart shaped cinnamon roll.

There's a card inside, too. As I slide it out of the red envelope, a smile touches my lips. A cute little cinnamon stick is waving at me with a gloved hand. I gently flip the card open and see Mika's neat, cursive handwriting:

A sweet treat for my sweet friend

Yours, Mika

Truong pops his head out of his cubicle. "Is that from my Mikquisha?" He points to the box and I nod.

"You bitch!" he squeals, feigning outrage. But I can tell that he's happy for me from the twinkle in his eyes.

I babble happily, "He signed the card 'Yours, Mika'."

I know it's silly. But I ascribe all sorts of meaning to it. Jason Mraz's *I'm Yours* anthem replays in my lovesick head. I'm so elated that everything seems so rosy, so blissful.

In a hazy love trance, I log in to my phone.

Beep!

"Thanks for calling Lightning Speed Communications. This is Maddy. How can I help?" I ask jubilantly.

Tra La La. Valentine's Day is such a wonderful day.

I even remember to use the Telemarketing Sales Rule script, which is the Permission to Sell Script, or the PiSS script, as I call it. Quite honestly, I often forget to mention that dreaded script, even though they drill it into my head to Sell, Sell, Sell!

At first, the mere act of pitching a sales offer was terrifyingly painful. But over time . . . well, let's just say I'm numb to the pain now. It's do or die.

So I *do*.

Half the time at least, just enough so I don't get myself fired.

The caller informs me that she's having problems accessing the internet.

"Ma'am, I'd be happy to assist you with that. Now, while I'm pulling up your information, if I see a product or a service that may be beneficial to you, is it okay if I mention it at the end of the call?" I ask, cringing at the same time.

Her response comes in a puzzled tone. "Whad'ya mean?"

"Exactly what I just said," I say, keeping poised. "If I see a product or a service that may be beneficial to you, is it okay if I mention it at the end of the call?"

"Oh dear," she apologizes, guilt co-mingling with frustration creeping into her voice. "Sugar, I still haven't the slightest idea whatcha harping aboot."

I repeat the TSR script for the third time, but this time around, I word it a teeny bit differently. "Ma'am, if there is a product or a service that may help you save time and money, is it all right if I tell you about it later on?"

"I'm *sooo sooo* sorry." She releases a nervous laugh. "I *still* don't understand whatcha going on aboot!"

Something inside me becomes unhinged. "I WANT TO SELL YOU SOMETHING. DO I HAVE YOUR PERMISSION?"

Gosh. I don't mean to spell it out for her. It just sounds so *crass* when put like that.

"Oh me goodnees-eh. Well why didn'tcha just say so in da first place? Sure, sure," she tweets.

As it turns out, the caller, Marlene Dushek, is a really sweet old lady and I immediately detect her Wisconsin accent.

"So," my voice softens like it always does when I'm confronted with sweet old ladies; they tend to bring out the best in me. "Are you from Wisconsin, Miss Dushek?" I ask amiably.

She chuckles heartily. "You betcha! I'm a cheese head through and through. And a Packer fan, too, don't-cha-know?"

"Go Packers!" I cheer. "And which part of Wisconsin?"

"Oconomowoc," she says in a heavy Wisconsinite accent. "It's a varrry nice place up narth. And I've lived here for over seventy years."

I stifle a laugh. To most Wisconsinites, everything is 'up north.' I spent many muggy summers in Green Bay with my Aunt Sally, and whenever I asked her where we were going, her reply was always, "Up narth." No matter if we were headed just down the street, or to the south, east or west, her compass only pointed one direction—North.

"Miss Dushek," I say, veering it back to business, "what can I help you with today?"

"Yah. I've been stuck on yer website furrr weee hours. And I can't get on tuh any ooother sites."

I decide to try the oldest trick in the book. "Miss Dushek, can you please reboot your computer?"

"Oh-kie doh-kie," she chirrups. "If you don't mind eh, I'll just do some dishes while my komputarrr boots up."

"Sure go right ahead," I say with a smile in my voice.

I hear the faucet cranking, followed by the sound of gushing water, and in the background, I hear the rollicking rhythms and heavy accordion sounds of polka music. This polka song sounds like an upbeat mariachi band at a wedding.

Absently, I pick up my pen and doodle on my notepad.

I heart Mika   I heart Mika   I heart Mika

Then I draw swirly flowers and creeping vines all around it. After filling up a page chock full of fancy swirls, squiggly lines and doodles, all proclaiming my love for Mika, I check in with Miss Dushek. "Has your computer booted up ma'am?"

"Oh yeah! It did. I'm *sooooo* varrry sorry, I *fergahht* that you were still on hold," she chirrups, amidst the sound of ceramic dishes clanking about.

"And did that fix the problem?"

"You bet-cha! Thank you so much. You did good. And thank you for being so patient with me. Now dearie, I'd simply love to send you some of my famous homemade salsa."

"Trust me Miss Dushek, I'd love to try your salsa. But I'm clear out in Idaho and even if I did live in Wisconsin, it's against company policy to accept gifts."

"That's such a silly policy," she tinkles. "Now why don'tcha tell me more aboot whatcha wish to sell. I'm all ears now."

Since she has given me the green light, I pitch the sale, "Well, ma'am, we're also a cell phone provider and if you sign up for our service and bundle it with your DSL bill, it'll help you save some money."

"Oh. But I am blind as a bat. I think I need dat special kinda phone furr older folks. Ya-know, one of 'em Jitterbug phones?"

I'm really not an aggressive seller, so I say, "That's okay, Miss Dushek, whatever works for you."

"Thanks again, sweetie," she coos and hangs up.

Over my lunch break, Kars and I traipse over to Mika's cubicle. Hovering by his side, I tap him lightly on the shoulder. He looks up, catches my eye and smiles. I can tell that he's on a call, so I mouth, "Do you want to join us for lunch?"

He jabs his MUTE button on the phone. "I can't," he says ruefully. "I'm afraid I'll be stuck on this call for a while. This caller's system is FUBAR."

Kars and I immediately get it.

FUBAR = Fucked Up Beyond All Repair or Fucked Up Beyond All Recognition.

"Okay, see ya later then," I bid him adieu.

When we're safely out of earshot, I grumble, "I haven't even gotten a chance to thank him."

Kars tilts her chin. "Thank him for what?"

"Oh, that reminds me! Wait here a sec."

I nip back to my cubicle and fetch my heart shaped cinnamon roll, then I bound back to Kars and proudly display the treat in the palm of my hand. "See!" I say rapturously.

My eyes shimmer at the sight of my Valentine gift. It's as if I'm gazing at a sparkling De Beers diamond.

I gush, "This is my *Denny & George scarf* moment."

"Nice," says Kars, clearly impressed. "See! I told you that he likes you. Now are you going to eat it or not?"

I gaze at her uncertainly. "Maybe I should freeze dry it so I can keep it forever."

She rolls her eyes. "Oh, just eat the damn thing."

Stubbornly, I shake my head.

She whips out her iPhone and snaps a picture. "There! Now you can eat it. I'll send you the pic so you can scrapbook it."

"Thanks, Kars!" I take a huge bite and smack my sugar coated lips. Mmmm. Mika sure knows the way to my heart.

Four hours later, I have yet to thank my benevolent benefactor. I agonize and wait until my shift ends. And when it finally does, I head over to Mika's cube with the sole intention of giving him a proper thank-you, which in my mind involves a hug and a peck on the cheek. After that, I envisage us driving off into the sunset.

Strangely, when I arrive at Mika's desk, he's gone.

I glance furtively around but he's nowhere in sight.

Kars is soon beside me. "C'mon, Maddy, I just saw Mika leave a few minutes ago. Maybe we can catch up with him outside."

My face instantly lights up and we rumba out of the building.

Outside, my world slows down to a complete standstill. I spot *them*—Mika and some girl, who is hanging and clinging onto his arm like a baby orangutan.

At once, I feel shots of territorial pangs rip through my veins. It doesn't help that she's drop dead gorgeous. But she's not a classic beauty like Ingeborg.

Nope. Far from it. She looks like a chick from a *Girls Gone Wild* commercial that's forced down my throat on late night TV.

In short, she's skanky.

A gorgeous skank, but skanky nonetheless.

Skank woman is wearing Daisy Duke shorts, even though there's a foot of snow on the ground and it's minus two hundred degrees.

Oh, and her skin is the color of a tangerine.

Spray on fake tan gone wrong. Overdone and over baked.

And her stringy hair is definitely over peroxided.

Frozen to the spot, I feel a sharp metallic taste in my mouth, mildly sickened by the sight of Mika and Mystery Chick.

I watch them make their way across the parking lot, headed in the direction of Mika's car.

Gallantly, he opens the door for the tangerine and she slides into the passenger seat in a very uncouth manner. Her legs splay wide open, like a beaver trap.

Mika jogs over to his side of the car and hops in.

Seconds later, the engine roars to life and his car peels away. They zoom off into the stark night while I'm left standing there with my hair billowing in the biting wind.

Sniffles. That was supposed to be me and Mika driving off into the night.

Kars clucks like a flustered Mother Hen. "Oh, Maddy. I'm sure that slut is just a friend of his."

Swallowing hard, I manage a sardonic smile. "Yeah, just like *I'm* a friend of his," I say bitterly.

Kars gives me a respectful few minutes of silence, and I use it to gather my thoughts and pull myself together.

Right here, right now, I resolve to make some changes.

Any romantic feelings I have for Mika, I shall squash into the deep recesses of my heart.

There are plenty more fish in the sea. And this time, I need to find myself a local trout from a river nearby. Maybe even a farm raised catfish or tilapia.

Humph. What I surely do *not* need is some overrated Belgian swordfish from the Atlantic Ocean.

Kars gently pats my arm. "Let's go home, Maddy."

"Okay," I say in a small voice, feeling utterly broken.

Later that night, I throw myself a pity party. I fold up on my bed, licking my wounds and hugging my sorrows to my chest.

Outside, the heavens open up and rain begins to pour.

Listening to the dismal sound of raindrops pattering against the windowpanes, I allow myself to descend into a brief foray of sadness.

I feel an inexplicable knot in my chest. My eyes fill in spite of myself and salty tears spill down my face, stinging my raw cheeks, sopping my pillow.

Abruptly, my BlackBerry blares with the voice of AR Rahman belting out *Jai Ho*.

Ah yes, I switched my ringtone. A new year, a new ringtone. A new year, a new man.

I need to force Mika out of my mind.

I hereby declare the Mika love fest over and done with!

I have a feeling it's *him* calling. He's been calling me every night. Sometimes to talk, sometimes just to say good night, and I've always looked forward to his phone calls.

But not tonight.

I refuse to answer and let it go to voice mail. Seconds later, the music stops and I glance at my phone.

'You Have 1 New Voice Mail.'

Curiosity gets the better of me. I dial in and listen.

Mika's deep timbered voice floods my ears. "Maddy, I hope you like your gift. I'm sorry I was tied up all day; it's just been one of those days where every caller was upset about something." Pause. "Anyway, call me."

I delete the voice mail. And I don't call him back.

This whole time, I'd been grasping at the straws, hoping and searching for something that does not exist. Well, it exists. But only on my part.

Sigh. What more can I say? I am in love with a man who is in love with a citrus fruit.

Today, Cupid's arrow has struck me.

But instead of going *Ahhhhh*, reeling with joy and love, I am yelping *Owwww*, writhing from pain and yearning.

Oh, how it hurts to be in love!

Eighteen

The next day, I find myself staring impassively at my cubicle wall. Resting my elbows on the desk, I silently brood while waiting for a call. It's pretty slow today. It's the day after Singles Awareness Day and all these couples are just too darn exhausted to call in after spending the night locked up in their love boudoirs, caught in the throes of passion.

No complaints here.

At least something good comes out of that evil day.

"Truong, your Mikquisha is taken," I say sullenly.

He adjust his silk scarf. "My Mikquisha? More like *your* Mikquisha."

"Nope," I say despondently. "Not anymore."

His expression softens. "Oh, what's wrong, Maddy? Tell Mama Truong all about it."

After a pause, I say, "I saw him with a girl yesterday."

"Describe her," he instructs firmly.

"Gorgeous. Long stringy blond hair. A bleach-o-saurus and a tan-o-saurus and—"

He cuts me off, "I know who that bitch is! Orange Slut with Split Ends. Her name is Tatiana Green."

"Tatiana Green?" I snort briefly. "She's more orange than green. Her name should be Tatiana Tangerine."

Truong emits a gleeful chortle.

"But wait!" I cry. "How do you know her?"

Then I realize—how can he not? Truong is privy to everything that goes on in this call center. He isn't called the ABC or the AP wire for nothing.

Truong studies his cuticles. "Oh, I have my sources," he says with candor. Then he whips out a purple filer and sands his nails with vigor.

A plume of nail dust settles on my desk.

So annoying.

Truong also clips his fingernails in the middle of calls, which I find absolutely repulsive. I personally would never floss, pick my nose, use Q-tips, pop my blackheads or shave my pits at work. That is why it is called *personal* hygiene.

I'll be conversing with my callers, and in the background I'll hear the maddening *Clip Clip Clip Clip* sounds resonating in my ears, sounding very much like Japanese water torture. And before I know it, fingernail shrapnel will be zinging in all directions. My work space is fraught with danger!

Seriously, I really don't think I'm overreacting when Truong's essentially sending large organic bits of himself my way.

I'm dreading the summer time; that's when he'll waltz into work in flip flops and clip his toenails. Ugh! That's the problem with Truong. He brings in his whole grooming kit and operates Truong's Nail Salon in his cubicle.

Although Truong's grooming habits bug the hell out of me, I'm trying my *darndest* to act like a tolerant neighbor. Well, that is until a fingernail scrap lands inside my mouth while I'm in the midst of yawning.

"Truong! Cut it out!" I sputter and spit out his nail. "Please, this is not Truong's Nail Salon," I remind him for the umpteenth time.

"Okay, I'm done. I'm closing shop." He stows the clipper and filer away. "By the way, that's why you're supposed to yawn with your mouth closed."

"That's technically impossible," I retort.

"Whatever! Just cover your mouth next time," he chides, like it's *my* fault that his fingernail landed inside my mouth.

Moments later, Truong roots around in his Marc Jacobs man purse and fishes out a bottle of nail polish. After giving the bottle a good shake, he unscrews the cap and begins to give himself a manicure.

"Thank you for fumigating this place," I say with a trace of sarcasm.

He ignores my jab. "It's Chanel Vendetta," he intones like a vindictive vixen.

I check out his raven black nails. "Nice. Very Adam Lambert."

My gaze shifts over to his pinky. "Hey, Truong, why is your pinky nail so long?"

"For digging ear wax, nose wax and eye wax," he says without missing a beat.

I make a disgusted face.

"I'm just kidding! Although I know that's what you were probably thinking. Am I right?" He looks me squarely in the eyes.

I shake my head but it's transparently obvious that I'm lying.

He dips the brush into the bottle. "It's actually for good luck."

"I see. But you know what some people will assume it's for?"

"What?" he asks without looking up.

"Scooping up cocaine for a quick bump."

This time, Truong looks up. "*Girrrrl*, I am no druggie! That shit does not fly with me. I've never done drugs in my life," he says huffily. "But you want to know who's a coke head?"

Feeling a bit restless, I swivel my chair, spinning it round and round in circles. "Who?" I ask dizzily.

"Tatiana," he deadpans.

I shoot him a speculative look. "How do you know?"

He shoots back one of his infamous *I-know-I'm-the-shit* sort of looks. "Mama Truong knows *everything*."

"Well, spill the goods then, Mama."

He holds his hand up eye level and appraises his work. "She and I went to the same high school, and I caught her doing blow plenty of times."

Intrigued, I lean forward in my chair. "Tell me more."

"That Tatiana is one skanky hoe. That hoe slept with the entire high school football team *and* cheerleading squad."

I give him a wide-eyed look of disbelief. "No way!"

"*Way.* Girl she so *did*. That chick is one hot mess." Truong inclines his head, like he always does when he is about to impart some juicy bits of gossip. "She works in the cafeteria downstairs because she's got a felony record. They won't hire her up here. *No, no, no.* That bitch is gang-sta man! She's done time in the slammer."

"Time in the clink?" I gasp, "For what?"

He blows on his fresh manicure. "She stole someone's identity, and she got busted with a DUI."

I let out a short gasp.

Truong shakes his head. "I can't believe *our* Mikquisha would go out with a stupid, skanky slut like that."

I can't believe it either. But Truong has sparked my interest. I need to satiate my ardent curiosity and find out more about this Tatiana character. "Truong, when's your lunch?"

He glances at his Cartier. "Right now."

"Me too. Do you want to go down to the cafeteria?"

He smiles a wicked little smile. "Hell yeah, sista! Let's go check out Tatiana the Tangerine."

The cafeteria is buzzing with activity and we're standing in line, waiting to be served by the Tangerine. A scruffy, unkempt man, sporting uneven side burns and a mangy twelve foot long ZZ Top beard, is queuing up right in front of us. Poor guy. He appears to be suffering from a serious case of persistent eczema. His skin is peeling and shedding all over the place.

It is now the unabomber's turn to be served.

He lurches forward and leers at Tatiana lasciviously.

Tatiana flutters her fake lashes and flashes the unabomber a coquettish grin. "Hi, handsome," she gushes.

Um, if that isn't full blown flirtation, then I don't know what is. Doesn't Tatiana realize that she's not a waitress at Hooters?

D'oh! You don't get tipped at a cafeteria for being a floozie. In fact, you don't get tipped at a cafeteria *period.*

"Hey-ya doll, I'd like some tater tots *purty puhlease*," the unabomber drawls like a Confederate Yankee.

"Comin' right up, big boy," Tatiana coos in a syrupy voice. She scoops up a hefty ton of tater tots and plops it onto his plate. "Is that all?" she asks saucily, wiggling her butt.

"Can ya get me a to-go box, sexy?" he drools. Apparently, Tatiana's incessant flirting is not lost on him.

"Sure thing, cutie!" Tatiana winks and spins around to grab a Styrofoam box.

Truong and I gawp. OMG.

Tatiana's low-rise jeans ride so low that her fishnet thong and butterfly tattoo is on display for the world to see.

Fishnet thongs? Why even bother wearing undies?

Meanwhile, the unabomber is panting like a dog in heat.

"Here you go, sweetsie." Tatiana blows him a sensuous kiss before he slithers away. "Who's next?" she chirps.

As soon as her eyes rest on me, her whole demeanor instantly shifts. It's so palatably different that I can almost taste the hostility in my mouth. "What can I get you?" she huffs.

"Some tater tots," I say politely and offer her a kind smile.

I will not judge. For all I know, she could be a very nice person underneath all that spray tan.

Tatiana makes an irritated sound. Then she scoops up three measly tater tots and plops them onto a plate.

"May I please have more?" My tone is patient and courteous.

"No!" she sneers and thrusts the plate at me, dismissing me like I'm some sort of insignificant insect.

I remain glued to the spot, much too shaken to retaliate.

The unabomber's plate was swimming with tater tots, and I only get a few scraps?

Tatiana flicks her stringy peroxided hair over her shoulder and turns her attention to Truong. My jaw literally drops when she gives him the same appalling treatment.

WTF?!? We have done nothing to her (well at least not *yet*; I'm fully confident that Truong can be a bitch enough for the both of us). What is Miss Tangerine's problem? Truong and I may not be walking testosterones, but we're still human beings nonetheless.

"What do you want?" Tatiana's tone is sharp and rude. "Hurry up! I haven't got all day here."

Big mistake. Big, BIG mistake. Queen Truong takes shit from nobody! She has undeniably awakened the sleeping dragon.

"Some tater tots." Truong narrows his steely eyes at her.

Tatiana returns his contemptuous gaze and slaps two tater tots onto a plate.

"Bitch! You better give me more tater tots," he screams in a blood curling voice.

There is a moment of still silence in the cafeteria as several heads turn curiously to check out the commotion. Little do they know that the drama has only just begun.

Tatiana glares at Truong scornfully. Then she picks up *one* puny tater tot and plops it onto the plate.

The tater tot drops with a sickening thud.

"There ya go!" she sneers.

Truong goes ballistic. "Now you look at me, Miss Tan-o-rexia Nervosa!"

Tatiana remains intentionally obtuse. "Fuck you, faggot," she spits and flips Truong a birdie.

Truong flies into a blind rage. "Is that all you've got, bitch? You give me the finger and call me an eff-ing fag? You know what? That lame tattoo of a dead moth that's on your back is *so* befitting! It's what I call a *tramp stamp*. And it's *so* nineties."

Tatiana's face contorts.

But Truong is far from finished. When Truong wants to bitch, he can bitch up a Katrina level storm. "And please do me a favor and throw on some intense Pro V repair treatment. I am sick of looking at your split ends."

Slightly dazed, Tatiana touches her parched hair.

"And news flash! You're no Kim Kardashian. If I were you, I'd cover up that sorry excuse for an ass. Now you take these tater tots and stuff 'em up your nonexistent, cellulite, ricotta cheese behind!"

With that parting shot, Truong chucks the plate of tater tots at Tatiana's face and grabs my arm. "C'mon. Let's go, Maddy," he commands and storms off in a fury.

As I'm being dragged away by Truong, I peer over my shoulder.

Tatiana appears flummoxed, and for a fleeting moment, my heart goes out to her.

But she quickly recovers. Straightening herself, she begins pelting us with tater tots with an almost deadly precision. The flying tater tots go whizzing over our heads like hot bullets.

Okay, now I don't feel sorry for her anymore.

Truong and I break into a run, dodging tater tots, shrieking hysterically and ducking for cover.

When we're safely out of Tatiana's tater shot, Truong bursts into rhyme. "There's some hoes in this house. There's some hoes in this house. There's some hoes in this house," he raps in a low, grating voice.

Gasping for breath, I tease, "Calm down, MC Truong. Now do you mean holes, hoes or whores?"

"She's a whore," he hisses. "But back in the hood, we say hoe!"

"*Okay.*" I snicker.

"Fo shizzle," he foshizzes, crossing his arms.

Then he busts out chops to a different rap. "Got lice bitch? Got lice? Got Kikkoman spice in your flied lice?"

I double over.

"Westsiiide, Wu-Tang," he grunts gangsta style. Then he flicks his scarf around his neck in a dramatic fashion, and instantly all his thug-like credibility evaporates into thin air.

"Maddy, that Tatiana is one nasty bitch. And what the hell is wrong with Mika? Why would he go out with a messed up chick like that? I'm completely gobsmacked!"

I shrug morosely. I'm gobsmacked myself.

Sometime later, I'm logging in to my computer when an alarming thought suddenly strikes me. Tatiana is a *real* threat. Ingeborg was just an empty threat, like the Weapons of Mass Destruction. As much as I searched, I could not find a single mean bone in her body.

That girl is a true saint.

But Tatiana the Tangerine on the other hand is *pure evil*. A Kim Jong-il nuclear threat. Or is it now Kim Jong-un? And then there is the older son, Kim Jong-nam.

Hmm, I need to get my Kim Jongs straight.

Truong interrupts my highly charged political thoughts. "Will you fight for Mikquisha? I say we do! Let's start a war, Maddy!" He pumps his fist, fired up and all gung-ho. "Hell, she's no competition! She's just a citrus fruit!"

"No," I say disconcertedly."

"Why not?" he demands.

"I already gave up on him yesterday."

After a pause, Truong mutters, "Yeah, that tacky tangerine will bring too much drama into your life."

"No drama for me." I sigh deeply. "I prefer to sail in tranquil waters."

Truong begins humming the melody to Mary J. Blige's *No More Drama*. Then he starts singing soulfully, hopping on board the Soul Train, pointing at me.

Taking his cue, I croon the chorus, punctuating my words with big bends and tiny dips.

Truong groans, hands in the air, belting out the lyrics in a weary, evocative manner.

Consumed with emotion, I sing with raw conviction and find myself swaying from side to side like Stevie Wonder.

Beep!

"Thanks for calling Lightning Speed . . ."

Nineteen

The words of the great poet and playwright ring loud and clear. The Mika that I'd thought I knew has died. He is a complete stranger to me now. All the things I'd believed to be true about him are thrown into doubt.

Things have sort of tapered off with us.

And to be quite honest, after that incident with Tatiana and the tater tots, I refuse to have anything to do with her. If she's the sort of girl that Mika is into, well maybe he's just not the sort of guy for me, friend or otherwise. I'm still cordial with Mika, but every time I see him, the air is zinged with awkwardness.

And so I try my best to avoid him. Whenever our paths cross, I make a quick about-face and take off in another direction.

Mika has yet to confront me about my erratic behavior, but he's been withdrawn and detached lately. Sometimes he looks sullen, almost broody. I catch him leaving with the tangerine every day; therefore, things must be progressing nicely between man and fruit. Right this minute, in the parking lot, I'm forced to witness them yet again.

"Just look at that hoochie mama," Karsynn says with revulsion. "That skirt is so short you can almost see her coochie."

Tatiana climbs into Mika's car and indeed her skirt rides up, exposing her coochie.

Hey! *That* must be how the word 'hoochie' came about!

Hooker + coochie = Hoochie.

I share my epiphany with Kars and she smirks. "Makes perfect sense. Anyway, let's not get started on that hoochie. I know how much she bugs you."

"I may not like her, but she doesn't bug me *that* much. What bugs me is the fact that Mika is dating her."

"Oh, don't get your panties in a wad over that hoochie who doesn't even wear panties. And what makes you think Mika is even dating her? It's never been verified."

"Well, it's never been falsified either," I retort.

"I think you need to have a talk with Mika and just flat out ask him."

"I can't . . ." I let out a ragged breath. "It's too weird. We haven't spoken in days. I've, um, sort of been avoiding him."

"Why?" Karsynn demands. "Poor boy doesn't even know what he's done wrong."

"I don't know." I sigh dramatically. "I just thought that maybe he *felt* something for me. And seeing him with someone else just confuses things."

Suddenly my phone blasts with Katy Perry rocking out in full angst to *Hot 'n Cold*. Reaching for my BlackBerry, I answer, "Hi, Truong." Pause. "Okay." I hang up. "Truong is bringing lunch for us tomorrow."

"Sweet! I won't need to go to the cafeteria, which means I won't have to deal with that hoochie mama." Then Karsynn abruptly exclaims, "Hey! You changed your ring tone."

I shrug it off as if to say, "Yeah, what's the big deal?"

"Oh, Maddy, you're such a dingbat! Mika has been *hot, hot, hot* for you the whole time. You're the one who's *cold,* Miss Ice Queen."

"I'm not cold!" I cry defensively. "Okay. Maybe I had my guard up a little at first, but I almost pulled the trigger. I almost told him I was more than a bit in love with him."

"What? When?"

"On Christmas."

"Well why didn't you?" she counters.

"Ingeborg's vodka. It was my best friend *and* my worst enemy. It emboldened me, but before I could pour my heart out, I puked my guts out," I mutter glumly, still burning from shame at the memory.

Karsynn collapses onto my shoulder, giggling. "How come I wasn't there to hold back your hair?"

"Hullo, don't you remember? Kars, you were hunched over the toilet *all* night. And not only did I hold your hair back, I braided it, too."

Kars scrunches up her face. "I don't recall." After a beat, she asks, "What kind of braid?"

I bite back a smile. "Princess Leia."

"*Aww*," she gushes. "You're such a good friend, Mads."

"You bet I am."

We walk in companionable silence.

After an unreadable minute, Kars says quietly, "Just talk to Mika. You'll see, everything will work out just fine."

I admire her cock-eyed optimism. "I'll think about it," I say, just so she'll drop the subject.

Beep!

"Thank you for calling Lightning Speed Communications, my name is Maddy. How can I help?"

"Hi, Samantha, my username is not working," says the caller and, I don't even bother correcting him.

Sigh. I gave up a *long, long* time ago. I've had customers call me Theresa, Sylvia, Amy, Amanda, Kimmy, Natalie, Susan and Jessica. And none of those names sound remotely like Maddy.

"I can help you with that, sir," I say and take him through the whole authentication rigmarole.

Once that is out of the way, I probe, "Sir, what username did you type in?"

"Ilovebodyodour67," he says in a kind and gentle voice.

A loud snort escapes me. I compare his username against our records. "Sir, you *are* typing in the right username. Can you please make sure that it's in lowercase letters?"

A beat of silence ensues.

Finally, he speaks. "I can't."

I blink. "Huh? Why not?"

"All the keys on my keyboard are in uppercase letters."

I rub my temples. "Sir, can you please make sure that your Caps Lock is not turned on."

A beat. Another beat.

"I'm so sorry, Samantha, but what do you mean by that?"

Beam me up, Scotty.

I help navigate him through that simple task, and it literally takes him twenty minutes to turn the Caps Lock off. Regrettably, that doesn't fix the problem.

"Sir, when you type your username, do any numbers appear?"

"No numbers are showing up. But I *am* typing 67."

"Okay, sir, that means your Num Lock key is turned off and I need you to turn it back on."

"How do I do that?" he asks in a clueless voice.

I steel myself and walk him through that very task. But it is akin to leading a blind donkey out of a cave.

"I still don't see it," he tells me for the umpteenth time.

"It's on the right-hand side of your keyboard, right above the number seven."

"I'm so sorry, Samantha, but I still don't see it."

"Sir, I'm really trying here—" I break off and inhale sharply.

"Don't worry, Samantha, I know you can help me fix this. So please don't give up on me. You can do it. I *know* you can."

My voice falters. "Sir, I appreciate your vote of confidence, but there's only so much I can do."

"What would you like me to do, Samantha? I'll do whatever you tell me to do," he says obediently.

I grit my teeth. "Sir, can you *please* just open your eyes and *look?*"

"Wait! Is it *this* Num Lock key?" he cries excitedly.

Relief washes over me. "Yes! There is only one Num Lock key. Push that key," I say to the Numskull.

"But the green light above it is now turned on."

Closing my eyes, I mutter, "Yes, sir, it's supposed to be."

"Oh!" he says, seemingly surprised.

"Okay, you're all set now. Is there anything else?" I ask, ready to wrap up the call.

"Yes, Samantha, as a matter of fact, there is. If I need to call back with a problem, how late are you open?"

"We're open twenty-four seven," I inform him briskly.

"Huh? I'm sorry, but can you please explain, in simple and plain English, exactly what that means?"

"It means we are open twenty-four hours a day, seven days a week, three hundred and sixty-five days a year," I explain good-naturedly.

He-Who-Loves-BO seems pleased with my answer. But then he hits me with this next mind numbing question. "Um, what time zone is that? Eastern, mountain or pacific?"

I blink. A couple of times
?????????????????????

When I finally find my voice, I say, "Um . . . all of them?"

"I am so sorry, Samantha, but I still don't follow what you're saying. Now you're open twenty-four hours a day in what *specific* time zone?"

I decide to simplify things for him. "Well, sir, what time zone do *you* live in?"

"Um . . . eastern?" he says uncertainly, like he's a contestant and I'm a game show host quizzing him live on *Are You Smarter than a 5th Grader.*

"Well in that case, we are open twenty-four hours a day, Eastern time." I scratch my head at how ludicrous that sounds. But Jeepers! That is the only way I could get through him.

"You are? Well that is wonderful. Thank you for all your help, Samantha. You've been super. Have yourself a fabulous day," he says in a chipper voice.

"You're very welcome, and thanks for calling Lightning Speed Communications."

Now, I have got a pretty high tolerance for stupidity. But that has got to be *the* dumbest person I have ever spoken to. I daresay he was dumber than algae! Heck, I am not even that smart, but he is so dumb that in comparison, I come off looking like some sort of astrophysicist who just won the Nobel Prize for quantifying the universe.

But in his defense, he was upbeat and positive throughout the call, and he sounded like a very happy man.

Ah . . . ignorance is bliss.

Plus, he was so incredibly nice, and oftentimes niceness can take a person a lot further in life. I imagine Mister I-Love-BO floating through life in a happy bubble, meandering aimlessly through smelly, sweaty gyms.

It's my lunch time! Very swiftly, I log off the phone before another call comes through. Truong is already on his lunch break and browsing the internet.

"Truong, I just spoke to a guy whose username is I Love BO."

He chortles gleefully. "I'd once dated a guy with really bad BO. Let me tell you, Maddy, it was so *bad*. You would not believe the stench! But Pepé Le Pew was super hawt, and so we dated for a week until I could *not* take it anymore. So I told him very nicely that I had serious issues with his BO, and that he really needed to take a shower."

"Did you guys still date after that?"

"No. But months later, we bumped into each other and he thanked me profusely for bringing it to his attention. I'm such a Good Samaritan," he says with a virtuous glow.

"What? He thanked you for bringing it to his attention? Are you telling me he didn't know that he needed to shower?" I say in my most sardonic voice and smirk. "Wow!"

"Cut it out you ninny!"

I reach for my water bottle and take a sip of water. "What are you browsing, Truong?"

"Just the latest news on Prop 8," he says distractedly.

I pause thoughtfully. "Do you hope to get married someday?"

"Oh *hells no*," he cries. "I mean, of course I want my peeps to be able to get married, but I personally do *not* want to get hitched. No, no, no. No marriage for me."

This takes me by surprise. "But why not?"

"Why should I buy the whole pig when all I want is a little sausage?"

I let out a howl of laughter.

Kars perches on my desk. "What are you guys talking about?"

"Pigs and sausages," says Truong, without missing a beat.

I turn to Karsynn and explain, "Truong was just telling me all about his mantra in life."

Kars purses her lips. "I've got a new mantra myself, thanks to Doctor Mares."

Janis had forced Kars to seek therapy shortly after her breakup with Bob. So once a week, Kars visits her psychologist and I'm all for it. It is high time she gets some help so she stops dating these pathetic Potato Head Players who aren't worthy of her.

"That's awesome, Kars," I enthuse. "What is your mantra?"

She crosses her arms and says, "Insanity is doing the same thing over and over again, and expecting different results each time. It's an Einstein quote."

"Oh, I have one along those lines," I cry. "Burn me once, shame on you—"

"Burn me twice, shame on me," Kars finishes with a smile.

"Ditto!" Truong exclaims.

Kars appears to be doing just fine, when all of a sudden, she makes an exasperated sound. "What the hell is wrong with me? I want to be released from the shackles of Douchebag Desire!"

I cast her a meaningful look. "It takes time, Karsynn. But you will. *You will,*" I repeat with conviction.

"Do you think I'm a quack? I mean, I'm a psych major myself, and here I am seeing a psychologist."

"No! Of course not," I say at once. "Just think of it this way, a hairdresser always gets her hair cut by someone else and—"

"Not true," Truong interjects and points out, "My cousin is a hair stylist and she cuts her own hair."

"Oh shush, Truong." Turning to Kars, I say, "He is missing my point. Kars, if you need help, then you need to keep seeing your psychologist. You can't treat yourself and be objective about it."

Taking my cue, Truong echoes, "Yeah, you should keep seeing your psychologist. I think it is helping and I just love your new mant*rrr*a."

I seize him fiercely by the shoulders. "Truong! You just said it!" I exclaim breathlessly. "You just enunciated the letter R. Say it again. Say it again."

"Mant*r*a," says Truong, beaming at me like a baby who had just uttered his first word.

"You did it!" I cry ecstatically and slap him a high five.

Kars thumps his back. "Respect, man! Big ups! Now say 'shrimp fried rice'."

"Sh*r*imp f*r*ied *r*ice," says Truong, enunciating each and every syllable. It sounds as crisp and as clear as Eliza Doolittle in *My Fair Lady* when she'd recited *The Rain in Spain Falls Mainly in the Plains.*

Ahhh, his words are like music to my ears. Like a Puccini and Bellini aria. Like Hamlet's Second Soliloquy. Feeling a sudden swell of emotion, I fling my arms around him. "I'm so proud of you, Truong!"

His face creases into a triumphant grin. "Speaking of which, guess what I brought today? And, I've got plenty to share."

"SHRIMP FRIED RICE!" Kars and I whoop in unison.

"Correctomundo!" he exclaims. "Let's go chow down."

In a celebratory mood, the three of us sashay to the break room and nuke our fried rice in microwave ovens that can only be described as older than dirt. Seriously, these microwave ovens should be locked up in the Smithsonian museum. If I don't die from this job, I'll die from being exposed to the hazardous radiation that leaks out of these archaic ovens.

Minutes later, we scarf down our Chernobyl shrimp fried rice with gusto. After our satisfying, albeit radioactive, meal, Kars lets out a loud belch, without bothering to stifle the sound, whereupon Truong gives her a slight nod, recognizing it for the accolade that it is. "Good one," he says.

"Time for dessert," I announce airily.

"Dessert?" My eating companions light up at the sound of that beautiful word.

"Uh-huh, I've got some popsicles in the lactation room. Stay right here, I'll go and get 'em."

Truong looks at me with a slightly disturbed expression. "Um, why are you storing food in a room where these fertile women mutate into cows? Their boobs turn into milk udders! It's utterly, correction—*udder-ly* gross."

Kars leaps to my defense, letting Truong in on the best kept secret in this call center. "Dude, the lactation room has the cleanest fridge in the building. And no one will steal your food if you store it there."

"Girl, it is *so* not worth it. It's way too freaky deaky! Plus, I do *not* want to walk in on some grouchy woman with an alien device attached to her boob udder. Have you ever seen that shit? It's frightening!" He shudders.

"Truong," I say mildly, "even if you want to store food in the lactation room, you can't. You're a guy and that room is strictly for women. Anyway, wait here. I'll go get our popsicles."

"Strawberry for me," hollers Kars.

"Lime," Truong barks his order.

"Be right back," I say and nip to the lactation room.

Bursting through the door, I stop cold in my tracks.

Mika is fast asleep on a lounge chair. *Just great!* He's the last person I expect to see here, and the one person I'm trying so hard to avoid.

Spinning around, I'm about to make my hasty retreat when my BFF instincts kick in. If Angela walks in on Mika, it surely won't bode well for him.

Angela walks around barefoot and pregnant all the time. She has twelve kids, with another bun in the oven. Not surprisingly, she's constantly cranky and mean-spirited.

Honestly, that woman should consider getting neutered.

And she monopolizes the lactation room, treating it as if it were her own hotel room.

I *must* get Mika out of here before Angela sees him.

Standing next to him, I hesitate.

My heart softens just watching him in his deep slumber.

Poor Mika . . . he looks worn around the gills.

His hair is rumpled and dark circles rim his eyes.

Gently, I rouse him awake. "Mika, what are you doing here?"

He stirs and sits up. "Huh? Oh, I was up studying late for my finals." He rubs his eyes. "I was so tired . . . *yawn* . . . I stumbled into the first empty room I could find."

"C'mon Mika, we must go now," I say with a sense of urgency.

"What's the hurry?" A slow and lazy smile crooks his lips. He pats the leather chair, indicating that I should take a seat. "You should try this chair. It's so plush. And it even reclines."

He proceeds to do a little demonstration. Lifting the lever, he leans backward and forward in an exaggerated manner. "See?"

"Mika, this is a lactation room; that comfy chair you're sitting on is for nursing moms."

"Whhhhaa?" His voice is scratchy with sleep.

"This room is for women only. You can get in trouble for being here. It's like a man being caught in the ladies restroom, and if Angela catches you in here, she'll report you to HR," I say in a hushed voice.

"But why are *you* in here, Maddy? Are you lactating?"

"No!" I blanch.

He rakes a hand through his hair. "So why *are* you here then?"

"That reminds me." I throw open the door to the mini freezer and fish out my box of Dreyer's popsicles. "Want one?" I offer awkwardly. We haven't spoken in weeks, and here I am in the lactation room, offering him a popsicle.

He blinks.

"Um, it's loaded with real fruit, not fat."

A smile tugs at his lips. "I prefer ice-cream bars myself. But sure, I'll have a popsicle." He extends his hand. "Hit me with any flavor."

"C'mon." I steer him out. "First we need to get you out of here before you're incriminated, *then* you can have a popsicle."

Covertly, I pop my head out to make sure the coast is clear.

It is. I motion for Mika to make his exit.

Once we're safely out of the milk room, I thrust a popsicle into his hand.

"Maddy," he hesitates, "I hope this popsicle is a truce offering."

"What are you talking about?" My voice pitches higher.

"Look," he says, wearing a strained expression. "I *know* you've been avoiding me. And I've been giving you some space . . . but we really *do* need to talk."

"Um, okay," I say, averting his eyes. "Call me tonight? I have to run these popsicles to the break room before they melt. Kars and Truong are waiting for their desserts."

His hand reaches out as if to touch my face, but he seems to think better of it. Dropping his hand to the side, he sighs. "What's wrong, Maddy?"

"Nuh-nothing," I stammer.

"I'll call you tonight, then. Is ten thirty okay?" He scrutinizes me with his dark, penetrating eyes, and I suddenly feel very shy.

I nod in affirmation. "See ya," I say and skedaddle off.

Twenty

"I'm on the phone!" I cry when Kars barges into my room.

"Still?" she groans and slams the door.

Mika and I resume talking.

"So . . ." I nibble my inner lip. "You were saying?"

He clears his throat. "I'm sorry if I scared you off with the Valentine gift but—"

"Wait!" I interject. "What are you talking about? I *loved* my gift; I thought it was the most thoughtful gift ever."

"Really?" he says, seemingly surprised. "Then why have you been avoiding me?"

"I haven't been avoiding you."

"Yeah, you have." There is a slight hard edge to his voice.

I hesitate, "I just felt confused about things."

"What things?" he probes.

I wipe my sweaty palms on my jeans. I certainly don't want to come across like some *fatal-attraction-bunny-in-the-stew-pot* sort of woman.

"I . . . err, saw you with Tatiana," I say in an attempt to gauge his feelings for her.

"Oh, you know Tatiana? She's a sweetheart, isn't she?"

I find myself laughing hysterically. "*Sweetheart?!?*"

He adds, "I know she's a bit different, but she's grown on me."

"Um-hmmmm," I mutter with a trace of sarcasm, but Mika entirely misses it.

Yeah, I bet she's grown on him—like a colony of e-coli bacteria that grows on a raw chicken carcass. She's toxic!

"I've been giving her a ride to work. She lives on campus and she doesn't own a car," he says, still oblivious to the hate vibes I'm emanating through the phone.

Humph. From what I've heard, she has a DUI. That's why she can't drive. Tatiana has certainly got the wool pulled over Mika's eyes if he seems to think she's all THAT.

"Maddy, are you still there?"

"Yeah, I am." I grind my teeth to keep from saying, "Tatiana is a snarky bitch! Why can't you *see* that?"

"So . . ." he trails off.

"So . . ." I echo. "Um, is that the extent of your relationship with Tatiana?" As much as I try to keep my voice steady, it falters.

I know that it's best to get it all out in the open, but a part of me is afraid to hear his answer. My stomach is in knots.

"What are you talking about?" He sounds a bit affronted.

There is a taut silence. My nails dig sharply into my palms.

Eventually, he says in a low and deliberate voice, "No, I am not dating her, if that's what you mean."

I cover the receiver so he can't hear me whooping, "WOOT! WOOT! Mika is not dating that Orange Slut with Split Ends!"

"Madison," he breathes my name. "Are you jealous of her? Because there's really noth—"

"NO!" I interject forcefully. "No," I repeat softly this time. "Of course not. I mean . . . we're just friends, right?"

"Yeah," he says simply. "Friends."

Flopping back onto my pillow, I close my eyes in exasperation. "Of course." I bite my inner lip, disappointment striking me like a blow to the stomach.

"So, are we okay now?" he asks softly.

"We're okay," I say stiffly.

"Maddy, I'll stop giving her a ride to work if it bothers you."

"*Pssh!* Why would it bother me? She's a *sweetheart*, right?" I almost gag in the process. "So give her a ride. I don't care."

But inside, I do care. I'm afraid she'll cast him under some voodoo spell of hers.

After a hesitant pause, he asks, "You sure?"

"Positive," I say and clear my throat. "So, um what else do you think of Tatiana?" I ask in an innocent voice. "I mean, I know you think she's a sweetheart and all that, but do you think she's pretty, too?"

"I don't *think* about her. Period," he says with such force and conviction that it takes me by surprise.

Good answer. It is the answer I've been longing to hear. So I brush Tatiana off as just a minor hiccup in our fledging friendship.

We talk for hours, exchanging tidbits of this and that, covering every moment of our brief time apart. Burning up the minutes on our phones, we tacitly avoid any mention of Tatiana.

Unbeknownst to me, when I'd bragged on my resume that I was an excellent multitasker, I would actually turn out to become one; wonders never cease! Working in this call center has turned me into a multitasking queen. Here's an example:

Beep!

"Thanks for calling Lightning Speed Communications. This is Maddy. How can I help you?" I ask, while reading chapter eight of *The Da Vinci Code*. MUTE.

Then I listen to the caller, read a paragraph and crunch on a Hershey's bar. After taking a moment to chew and swallow, I release the MUTE key. "I'll be happy to assist with that," I say briskly.

And if I get a caller who just wants to bitch, moan and listen to himself talk forever and a day, just like this caller that I have on the line right now, well all the better!

I jab the MUTE button, tune him out and read several more paragraphs. This part is juicy! Langdon has solved another enigmatic riddle and the Priory of Sion are on to him.

In the past few months, I've read the entire *Shopaholic* series, *The Hunger Games* trilogy, Khaled Hosseini's novels, Paullina Simon's *The Bronze Horseman* and all its sequels, Nicholas Sparks' tear-jerkers, Jodi Picoult's controversial books, and now Dan Brown's mind gripping thrillers.

The problem is, Dan Brown has got me gung-ho on conspiracy theories—the secret brotherhood of the Illuminati, the fraternal order of the Freemasons. So riveting and such fascinating stuff.

And truth be told, I think there's a conspiracy going on in this call center. Last week, this company spent millions of moolahs buying up air time space on TV and radio to launch their new ad campaign. Their new slogan: Lightning Speed Communications, We Service All Your Needs in Lightning Time.

Groan. I know. It is so *stooooopid!*

I brushed off that silly ad campaign, but I really should have paid more attention. It was the purveyor of bad things to come.

Today, everyone on the floor received this apocalyptic email:

From: Corporate Headquarters
To: All Customer Service/ Tech Support Agents.
Subject: Our new ad campaign.

We have proudly launched our new ad campaign—We Service All Your Needs in Lightning Time. In order for our campaign to be a success, we will focus on your AHT (Average Handle Time). This is something that all the Team Leads and Supervisors will be watching out for. If they see that your call goes over 2 minutes, they will come and check on you. We will also be watching Not Ready since every second of Not Ready will increase your AHT, and you should typically never be in Not Ready for more than 5 seconds. Keep in mind that the AHT goal is 2 minutes. Please adhere to this policy; failure to do so will result in an informal warning, followed by a formal written warning, and subsequent termination. Thank you for all your hard work.

Siegfried Miles, CEO
Corporate HQ

I stare at the appalling email. "My AHT is seven minutes," I cry. "What's yours, Truong?"

"Mine's six." He exhales sharply. "We are *so* fucked."

I pound my fist on the desk. "I got another relay call today so that will jack up my handle time!"

"Next time you get a relay call, just hang up." Truong plonks a maki roll in his mouth.

I nibble my lips. "I'll get fired if I get caught."

"Well, that's what I'll do," says Truong. "Hang up on the handicapped to save my job."

My conscience immediately kicks in. "But I really don't want to hang up on them. It's not their fault that they are deaf or dumb, I mean *mute*," I hastily correct myself. "Don't you think *dumb* is such a degrading word?"

"You can call them whatever you want." He sniggers. "They can't answer you back!"

"Truong! You are going to Hell in a handbasket."

Lurching forward, I playfully tug his scarf and he theatrically feigns his death. After goofing around, the reality of the situation begins to sink in.

"What they're asking us to do is *impossible*," he implores.

"I know! Troubleshooting takes time. Listening to customers' complaints takes time, selling takes time. Let me have another one of those Spider rolls." I reach across with my chopsticks and plunk a roll in my mouth.

Truong strokes an imaginary Confucius beard. "Just you wait and see. When they find out that *no one* can meet this ridiculous 'two minute AHT goal,' they will change it!" he proffers.

A week goes by and the Average Handle Time is still stuck at two minutes. It's near pandemonium; everyone is in a wild panic. The AHT for the entire call center hovers at six minutes, give or take a minute. I know this for a fact because management sends out everyone's stats on a daily basis. Last week, the overall AHT for this center was 6.5 minutes.

And they want us to drop it down to 2 minutes?

Are they loco?

"Truong! What will they do? Fire everybody?"

"I don't know." He fidgets with his scarf. "I don't want to lose my job. Heck, it's a full blown recession now."

"Hell, if I lose mine, it'll be a depression."

A shadow of a frown touches his forehead. "They *have* to lower the handle time."

"They won't," I say glumly. "I heard this rumor that they can't lower it. In that stupid ad campaign, the caption says we service all calls in two minutes or less. So they can't retract the ad now; it's too late! They've already spent way too much money."

Truong shakes his head at the company's sheer idiocy. "Well, they'll *have* to do something."

And then it happened.

On Tuesday morning, the server crashed. All our systems are down. Kaput. I cannot log in to a single app. Not one!

It is complete bedlam and utter chaos in here. Armageddon.

All the supervisors and leads are running around in circles like the sky is falling, screaming out orders, "Use down scripts! Use down scripts!"

Beep!

"Thank you for calling Lightning Speed. I'm so sorry, but our systems are currently down. Is there a general question that I can help you with?"

"Nope," says the caller and promptly hangs up.

Beep!

And on and on and on it goes.

I use 'Down Scripts' on every single call, while simultaneously reading *The Da Vinci Code*. This is fantastic! I don't even have to use one ounce of my brain to think and troubleshoot.

I can just read my novel and repeat the same sentence over and over again, like a broken tape recorder.

Sometimes, just for shits and giggles, I make sure I sound extra robotic so the callers think they're talking to an automated attendant and hang up. This is too good to be true.

Suddenly, Hillary barks over my shoulder, "You cannot say that our systems are down, you are *supposed* to say that our systems are UNAVAILABLE. That is the mandatory script."

I blink.

She continues frenetically, "If you say that our systems are down, it causes undue panic. Like if there is a bomb on the plane, the pilot does *not* tell the passengers that there is a bomb on board. He merely informs them that there is 'a situation'. Same thing here! Our systems are NOT DOWN! And if you tell the callers that our systems are down, you will get a big fat zero on your quality scores!"

"Got it. The systems are unavailable," I say to placate her.

She forges on, "And if the callers ask when our systems will be back up, let them know that we do *not* have an ETA."

I smile and nod obediently.

Beep!

"Thank you for calling Lightning Speed. I'm so sorry but our systems are currently unavailable. Is there a general question I can help you with?"

"So your systems are down," states the caller.

"Um . . . *no,* sir. Our systems are unavailable."

"Yeah, so they're down," insists the caller.

"No," I protest. "They're unavailable."

"What the hell is that supposed to mean?" he demands.

"It means our systems are not available."

He makes an exasperated sound. "When will it be back up?"

"Sorry, sir, we don't have an ETA."

"Now what does that mean?" he huffs.

"It's an abbreviation for Estimated Time of Arrival."

Sheesh. Now we're supposed to talk like air traffic controllers.

Hmm, shouldn't it be ETR? Estimated Time of Repair?

Click!

Aside from that snafu, it has been a rather swell day at work; and by the end of my shift, I've finished reading the entire novel.

Before logging off, I check my stats report.

Holy Sacred Indian Cow! My Average Handle Time for today is eight seconds! And that bumps up my overall handle time to two minutes!

"Truong!" I cry excitedly. "Have you checked your stats yet?"

"Sure have, darling. I love it when the server goes down; makes my stats look *fab.*"

My eyes narrow suspiciously. "Do you think they rigged it?"

Truong stares at me in blank astonishment. "What the hell are you talking about?"

I say in a hushed voice, "I think they planned this! They made the server crash on *purpose* to help improve our handle time."

How sneaky! I am amazed by their shrewdness.

This is *so* surreal. And what a brilliant idea!

"It's a *conspiracy,*" I hiss.

"Maddy," he says mildly, "quit reading those silly Dan Brown novels."

Twenty One

This week, Lightning Speed launched Security Questions, and all day long, I've been fielding calls from customers who either do not recall setting up their questions, or do not recall the answers to the questions that *they* themselves picked.

Go figure. I'm convinced that half the population suffers from acute Alzheimer's and dementia.

Beep!

"Thanks for calling Lightning Speed Communications, this is Maddy. How can I help?"

"My name is Rajeswari Veerakukatanarasimharajuvaripeta and these Security Questions are so annoying. I don't remember setting them up, and now I'm locked out of my account."

"I'm so sorry to hear that Mister, um, Venkaqruisi, err . . . piqua," I fumble, "but these are questions that you at one time chose and answered."

"I said that I did NOT set them up!" he blasts. "I SWEAR ON MY MOTHER'S GRAVE!"

"Sir, if you can answer one of your Security Questions over the phone, I can get you back online."

"Go ahead!" he growls. "Ask me the damn question!"

"Okay. Where did you go on your first date?"

"I picked that question?" he spits haughtily.

"Yes, sir, you did," I inform him evenly.

"Shhhhhhiiiiiiiiiiiiit, I don't know. My bedroom?"

I gag. *Some date.*

After typing in his answer, my app tells me it's a no-go. "Sorry. That's incorrect. Would you like to go to the next question?"

"Yeah, yeah," he mutters, highly agitated at this point.

"Question number two: What is your dream occupation?"

Long pause.

"Bus driver?" he manages at last.

"Sorry, but that is the wrong answer. Would you like to go to the next question?"

"How can that be wrong?" he demands, huffing and puffing.

"Um, because that was not the answer you originally gave?" I say in a neutral tone.

"This is complete BULLSHIT! Next question!"

"Okay, question number three: What song did you dance to on your wedding night?"

"Which one? I've been married *four* times."

"Sir, once again, you picked these questions. So *you* tell me."

He scoffs with rage, "HOW THE HELL SHOULD I KNOW?"

I forge on, "All right, here is the last question: What was the model year of your first car?"

"Well I bought my car in 2008," he says grumpily.

I rub my temples. "Sir, the model year refers to the year your car was built, *not* the year you bought it."

"Oh! 2002 Chrysler!"

"Thank you. That was the right answer." *Phew.*

I unlock his account and he's able to get back online.

Cough. And he swore on his mother's grave that he *never* set up his Security Questions. Shame on Mister *whatshisname.*

Beep!

"Thanks for calling Lightning Speed, this is Maddy," I say listlessly. "What can I do for you today?"

"These Security Questions are driving me crazy. I need help setting them up."

"I can help, ma'am. What seems to be the problem?"

"It's patronizing me! It refuses to take my answers."

"Now tell me, what are the questions you're choosing?"

"Well, the first one is: What's your oldest sibling's birthday?"

"Ma'am, can you please make sure that your answer is in the right format?"

A beat. Another beat. Still no answer.

"Um, what format is it specifying?" I persist.

"It says MMDD. But I've entered my sister's birthday and it won't accept it!"

"Well, what answer did you give?"

"0581978."

"So, is her birthday on May eighth?"

"Yes," she concurs, flustered at this point.

"Then you need to enter 0508."

"Oh!" she cries like it's a revelation. "Since I have you on the line, can you please stay with me until I complete this?"

"Of course I can," I say graciously.

"Here's the next question that I'm choosing: What is your favorite book? And I'm typing in the Bible for my answer."

"Um, ma'am, that is pretty easy to guess. According to polls, that is what forty percent of users list as their favorite book and any hacker could easily figure that out. It would be more secure if your answer is a bit harder for someone to guess."

"Then I won't remember it," she says with an aggrieved air.

I breathe out a heavy sigh. These stinking Security Questions are far from being foolproof. Some of the answers she provides could be posted on her Facebook page. Any teenager high on pot could easily access her info with just a few mouse clicks.

Eventually, she concedes. "I've typed in a different answer. I put down *The Book of Mormon*. And here is the next question I'm selecting: What is the name of the hospital in which you were born? And I am typing in Saint Jude."

"Now that is a tricky one. Keep in mind that you need to remember *exactly* how you spell it. For instance, saint can be spelled St, or Saint, or St followed by a period."

"The crap I have to remember," she gripes. "I've already got over fifty passwords, and if I have to remember one more password or security question, my head will crack open!"

"I know." My voice drips with empathy. "We've got so many passwords to keep track of these days."

"You got that right. *Shoot*. I'll probably be calling you again."

I shake my head. I'm sure she will be.

Beep!

"Thanks for calling Lightning Speed Communications, this is Maddy, how can I assist?"

"My Security Questions are locked. This is frustrating, man. It used to be so much easier. Why did y'all have to go and change the dang thing?"

"I'm sorry, sir, it's a new security procedure. But I can get you back online if you can answer one of your Security Questions over the phone."

He groans with displeasure. "Ask me the question."

"Okay. When you first flew in an airplane, what was your destination?"

"I believe it was Chicago, Illinois," he says.

"Sir, when you originally answered this question, did you type Chicago, or Chicago space Illinois, or Chicago comma Illinois, or Chicago IL? I have to key in your answer and if the spelling is not an *exact* match, my system will tell me it's wrong."

"Gotcha! I think I put down Chicago comma Illinois."

I submit his answer and wait. "Sorry sir, it's incorrect."

"This is ridiculous!" he hisses and I don't disagree.

But since day one of working here, I've learned to *never ever* give the callers the benefit of the doubt.

So I probe, "Sir, can you please tell me how you would have spelled Chicago, Illinois?"

He emits a loud exaggerated snort, taking slight offense to my question. "Humph, just like how it's supposed to be spelled—C-h-i-c-a-h-g-o I-l-l-a-n-o-i-s-e."

I stifle a giggle. "Okay, let me try that."

I submit his answer and wait for my system to verify it.

"That is the right answer."

"See!" he says in an accusatory tone. "Why don't *you* learn how to spell next time!"

I close my eyes briefly and reset his Security Questions. Some battles are just not worth fighting.

I'm just glad that he didn't have to spell Mississippi or Massachusetts.

Beep!

Before I can rattle off my usual greeting, the caller ruptures my eardrums, "DO I HAVE TO ANSWER THESE BLASTED SECURITY QUESTIONS?"

"Yes, sir, you do," I say patiently.

"WHY?" He huffs and heaves, like he's about to suffer a coronary.

"It's for your protection sir," I inform him kindly.

"I DO NOT WANT THE EXTRA PROTECTION!"

"I'm so sorry sir, but if you want to use our service, then you don't have a choice," I say in my most apologetic voice.

"FINE THEN! I'LL JUST ANSWER '*DON'T KNOW*' FOR EVERY SINGLE QUESTION!"

Click!

I was about to inform him that if he enters the same answer more than once, our system will reject it. But he didn't give me a chance. Oh well, he'll just have to discover that on his own.

Or, he'll be calling us back.

After taking more than a hundred Security Questions-related calls, I am frazzled to bits.

I hate Security Questions as much as the callers do.

And I hate this job.

Midway through assisting another caller with, you guessed it—her Security Questions, I hear the high-pitched, screeching noise of the fire alarm going off.

YESSSSSSS!!! IT'S A FIRE DRILL!!!

"I'm sorry, ma'am, but you'll have to call back in about an hour 'cause the fire alarm just went off," I say with a big, fat smile on my face and promptly jam the Log Out button.

I scan the floor for my buddies. But they're nowhere in sight.

Hmm. They must have already bolted.

Traipsing happily toward the exit stairwell, I merge into the mass exodus.

Karsynn is sitting on a patch of brown grass, basking in the sunlight. "Isn't this great?" she trills.

"Sure is," I enthuse, watching a fire truck swing by the curb.

Minutes later, Truong, Mika, Ingeborg and Archie join us on our private oasis, and for the next fifty-five minutes, we lounge under an azure blue sky, enjoying fresh air and good company.

"I sure wish we had fire drills every day," I murmur lazily, glorifying in the feel of the sun on my cheeks, its lulling warmth making my eyelids drowsy.

Truong sticks a blade of grass in his mouth. "My wish is for that building to burn down to the ground." He quickly adds, "When nobody is inside it, of course. Now wouldn't that be nice?"

Everyone echoes his sentiments.

Sigh. I guess you know you really hate your job when you're wishing for disaster and destruction to strike *just* so you don't have to go into work.

Beep!

"Thanks for calling Lightning Speed Communications, this is Maddy. How can I assist?"

"I need help with QuickBooks," demands the caller. "I can't get QuickBooks to connect to the internet."

I probe for more, "Can you connect to any websites when you use your browser?"

"Yes." His voice is laced with irritation.

"In that case, it's a QuickBooks issue. The QuickBooks.exe file is blocked from accessing the internet, so you'll need to contact Intuit or QuickBooks for support. Or it could very well be your firewall blocking you, in which case you'll need to contact Norton or McAfee."

"I don't mean to take it out on you *but* I DID NOT EXPECT TO BE TRANSFERRED ALL OVER THE PLACE FOR HALF A FOCKIN HOUR JUST SO YOU CAN TELL ME THIS! THIS IS COMPLETE BULLSHIT!"

Now why do you say that you don't mean to take it out on me? Why? What for? You say that, and then you turn around and take a mega shit on me.

"I'm so sorry, sir, but QuickBooks is a third party software which we do not support. As much as I'd like to help you, I can't; so you'll need to contact QuickBooks directly."

"THANKS FOR NOTHING!" he blasts.

"Um, before you go, is it okay if I mention a product or a service that may be beneficial to you?" I ask meekly; my voice is strangled to say the least.

But I *have* to say the dreaded TSR script. Otherwise, I'll be on a formal warning if the KGB spies are listening.

I hold my breath. I can hear his heavy breathing on the line.

"WHATEVER!" he barks.

"Um, is that a *Yes* or is that a *No?*" I swallow hard.

"Let me get this straight young lady. You haven't even helped me with my issue, and here you're trying to sell me something? ARE YOU TRYING TO ANTAGONIZE ME?"

"Yes, um, I mean n-no," I stammer. "What I'm trying to say is *yes*, I am trying to sell you something but *no*, I'm not trying to antagonize you. But if I don't read you the sales script, and if I don't probe you for more when your answer is *'whatever,'* then I'll be docked down by Quality Assurance if this call is monitored."

He goes ape shit. "THAT IS THE STUPIDEST THING I'VE EVER HEARD. TELL YOUR QUALITY ASSURANCE PEOPLE TO GO FUCK THEMSELVES!"

"Sir, I can definitely submit a customer feedback for you. That is, um, if you'd like me to," I say, consumed with hope.

"DO THAT. And capitalize the word FUCK!"

Click!

Wow! I feel like I've just hit the jack pot.

I've been waiting to tell the Quality Assurance Assholes to go fuck themselves since day one.

And now, I *can*—on a customer's behalf!

With glee and utmost pleasure, I click the Customer Feedback link located on our internal website and begin feverishly tapping away at my keyboard.

Department: Quality Assurance
Subject: Customer Feedback

Notes: Customer is very upset with our policy Re: Selling on every single call. Sometimes it is simply not appropriate. Per the customer, you people (meaning the Quality Assurance group) need to go FUCK yourselves.

Rubbing my palms together and with a million dollar smile plastered on my face, I click submit.

That felt *soooooooooooo* good.

The Quality Assurance agents in this call center are like the Sicilian Mafioso. They run amok on a power trip, terrorizing us with failed monitors and shoddy quality scores. It's a classic case of an over abuse of power. Instead of helping us perform our jobs, they hinder us.

Seriously, I get marked down for every petty, ridiculous and egregious thing. The Quality Assurance agents go through a long check list:

#1. Did you thank the customer for calling?
#2. Did you say, "Yes, I can help you with that."

And on and on it goes.

Recently, I got marked down because I said, "Yes, I can look into that matter for you." Essentially, it's the *same* as informing the caller, "Yes, I can help you with that."

But *nooooooo, n*ot to the QA mob and their convoluted logic. They struck me down hard for not using the *exact* and *precise* wording. My failed monitors used to anger me to no end, but now I just find it downright laughable.

The QA Assholes don't use their brains, instead relying on a stupid and restrictive check list. The check list is merely there to serve as a guideline, and it's certainly not meant to replace their brains. But in the QA mob's case, I guess you can't replace something that you don't already have.

Truong calls them the KGB, and quite aptly so. They're the secret police of this fascist regime. Every single word we utter is subject to their scrutiny.

We're held hostage by the KGB and their crazy cronies; they suppress our voices, our ideological subversion, and worst of all, they suppress who we are as human beings.

Consequently, my calls end up sounding scripted, like a robot with no life, no emotions.

I've already been slapped with two failed monitors this month. What's next?

"Maddy," growls The Führer. "Log out of your phone and come see me at my desk."

Egad! I spoke too soon.

I march to her cubicle with a sense of foreboding. "You wanted to see me?" I hover anxiously by her side.

"Sit!" Her face hardens and she whips out a black folder.

Cautiously, I take a seat.

She yanks my Performance Review out of the black folder and slams her fist on the desk like a sledgehammer. "Look at this! Just *look* at this will you? You have NOT made your sales quota this month, and you barely scraped through last month!"

A cry of fear escapes my lips.

"On top of that, you've had several failed QA monitors. When your stats look bad, I look bad!" She gnashes her teeth.

"So far, I've been very lenient and merciful in spite of your unacceptable performance. But not anymore!"

I manage a feeble smile. Merciful? Um, if that's her mercy, I'd hate to see her vengeance.

"Your quality has to be on par, too!" She shoots me a vicious look. "Remember, SERVICE OVER SALES!"

I bob my head up and down, obediently playing along.

Riiiiight. Then how come seventy percent of my Performance Review—which incidentally, is what determines my raise next year—is based entirely on sales? Only ten percent is based on my quality scores.

Service over Sales? *Pssh!* Horseshit!

"And your handle time is way too high! Keep your calls within two minutes! Lower handle time equals more calls. The more calls you take, the more you can sell. Get it?" she shrills.

"Uh-huh," I squeak.

"And explain all this tardiness!" she barrels on. "How come you logged in from your break one minute late yesterday and two minutes late on Tuesday? EXPLAIN YOURSELF!"

Heck. I'm not going to tell her the *real* reason. You see, I have a hard time going 'number two' on the floor I work on (the third floor). I'm a very private person and try as I may, I just cannot go poo when my co-workers are whooshing in and out of the toilet.

And so I use the restroom located on the thirteenth floor. It's always vacant, allowing me to do my business in absolute peace, privacy and tranquility.

Perversely, Truong had once admitted that he never goes 'number two' at work. He said, "I just hold it in until I get home."

I'd stared at him as if he was bonkers. Then I asked, "What if you have an EXPLOSION in your chair?"

Truong had just stared at me as if I was the one who was bonkers.

I'm sorry, but I can't hold it in. I think I'd DIE if I did. When you gotta go, *you gotta go.*

The only problem is, a fifteen minute break does not afford me ample time to use the restroom located on the thirteenth floor. Mind you, I sprint up and down the stairs at the speed of a gazelle. And sometimes I make it back on time, sometimes I don't. Trust me; I even tried taking the lift once, but it ended up taking much longer.

Hillary's eyes burn with rage. "SO?" The Führer demands an answer, "WHY WERE YOU LATE?"

I twist my fingers, trying to come up with something that will placate her. After a tentative pause, I manage, "I was going over the sales integrity CBT (Computer Based Training) to, um, make sure I'm in compliance with all the rules and regulations we have to abide by, you know, when selling over the phones, and um, I just somehow lost track of time . . ." I trail off unsteadily. "But I *had* to do it! It was my fiduciary obligation," I expostulate.

The fire in her eyes is extinguished—at least for now.

Phew! That always seems to do the trick.

Mention words like Regulation, Compliance, Sales, Obligation and it immediately quells her anger somewhat.

Hillary harrumphs and steers the topic back to my poor sales performance. "Just look at these atrocious sales numbers! They are completely unacceptable!"

I gulp and wheel my chair back several inches.

Her capacious nostrils flare with annoyance. "So, what do you have to say for yourself?"

I sit numbly in my chair. "Um, I . . . err, tried?"

"WELL YOU ARE NOT TRYING HARD ENOUGH! I have listened to your monitors and YOU HAVE NOT BEEN SELLING ON EVERY SINGLE CALL!"

"But, sometimes I can't," I say timidly.

"Excuses, excuses!" she spits. "This week, I'll be doing side-by-sides with you, starting right now."

She marches me to my cubicle, pulls up a chair next to mine, throws on her headset and Y-jacks onto my headset.

I feel trapped.

Beep!

"Thanks for calling Lightning Speed Communications, this is Maddy. How can I help?"

"I need to pay my cell phone bill," says the caller.

"I'm sorry, sir, but you've got the wrong department."

"My fault." He chortles briefly. "I'm on chemo right now and my mind is just not in the right place."

"Don't worry about it, sir," I say amiably. "People get lost in the tree of numbers all the time. Let me just get you over to a billing sp—" I pause mid-sentence as Hilary is shooting me a scathing look.

I push MUTE and turn to her. "What?"

"Pitch a sales offer!" she orders so severely that the veins on her forehead are pulsating and popping.

"Hillary, he has cancer," I beseech, my eyes begging her. "He's sick and he may have months, maybe only days to live."

"I—do—not—care!" Her tone is cold and remorseless.

Resigning myself, I release the MUTE key.

"Sir, before I transfer you to a billing specialist, is it okay if I mention a product or a service that may be beneficial to you?" I cringe at my very own words.

"Darlin', I am a dying man. There is nothing else I need but God's love." He chuckles heartily.

Instantly, I am filled with remorse. And I berate myself for allowing Hillary to bully me into pitching a sale to a man who is terminally ill and about to meet his Maker.

There really are no 'right words' to say to him. His situation is horrible and death is final. I used to take offense when people would say that my dad was going off to a better place, or that his pain would soon be over with. I know they were well-meaning, but I would rather they had said nothing at all.

The Führer is still on my case.

"Say something!" she hisses. "*Empathize* with the caller."

This caller seems so positive and the last thing I want to say to him is something pitiful like, "I'm sorry," so I try to match his upbeat mood. "Sir, will you please put a good word up there for me when you see God and Saint Pete?"

"I sure will," he says with a smile in his voice. "What is your name again?"

"Madison Lee," I say and he's the very first caller to whom I have disclosed my full name.

"Will do," he says kindly.

After transferring him over to the payment center, I turn to Hillary. "See!" I say steadfastly. "It's *not* possible to sell on every call. Sometimes, it's just not right. He's a dying man Hillary."

The Führer is without a soul. "If you did not make the offer, then how would you have known if he would have said 'Yes' or 'No'?" She raises her unibrow, making her meaning quite clear.

I drop it. It's pointless . . . just like talking to a brick wall.

She's clearly brainwashed like the rest of them.

Anxiously, I sit and wait for another call to come through.

It's summer time and the call volume tends to drop during the warmer months, and spike during the colder ones. And right now, it's super slow.

Hilary seems annoyed that it has slowed down. She glares at me belligerently, as if it is *my* fault that there aren't any calls in queue. Gosh. Her eyes are ablaze like red hot coals.

Squirming in my seat, I mutter, "Um, Hillary . . . will you please stop yelling at me?"

"I'm not yelling at you," she snaps.

"Yes you are. You-you're yelling at me with your *eyes.*"

Beep!

I sag with relief. "Thanks for calling . . ."

By the end of my shift, I am having serious thoughts of suicide, and for some odd reason, my left eye hurts like crazy. I briefly close my eyes, hoping that the mere act of shielding it from the bright lights will offer some sort of relief from the acute burning sensation. It feels like someone is stabbing my eye with a blunt screwdriver.

I'm stumbling down the stairs with my vision impaired, when Mika is suddenly beside me.

"Hey," he says, slowing down to match my pace.

I squint. "Hey."

He immediately notices something amiss. "Are you okay? You look a little tired."

I sigh. "I'm all right. Hillary's been doing side-by-sides with me all day."

He makes an apologetic grimace.

"Mika, is it okay with you if we skip your tutoring session this weekend? I don't know why, but my left eye is bugging the hell outta me."

"Sure. Of course we can skip it." He stops abruptly, cups my face and gently tilts up my chin. Bending his face to my upturned face, he studies my left eye. "Hmm. It looks pretty red."

Instinctively, I touch it and wince. "It does?" I ask, squinching my mangled eye. I probably look like a mad Mongoloid.

A look of concern clouds his face. "Yeah, you better go home and get plenty of rest, okay?"

"Okay," I mutter, bumbling my way down the stairs. "What about you? What are you doing tonight?"

He props the door open. "Nothing exciting. I have a hundred page thesis to write."

We stroll out side by side into the sweet, balmy summer night and a welcoming breeze kisses my cheeks.

Mika escorts me to my car. "I'll call you tonight?"

"Sure." I stall for time, swinging my bag from side to side. "Are you heading home right now?"

Another breeze sweeps in and tiny wisps of hair tickle his forehead. "Yeah." He smiles. "Why?"

I clear my throat. "Um, don't you have to wait for Tatiana?"

He rakes a hand through his wind-rumpled hair. "As a matter of fact, I don't. Tatiana's hooked up with Adnan, so *he* gives her a ride now," he says with a hint of relief in his voice.

"Adnan? The security guy?" I ask, surprised yet undeniably pleased. "Are you for real?"

Mika confirms this with a nod, and waits for me to slide into my car before firmly shutting the door behind me.

I roll down my window. "Do you want to go hiking up in Cherry Creek tomorrow?" I ask on a whim.

"Sure." He leans forward and lightly brushes my hair from my eyes. "We'll figure out the details when I call you tonight, 'K?"

"Okay." I find myself grinning stupidly.

For a brief moment, our eyes lock and he gives me a strange, and serious look. The moonlight flicks on his face, and after several beats he steps back and says, "Take care of that eye of yours."

"I'll try." I switch on the ignition.

Although there is an acute burning sensation in my left eye, and the earlier part of my day was total crap (thanks to Hillary), I feel my spirits soar. "Ta-Ta, Tatiana," I think out loud.

As I'm driving away in a haze of delight, I glance at my rear view mirror and see that Mika is standing in the middle of the parking lot, watching me.

Unblinking, I watch him watching me until all I can make of him is a tiny speck of dust.

It's a scorcher! It seriously feels like someone is holding a Conair hair dryer up to my face. We are marinating in this heat, and I'm pretty sure I can make beef jerky on the grill without even turning it on.

In spite of the insufferable heat, Mika and I are enjoying our hike through Cherry Creek. The trail follows the creek upstream, taking us through a tapestry of trees and wildlife.

After hiking for almost an hour, we stop under a shady Aspen tree to replenish our fluids. Standing there side by side, we find ourselves gazing out at the golden sky, robed by the mid-afternoon rays.

Mika turns to me, sun glinting in his hair. "I've got a little surprise for you."

My face lights up. "You do?"

"Close your eyes," he instructs. "And open your hands."

Placing my faith in him, I squeeze my eyes tightly shut and keep my hands wide open. Seconds later, I feel something small and scaly wiggling about in the palms of my hands.

I smile. It brings back fond and happy memories. I don't even need to open my eyes and I know exactly what it is.

It's a sagebrush lizard.

"Okay, you can open your eyes now."

Upon doing so, I dissolve into a gooey mush.

It's a *baby* sagebrush lizard. The tiny reptile pulls on all of my heartstrings.

"*Aww* you're so adorable." My palms curl up and I coddle it close to my heart. "Thank you, Mika," I gush, choking with emotion.

Right this very second, I want to fling my arms around Mika and never let him go.

He kneels down beside me, and for a little while, we gaze adoringly at the lizard like it's our firstborn child.

"Hi, buddy. You're still a little skittish, aren't you?" I lightly tap the lizard's head and grandiloquently anoint him, "I shall hereby name you Ewan McGregor."

Mika chuckles. "Ewan McGregor?"

"Yeah, I always name my lizards after famous celebs."

A faint look of amusement lights his face. "So what will you do with Sir Ewan McGregor?"

"Just hold him for a few more minutes and then I'll set him free," I say, feeling radiantly happy.

Meanwhile, Ewan still seems skittish. Making cooing sounds, I stroke him lightly on the underside, and Ewan begins to relax under my hands.

I'll have to give myself credit when credit is due. I am a Lizard Whisperer.

Mika stares at me, unblinking. "How did you do that?"

I show him. And pretty soon, he's gotten the hang of it.

Gently, he rubs Ewan's belly, much to the reptile's enjoyment. "This little fellow here is pretty tame," he says, carefully handing the lizard back to me.

I coddle little Ewan for several more minutes and breathe out a sated sigh. Then, reluctantly, I kneel on the ground and set him free.

Brushing the dirt off my knees, I watch Ewan scurry about and in the blink of an eye, he scuttles off into the nearest shrub.

A sagebrush of course.

I look up and catch Mika gazing at me with affection.

"Thanks again." On impulse, I throw my arms around him and embrace him in a burly bear hug.

He buries me in his arms and whispers into hair, "Anytime."

Cradled against his chest, I grin with contentment, allowing myself to be smothered by him.

Out of the woodwork, a bearded hiker tramples by the beaten path and we spring apart like guilty lovers. Then we resume our hike, pretending like the embrace had never happened.

Twenty Two

When I troop into work on Monday, Hillary is noticeably absent from her spy tower.

I nudge Truong. "Where is our Lord and master?"

He snickers. "She took off on her broom an hour ago. They sent her to the California headquarters for some meetings."

My heart leaps joyfully. *Yesssss.* No more side-by-sides with Hillary!

"Oh!" he exclaims and adds, "She also wanted me to tell you that she'll be back in two days, and she'll be doing side-by-sides with you for the next six weeks."

The merriment instantly dies out of my face. And a premonition of death flashes before my eyes.

I take a moment to compose myself. That's okay. I won't let Hillary dampen my enthusiasm. Last I checked, all my monitors have been completed. A total of twelve calls are monitored by the Quality Assurance Assholes each month, and today, being the 31st of July, they've all been reviewed and I'm covered.

YAY! None of my calls will be monitored today!

Beep!

"Thanks for calling Lightning Speed Communications, this is Maddy. How can I help?" I rattle off my usual greeting and feel my shoulders begin to relax.

No monitors. No Hillary. What more can a gal ask for?

"Hello, this is Blinky from the Billings department. I need to transfer a customer who needs help with his online access."

"Is this Blinky Fiore?"

"The very one. Is this Madison? Maddy the Minx from my training class?"

"That's me!" I squeal with delight. "I can't believe it's you Blinky! It's been *so* long."

Blinky was in my training class, and she had to leave rather abruptly during our third week of training, because her twins were born two months prematurely.

Everyone in class loved Blinky; she always had us in stitches and her spot on imitations of Glenn the Bland trainer brought the house down. She is also legendary for her hoots. It starts out as a mild giggle, then it crescendos into a high-pitched hoot *slash* shriek of epic proportions. Belinda is actually her real name, but she prefers to be called Blinky, after the three-eyed orange fish from the Simpsons, mutated by a nearby nuclear plant.

Ordinarily, I would have to keep everything business-like and robot-like, but since I'm fully covered on my QA monitors, I can act like a normal person and interact with my long lost friend.

"Maddy!" she booms. "It's so good to hear your voice again."

"You, too, Blinky! How are your twins?"

"Homer and Marge are doing just great. Did you see the first batch of pictures I posted on Facebook?"

"Yes. They are so flippin' cute. When will you post more pics?"

"Soon. I hauled them over to Kiddie Kandids today."

"I can't wait to see," I gush.

Truong scoffs, "I can't stand it when people post pics of their newly born naked rats on Facebook. I like my newsfeed to be a baby free zone."

I roll my eyes at him. I simply adore baby pics!

My cubicle calendar features pictures of happy, cherubic babies posing in flower pots and wheelbarrows.

"How are things over there in customer service?" asks Blinky.

I laugh mirthlessly. "Not that great."

"That's too bad," she tuts. "Whose team are you on?"

"Hillary's Third Reich," I groan morosely.

She hoots like a hyena. "Ah yes, I've heard that she's the Not Ready Nazi. I have to ask you though, when she walks into a room, do you click your heels and clap your thighs together, and yell HEIL HILLARY?"

"No, but I'm still a P.O.W in this labor camp, and Hillary is still a fascist pig."

Sometimes, I wish I was in a different department. Blinky is *so* lucky to be in Billings. After she returned from maternity leave, she managed to get transferred.

"Do you like it over there in Billings, Blinks?"

"It's okay. At least my supervisor is nothing like yours. But it kind of sucks; we have to sell over here, too."

"You do?" I cry in astonishment. I was under the impression they didn't have to sell. "Sell what?"

"Credit cards," she moans peevishly. "Some of my callers have a hard time even paying their bills, and I'm still forced to sell them credit cards."

I shake my head. "I guess there's no escaping it."

"No there isn't," she says with an aggrieved air, imprisoned, too, by this madness.

"Okay, I guess you better transfer the caller," I say ruefully.

I could go on chatting with Blinky forever, but I don't want the poor customer to be on hold for much longer.

She breathes out a heavy sigh. "Yeah, I guess I better."

"It's been great catching up with you, Blinky."

"You, too! And try to stay alive over there."

"I'll try," I say half-heartedly.

"Next time Hillary is mean to you, say this: *Halt! Lassen sie mich die unterlagen für ihren schnurrbart sehen.*"

I stifle a laugh. "What does that mean?"

She hoots. "It means '*Halt! Let me see the documentation for your moustache*'." Then she immediately brings the caller on the line, and her tone is all serious and business-like. "Sir, thank you so much for holding. I have Maddy on the line with us now. She's a very good friend of mine, and she'll be assisting you from here."

"Bye-bye, Blinky," I manage between sputters, laughing like a loon, trying hard to compose myself so I can assist the caller.

This past week has pretty been rough, with my left eye getting progressively worse. It's red, it's sore, and it hurts like crazy. At first, I had chalked it up to computer eye fatigue for the simple fact that my job requires me to stare at a monitor for eight hours a day. But by Thursday, my left eye is so severely inflamed and the pain is so unbearable, that I just *know* something is seriously wrong. I immediately make an appointment with an ophthalmologist and the receptionist at his clinic manages to squeeze me into a slot tomorrow.

The next morning, Kars gives me a ride to the eye doc's office. My vision has become so impaired that I'm almost certain I'd cause a pile up on the freeway if I'm at the wheel.

We arrive at Okelberry Vision Center unharmed and intact.

In the waiting room, I find myself observing the folks around me (through my one good eye), and I'm shocked. Aside from me and Karsynn, not a single person here is under sixty.

Kars nudges me. "*Psssst.* You're here along with all the senior citizens suffering from age-related macular degeneration. They're here for cataract surgery!" She snorts derisively. "Just like you!"

I shoot daggers her way, but it doesn't really have the desired effect when pus is oozing out of one eye.

Flummoxed, Kars hands me a Kleenex. "Calm down, Maddy. I don't want you going blind on me, ya hear?"

"Madison Lee?" The nurse looks up from her clipboard.

I stand up and walk into a dark den.

After I relay all my symptoms to Dr. Okelberry, he performs a slit eye exam on my butchered orb. Minutes later, he diagnoses me with Ocular Herpes, also known as Herpes of the Eye.

"Herpes? I cannot have herpes!" Is the first thing that flies out of my mouth.

He offers me a kind smile. "It is nothing to worry about. The Herpes Simplex virus is a pretty common virus. It's the same virus that causes the cold sores that you get in your mouth."

"Oh," I say with a puzzled frown. "But what causes it?"

"Stress can trigger it," he says. "Now have you been stressed at all lately?"

Hillary had been doing side-by-sides with me for the past several weeks. On top of that, I'd had all these unattainable sales quotas I was forced to meet. So, to answer his question, "Yes, I have been feeling considerably *over stressed* lately."

Dr. Okelberry prescribes some antiviral eye drops to treat my infected eye and sends me on my way home. I spend my entire weekend holed up in my dungeon of a room, with the lights switched off and the venetian blinds shut, willing the horrible Herpes to go away.

On Monday, I troop into work with an eye patch, much like Tom Cruise in *Valkyrie*. A word to the wise—wearing an eye patch is extremely uncomfortable. But I've no choice. I need to shield my Herpes eye from the glaring outdoor sunlight, as well as the garish indoor fluorescent lighting.

Truong's chin drops at the sight of me. "What the balls?!?"

"I have Ocular Herpes," I say, straining to see out of one eye.

There is a moment of still silence as he blatantly stares at my eye patch. Then he throws his head back and roars with laughter. "Maddy, please don't go around saying that you have Ocular Herpes. People will think that you got poked in the eye with your boyfriend's snake."

I roll my one good eye. "Shut up, Truong! I don't even have a boyfriend. Besides, I have *Ocular* herpes. And it's *not* the same as the STD."

"It *is* a STD if you got poked in the eye with Mika's snake," he taunts. "Oh my God, I cannot believe Mika gave you herpes."

"Stop saying that!" I hiss and steal a quick glance at Mika, who thankfully appears to be preoccupied with a call.

Good. I don't want him seeing me like this.

Truong arches an eyebrow. "Speaking of snakes, do you think Mika has an anaconda or a rattlesnake in his trousers?"

I shake my head in utter amazement. Typical. This is classic Truong. He'll veer the topic to penises, balls, and asses whenever the opportunity arises.

Hurriedly, I log in to my apps before The Führer cracks her whip.

While my Crystal Ball app is chugging along, Truong turns to me and asks, "What type of snake do you think I have?" Truong asks, while rearranging his silk scarf. "Flatter me, Maddy."

Truong is *totally* asking for it. "Snake? You mean *worm*?"

His eyes widen like a hurt puppy. Stepping forward, he swats me in the face with his scarf, whipping it like Bruce Lee with a nunchuck.

"Stop it!" I protest, half laughing.

Eventually, Truong stops with a "Hi-Yah!" Then bizarrely, he begins quoting Bruce Lee, "Maddy, you need to empty your mind; be formless, shapeless like water. Now you put water into a cup, it becomes the cup; you put water into a bottle, it becomes the bottle; you put it into a teapot, it becomes the teapot. Water can flow, or it can crash. Be water, my Maddy friend."

I blink. On impulse, I reach for my bottle of Evian and chuck the contents in his face.

For several seconds, Truong fixes me with a murderous glare as water drips down his face. Suddenly, he lurches forward—

Beep!

He freezes mid-air and I flash him a toothy grin.

"Thanks for calling Lightning Speed Communications. This is Maddy. How can I help?"

"Can you *speak up* young lady? I cannot hear a *word* you're saying," croaks the caller.

I crank up the volume. Way, way up to its highest setting.

"Thank you for calling. My name is Maddy, what can I do for you?" I say, this time an octave higher.

"I still can't hear you," the caller shrills with irritation.

"THANKS FOR CALLING. THIS IS MADDY. HOW CAN I HELP?" I practically yell.

"That's a little better," mutters the caller.

Sheesh. And so for the rest of the call, I find myself screaming at the top of my lungs. Why oh why don't these deaf people get some hearing aids so I don't have to yell at them? I'm a mild mannered, soft spoken person, and it's not my nature to yell. And, it's starting to *get* to me. All this yelling is so darn exhausting.

I pop a lemon mint Ricola and suck on it to soothe my aching throat.

This job has also made me partially deaf. I can barely hear out of my right ear—the ear my headpiece is glued to for eight hours a day. Sometimes, I hear a sharp ringing sound and I've had to amp up the volume on my headset, *just* so I can hear my callers. And even so, there are times when they sound so far away. Like when you put a seashell up to your ear and listen really hard, you hear the ocean. That's what some of my calls sound like . . . big waves crashing against the shore.

Beep!

"Thanks for calling Lightning Speed Communications, this is Maddy. What can I do for you today?"

"I can barely hear you," says the caller crossly.

I draw in my breath with a hiss. Oh God, no. Not *another* deaf person. But this is even worse. "I can barely hear you either." I raise my voice several decibels.

"I need help with my . . ." The caller's voice sounds so faded and garbled that I miss half of what he's saying.

"What did you just say again, sir?" I strain my ears to listen.

"What did *you* just say?" he fires back in an agitated tone.

This goes on for an hour. This exacerbating *ridiculosity!*

During a brief interval, the caller gasps in surprise, "Oh! I've been holding the phone UPSIDE DOWN!"

I slap my forehead.

He chortles, seemingly tickled by this. "And here I thought I was going deaf."

I find myself laughing deliriously. And here I thought *I* was going *deafer.* When I'd signed up for this job, I knew that being yelled at was par for the course. But I did *not* anticipate this at all. Having to scream at customers who talk with their phones upside down? Callers who are literally deaf. *Deaf I tell you!*

And I most certainly did *not* expect to become deaf myself.

Or partially blind for that matter.

Perhaps this is a sign that I need to move on. I've been on the phones for almost a year now, and I feel brain dead. I don't even have to think anymore and I'm certain I can do my job blindfolded, with both hands tied behind my back. If it wasn't for the novels I read that bring me a much needed escape, and for Truong's delightful and enigmatic company, I'd probably die of boredom.

Honestly, my job is so easy that even a monkey could do it.

Actually, a monkey could probably do it better.

And like Tiger Woods, once I've conquered something, I get bored and restless and desire to conquer something else. Only difference is, I aim to conquer higher than Tiger does . . . something other than strippers and Vegas cocktail waitresses.

Plus, Hillary still insists on doing side-by-sides with me, and it's catapulting me into a nut house.

And there are other issues that irk me, namely having to sell. If I don't make my sales quotas for three months in a row, I'm fired. Just like that.

So it's time I jump ship or sink with it.

Sitting up straighter, I square my shoulders and resolve that it's time for change!

Onward and upward!

And I know just the place I want to go.

"Hey, Truong. Did you see the two postings for Second Level Techs? I think I'm going to apply."

Lately, I've been eyeing the wireless headsets that these smug technicians parade around in.

They are the envy of all the minions who covet their wireless headsets. They have the freedom to roam and wander wherever their hearts desire, whilst the rest of us are chained to our desks by our non-wireless headsets.

At the mere sight of a wireless headset, my pulse quickens and my palms get sweaty. I feel faint, breathless. I feel all hot, heavy and bothered. *Ahh* . . . my lust for one has never ceased.

I dream of one and I drool for one. I must have one. I *MUST!*

Suddenly, a techie saunters by with a wireless headset, and I stand stock still with a look of pure rapture on my face. *YOU WILL BE MINE WIRELESS HEADSET. Angry fist shake. YOU WILL!*

I'm still waiting for a response from Bruce Lee, but he's been oddly quiet. "Truong," I croak, my voice cracking and splitting.

Nothing. No reply.

"TRUONG!" I shout with a strained expression.

Finally, he shoots me one of his infamous *I'm-far-too-busy-for-this-conversation* looks.

"Please don't make me yell, okay? I've been yelling at all these deaf callers all day." I pop another Ricola in my mouth. "So did you see the posting or not?"

His response is tepid to say the least. "Uh-huh, why?"

"I *need* a wireless headset," I say with dire passion. "And the best part about being a second level techie is that you don't have to sell!"

But Truong doesn't appear to be sold on the idea. In fact, I'm rather taken aback when he turns weepy and whiny. "But if you get the techie position, you won't sit by me no more. Don't leave me, bitch." He pouts profusely.

"It won't matter," I assure him. "Hullo? With a wireless, I can stop by and visit you anytime!"

"Sure you will," he says dubiously.

"Hey!" I have a brain wave. "Why don't you apply, too?"

"Me? No," he says dismissively. "They make you take a test and I probably won't pass it."

"C'mon, Truong," I beg, falling to my knees. "This job is just so stressful. We have all these unrealistic sales quotas and, by the way, this job is making me deaf. Maybe even partially blind." I point to my eye patch. "And don't you want a change? A challenge?"

His hand flies up in protest. "No! No! I like my job now. I don't have to think and I like it that way. Thinking hurts my brain, plus I don't mind the selling part. I'm actually quite good at it."

Humph. He is resisting. I decide to switch tactics by dangling a big fat carrot in front of him. "With a wireless headset, you'll be able to use the restroom *and* take calls. Imagine that! You won't have to *hold it in* anymore."

Truong considers this briefly. After hemming and hawing, he says, "No, there's no way I can pass the test. I suck at math."

"Fine. But I'm still going to apply," I say steadfastly.

Single minded in my quest for a wireless headset, I fervidly fill out the online application.

"You're making a big mistake," he tuts and shoots me a look of forewarning. "Those techies are arrogant bastards. They act as if they're in their own exclusive country club. *Really.* They think they're better than everyone else."

"Well they *are* better than everyone else," I quip. "They have wireless headsets and we don't!"

Over my break, I ambush Kars and begin recruiting her.

"C'mon Kars!" I seize her fiercely by the shoulders. "Think of all the fun and freedom we can have with a wireless headset."

"But I don't want to be on the phones anymore," she howls in protest. "They posted seven team lead positions and I'm going for it."

"Tsch-tsch." I shake my head. "It's *so* hard to get a team lead position. There's too much politics involved, and you have to suck up to all the right people."

"And I have, trust me. I've been puffing like a chimney to get in their good gra—" she breaks off when she meets my eye.

"Kars!" I chide. "I thought you quit smoking?"

"I did, but I started again as soon as they posted the position. Maddy, I *need* to be a team lead; it's my only way out. I hate being on the phones."

I give her a tight-lipped smile. "As soon as you get the lead position, you'll quit smoking again, right?"

Kars crosses her heart. "Right. It's only temporary since I'm immersing myself in their lifestyle. But once they see that I'm one of *them*, I should be able to ace the interview and secure the position," she says like she's some sort of covert FBI agent on a clandestine operation. She lowers her voice, "I'm incognito. You know the saying—if it looks like a duck and walks like a duck . . ."

"You're a goose." I smirk. "A goose disguised as a duck."

"What's good for the goose is good for the gander," she quips.

And she's right. If she snags the lead position, it will surely bode well for all us goslings. She'll be the Mother Goose, looking out for her feisty flock.

Kars interrupts my thoughts. "The smoking part is easy. The hardest part for me is acting like a complete flooze ball, flirting and slutting myself out, stroking all these managers' egos."

That very second, Richard Just-Call-Me-Dick Jones ambles by, and Kars completely transforms herself.

"Oooooh, Diiiiiiiiiiiiiiickkkk," she coos in a high-pitched, whiny, nails-on-chalkboard voice. "That tip you gave us on selling, you know, asking the callers '*What is your hesitation?*' Well it's been working wonders for me! My sales have practically quadrupled!"

Dick puffs his chest out like a puffer fish. "Well, I am *so* glad that's been working for you. Back in the day, when I was in the trenches like you, that sales pitch of mine sealed plenty of deals for me. I was the top sales performer for Fanny Farm Insurance."

Karsynn's eyes widen like hard boiled eggs. She emits a gay, tinkling laugh. "You were?" she enthuses, suddenly becoming buoyant, tossing her hair this way and that. "Wow! You're so amaaaazzzzzzzzzzzing."

Dick straightens himself, his eyes shining with self-importance. He addresses Kars, "And what is your name again?"

"I'm Kars," she breathes evocatively. "Karsynn Higginbotham, and I recently applied for the team lead position," she adds in a syrupy voice.

"Well I'm glad to see that we've got some good candidates." He gives her a big fat wink and plods off.

I blink. *Err . . . did that just happen?*

Karsynn wheezes and collapses into a ball. "Whoa! It ain't easy being an airhead."

I mimic Karsynn by using a nasally, helium-filled, cat claws-scraping-car-hood voice, "Oooooooooooo, Diiiiiiiiiiick, my sales have practically quadrupled. You're so amaaaazzzzzzzzzzzing."

Kars delivers a solid punch to my arm. "It's politics baby. Plus I've got no choice. You should see the *real* Call Center Termites that I'm up against for the team lead position."

I shoot her a quizzical look. "Call Center Termites?"

"Yeah, these incompetent bimbos who chew on the managers' wood. And you know what? They don't stop there! They chew on everybody's wood—the team leads, the supervisors, the directors, anyone and everyone who can help them get ahead. Soon we'll have such a severe infestation of these completely inept termites who haven't the foggiest idea how to do their jobs once they're promoted, that this whole freakin' structure will be on the brink of collapse!" She flings her arms, gesturing wildly as she finishes off her tirade.

"Okay, Kars, calm down now. Take a deep breath."

She stops and catches her breath. "You worry about scoring the techie position, and I'll worry about securing the lead position. Now," she tuts, "have you got all your ducks in a row?"

"I've got all my ducks in a row," I say indignantly.

"Well make sure they're in a *perfect* row. You've got some stiff competition yourself."

"Who?" My interest is piqued for obvious reasons.

"Mika!" she exclaims, thumping my back.

I curse under my breath, "Dammit!"

"Don't worry, Maddy! You, me and Mika will be going places. We're the unstoppable trio of musketeers, and we shall sally forth and conquer this call center!" Raising an imaginary sword, she bellows, "ALL FOR ONE, AND ONE FOR ALL!"

My head is still reeling from the fact that I'll be up against Mika for the techie position.

"Well, Maddy, I've got plenty more schmoozing to do, and I've got to keep a close eye on my competition. Like they say, keep your enemies close, but keep the Call Center Termites closer." Bouncing away with the buoyancy of a cheerleader, she wields an imaginary sword and bellows once more, "Remember what I said—ALL FOR ONE, AND ONE FOR ALL!"

I stare after her open-mouthed.

What is the world coming to? Rambo Girl has morphed into Barbie Musketeer, and she reeks of Marlboro and mints.

Oy Vey! Several weeks later, I'm still waiting with bated breath. Did I get the job? Did I *not* get it? I just want to *know.*

Nothing. Not a peep.

I start ticking off the days in my head. I *need* that job. It's my one-way ticket out of this Hell hole. It's my pot of gold at the end of a rainbow that's quickly fading away.

Finally, right before I leave for work, I get the call from HR.

A huge wave of euphoria washes over me and I almost have to pinch myself twice. Is this a mockery or is this a dream?

Overcome by the news, I decide to keep it all to myself. I'm a trifle worried that the evil fairies will swoop in and snatch my dream away if I utter a word.

Sometime later, I float into the office through a fuzzy haze of disbelief. Dazedly, I pull up Outlook and check my email.

It's official.

This announcement was sent out to the floor:

From: Human Resources
To: All Employees
Subject: Promotions

We would like to congratulate January Jones, April Flowers, Jewel De'Nyle, Wendy D. Whoppers, Pamela Pornero, Karsynn Higginbotham, Amy E. Areola and Kylie K. Kleevage, who have all accepted positions as team leads.

Madison Lee and Jamal Jackson have both accepted positions as Second Level Technicians.

Mika Harkett has accepted the Third Level Technician position.

Each of these individuals brings a wealth of knowledge and experience to their jobs. Please join us in congratulating them.

Linda Parker,
Human Resources

It's for real! And it's finally sinking in. I'm simply giddy with happiness and relief. The test I had to take was semi-difficult, yet somehow I'd managed to score an eighty-five percent—a pass.

Mika, I had found out, scored a perfect one hundred. Although when I'd asked him how he fared, his face twitched uneasily, almost like he was half-embarrassed to tell me. But I'm not in the least bit surprised that he aced the test; it simply attests to his brilliance. And allegedly, because of Mika's perfect score, they'd offered him the Third Level Technician post.

"I got the job!" I smother a triumphant grin and pinch myself yet again. I'm now officially a Second Level Techie and the proud owner of a wireless headset. *Ahhhh,* it feels downright euphoric. It's the most wonderful and exhilarating feeling in the world.

Linda from HR shuffles by and thrusts a wireless headset into my hands. "Here you go, Maddy. You report to Douglas Gomez tomorrow."

I stare at Linda wide-eyed, like she just dropped a bejeweled Fabergé egg into my waiting palms.

"I've had Scheduling Ops take you off the phone for twenty minutes so you can test out your new headset. Now don't have *too* much fun." She winks and disappears on her rounds.

Slowly and almost reverentially, I turn the headset around in my hands, marveling at its exquisiteness.

Yeah! I need to test this baby out!

Let's see how far this baby can go! I can't wait to gloat about my new headset. I'm going to rub it and smear it in Truong's face.

It's just too bad he's nowhere to be found.

I poke my head over my cubicle wall. "Hey, Tiny, have you seen Truong?"

"Yeah," he grunts. "I think he ran to the break room to store his food. Oh and by the way girl, congrats on your promotion!"

"Thank you, Tiny." I flash him a bright smile and adjust my headset so it sits comfortably in my ear.

Strutting to the break room, I fetch plenty of stares. All the lowly minions eye my wireless headset with a mixture of envy and admiration. Hahahahaha. Look at me everybody. *Look at me!*

It's like kindergarten all over again and I have the shiny toy that all the other kids covet.

After swanning around for a bit, I step into the break room. *"Oh, Truooonnnng,"* I coo. "Look what I've got!" I toss my hair over my shoulder so my headset is in full view, in all its crowning glory.

"Wassup traitor?" He shoots me a smile of inconvenience and slams the fridge with deliberate force.

"Oh, get over it, will you!" I say with a laugh. "Quit ruining my mojo! C'mon, I want to test the range on this thing."

Truong blatantly stares at my headset. After *Oooooohhhh-ing* and *Ahhhhhhhhhhh-ing,* he says, "It looks a helluva lot better than mine. It's like a Bluetooth headset."

"I know!" I twirl merrily. "See, no wires!"

"Mmmm. I like how you don't have a nasty looking metal band wrapped over your head," he says in a quiet voice.

"You *like?"* I taunt.

He begins circling around me like a shark.

Truong is such a glamour queen. He is all about fashion and hair, and he thinks more mousse is better than less mousse, hence his hair is like an elaborate concrete coiffure.

I strike an elegant pose. "If you had one of these babies, your spiky hair wouldn't be squished in the middle."

Suddenly, Truong pounces on me like a panther. He mauls me and paws me, making a desperate lunge for my headset.

Like a sabre-toothed tiger, I fiercely fight him off.

"Hah! You can have my headset when you pry it out of my cold dead hands!" I huff and hustle.

After a mad scramble and scuffle, he graciously gives up.

"This baby is *mine, mine, mine*," I sing triumphantly. "Okay, I'll dial your extension and we'll test this baby out. You on?"

"I'm on," he says gamely.

We dart back to our cubicles and I dial his extension. "Truong, are you there?"

"Hey, Dum Dum, I'm here. Looking right at you," he sniggers from the cubicle next to me.

"Well enjoy my company while it lasts you Ding-a-Ling. I'll be moving desks tomorrow. Okay, now I'm heading back to the break room," I say in a giddy voice.

Upon setting foot in the break room, I check in with Truong.

"Can you hear me now?"

"Loud and clear," he says, giggling in my ear.

Next, I head for the restroom. "Can you hear me now?"

"Sure can. But don't stay in the toilet!" he shrieks. "I don't want to hear you doing your nasty bizzznessss."

"Already out the door," I tweet. "Now I'm taking the stairs all the way down to the cafeteria."

"Yes!" he cheers and fires out his orders, "Get me a diet coke from the fountain. If they're still serving tater tots, get me some! And don't forget to get me a fork, some ketchup and a couple of napkins. Thanks, doll ."

"Truong, I'm not your maid. Plus I don't have time. Linda only gave me twenty minutes off the bleepin' phones to test out this headset."

He clears his throat. "Um, when Linda asked you to test it out, I'm pretty sure she didn't have *this* in mind."

"I know. And no tater tots! I really don't want to deal with Miss Tropicana Orange Juice right now."

"*Girrrrl*, that bitch doesn't deserve to be called Tropicana OJ. She's that cheap, generic Wal-Mart brand. You know, the fake frozen concentrates that you get in a can, and you have to mix it all up with water."

"Ugh, those things are nasty."

He snickers. "*She's* nasty!"

"Okay, I'm in the cafeteria. Can you hear me now?"

"I can, but you're starting to sound a little faint."

"Stay with me, Truong. I'm heading out to the parking lot now," I wheeze as I jog out of the building.

Minutes later, I check back with Truong. "What about now? Can you hear me now?" I ask, leaning against my rust bucket Subaru.

"Holy Crapanoly!" he squeals. "I can! It's a bit staticky, but I can still hear you!"

I'm standing in the middle of the parking lot with my wireless headset glued to my ear and a silly grin pasted on my face.

Arms outstretched, I twirl around and around and around, feeling a rush of thrilling emotions.

In this rare and lucid moment, the iconic image of Julie Andrews pops in my head, the image that still gives me goose bumps. The image that captured her glowing rapture as the cameras panned and swooped through cotton clouds and across the snow covered Swiss Alps.

Flapping my arms like a bird, I burst into song, "The hills are alive, with the sound of *muuuuuuuuuuuusic.*"

I feel invigorated and liberated, much like Fraulein Maria on that lush, green mountain top.

FREEEEEEEEEEEEEDOM!!!

Merrily, I'm moseying about the Lightning Speed parking lot as if I were in Salzburg, Austria. Without a care in the world, I'm flouncing and romping along my imaginary hillside. Suddenly, I hear Truong's scratchy voice crackling in my ear.

"Quit futzing around, you have exactly five minutes left."

I race back into the building with surprising speed.

Sprinting up the stairs, I slam straight into Mika and almost topple backward in the process.

He slides his arms around to steady me. "You okay?"

"I think so." My voice is wobbly.

Gosh. His abs are rock hard. I feel like I've just slammed into a freight truck. I'm still seeing stars when Mika startles me with his outburst. "Maddy! Congrats! I told you you'd get it."

I flick my hand in a *yeah-whatever* gesture. "I was up against you, so I wasn't so sure."

He shucks, "C'mon, there were two postings; I knew we'd *both* get it."

I elbow him playfully. "Congrats to you, too, Mister Big Shot! You're a Third Level Techie now. A bona fide star. Me?

I'm just a pitiful low level tech. And when I don't know what the heck I'm doing, I'll be calling you round the clock."

He tips an imaginary top hat and executes a gallant bow, Fitzwilliam Darcy style. "And I will be at your service."

Hmm, no wonder they just called him Darcy. Fitzwilliam? I'm still laughing at Mika's theatrics when I hear Truong's voice crackling in my ear. "You've got exactly two minutes left, Miss Flirty Pants."

"I have to run," I say at once.

"Wait a sec." He halts me. "How come you didn't call me when you found out about the job? I got the call from HR this morning, so I'm sure you got it, too."

I cast him a meaningful look. "I wanted to tell you in person." I don't know why, but I tell him this because I want him to feel special. And he does.

His face breaks into a glorious grin.

I clear my throat and turn the tables on him. "Ahem, and why didn't you call me when *you* found out?"

"Same reason," he says, holding my gaze for far longer than necessary.

I palm my face. It feels warm. Very warm.

"I really *must* go! Otherwise there'll be a *fatwa* on my head."

He steps aside. "I'll call you tonight?"

"K', later," I say and fly up the stairs, this time with my chin up, to avoid any more head on collisions.

Twenty Three

The next several months pass without incident and I throw myself into my work with fierce determination. Being a second level technician has its definite perks, especially when I have an awesome supervisor. Thank the Lord I no longer answer to The Führer. I'd finally escaped her Gulag camp and I still, to this precise moment, feel a heady sense of freedom.

My new supervisor, Douglas Gomez, is known as the Yoda in this call center, and I can see why. He is a brilliant mentor and guide. He is my maestro, and I blossom under his tutelage.

The instant I'd expressed my ardor for writing, Douglas put me on a special project. And so a large part of my job now consists of writing user guidelines for our knowledge base.

I'd since learned that this style of writing is called technical writing. Just like poetry writing, technical writing is an art form in and of itself. Instead of the speaker-audience relationship that I am used to, this style of writing tends to be more of a teacher-student relationship. Consequently, there is a fine line I have to toe. On one hand, I have to be careful not to dumb down to my readers; and on the other hand, I don't want to leave out too much information to the point that my documentation hardly makes any sense at all.

Tech writing was a bit daunting at first, but I dove right into it and honed my skills every day, learning to develop my own bare bones style of writing and define my own voice.

A lot of my time is spent organizing complex material in a logical manner, and I'd even picked up Visio, which is a great tool for creating diagrams. Whenever I'd incorporate graphics in my documentation, I'd immediately score a hundred points with my readers.

Another part of my job involves interacting with third level engineers, and my go-to tech is Mika. This is the fun part as I get to play the role of journalist slash investigative reporter and extract as much information from him as possible.

Mika has been beyond helpful and patient with me, but he occasionally slips and starts speaking in *code,* and I find myself having to ask him all the 'dumb' technical questions. But truly, that is the only way I can thoroughly understand a subject. After all, I can't write about something I only half understand. And with Mika as my faithful guide, and with me constantly poking and prodding him for more, there is no stone, rock or pebble left unturned.

Still, I am a rookie in this field of writing, and when Douglas is unsatisfied with my work, he sends me back to the drawing board where I'd have to rewrite a second, third, and sometimes even a fourth draft. But I love the challenge, I love sinking my teeth into a juicy project; and most of all, I love writing again.

It is such a wonderful release.

After a long day at work toiling away in my windowless cubicle, I stroll out into the night, leaving the call center behind. A pale, watery sun is setting behind the clouds, and the air is chilly with a hint of frost.

Leisurely, I plod along the sidewalk, listening to the sound of dried leaves crunching beneath my Uggs. For a brief moment, I stop and admire the stunning backdrop. Leaves have matured into fiery colors of bliss. Fall is such a sexy season. An explosion of visceral colors—spicy reds, burnt oranges and mango maroons decorate the trees and the tarmac.

As I'm driving home through the suburbs, I'm reminded that Halloween is just around the corner. Ghouls, bats and cobwebs hang from the gallows; jack-o-lanterns and tombstones adorn the suburban lawns. I find myself cringing when I drive by a blood soaked guillotine, complete with a freshly bludgeoned head.

Now that is a little *too* gory for my taste.

Several days later at work, I'm treated to the sight of something *much* gorier. Great Scott! A great number of my co-workers take Halloween very seriously.

A little *too* seriously if you ask me.

Two days ago, management had sent out an email stating that we could all come into work on Halloween dressed in costumes. And already, I have spotted ten Lady Gagas, and over a dozen scary looking, blood curling trannies.

Apparently, I've completely underestimated the vast number of men who'd jump at the chance to dress as women. And what's even *more* disturbing is, these men actually look *better* dressed as women.

Our site manager, Richard Just-Call-Me-Dick Jones, struts by in sparkly silver stripper heels, fully decked out in a red mini, blousy top and Farah Fawcett wig.

Dick looks like an orangutan from the Malaysian jungles. An orangutan that's wearing *way* too much rouge and red lipstick.

When Dick Jones is in his customary khaki pants and bright polo shirts, he's a dead ringer for Gary Busey. Trust me, his *eww* factor is way up there. But as a woman, he's passably attractive, perhaps even good enough for Bangkok's infamous Patpong Street.

The orangutan look suits him.

Tiny's head pops out of his cubicle, and I'm shocked to see that he, *too,* is dressed in drag.

"Why aren't you dressed in costume, Maddy?" Tiny adjusts his Rihanna-inspired wig, then he whips out an umbrella and sings the chorus to, you guessed it—*Umbrella.*

I'm wiping tears from my eyes when five Call Center Termites sashay by, fully slutted out in ultra-revealing, breath-restricting German barmaid costumes.

How cliché. Halloween has become an opportunity for girls to dress like total sluts for a day. I don't mean to be a party pooper, but when I come into work, I like to dress comfortably. My daily uniform consists of dark skinny jeans,

Anthropologie tops, and Ugg boots. Truong insists on calling my boots Fuggly; to which I say, "Viva la Ugg!" I love my Uggs no matter what the haters may say.

Truong waddles over in a huge cardboard box with cut outs for his arms and head.

I gawk at his costume. "What the hell are you?"

"I am a light switch," he says with flair.

"A light switch?" I say and stare. "I don't get it."

Truong takes my hand and guides it to the plastic tube that's haphazardly taped onto the box. "Flick the switch and TURN ME ON BABY!" He flashes a hundred watt smile.

"How cheesy," I say, smiling in spite of myself. "But I'll give you props for being cheap and creative."

Then he gives me a once over, and his smile instantly recedes. "Why didn't you dress up?"

"I did," I say indignantly. "I'm a werewolf from Team Jacob's wolf pack."

"But, Maddy, where are your fangs? Your fur? Your wolf face?"

"D'oh! It's not a full moon tonight. I only turn into a werewolf when there's a full moon."

But Truong is paying me no heed. He is far too busy drooling and ogling over something . . . or someone.

I whirl around to see what all the fuss is about.

It's Mika.

He swaggers toward us, fully decked out in cowboy gear from head to toe. Truong and I blatantly stare, losing ourselves in his rugged beauty.

Mika's hair is slicked back, and he's handsomely outfitted in a denim shirt and a caramel suede vest fringed with tassels that sway to the rocking motions of his body.

As I cast my gaze downwards, my eyes clap on *the* fattest Texas-star belt buckle holding up his faded Levi's.

Holy Cowboy! Yee-Haw! Even his boots are donned with silver spurs that go jingle, jangle, jingle.

Mika cocks his head to one side. "Howdy y'all."

Without warning, he quick-draws and I find myself staring into the barrels of two identical water pistols.

A split second later, he rotates his wrists, showing off a fancy gun twirling display. Then he expertly slides the pistols into his leather holsters and drawls, "Welcome to the Wild, Wild West."

"Howdy, cowboy." Truong fawns all over Mika. "I know who you are! You're Jack Twist from *BROKEBACK MOUNTAIN!*"

Mika laughs and protests, "No, I'm Clint Eastwood from *The Good, the Bad and the Ugly.*"

"Nuh-uh," Truong dismisses with a wolfish grin. "You're Jake Gyllenhaal from *Brokeback Mountain.*" Sighing theatrically, he purrs, "You even have his sexy lips, sweetie."

Mika shoots me a long suffering look.

Beep!

Bummer! Visiting time is over.

I throw Mika a rueful look and sprint back to my cubicle with my wireless headset in tow.

Even though I am a techie, I haven't truly escaped the phones. Whenever we're swamped with calls, Douglas throws me back into the queue to help out, and today is no exception.

"Thank you for calling Lightning Speed Communications, my name is Maddy. What can I do for you today?"

Heavy breathing. "Well for starters," says the caller, "you could *do* me."

O-*kay*, so I've got a pervo on my hands.

I ignore his sleazy comment. "Sir, may I have your first and last name please?"

"My name is Long Ngock Nguyen. However, the N in Ngock is silent. So it's pronounced Long *Cock* Nguyen. But you can just call me Long Cock," he insists in a greasy voice.

Long Cock?!? This is worse than the Richards who prefer to be called Dicks. MUTE.

"Truong!" I holler from across the room; he now sits ten rows away from me.

"What?" he shrills with a hint of annoyance.

I wave my arms in the air, motioning for him to come over.

Reluctantly, he disentangles himself from Mika and prances over. "This better be good! You just wrenched me from the arms of my cowboy lover." He pulls a face.

"Trust me! It is. And guess what? I'm talking to your long lost brother Long Cock Nguyen."

"No *way*," he cries in disbelief.

Out of the corner of my eye, I catch Mika furtively sneaking away. Good for him; he's made his escape from the light switch.

Meanwhile, Truong is peering at my screen. "Well, Nguyen is a pretty common Vietnamese name. But Long Cock eh?" he says, clearly impressed.

And for the rest of the call, I try my best to ignore Long Cock's lewd comments and sexual innuendos. "You sound so sexy and so sweet. I love the sound of your voice. How old are you?"

Ugh! This guy is revolting! Why doesn't he just call the phone sex line? To get him off my back, I inform him that I'm ninety nine years old and suffering from incontinence.

"I don't believe ya for a second sweetheart. You sound about sixteen! What are you doing tonight? Are you going to party it up? What will you wear? C'mon darlin', fulfill my fantasies."

Is this guy for real?

I veer the conversation back to business. "What is the reason for your call, sir?" I ask blandly.

"You want to know what I'll be wearing tonight?" he asks and I remain silent. I really don't care, nor do I wish to know.

He tells me anyway. "I'll be dressing up as one giant gift box with a big bow wrapped around my head. And on the tag it shall say 'To: Women, From: God'. Get it?" He sniggers derisively. "I'm God's greatest gift to womankind."

Surely this guy *cannot* be for real.

"Is there anything else." I phrase it more as a statement than a question. It's my wrap up line for saying, "Take a hike!"

But Long Cock doesn't take the hint. He yaps on and on about all these costumes he fantasizes—French Maid, Naughty Nurse, Naughty Schoolgirl . . . I tune myself out to all of it.

"Is there anything else?" I interrupt bluntly. And every time he spews his smut, I interject and repeat myself over and over again, "Anything else? Anything else? Anything else?"

Finally he concedes, but he gives me the corniest line *ever*. One I've heard over a gazillion jillion times.

"Yeah babes, how about the winning lottery ticket number?"

I force a stilted laugh. "Oh, you're *so* funny," I say in a dry voice.

What a cornball!

He snorts loudly, like it's the funniest joke he's ever told. "Or you could put a million dollars into my bank account."

Um, now why the hell would I do that? First of all, if I had a million dollars, I wouldn't be working in this dump, listening to pervs like you.

I exhale sharply. "Well, if that's everything, sir, thank you for calling," I say and promptly disconnect the call.

Swiveling around, I find Truong still hovering by my side, and he's wearing a slight frown on his usually good-natured face.

"What's up, Truong? Why so glum?"

"I wish my mama would've named me Long Cock."

Oh brother.

The circus at work follows me back to my apartment. I saunter into the living room to find Karsynn dressed as Marie Antoinette in full regalia. "Kars, is this why you skipped work today?"

"Uh-huh. I've been busy prepping for my debut as the Queen Consort of France," she says, tittering in six-inched platforms.

"Kars, you look like an albino monkey. And those shoes are a little ridiculous. How can you even walk in them?"

"I can and I will," she says adamantly. "You know how short I am, and I refuse to live my life as a Hobbit. Anyway, c'mon! Let's storm the Bastille!" she roars, pumped up and ready to party.

I flop onto the sofa. "I'm staying in tonight."

"Don't be such a bore Maddy. What are your plans?"

"Nothing much really. Mika is coming over and he's bringing a movie."

"Well don't wait up for me." She whips out an elaborate lacy fan and begins vigorously fanning her face. "I am going to evoke another French Revolution."

I raise my eyes to the ceiling. "Kars, the French Revolution is what led to Marie Antoinette's death. Her people convicted her of treason, sent her to the guillotine and sliced off her head."

"*Mon Dieu*," she gasps in horror. "*Zut alors.*"

Knock! Knock!

"*Sacré bleu.* That must be my *Dauphin*." Swishing her train across the room, she makes her royal exit. "*Au revoir les enfants. Bisous. J'adore.* I'm here, my darling *Dauphin*," she tinkles. "Marie Antoinette *la Dauphine de France.*"

Hours later, the doorbell buzzes and I pad to the front door in my worn out bunny slippers which are collectively missing one eye, two ears and a nose. Cracking the door ajar, I catch a whiff of Mika.

I inhale his sweet, intoxicating scent. He smells of soap. Fresh, crisp and breezy . . . ocean breezy.

"C'mon in," I say with a pleasant smile.

He holds up a DVD. "I rented *3:10 to Yuma.* Hope that's okay with you. It's a western."

"Good choice!" I exclaim, as I'd much rather watch a western over a horror flick any day. "Make yourself at home; I just need to go grab some popcorn out of the microwave."

I dart to the kitchen, and in a hop and a skip, I am back in the living room. I find Mika on the sofa, messing with the controls.

The main menu is on the TV screen and he's surfing through the options, programming the receiver so the movie plays in Dolby Digital Surround mode.

Oh, he's such a man.

I ease myself onto the sofa and wedge the bag of popcorn in between us. Next, I cover our feet with a wooly afghan and settle back into the cushions.

"Okay, let's start the movie," I say eagerly.

The movie moves at a good pace, and the characters quickly captivate me. Russell Crowe plays the bad guy turned good guy, and like most Westerns, this movie is all about the measure of a man. How far will he go to fight for justice?

Two hours later, the movie ends and the credits roll. I sneak a peek at Mika and suspend belief for a moment. I imagine the two of us in a dry and dusty desert in some old mid-western town. Somewhere in the distance, I hear the familiar whistling tune that's played in all the old spaghetti westerns. The sound effect blared right before a showdown— Nah Nah Nah Naaaaaaaaaah NEOW NEOW NEOW.

Or is it Woo Woo Woo Wooooooooo WEOW WEOW WEOW?

Anyway, you catch my drift.

"There's a new sheriff back in town," I drawl sassily, like I'm the seasoned gunslinger and Mika is the young punk stirring up trouble in my jurisdiction.

Our eyes lock.

There is a minute of silence as we stare each other down.

Our hands hover anxiously by our sides, ready to draw.

I don't blink and neither does he.

Then all of a sudden, the scene turns Bollywood.

Consumed with raw passion, we throw down our weapons and run to each other. In slow motion.

Our bodies collide and we lock ourselves in a steamy embrace. Our lips mesh in a scalding kiss.

Abruptly, I'm jolted out of my Western-turned-Bollywood flick when I hear Mika ask, "Did you like the movie?"

"Yeah, it was pretty good. Although, I miss watching comedies and *not* hearing you laugh."

He chuckles, and of course, no sound is emitted. After a long minute, he says, "So . . ."

"So . . ." I nervously adjust myself on the sofa. Our toes lightly brush and we immediately jolt apart.

His eyes crinkle at the corners. "Your toes feel like icicles."

"And yours feel like hot coals," I say with a silly grin.

We enjoy a brief and playful banter. "Would you like me to warm up your toes?" he asks.

I tilt my brow. "Would you *really* want to warm up my toes?"

"I'd love nothing else," he says evenly.

My toes curl up in anticipation.

Seconds later, I feel his toes rubbing against mine, creating friction and instant warmth.

"Better now?"

I nod and tuck my feet under me.

Mika crosses the room and ejects the DVD from the player.

I play for time. "So what are your plans now?"

"Call of Duty: Black Ops awaits me." He straightens himself and flexes his arms like Chuck Norris.

"You're in the marine corps reserve?"

He laughs. "No. It's a Xbox game. And what about you?"

"Oh, I'm staying in." I stretch out my arms and legs. "I've got to book my ticket before the prices go up."

"Book what ticket?"

"My plane ticket. I'm going home for Thanksgiving." After a thoughtful pause, I ask, "Do you have any Thanksgiving plans?"

"I plan to be holed up in my dorm room since mostly everything will be closed. But the campus cafeteria will be open and they serve some pretty good turkey."

"What?" I gawp. "Cafeteria food is like cat food. You need to have a *real* Thanksgiving meal."

He shrugs like it's no big deal.

"Hey, why don't you come home with me? It'll be fun and I can show you around Chicago."

To my surprise, Mika concedes without a fight. "Okay. Don't you remember? I'd promised you I would."

"Yes, you did. At the pizzeria. Great! It's a done deal then!"

He smiles an endearing smile. "When do we leave?"

"In about three and a half weeks." I hop off the sofa and fire up my laptop. "C'mon Mika, let's book our tickets.

Twenty Four

"You grew up here? This place is incredible!" Mika's awestruck eyes sweep the interior space of my home.

Leaning against the kitchen counter, I shrug. "Sort of a cross between Frank Lloyd Wright and Jeff Lewis, don't you think?"

He continues exploring the floor plan. "This place is *huge*; you didn't tell me you lived in a five star resort."

My gaze travels across the open and spacious room. "I guess you could say it's *capacious*," I say facetiously.

Meanwhile, Mika is conducting his own tour, his eyes keen and intense as he wanders around.

I find myself rifling through the stack of mail on the kitchen counter. A student loan statement, a student loan statement, another student loan statement.

Minutes later, Mika asks, "Can I check out the patio area?"

"Sure." I set aside my student loan statements. "I'll join you."

Mika slides the glass door and we step out.

"I like this." He grips the steel railing. "I like how this entire deck is wrapped around that giant oak tree."

"Yeah, my dad was all about sharing his living space with nature. He was a tree hugger . . . like you are."

"Tree humper, polar bear lover, forest freak, Eco Nazi." He gives a short shrug. "I've heard worse."

"No, I said tree *hugger*, not humper." I laugh, gesturing to his Earth Day T-shirt.

He glances down at his shirt and smiles. "Yep. We're all in this together. We must take steps to conserve energy and reduce our carbon footprint," he lectures in a comical tone.

"*Okay*." I elbow him playfully.

Mika can be such a colossal dork at times, but I find it so endearing.

For a little while, we rest our elbows on the railing and gaze out into the distance.

"See that hill over there? Me and my dad used to belly-slam our sleds down that hill."

He shoots me a sidelong glance. "I wish I could've met him."

I return his gaze and smile wistfully. "Me too."

Mika and my dad would have surely hit it off. My mom is not even here to welcome me home. To welcome *us* home.

I pull my cardigan tightly around me. "Let's go inside, Mika. I can show you your room." I usher him indoors, away from the ominous winds.

While Mika disappears to gather his things, I cross the living room and head for the kitchen. I'm about to grab a drink out of the fridge when a yellow Post-it note catches my eye.

I peel the note off the fridge.

Hi honey,

Sorry I couldn't be there. I'm at work, not sure when I'll be home tonight. See you tomorrow?

Love, mom

I breathe out a heavy sigh. Just like old times. Crumpling the note in one hand, I hurl it into the trash.

Seconds later, Mika finds me in the kitchen. "Lead the way," he says, lugging a clunky Samsonite suitcase.

Since we're only visiting for a couple days, I had packed light. And the fact that Mika had packed an entire suitcase somewhat baffles me. "What have you got in your suitcase? A dead body?" I raise a delicate brow.

"Something like that," he says in all seriousness.

It takes us approximately five minutes to trek to the far end of the east wing, and Mika makes some smart comment about me living in a manor, calling it Maddy's Manor.

"Here's the guestroom," I announce airily.

At one time, this used to be my playroom. And true to the design of Frank Lloyd Wright, colossal stained glass windows dominate the space, sending shards of rainbows across the room.

While my dad had tried his best to mimic the style and design of the famed architect, the result isn't always comfortable, nor is it practical. I immediately feel a draft in the room.

"There's some thick quilts in there if you get cold." I gesture toward a wooden chest.

He nods, depositing his suitcase at the foot of the bed.

"Make yourself at home. Grab whatever you want from the fridge; my mom's stocked it up. I'll go hop in the shower now and then we can grab a bite to eat."

"Sounds good. Will your mom be joining us?"

"Nope," I say with a slight frown. "Not tonight, anyway. She's at work, but she'll be here for our Thanksgiving feast tomorrow."

He shrugs off his jacket. "I'd like to take a shower, too. Not with you, I mean," he quickly adds. He winks playfully. "But if you want to save water and conserve energy, we could always shower together. We'd only be helping out Mother Nature."

I release a nervous laugh. "Um, as you can see, you've got a bathroom in here and the towels are in the closet to your right."

He undresses and starts shirtless for the bathroom.

Eyeing his half naked body, I clear my throat. "I'll leave you to it, then."

I bound athletically up the stairs two at a time, fly into my bathroom, fling off all my clothes and step into a scalding hot shower. I'm lathering soap all over my body when my mind elicits erotic images of Mika in *his* shower.

Unwittingly, I envisage hot water sluicing over his shoulders, coursing past his washboard abs, dripping down his muscular legs . . . drops of water glistening and clinging to the tuft of fuzz between his—Eeps! An image of an elephant trunk pops into my head.

Shaking off that disturbing image, I step out of the shower.

As I'm toweling myself dry, I smirk at the thought that while my body feels squeaky clean, my mind is filthier than ever.

Emerging from the steamy bathroom, I hastily throw on my usual attire. Next, I rummage through my closet and drag out my reliable North Face parka, the one that makes me look like a grotesquely engorged Michelin Man.

Waddling down the stairs, I find Mika looking resplendent in a suit.

A very Gucci looking suit.

A light bulb goes off in my head. "Oh! That's why you packed such an enormous suitcase!"

"Hey, a wrinkled suit is a fashion faux pas."

Much to my chagrin, when Mika takes note of my attire, he chides, "Maddy, go change!"

I dither on the stairs. "What's wrong with what I'm wearing?"

"I'm taking you to a fancy restaurant."

"Why?"

"Why not?" he retorts.

"Um, okay," I hesitate. "I guess I'll go up and change then."

He shoots me a winsome smile.

Decisions, decisions. What to wear? After much deliberation, I finally settle on a Tracy Reese dress. The chic bodice is a throwback to the Chanel classics, and the Oscar de la Renta-ish skirt is detailed with intricate embroidery.

I feel very 'old Hollywood' glam in this pretty frock.

Next, for my makeup, I opt for the *au naturale* look. I want my skin to appear dewy and luminous. But creating the natural look is no easy feat. In fact, it is a laudable triumph of great difficulty. It takes loads and loads and *loads* of makeup to achieve *ze au naturale* look. As I'm caking on my fourth coat of foundation, I check the time.

Oh, snap! Mika has been waiting downstairs for almost half an hour. Time to switch things into high gear.

I inspect my appearance in the mirror. My lips look understated with my nude lip gloss.

But tonight, I feel bold.

I glide on some killer red lipstick and fluff up my hair. After slipping on a pair of dark sheer tights, I hop over to the shoe rack and wriggle my feet into my Miss L Fire blood red Hedy heels.

It's sex on heels, adding a touch of *vavavoom* to my outfit.

Okay, now I'm ready.

Strutting down the stairs, I unfurl with the power of a femme fatale. The right dress and shoes can make any woman feel like a million bucks. I bet if Hillary Clinton ditched the pantsuits and donned a pretty frock from time to time, she'd be a less grouchy Secretary of State. And with a different attitude, perhaps she could broker a peace agreement in the Mideast between Israel and Palestine.

Mika is standing in the foyer with both hands in his pockets.

As I gracefully descend the stairs, his eyes rake me from head to toe, traveling slowly and deliberately, almost sensually.

Straightening himself, he shoots me an appreciative smile.

"You look gorgeous," he says in a thick voice.

I gaze at him from half lowered eyelids. "Thanks, so do you."

"I've made reservations at Bri," he says with aplomb. "And I've called a cab; it's waiting outside."

Gallantly, Mika helps me into my coat and whisks me out the front door.

Our cabbie is a rather jovial Indian man named Vijay Singh. Driving at breakneck speed, Vijay strikes up a conversation about the sour economy. "This recession is terrible. My daughter, Gita, graduated from college months ago and she's still jobless."

"What did she major in?" I ask politely.

"Philosophy," says Vijay, swerving in and out of traffic.

Well no wonder, I think to myself. That has got to be the most pointless degree ever. All you can ever do with a degree like that is teach philosophy or philosophize, asking yourself mindless questions like, "If an ambulance is on its way to save someone and runs someone else over, should it stop to help that person?"

A good friend of mine, Descartes, has a PhD in philosophy. He was a pothead, *still is*, and he now works at Blockbuster.

But then again, who am I to even talk? What good did my journalism degree do? I'm stuck in a frickin' call center.

"I myself have a master's degree from Delhi University," says Vijay and slams on the brakes, just barley avoiding a head-on collision.

We lurch sickeningly forward and then flop backward like a pair of rag dolls. "That's cool. How long have you been driving a cab?" Mika asks, gripping the sides.

"For far too long." Vijay chortles. "When I'd started driving a cab eight years ago, I told myself it's nothing permanent. Short term only! But then the years start to pass." He stops and pounds his fist on the horn. "And now with the economy going down the drain like this, I'm just thankful I can put food on the table."

Staring numbly at the bright lights whizzing by outside, I grimly reflect upon my own predicament. I certainly don't want to end up working at that call center forever. Already, I've been feeling considerably burnt out. Over the past few weeks, the call volume spiked and I was forced back on the phones again.

This Thanksgiving break is a much needed one. I was coiled so tightly that I was about ready to snap. But at the same time, I feel the same way Vijay does, grateful that I at least *have* a job.

"Vijay, if you ever want to make a career change, come out to Pocatello," I offer. "You can get a job at a call center."

He glances at the rearview mirror. "Actually madam, being a cab driver is not so bad after all. I enjoy working all by myself."

For a brief moment, I consider what it must be like to be a cabbie. How liberating! I wouldn't have to talk to customers all day long. Vijay is chatting with us on his own accord. It's his prerogative if or not he wants to talk. And if I was at the wheel, it'd be *my* prerogative if I'd want to talk or not. Plus, driving always has such a calming effect on me.

Mika seems to have a keen sense of knowing what's brewing about in my head. "You could *not* be a cab driver."

"Why not?" I huff.

"I've seen the way you drive, weaving in and out, cutting other cars by an inch, flying over speed bumps. When you're at the wheel, I'm constantly pressing the phantom brake pedal."

"Actually," Vijay chimes in, "she'd make an excellent cabbie."

"See!" I smother a triumphant grin.

Traffic slows to a crawl, but Vijay is undeterred. He zips in and out of traffic, swerves around corners, jumps over curbs and drives down sidewalks. Minutes later, he violently swings the cab onto the side of the road.

"Here we are at Bri!" He flashes a toothy grin. "Very popular among the locals. And by the way, you two look like a *beau-ti-ful* couple. Enjoy your evening," he says regally.

"Thanks, Vijay. It was so nice to meet you," I say, inching across the back seat.

For some odd reason, I don't correct Vijay about us being a 'couple.'

And neither does Mika, I observe.

Mika pays the fare and I notice him slipping Vijay a hefty tip.

Chalk another point for Mika. I'm so glad he's not a tightwad and a cheapskate.

Sauntering into Bri, I realize that Mika is anything *but* cheap.

My goodness! This place is going to break his Belgian bank account.

My bug eyes sweep across the golden gilded room and I find myself mesmerized by its opulence and grandeur. It's splendidly baroque and ornately orchestrated. Crystal chandeliers drip from the ceilings, tufted chairs are tucked into alcoves, a roaring fire glimmers and glows in the score of reflections in the room.

Inclining my head toward Mika, I whisper, "I didn't know we were attending the Tsar Ball at Catherine Palace."

He places his hand on the small of my back. "I couldn't afford the plane ticket to Saint Petersburg, so this will have to suffice."

Within minutes, we're seated by a burlesque-y hostess who bears a striking resemblance to Dita Von Teese.

I stare after Dita as she sashays off. Leaning forward, I ask in a hushed voice, "Mika, do you think she's hot?"

"I think you're hot," he says without missing a beat.

I scoff at his deflection. "You didn't answer my question."

Smiling, he shakes his head and consults the menu.

I do the same.

Seconds later, he pops his head over the tall menu. "Shall we go for the tasting menu?"

"Let's go for it," I say robustly.

As if on cue, two posh waiters materialize at our table and introduce themselves as Juan and Steve.

Juan takes our orders and nods approvingly. "Our chefs only use the freshest, local ingredients."

Steve concurs with his team mate. "Yesssss. And all the food prepared here is organic *and* sustainable."

My eyes shimmer. "Sustainable? How splendid!"

At first the trend was organic food, and now a new one has snuck up on me—*Sustainable!*

And I'm a complete sucker for it all. Trust Mika, being an eco-friendly guy, to pick a green restaurant.

After our orders are placed, Juan and Steve magically fade into the wallpaper. Leaning back against my plush chair, I gaze at the Jackson Pollock-like artworks that line the walls.

Bach's *Brandenburg Concerto Number 2 in F major* is playing softly in the background, set in perfect harmony to the romantic and whimsical ambiance.

Wait a minute.

Or is this *Concerto Number 3 in G major?*

I perk my ears up, straining to listen. But I can no longer tell.

To my absolute horror, I discover that I am tone deaf.

Egad! My ears have been ravaged by that call center! Eight years of piano lessons all washed down the drain!

Mika watches me closely, and I can tell by the look on his face that he's slightly alarmed by my state of distress. He clears his throat. "So, what do you think of this place?"

"What'd you say?" I rub my damaged ears, and soothe myself with the thought that although Beethoven was tone deaf, he was one of the greatest pianists of all time.

"What do you think of this place?" he repeats.

Basking in the candlelight, I gush, "It's magical."

Moments later, Juan and Steve appear by our sides and serve our first *entrée* simultaneously. They lift the silver lids off the platters in perfect synch, as synchronized as two dolphins at SeaWorld. Their timing is perfect and their tricks flawless.

Wow. This place is surreal, like a cross between SeaWorld and fine dining. And come to think of it, they *do* have such a thing at SeaWorld. It's called Dinner with Shamu. Only difference is, this is *fine dining* with our waiters Steve and Juan.

The first entrée is Escargots à la Bourguignonne.

"Um . . ." I stare uncertainly at the escargot that's swimming in some sort of garlic buttery sauce. "Mika, you can have mine if you want."

He spoons a snail into his mouth. "You don't like escargot?"

The look on my face says it all. "Don't you love euphemisms? If they called it snails, I bet you no one would eat it."

"I would." He takes another bite to prove his point. "You don't know what you're missing, Maddy."

"Yeah I do," I say with a faint smirk. "Sorry, Mika, but I'm pretty ghetto. I don't have a sophisticated palette like you."

"You? Ghetto? You live in an architectural dream."

"Well, my parents were well off, but they worked full time and neither of them cooked. I mainly lived on frozen pizzas, hot dogs, and mac and cheese."

"That's it?" He looks appalled. "I grew up poor, but only in the material sense of the word. My mum made a feast out of every meal. We spent lots of time discussing food, preparing food *and* consuming food."

I lean my elbows forward in fascination. "So what did you eat most of the time?"

"My mum's homemade meatballs in sweet cherry sauce," he says with a smile. "And you?"

"Hot dogs cold, right out of the fridge," I admit, slightly embarrassed.

"You speak of euphemisms, but don't you know that a hot dog is pig snout, pig liver, pig kidney, pig fat and scrap that's ground up, stuffed and squeezed into casings made of animal intestines? You'll eat *that* but you won't eat a snail," he taunts.

"Fine," I concede. "I'll try a snail." I fork the tiniest escargot, squeeze my eyes shut, and force the slimy thing down my throat.

He stares at me expectantly. "So?"

My face contorts. "The texture is a bit strange, but the garlic buttery sauce sort of makes it edible."

"Well, I'm glad you at least tried it."

The next course is Grilled Portobello Mushrooms and Alaskan King Crab Legs served with a red wine reduction.

"Now this is a humongous fungus!" I stifle a laugh.

A smile crooks his lips. "I've never understood why they call skinny, spindly crab legs King Crabs."

"I know," I concur. "They should call it Poor Man's Crab legs, or Anorexic Crabs."

Sometime later, our next dish arrives—Pan Roasted Breast of Squab over Beet Salad and Oven Dried Black Figs.

"Enjoy your street pigeon and weeds," Mika says cheekily.

"Mmmm." I crunch on a lettuce. "I love rabbit food. And as for this birdy, it's payback time for all the icky pigeon droppings."

Mika takes a bite off his rat with wings. "Sorry pigeon, this is for firing your mess all over my car."

After all that pigeon bashing, I'm suddenly consumed with guilt. "You know what? Pigeons are also symbols of peace," I say, paying tribute to my meal.

Mika matches my somber mood. "Pigeons are credited with saving thousands of soldiers' lives in World War One and Two."

"How?" I ask, nibbling on my salad greens.

"They were used to carry messages. Pigeons can fly at high speeds for miles and miles without stopping for food and water."

For a little while, we lapse into silence.

"You know what?" I say in a sage voice. "I think we *should* call this hero with wings a squab. That way I'm not reminded of the fact that I'm eating a patriotic, lifesaving pigeon."

"Okay, no more deconstructing euphemisms," Mika agrees wholeheartedly. "They're around for a reason."

Our fourth course is soon placed before us, this time it's Citrus Marinated Salmon with a Confit of Navel Oranges, topped with Sustainable Sturgeon Caviar and Pea Shoot Coulis.

Now let me start with my one caveat—I really detest caviar. But as I cautiously spoon some pearly eggs into my mouth, it pops with a flavor that's surprisingly pleasing to my palate.

The food here may *sound* pretentious, but it certainly doesn't *taste* pretentious.

We relish and savor every bite, praising and applauding the dishes along the way.

The last three courses are all desserts. And the first one up is White Chocolate Bread Pudding drizzled with Bourbon Caramel Sauce. It is to *die* for.

I breathe out a sated sigh. "Mika, you're the best! I've never had food like this before. Thanks so much for bringing me here," I say preemptively.

He beams at me. "You deserve it!"

"What did I do?" I spoon a voluptuous portion of pudding into my mouth.

"Well, you spent a lot of time tutoring me, and you helped me out with my papers."

I wave my hand dismissively. "I hardly did anything. And if you thank me for tutoring you one more time, I'll eat my own head. Actually, you have to eat a tenner."

"Well you did," he insists. "You have mad talent, Maddy. You could even earn some extra money on the side if you wrote for an essay mill."

I stare agog at the next dessert that is placed in front of us.

Juan announces, "Triple Molten Chocolate Lava Cake served with a side of hand churned chocolate ice cream."

It is literally a detonation of chocolate. And it is dynamite!

Mika smiles at me indulgently. "You can have some of mine."

"Sure," I say without hesitating, and he slides his oozing plate of chocolate my way. "You were saying?"

"Have you ever considered writing for an essay mill?"

I lick chocolate sauce off my bottom lip. "What's that?"

"You don't know?" he asks, mildly surprised and I shake my head. "It's a ghostwriting service," he explains. "College students pay big money to have these essay mills churn out their term papers."

"How much do these papers go for?"

"Well a friend of mine paid fifty bucks per page, and his paper turned out to be well over a hundred pages long."

"Whoa! That's *way* more than what some *New York Times* bestsellers are paid per page. Now have *you* ever bought a paper from one of these essay mills?"

"No," he says with conviction, and I believe him.

He continues, "I may struggle with writing but I enjoy doing the research. Anyway, that was a dumb idea. Don't sell yourself short. You shouldn't waste your talents writing for an essay mill." After a pause he adds, "You shouldn't waste it at that call center either."

The last dessert is elegantly placed in front of me: Raspberry Champagne Sorbet topped with fresh mint.

Just perfect for cleansing my palette!

"Well?" he urges. "I know how much you hate working at that call center. Why don't you explore your options elsewhere? Do something you love."

"Well," I hesitate, "I applied for a tech writing job with Ajon; they design software for medical devices."

"Really, Maddy? That's great! Have you heard back?"

I shake my head and pop a mint leaf in my mouth. "I only just applied a few days ago. Anyway, I'm not even sure if I'll take the job if I get it."

Mika reaches for his napkin and wipes his mouth with vigor.

I'm so glad he doesn't dab. I find it so prissy when men do the demure dabbing thing.

After setting his napkin on the table, he startles me with his outburst. "Are you kidding me, Maddy? If you get an offer *take* it."

"I'm still thinking about it," I say, and promptly change the subject. "Shall we get going?"

He nods and whips out his Visa. Discreetly, our waiter, Steve, swoops in, slips the leather booklet into his hand and disappears around the corner.

"Thanks again for the awesome meal!"

"You're very welcome," he says graciously. "What's next?"

"Well, it's a good thing this place is downtown. I want you to feel the spirit of this city, so I say we take on Chicago by foot."

He pokes his nonexistent belly and chuckles. "After all that eating, walking sounds good to me."

Steve returns with the bill and Mika signs the receipt.

I sneak a peek and gasp, "Mika! That is too much. You can feed everyone in Botswana with that money. Let me at least pay for half."

"No!" he protests.

"Yes!" I insist.

"No!"

"Yes!"

"No!"

"Okay," I grudgingly give in.

After settling the bill, he asks, "So where's Botswana?"

"In Africa."

"Hmmm," he muses aloud. "Is Botswana the poorest country in the world?"

"No, I think the poorest country is Zimbabwe. It has a ninety sextillion percent inflation."

"Sextillion," he echoes. "Is that like a billion trillion?"

I nod in what I hope is an intelligent manner. "I think so. I know they had one of the largest bank notes in history—the one hundred trillion dollar bill!"

He laughs. "I'd like to buy some Zimbabwean eggs. Oh sure, that'll just be one hundred billion dollars."

I giggle. "They actually got rid of the Zimbabwean dollar last year. Their government got tired of printing new money."

"Or," he points out, "they could've just run out of paper."

"True." I smile.

He smiles back. "So if Zimbabwe is the poorest country in the world, then why'd you say I could feed the whole of Botswana?"

I give a short shrug. "I just like saying Botswana. Anyway, we should get going."

Juan appears in a flash and pulls out my chair.

"Thanks, Juan," I say gregariously. "Thanks, Steve."

"Thanks for the excellent service," Mika adds heartily.

Our tuxedoed waiters stand together with their perfect postures. With a cordial nod, they execute a final bow of impeccable grace.

What a performance!

Mika and I bundle up and roll out into the crisp, clear night.

"This area is also known as the Loop," I say as we stroll down the strip.

Since Christmas is only a month away, Michigan Avenue has become a magnificent mile of lights. Christmas lights weave and entwine the trees and branches, illuminating blankets of white snow.

Macy's and Marshall Field's gargantuan window displays are dolled up with vibrant, colorful creations, unfolding the magic and splendor of the season.

We promenade side by side, absorbing everything: the throngs of people out shopping, a Salvation Army volunteer tinkling the donations bell, fantasy-like decorations that adorn every space, the jolly ol' sounds of Christmas music emanating from the retail stores, the lights, the lights and the *lights*.

It feels like the most Christmas-y moment ever, bar none.

And it's not even Christmas!

Mika says animatedly, "What a way to kick off the holidays."

I laugh joyously, imbued with the holiday spirit. "I'm so glad you came."

He links his arm through mine. "Phenomenal dinner, nice walk under the lights. We should do this more often."

"I know." I pat his arm affectionately. "We should."

But inside, I doubt that we will.

Mika will soon return to The Land of Waffles, while I'll still be stuck in The Valley of Potatoes. For now at least, I briefly close my eyes and remember this moment.

Twenty Five

The sweet, decadent aromas of Thanksgiving permeate the halls. The smell of an oven-roasted turkey dripping with gravy, fluffy mashed potatoes, freshly baked pumpkin pie, and my all-time favorite—sweet potatoes mushed up with a pound and a half of *real* butter, dusted with brown sugar, and sprinkled with pecans. It's artery clogging, calorie packing and waist expanding, but it's *so* worth it.

My mom doesn't cook, but she has a tendency to go overboard with small dinner parties. Today, she's hired two personal chefs along with an army of sous-chefs; and they're busy chopping, peeling, dicing, cooking and prepping.

Catching a buzz from their hustle and bustle, I grab a box of matches and sidle out of the jam-packed kitchen. I may as well make myself useful elsewhere. There are too many cooks in this kitchen and I don't want to spoil the broth.

Twelve rustic candles make up the centerpiece of the oblong dining table. Striking a match, I light the candles one by one and instantly feel invigorated by the scents of autumn; the smell of an Indian Summer's slow farewell.

Feeling someone's eyes upon me, I look up and catch Mika watching me with interest. I return his gaze, staring at him with a sort of insolent appreciation.

Leaning heavily against the doorframe, he's dressed casually yet impeccably in black slacks, black button-down shirt, black leather belt, and black leather shoes.

He's bringing sexy back, and I'm loving his swagger.

"You look lovely, Maddy. Nice dress."

"Thanks."

My dress is boldly embellished with a huge rosette appliqué, and it could have gone one of two ways with this dress: incredibly kooky or incredibly chic.

Methinks it errs on the latter, and I'm glad Mika seems to think so, too.

Even my T-strap heels are decorated with rosettes, and spring bouquet studs adorn my ears.

I'm a walking arboretum.

"So, what time will your relatives be here?"

"Anytime now," I hesitate. "Um, I have to warn you though, my Aunt Benedicta can be a bit snarky at times."

In Latin, Benedictus means 'blessed.' And my aunt sure is blessed. Blessed with arrogance, egotism and conceit. Some may consider those traits a curse, but not my Aunt Benedicta. She considers it a blessing from above.

"And her husband, Stuart, is the perfect match for her. He's super smarmy." And together those two are a frightful combination. "You'll see . . ." I crinkle my brows. "Even my cousin, Constance, is a constant pain in the rear."

Ding! Dong!

"By the way," I say hurriedly. "My Uncle Stuart has strabismus. Basically, he's cross-eyed. So, if you're not sure which eye to look at, just stare at his hairpiece, okay?"

"O-kay," he says tentatively.

"C'mon, Mika." I grab his arm. "Let's go meet them."

"Beatrice! So lovely to see you again," Aunt Benedicta clips in her fake British-Madonna accent.

"And you as well," tinkles my mom.

Then they swoop in and give each other the tepid two-cheek Euro air kiss. I swear sometimes, they address each other as if they were two strangers at a wedding.

Eyes sharp as needles, Aunt Benedicta spots me standing in the corner of the foyer. "Mah-dih-shon, *dah-ling*," she trills in her over the top soap opera voice.

I reach in for a hug, but she immediately halts me, causing her Tiffany bracelets to jangle up and down her sinewy, veiny arms. Then she puts up her face for an air kiss and I freeze.

Does the right side come first, or the left? Does it matter?

Like air guitar, air kisses just aren't the real deal, so I never bothered educating myself on the proper etiquette.

I wait for Aunt Benedicta to take the lead.

Grabbing my shoulders, she brushes her feathered lips on my right cheek, and then the left.

Okay, so the right side comes first. Got it.

Then her critical eyes fall on Mika. She sizes him up and down with shrewd evaluation.

I make the introductions. "Aunty Benedicta, this is my friend Mika."

"*Meeeeeee-kah*," she enunciates, contorting her mouth in an unnatural and unattractive manner.

They go *Muah, Muah* in the air like a pair of seasoned Europeans.

At least Mika is the real McCoy; my Aunt Benedicta is just a wannabe. And I can tell she's charmed. Over Mika's shoulder, she shoots me a look of surprise. One that says, "How did mousy Maddy manage to snag *this* guy?"

But then again, it could just be my overactive imagination since she *always* looks surprised. Sadly, in her attempt to freeze the aging process with endless Botox treatments and frequent facelifts, Aunty Benedicta's face looks frozen.

Not frozen in time, but in the moment.

It's in a perpetual state of no-emotions and no-expressions.

Correction. There is one expression: perpetual surprise.

Meanwhile, the air kissing debacle is far from over as Uncle Stuart and Constance make their rounds. Finally, after all that pretentious nonsense is done with, we settle ourselves in the living room.

Constance emerges from her curtain of jet black hair, and her eyes narrow at me contemptuously. From the look on her face, I can tell she's not a fan of my dress. She leans to her right and whispers something to her mom; then they look me up and down in a very impolite manner and exchange supercilious smirks.

Swallowing my annoyance, I force a smile. Then I incline my head toward Mika and whisper, "I can't stand my cousin and my aunt."

Mika's lips twist into a smile, but he adopts a neutral facade, remaining placid and polite.

I cast a disdainful eye in Constance's direction. She's dressed like a character straight out of a Tim Burton movie. Dark horn rimmed glasses adorn her shifty, rodent-like eyes, and she's got so much eyeliner caked on that she looks like a panda bear. Her makeup is a stark contrast to her pale, corpse-like skin. Everything about her is severe.

As usual, Uncle Stuart dominates the conversation and I find myself staring amusedly at his Donald Trump comb-over piece. The strawberry highlights clash with his salmon pink sweater. I'm sorry, but a grown man should *never ever* wear pink. No sane mom would ever dress her baby boy in pink, or paint his nursery pink. And any grown man who chooses to dress in pink is just plain *ridiculous* if you ask me.

As distracting as his silly hairpiece and girly attire may be, I try to tune myself in to the conversation that is swirling around me. When the economy was booming, Uncle Stuart had loved boasting about all the riches he was raking in from the stock market.

He'd fancied himself a mover and shaker, and hobnobbed with all the Wall Street head honchos and hedge fund managers. He'd also heavily invested in Madoff's ponzi scheme.

Now that the economy is tanking and Stuart has lost his high-flying job, all he ever does is whine about how much money he is losing, how his investments and 401K are dwindling to nothing.

We make all the appropriate sympathetic noises.

"Bernie Madoff has got blood on his hands," he growls.

"Um, didn't Steven Spielberg and Kevin Bacon invest with him, too?" I ask casually. It was something I had read in *US Weekly*.

Uncle Stuart shifts his anger to me. "Yes! But those are just stupid, gullible Hollywood celebrities. Let me tell you, lots of *smart* people got duped. Smart people like me!"

"I didn't say you weren't smart," I implore.

"You *implied* it," he grumbles and sulks like a two-year-old.

I roll my eyes and Uncle Stuart throws me a murderous look.

A bubble of laughter escapes my lips.

Hah! It's a good thing Uncle Stuart is cross-eyed. Although he's glaring at me, it appears as if he's glaring at Mika, who happens to be sitting next to me on the leather settee. Poor Mika has no idea why my Quasimodo Uncle is giving him the evil eye, and so he centers his full attention on Stuart's hairpiece.

I do the same.

For obvious reasons, conversation is driven to an absolute halt.

After an awkward silence, my mom clears her throat. "Let's adjourn to the dining area, shall we?"

"Let's," Aunt Benedicta concurs and struts to the dining room, flanked by her two toddlers.

A feast fit for a king is spread out before us.

My Quasimodo uncle pads heavily into the room and squashes his humongous rear into the chair next to Mika. Now if there is one thing Uncle Stuart loves, it is new company. To him, it is an opportunity to brag in their ears nonstop. And when he does not brag about himself, he brags about the next best thing—his evil daughter, a.k.a. the Devil's spawn. Just barely a minute into our meal, the brag session begins.

"Constance has just landed herself a fantastic job," he booms.

My ears instantly perk up.

Constance and I are only months apart in age, and ever since we were kids, Uncle Stuart has loved making comparisons between Constance and me. Of course, it was always in Constance's favor. Constance was always the faster swimmer, she always got better grades, and she attended the better college.

When she'd got admitted to Yale, it was all we ever heard about at every single holiday gathering. To add insult to injury, Constance also majored in Journalism, and so the comparisons have never stopped.

Uncle Stuart begins stroking Constance's hair like he's petting a prized panda bear. "Constance here is a foreign correspondent for CNN. She's following in the footsteps of Christiane Amanpour and Anderson Cooper."

From across the dining table, Constance shoots me one of her *I'm-better-than-you* smirks, preening like she's the gold medalist.

Keeping sangfroid, I treat her with taciturn indifference. On the surface, everything seems pleasant enough.

But I hate her.

And I wish she'd wipe that pompous smirk off her panda face.

Foreign correspondent, eh? Well I hope CNN deploys her to Afghanistan, or Syria, or Yemen.

"And what is it that *you* do Madison?" Uncle Stuart sneers.

I level my gaze with his. "I work at a call center."

"What a shame," clucks Aunty Benedicta, in a voice dripping with false empathy.

Uncle Stuart snarls in an accusatory tone, "Oh! So you're one of *those* people, aren't you?"

Slowly, I set my silverware down on the table. "And what do you mean by that?"

"You know, customer-*no*-service," he says patronizingly. Then he emits his signature scratchy laugh, reminiscent of the noise a dog makes right before it pukes.

After collecting himself, he shoots me a smarmy smile and adds, "No offense, kiddo."

I know exactly what he's trying to do. He's been doing this to me my whole life—trying to make me feel inadequate.

Constance laughs a mirthless laugh and my mom's eyebrows crease with concern when she catches the determined glint in my eye. Resentment and indignation boil inside me, and I have to consciously bite my tongue to repress the remarks I feel bubbling to the surface. But as tradition requires, a lady never speaks with her mouth full. And so, I patiently bide my time.

Crunching on my romaine lettuce, I allow myself to enjoy the tartness of the cranberries and the crispness of the leafy greens while I reflect upon the rampant stigma associated with my job.

I wasn't born yesterday. I'm fully aware that most people harbor a deep contempt and hatred toward customer service reps. But now that I'm on the other side of the invisible phone line, I understand. The pressure and stress that management puts on me to sell *and* keep my calls short, callers who yell at me because their world will end if their DSL service is down for ten seconds.

It often feels as if I'm being crushed and compressed from all sides. It takes a *helluva lot* to keep my composure, yet I always do my best. I am courteous, respectful and go above and beyond to be helpful, as long as the callers don't make it obvious that they wish for me to die a slow and painful death.

There is bad customer service but there is also *good* customer service, and I have always prided myself on the latter. And with Uncle Stuart's unprovoked attack, I feel marginalized, ostracized and victimized. Like I'm pushed against a wall.

I find myself in a situation where it's me versus them. A customer service rep versus the haters.

Oh, I know. I can be a bit dramatic and childish at times, but he started it! Plus, I feel this perverse need to defend myself, to defend the honor of customer service reps all around the world—in the States, in India, the Philippines, Botswana, Bolivia, Brazil, Malaysia, Russia, the Czech Republic.

I can't let him get away with talking smack about *my* people.

As the Lord had said to Moses and in the great words of Martin Luther King, "Let My People Go!"

Meanwhile, the tension at the table continues to crackle and mount. Projecting an image of unflappable calm, I raise my chin at my Quasimodo uncle. Acting like a true lady in the face of adversity, I say eloquently, "And you, Uncle Stuart, are one of *those* customers. And by that I mean brainless, idiotic, fart-brained fools who call in asking for help, yet think they know *everything*."

Uncle Stuart is incandescent with rage. "How dare you—"

Mika cuts in, "If I may, Stuart?"

"What?" hisses Quasimodo.

Mika gives him a steady look. "Are you currently employed?"

"No!" he snaps. "I was laid off nine months ago and—"

Mika boldly interrupts, "And are you collecting unemployment?"

Something inaudible sputters out of Uncle Stuart's mouth, which I take to mean a "Yes."

Mika says in a measured voice, "Well Maddy and I have jobs and we're not a burden on society." He shrugs and continues, "No one wants to work at a call center. But some of us just wind up working there, and we try to make the best of it, and Maddy here surely has. She's one of the nicest and brightest reps, and our callers love her." He darts me a warm look and announces with great pride, "You may or may not know this, but Maddy recently got promoted."

Uncle Stuart sneers scornfully, "Who the hell cares? I'd rather be unemployed for the rest of my life than work in a blasted call center. It is just *beneath* me."

Mika clears his throat, then continues in a tone that is authoritative and borderline sexy, "Look, Stuart, I'm really sorry that you lost your job, but when you hit a rough patch, you can either choose to be humiliated, or you can choose to learn humility. Perhaps working at a call center would do you some good. You could use a little humility."

Suddenly, my mom begins flapping and thrashing about in her chair. "Ackh, Kak, Kakh!"

I leap to my feet. "Mom, are you okay?"

"Achk! Kakh!" she hacks and sputters.

A gasp falls across the table as she continues choking to death, right before our very eyes.

At once, I clap her hard on her back and a cranberry comes flying out of her mouth. It ricochets across the table, clunks onto the white china and spins like a dreidel.

Everyone stops and stares.

A lowly cranberry has never looked so mesmerizing.

"I-I'm fine," my mom stammers and drains her glass of wine.

It pretty much goes downhill from there.

No one says a word for the rest of the meal; but there are plenty of pinched eyes, pained expressions and tightened lips.

And I *know* Aunt Benedicta is simply livid with me after my terse exchange with her Quasimodo husband. But try as she may to make a scowling Medusa face, she just looks *surprised.*

Constance has her usual hateful smirk pasted on her panda bear face and Uncle Stuart's Kim Chee expression remains unchanged. He is back to being a pickled cabbage, sulking with his pudgy arms crossed over his barrel chest, glaring at me with his crazy eyes.

How cute! My cross-eyed and cross-armed uncle.

Now all he needs to do is cross his legs and *Voilà!* He'd have the whole look complete.

I blow out an explosive sigh and catch Mika's eye.

He smiles broadly. Holding my gaze, he shoots me a look that says, "You *go* girl!"

I smile back at my comrade. "Mika, could you please pass me the gravy?"

"Of course," he says evenly.

As I reach for the gravy dish, our fingers lightly graze. We exchange a lingering look, one that seems loaded with potential meaning. And for the rest of the meal, his eyes never leave mine. Sparks seem to be shooting in all directions, and I am no longer aware of my Quasi relatives. I am no longer aware of anyone but the two of us.

Half an hour later, I'm standing on the front lawn, watching Aunt Benedicta and her crazy clan drive off into the stark night.

Mom takes me by surprise when she says, "Sorry, honey, I'm taking off as well. I'll see you tomorrow, 'k love?"

I blink. "Tomorrow?"

"Yes, Kirk works in the ER and his shift ends at midnight."

"Kirk? Mom, what happened to Vincent?"

"Oh, you were right," she says with a tinkling laugh. "I am *never* dating an Ob-Gyn again."

I stare after her open-mouthed as she slides into her Audi.

"See you kids tomorrow," she hollers out the window. Then she toots the horn twice and zooms off.

Mika elbows me playfully. "Well, that wasn't so bad, was it?"

"I guess it could've been a lot worse." I sigh. "And by the way, thanks for standing up to Quasimodo. That took some *kahunas*."

He shakes his head in polite disbelief. "Stuart sure is an interesting guy." After a stretch of silence, he says, "So, what do you want to do now?"

Laughing somewhat deliriously, I manage, "Are you kidding me? After all *that* drama, I want to do nothing."

"We can do nothing." He clears his throat. "We're all alone now in this big, empty house."

"Want to go hang out in my room?" I hear myself saying.

Our eyes lock and I smile at him with the timeless mystery of a Venetian courtesan. A *cortigiana onesta*. At least that's what I'm going for. For all I know, I probably exude the persona of a pariah dog in heat.

A faint smile passes over his face. "Sure," he acquiesces.

I'm lying on my bed, pushed up on one elbow, watching Mika flip through my high school yearbook. My yearbook is scribbled with soppy sayings like: *May your life be arithmetic. Joys added, Sorrows subtracted, Friends multiplied, Love undivided.*

And I distinctly recall the naughty line that Garrett Jennsen had penned in. Garrett is now a professional skateboarder, and I had the biggest crush on him my senior year. This is what he scrawled between the cracks of my yearbook, now riddled with a thousand creases: *Cows moo, ducks quack, but I am the first to sign your crack.*

Mika jerks his head up. "Who's Garrett Jensen?" he asks in a sort of proprietorial tone.

"No one special," I say simply.

"Humph," he grunts and flips the page.

I find myself cringing when he finds my picture.

Oh God. I look like the chief of the Nerd Herd.

Like most high school yearbooks, there's a designated spot for departing seniors to endow underclassmen with random nuggets of wisdom.

Mika reads the caption beneath my picture, "High school is like a lollipop; it sucks until it is gone."

Smiling knowingly, he leafs through the pages. He stops when he arrives at the 'Most Likely To' page. I bury my head in my pillow. *Oh no.* He's about to come across my embarrassing nomination. Peeking through my fingers, I quietly observe him.

His eyes skim the page, and they suddenly light up. He reads my blurb out loud, "Madison Lee, a.k.a. Word Girl— Most likely to be published." A slow grin breaks over his face. "You were Word Girl?"

I burn with shame. "I know, doesn't that spell *geek* all over? I'll never live that one down."

"I think it's cute," he says. "Okay, Word Girl, I have a question for you."

I sit up straight. "Shoot."

"Who *versus* whom? I'm never sure which word to use."

I twist my lips. "Well, that's a bit of a tricky one, since they're both pronouns, but—"

"Well is it *who* do you love or *whom* do you love?"

"The Rolling Stones actually got it wrong," I inform him. "This may come as a surprise, but it's *whom* do you love."

He sidles closer until we're just inches apart. Gazing into my eyes, he draws an imaginary line over my nose, traces my lips and looks at me as though memorizing my every feature. Touching his forehead to mine, he says in a low and intimate voice, "*You.*"

You . . . just one simple word, yet the tenderness in his voice is so overwhelming that I'm moved by his utter conviction.

Before I can react, he threads his fingers through my hair and pulls me into a warm and sensuous kiss.

Mmmm. Mika is such a good kisser. His lips are soft yet firm, and he varies the intensity and pressure . . . hungrily then gently, passionately then sweetly.

Somehow, some way, we manage to grope our way across my bed and slide under the cold sheets. He dips his head and seeks my lips, but I find myself yawning appallingly—long, drawn out yawns. Gosh. This is so embarrassing. As widespread lore has it, something in turkey induces sleepiness, and thanks to the hefty portions of bird I'd gobbled up at dinner, my eyelids feel so heavy . . .

Exhaustion washes over and claims me.

I'm in the midst of another heavy yawn when Mika smiles and strokes my hair. "It's okay . . . let's just rest," he says lovingly and drops a kiss on my forehead.

Lazily, I rest in the crook of his arm, snuggled under his chin. And for a long while I do not move, reveling in the joy of being close to him.

While the weather outside is soupy, we lie in my twin-sized bed, our arms and limbs entwined. I listen to his deep and even breathing, feeling incredibly sated and content. Drowsy with love and drowsy with food, I succumb to a deep and delicious sleep.

Twenty Six

"*It's furr-reeeeeeezing,*" I mutter under my frosty breath as the wind slams into my face. I can hardly breathe.

It's so cold that my eyes are watering and my nose is running like a leaky faucet. Another gust of wind whips into my face and my tears and snot freeze into icicles.

Winters here are notorious for being harsh. I *hate* the cold.

I'd take a summer scorcher over any wintery day.

This is Hell on earth! In *Dante's Inferno*, the innermost circle of Hell is portrayed as a frozen lake of blood and guilt.

And Dante Alighieri is right! I truly believe that Heaven is a warm place and Hell is butt ass cold.

Despite living in Illinois for most of my life, I still *cannot* take the cold here. All winter long, I fuss and complain about how cold and miserable it is. And today is one of those days.

Today is my *Dante's Inferno*.

"This is bone chilling *furr-reeze*." My teeth chatter incessantly as we plow through the tundra.

My scarf is dancing hysterically in the wind. Leaves, litter and debris are twisting and turning violently. In the near distance, I can hear the incessant snapping of flags, thrashing wildly in the storm.

Oh, how I long to be home right now. This was rather unexpected; the weatherman had forecasted a calm, twenty-degree winter day. This just proves that weathermen are as useless to me as a freezer in Antarctica. Their accuracy is almost 90% wrong.

We were hit by a freakish snowstorm as soon as we'd arrived at the Navy Pier. Seriously, we could not have picked a worse day to venture out on our first official date as a couple.

Yes, we are a couple! The cat and mouse game is finally over.

Since we're on my home turf, I'd wanted to show Mika some of Chi-town's popular attractions. The Navy Pier turns itself into a Winter Wonder Fest during the holiday season, and I thought it would be fun. It's Chicago's playground on Lake Michigan and boasts of good entertainment, an array of restaurants, and a fifteen story Ferris wheel that's open year round.

I had it all planned out in my head. First, we were going to grab a bite to eat at the famous Billy Goat Tavern, immortalized in the SNL skit where a short order cook, played by John Belushi, yelled out, "Cheezborger! Cheezborger! Cheezborger! No fries—chips! No Pepsi—Coke!" That skit is classic. And even if you didn't care for the whole Cheezborger shtick, the Billy Goat Tavern is still something to be experienced. There's nothing like a divey vintage diner that's full of history and lore.

So much for that.

The Billy Goat Tavern's parking lot was full, forcing us to park miles away. Big, BIG mistake. In this hellish snowstorm, neither man nor goat could ever make it there alive.

Secondly, I had envisioned the two of us strolling idyllically hand in hand, ice skating on the rink, going for romantic rides, kissing on the Ferris wheel.

So much for that. The Ferris wheel is closed.

Apparently, they're open year round, *weather permitting.*

"It's cold enough to freeze the balls off a brass monkey," Mika yells over the howling wind.

I nod, as I can no longer speak. My purple lips are frozen shut. *Brrrr.* I don't know about brass monkeys, but it sure feels like we're in that documentary film *The March of the Penguins.*

Mika and I huddle close together like Emperor penguins, marching against the brutal wind.

We are one against the force of nature.

This feels like the harshest place on earth and I am seriously questioning my ability to survive in this inhospitable terrain.

Out of nowhere, a hurricane-like wind swooshes in and pummels me into a tree. I anchor myself to it for dear life and shoot Mika a tortured look.

I can tell by the look on his face that he's suppressing an urge to laugh. Reaching for my hand, he firmly secures it and we break into a run, darting to the nearest safe haven, a place of impregnable safety—Starbucks.

At the register, I order a pumpkin spice latte and a blueberry scone; Mika opts for a Christmas blend latte and a chocolate cream cheese muffin.

We carry our treats to a dimly lit nook and begin defrosting.

I sip my latte, enjoying the feel of the creamy liquid trickling down my throat. *Ahhh*, it's like fuel for my body.

Mika pinches part of my scone, and I steal little chunks of his chocolate muffin. I love the intimacy of sharing food.

I rest my elbows on the table. "How's my scone?"

"Very buttery, but I like it. And how's my muffin?"

I pinch another bite. "Very chocolaty, but I love it."

We share an easygoing banter, and I finally find the guts to broach the topic that's been at the forefront of mind. There's no easy way to say it, so I just blurt it out, "Mika, how come it took you so long to make your move on me?"

After a pensive pause, he says, "Two reasons. One: I've always felt that the best relationships start out as great friendships." Holding my gaze, he continues, "We were good friends." He stops and smiles. "We *are* good friends, and I'd thought dating too soon might change things."

I take a long sip of my latte. "So things have changed now. Is that bad?"

"No," he says at once. "But we're starting out on something more substantial. I've gotten to know you so much better now, and I love everything about you, flaws and all."

"Flaws?" I sit up straighter. "What kind of flaws?" I release a nervous laugh and brace myself.

"Well, you'd lose your head if it wasn't screwed on tight."

I fling a napkin at him playfully.

"It's true," he says, not trying very hard to disguise the fact that he is laughing. "You have these big, beautiful doe-like eyes. But babes, I'm afraid they're just there for decoration only. You can't see jack."

I kick him under the table. "I can see!"

Unperturbed, my Shakespeare goes on professing, "I love how you're firm and fragile, lovely and unapologetic."

A warm glow envelops me. Mmm. I'm starting to like this.

"And I've been enchanted by your cute, sweet and shy persona since day one."

Smiling, I take a healthy swallow of lukewarm latte. "What else?" I ask, fishing for more compliments.

"And my petal." He reaches out and strokes my cheek. "You may look like a delicate flower, but you're as feisty as an old Ukrainian wife."

I splutter coffee into my cup.

"An old Ukrainian wife?" I demand huffily.

He chortles. "They're a force to be reckoned with. Haven't you heard the joke about the old Ukrainian wife?"

"Nope," I reply stonily.

He launches right into it, "An old Ukrainian man lies dying in his bed. Then suddenly, he sniffs the sweet aroma of pierogi and—"

"Wait," I cut in. "Do you like pierogi?"

"Nah. I'm not really a fan of boiled dumplings."

"Okay. Continue," I say with a flick of my wrist.

Mika's voice is animated as he regales the story of The Old Ukrainian Wife. "And even though the old man is near death's door, he musters all his remaining strength and crawls into the kitchen. There, he is beyond ecstatic to find three hundred of his favorite pierogi, spread out on the kitchen counter. It's a feast for his eyes. He thinks to himself that either he's died and gone to heaven, or this is one final act of love from his loyal wife of sixty years, ensuring that he leaves this earth a happy man. The frail, old man gathers all his remaining strength and flings himself at the kitchen counter. With trembling hands, he reaches for a pierogi. He's about to shove it into his drooling mouth, when all of a sudden KABAAAAM!"

I jerk my head. "What happened?"

"His wife smacks him with a wooden spoon and yells '*Piss off! Those are for the funeral.*' "

I burst into a spasm giggles. "Mika, if you were a dying man, I'd let you stuff your face with Belgian trippe sausages."

"Now that's one more thing I love about you—you remember things about me. And about others. You're thoughtful and kind, fiercely loyal . . . especially to Kars."

"Um, you said you love my flaws." I cough lightly. "What other flaws do I have?"

"None." His voice is colored with amusement.

"You sure? If there's anything else, I'd like to know."

"I'm sure." He gazes into my eyes and smiles. "I find everything about you endearing."

Since Mika is declaring his love for me, it seems only fair I reciprocate. "You know what I love most about you?"

His eyes crinkle at the corners. "What?"

"I love that you have the patience of a Dalai Lama."

He chuckles and shakes his head. "Maddy, I'd rather *not* be compared to a monk."

"And, I adore how when you laugh, no sound is emitted."

At that, he laughs and of course, it is silent.

"And has anyone ever told you that you look like Zac Levi and Zac Efron?"

He draws a blank. "Who's Zac Efron? And who's Zac Levi?"

I stare at him as if he'd just returned from Jupiter and Mars.

"Wait!" I exclaim. "Back to you and me. You said there were two reasons. What's reason number two?"

"Well, you had made it clear from the get-go that dating someone at the workplace was a bad idea. And the more I'd thought about it, you were right."

I blink. "But we're still working at the same place."

He sets down his cup. "Not anymore."

"What?" I gawp. "You quit?!?"

"I gave my two weeks' notice before we left. I've got a new job, Maddy. An engineering gig with Greenworth."

I can hear the exuberance and the passion in his voice as he goes on to tell me all about his new job. He continues, "And they'll even pay for my tuition if I want to go to grad school, which I surely plan on doing."

I stare at him, slightly alarmed. "You're leaving us?"

He cups my chin lightly. "Hey, we'll still be together, and from what it sounds like, you may be getting your own gig as well."

"Don't get me wrong, I'm happy for you. But it just seems like everything's moving so quickly. And I just feel sorta . . ." I struggle for the word, "scared?" I feel myself tense, slightly apprehensive about the future. "What if I get that job with Ajon and I turn out to be crap at it? I mean, compared to other seasoned tech writers, I'm probably not very good . . . maybe I should just stay where I am."

"Maddy, please don't get sucked into that black hole. Archie has worked in that call center for more than thirty years, back when Lightning Speed was just a phone company. Can you even imagine that? It may be something Arch enjoys, but I know *you*, Madison . . . you're like a wildflower. Actually, you're like a chrysalis trapped in the call center cocoon."

A smile tugs at my lips. "What's with all the flower and critter metaphors?"

"I've been reading Wordsworth," he says with a crisp nod and I shoot him a look that says, "Get real."

"I have," he insists. "But not by choice; I had to read it for a class." After a beat, he adds, "I even wrote a little poem about you."

"You have? Read it to me!" I order.

He smiles at me sheepishly and squeezes my hand. "Okay, but promise me you won't laugh."

I lie, "I promise."

He releases my hand and reaches in his pocket. I watch him dredge out a crumpled piece of paper. "It's a work in progress."

"Go on." I smile encouragingly.

After smoothing out the creases, he clears his throat. "It goes something like this . . .

When came the break of dawn,
Came to birth a delicate fawn,
She climbed up the hill so high,
But then heaved a sad, sad sigh,
For on the lake she saw swans,
And said to herself, 'I am only a fawn,
Oh, how I wish to be a swan.'

But she had grace and beauty so serene,
She had strength, agility and could run with the wind,
And the fawn soon grew into a majestic reindeer,
Sharp, witty and still so demure,
But she did not know, she would not believe,

That she could do anything her heart conceived.

Until one misty morning, she met a swashbuckling stag,
And together they journeyed to Lake Montague,
Said her stag, 'Reindeer, reindeer, look in the lake and see,
You're more beautiful and brilliant than a swan could ever
be.'

He stops and looks up. "Um, that's all I have for now."

For a moment, I remain speechless. No one has ever written a poem for me before.

I tilt my head to the side. "You wrote that for me?"

He nods, slightly bashful.

"I love it!" I gush with gusto. "I'm a reindeer? Why?"

He smiles an endearing smile. "Reindeers are the only female deer with antlers," he states matter-of-factly, spoken like a man who watches the Discovery Channel.

"You picture me with horns?" I make an exaggerated face.

"No! Not horns!" He laughs. "*Antlers*. Reindeers are gorgeous creatures," he says, sounding bizarrely like the late Steve Irwin. "And I find their antlers so majestic, and so regal."

I clear my throat. "In the poem, I . . . err . . . um, I assume that you're my swashbuckling stag?"

"Art imitating life," he admits with a lopsided grin.

Leaning forward, I peck him on the cheek. "Thanks. For the poem *and* for being my stag."

Abruptly, he veers it back to work. "Maddy, if Ajon offers you the tech writing gig, *take it*. I know you'll be good at it."

I bite my inner lip and remain silent.

He takes my hand and laces his fingers through mine. "When the timing is right, and when you feel comfortable with the idea, how do you feel about us moving in together?"

I'm slightly taken aback. Mika is laying all his cards on the table. And he sounds so serious about committing. *To me!*

"You mean you'd want to move out of the dorms?" I tease.

"Well, you can't live in the dorms when you are no longer a student," he deadpans.

"Mika!" I shriek ecstatically. "When are you graduating?"

He smiles broadly. "In a month."

My head is spinning with all this news.

"You're graduating, you're getting a new job *and* you want to move in with me?"

It's a lot to take in.

Seeing my open-mouthed expression, he treads lightly. "Let's just take it one day at a time, okay? You and me . . ."

I nod and toy with the crumbs on my plate.

"I'm getting another latte. Do you want anything else?" he asks and I shake my head. He consults the chalkboard menu on the wall. "Hmm. I can't decide what to get."

"Here, try my latte." I hold up my cup. "It's pumpkin spice."

My cup bears a trace of my Burt's Bees Watermelon lipstick.

Holding my gaze, he tilts the cup to his lips and sips from the exact same spot of my lipstick smear.

I swallow hard. That felt sexier than a kiss.

Mika returns my Styrofoam cup and I bury my nose in it, not trusting myself to speak.

He gazes out the window, his latte long forgotten. "It still looks brutal out there."

"Um hmm," I agree airily.

Still gazing outside, he says, "I don't think it's safe for us to be driving home in this weather."

"Umm hmmmm," I hum noncommittally. "I don't suppose so."

"So . . . should we get a room?"

"A room?" I part my lips and play dumb.

"They have hotels here, don't they?"

"I believe they do . . ." I trail off unsteadily.

His lips twist into a quirk smile. "Shall we go?"

"G-go where?" I ask like a blithering idiot.

He pins me with his gaze.

My heart is thumping away like hail on a windshield.

"Err . . . what about your latte? I thought you wanted to order another one?" I stall. "And don't you still want to go to the Billy Goat Tavern? Cheezborger! Cheezborger! Cheezborger! No fries—chips! No Pepsi—Coke!" I run my mouth like a mad woman.

What the hell is wrong with me?!?

Thankfully, Mika doesn't seem to notice my lapse in the sanity department.

"Forget about the latte," he says in a thick voice. "And forget about the Billy Goat Tavern."

And the rest . . . well let's just say that a lady doesn't kiss and tell. And since I'm not a lady, I'll say that he is *indeed* a stag, in every sense of the word.

Cough. Size is most certainly *not* an overrated commodity.

The next day, we take the red eye flight to Pocatello; or Poky, as the old-timers call it.

And to an unsettling degree, Poky is starting to feel a lot more like home.

Twenty Seven

Clank, clank, clank, clunk, clunk, clink, clank, clink, clunk.

"What the hell is that sound?" I ask in alarm. "Mika, take the wheel," I instruct and he swiftly complies.

Rolling down the window, I crane my neck back.

Oddly enough, I don't see anything unusual. But I can still hear that loud clunking noise.

"Maddy, just drive! Keep your eyes on the road," Mika orders in a stern voice.

Grudgingly, I peel my eyes away and try to focus on driving. But each time I step on the gas, my car just sputters, and I can still hear that damned clanking!

Mika grips the dashboard. "Pull over when you can."

Clank, clank, clank, clunk, clunk, CKLUNKTH.

Then silence.

Warily, I peer at the rearview mirror. To my absolute horror, my muffler is sitting right in the middle of the road. Cars and trucks are swerving in all directions to avoid it.

"My muffler!" I cry and swing my car to the curb.

Mika hops out. When the coast is clear, he makes a break for it. Shaking with laughter, he jogs back with my muffler. "Sorry, babes, but this thing has *way* surpassed its glory days."

That's a nice way of putting. "Can't I drive my car without a muffler?"

"You mean for good?" he asks in a perplexed voice and I nod.

"Um, no. It's not legal." He tosses the muffler onto the back seat. "Don't worry, I'll order you a new one."

"I can do it myself," I say a little too quickly. After all, I am used to taking care of myself; been doing it for years.

Mika ruffles my hair. "I know you can, but let me take care of it, okay?"

"Okay." I hit the gas and drive home in my muffler-less Subaru, praying that I don't get ticketed.

Going from being *friends* with Mika to *dating* Mika has been an easy transition. We still do all of the same things, the only difference is, we spend more time together and we're a lot more affectionate with each other. Every day, Mika gives me back rubs, shoulder rubs and leg rubs, and I love receiving them. After sitting in front of a computer for eight hours, my shoulders and neck are usually stiff, tense and knotted up.

"My back hurts," I'd simper and shoot Mika an injured princess look. That's all it takes! I'd be treated to a full on massage with long kneads and gentle strokes.

Now this may sound a little pre-emptive, but we have since moved in together, and I sometimes marvel at how much has changed in such a short amount of time.

Kars wasn't too bummed about me moving out since she has found a new best friend in Pamela Pornero, one of the Call Center Termites who had snagged the team lead position the same time she did.

Since becoming a lead, Kars now hangs out with the 'elite' squad. She claims it's all a ruse, but she's slowly warming up to the Bimbo Termites she'd once reviled. The very day I'd moved out, Pamela Pornero had moved right in.

But Kars and I remain close friends. We just move around in different circles. And I never tire of teasing her about her porn star flat mate.

For shits and giggles, Kars and I had once made up porn star names for ourselves. She was Karsynn Bangs and I was Maddy Cherry Poppins.

Conveniently, I still live in the same apartment complex as the Bangs-Pornero household. Just on a different floor— the first floor. The elevator here is always out of commission and after a brutal day at work, the last thing I want to do is mount twelve flights of stairs.

I do miss Kars, but I love my new flat mate.

Mika and I are happy homebodies. Tonight, like most nights, we find ourselves unwinding in our new apartment.

"How was work?" I ask and scoot over to make room for him on the sofa.

He plops down next to me, rests his head on my lap and tells me he's too tired to talk.

"C'mon, tell me." I tickle him playfully as he tries to snuggle up to me.

"Well, working at Greenworth is *way* better than working at Lightning Speed, but I'm on my feet all day long, and it can be taxing at times."

I lightly trace the edge of his jaw. "I'm sorry."

"Don't be." He burrows his head in my belly. "I like my job. Enough about me; how was work at the Lightning Speed call center?"

I groan with displeasure. "I wish lightning would strike that place down."

He laughs. "Suck it up! You won't have to work there much longer."

"You've got that right! Monday is my last day," I say with a mixture of awe and disbelief.

Momentarily, I find myself mentally revisiting the whirlwind of the past few weeks. Exactly fourteen days ago, I'd submitted my resignation after Ajon had presented me with a very enticing offer. I couldn't believe my deaf ears when they'd said they wanted to hire me and pay me seventy-five thousand dollars a year! I was overjoyed by their offer, but I'd remained undecided. For the first time in my life, I'd found myself at a crossroads, filled with sudden trepidation.

Should I stay with Lightning Speed? Or should I go with Ajon and become a tech writer?

Or should I pull a Frost and take the road less traveled by and write my own book?

For as much as I'd wanted to accept Ajon's offer, I was scared shitless. *What if I don't live up to their expectations? What if I'm not good enough?*

I'd kept laboring over my decision.

Thankfully Mika, Kars, Ingeborg and Truong were there to offer their undying support. Even my supervisor, Douglas, was thrilled for me. He'd put things into perspective when he'd said, "If you want to write, this call center is not for you. You've already reached the ceiling here, and I am confident you can go a lot further."

And I knew deep down inside that it was time for me to leave the call center. My dream was to become a writer, and I owed it to myself to pursue that dream.

Mika jolts me out of my reverie. "Let's not talk about work anymore." He sidles closer and I nestle comfortably into the curves of his arms. Closing my eyes, I relish our cozy existence.

"Hey, babes," he mutters. "I'll need to work on your car this weekend. The muffler I'd ordered came in today."

"Umm hmmm," I murmur lazily.

"Babes," he whispers.

"Mmmm?"

"My arm is numb. Can we switch positions?"

Sitting upright, we readjust ourselves on the sofa. Then Mika beings surfing the channels with one hand and musses my hair with the other.

Um, what does he think I am? An Irish Sheepdog? Lassie?

He has this annoying habit of stroking my hair. Actually, *squashing* my hair would be a better way to describe it, since it looks like a steamroller had just steamrolled my head.

And it doesn't help that I have straight, flat and BLEH hair that's completely lacking in vitality and volume. Every morning, I spend half an hour blow-drying it to give it an ounce of bounce, and then Mika just squashes it when he sees me.

I fluff up my hair. "Want to watch a DVD?"

"Sure," he says. "Whatcha' got?"

I pad across the room and slide the DVD into the player. "*Planet Earth.*"

The documentary unfolds. In one scene, a polar bear leaves his newly born cub in search of food, but it has no luck, thanks to global warming. By the time the polar bear finds his prey, it is too weak to hunt and too weak to go on.

And the next thing I know is, the film crew leaves papa polar bear to die. DIEEEEEEE!

"WHAT? Couldn't the film crew have done *something*?" I cry in righteous indignation. "They could've saved that polar bear's life. C'mon already! They could've air dropped papa bear some food!"

"Calm down." Mika begins stroking my hair. "They're letting nature play its course. That polar bear is in the wild."

I flip. "That's complete bullshit and you know it! If a film crew is there, they're no longer technically in the *wild*," I hiss, making air quotes with my fingers. "And you do not have helicopters zooming about and high-tech cameras filming in the *wild*. Plus, if I see some animal starving to death in the wild, you know what? I'll still help it! It makes no difference where it is. If an animal is dying and you are there to witness it, you're supposed to *do something*."

In another scene, a baby elephant gets separated from her mommy. Oh no! I feel a rising panic in my chest when the baby elephant follows the tracks—the *wrong* way.

And now the baby elephant is lost and guess what?

It is left to DIEEEEEEEEEE!

"NOOOOOooooooo!" I wail. "This is too freakin' messed up!"

Mika laughs and ruffles my hair.

"Sorry," I say, getting off the sofa. "But I can't watch this."

Mika tugs me back toward the sofa and gathers me firmly onto his lap. "I can watch this some other time." Then he nuzzles my neck, taking in the smell of my perfume. "I can think of better ways to be entertained."

"Oh yeah?" I whisper.

"Oh yeah." Standing up, he scoops me into his arms. "Urrrrggh," he grunts, showing off his brute strength.

I slide my arms around his neck. "Am I too heavy for you?"

"Uh-huh, must be from eating all those cinnamon rolls," he says in a teasing voice.

"Will you still love me if I turn into a chubby Cinnabon?"

"I'll love you more!" He drops a kiss on my lips. "You could use a little more meat on your bones." Heading for the bedroom, he carries me over the threshold like it's our honeymoon night and kicks the door shut. Then he plops me on the bed and jogs to the bathroom.

"Be right back, babes," he hollers over his shoulder.

I drape myself seductively across the damask duvet. Taking a deep breath, I fluff my hair and wait, jittery with anticipation.

Moments later, Mika emerges from the bathroom.

Holding out my arms, I bedazzle and bewitch him with my Jezebel charms, wearing a come-hither, sex-kittenish expression.

To my surprise, instead of sliding under the sheets with me, Mika hops onto his Stud Bar.

Heaving a big sigh, I resign myself and wait. It'll be another thirty minutes before he comes to bed.

Months ago, when Mika had mentioned in passing that he loved his Stud Bar, I'd assumed he frequented some seedy bar, and that thought didn't really sit well with me since the Mika I'd come to know and love just did *not* seem like the barfly type. Just to be certain, I'd googled 'Stud Bar' and a website popped up for a gay bar in Montreal. It was described as being one of the most virile establishments in town.

For obvious reasons, I was flummoxed beyond words.

Not only was it a bar, but um, it was also a gay bar?

In Montreal?

Now, after living together, I'd finally discovered that his much beloved Stud Bar is a steel, pull-up bar that mounts to the studs in the ceiling.

And every night before retiring to bed, he is up on that Stud Bar, doing thirty pull-ups followed by thirty chin-ups.

Just like tonight.

By the time my Stud Muffin is ready for bed, I am nodding off to sleep. "Mika . . ." I mutter drowsily into my pillow. "If you buff yourself up too much, your head will shrink *way* out of proportion to the rest of your body."

Slipping into bed beside me, he wraps the duvet around us and nuzzles me lovingly. Smothered in darkness, I can feel the strength of his wanting, and he proves that his *other* head is not in the least bit affected.

Ahhhhhh. Bliss. And double bliss. After some mind-blasting love making, Mika spoons me from behind and whispers a Scottish folk song in my ear. It's my favorite love song and I'd only mentioned it in passing once, yet he'd took it upon himself to memorize most of the lyrics.

Resting his chin on my shoulder, he sings in a hushed and sleepy voice . . .

My love is like a red, red rose,
That's newly sprung in June;

My love is like the melody,
That's sweetly played in tune.
So fair art thou, my bonnie lass,
So deep in love am I;
And I will love thee still, my dear,
'Til all the seas gang dry.
'Til all the seas gang dry, my dear,
And the rocks melt with the sun,
And I will love thee still, my dear,
While the sands of Life shall run.

PHWOAR! It's not Gaelic. But it's pretty damn close!

"Maddy," he whispers, "*mo chridhe*."

Gasp. *Mo chridhe* is Scottish Gaelic for *my heart*.

I think I may have just died and gone to heaven. Twice.

The weekend rolls by and Mika, my MacGyver, spends all his time in the garage, tinkering with my Subaru. And I've noticed that he's been putting gas in my car. It's such a small gesture, yet I'm undeniably touched. Being taken care of for a change, well it sort of feels . . . nice.

Before I know it, it is officially my last day at the Lightning Speed Call Center. Mika kindly took the day off from *his* work to share this momentous occasion with me. All I need to do is go in, sign some papers, gather my things and leave.

"You ready?" His face glows with elation.

"What are you so excited about?" I ask, grinning myself.

"Well, I'll be driving you to *that* place for the last time *and* you'll finally get to see what I've done to your car. C'mon, let's check it out."

"Wait," I say in a panic. "Have you seen my sunglasses?"

His mouth twitches. "It wasn't my turn to watch them, babes."

"I'm not amused."

Taking charge, he puts one hand under my elbow, steers me out the door and leads me to my car.

"Check out your new muffler," he gestures, pink with pride.

I stand frozen at the revelation. "Good Grief! Those suckers are gargantuous."

This is not a regular muffler. *No.* This is a rice burner muffler slash exhaust system.

Meanwhile, Mika is looking exceedingly pleased with himself. "Doesn't it look awesome?"

"Err, I guess." I manage a tepid smile.

Seriously, I could have bolted on a sewer pipe in lieu of that monstrosity of a muffler, and it probably would have looked the same. Actually, it would have looked better.

"Thanks, but um, it's not a stock muffler like I'd wanted."

"Why buy stock when you can buy aftermarket accessories for a better price?" he states matter-of-factly.

I am laughing inside. Oh my God. Mika has ordered me a fart can muffler. "Just in case you hadn't noticed, I drive a Subaru *not* a Honda Civic."

"This is a Magnaflow," he intones with a grandiose sweep of his arm.

As if I'd know the difference.

"This is *not* a ricer. Ricers are modified cars with all show and no go. This, my dear, is a tuner. Magnaflow mufflers have a much deeper and richer sound. It's a lot more muscular. Let's take it for a spin. You'll see," he says reassuringly.

We slide into my car and snap on our seatbelts. As I rev up the engine, I hear the ferocious roar of my new muffler coming to life.

On impulse, I floor it and we're soon flying down the freeway like fugitives in my souped up Subaru. Hahaha. I'm surprised to find myself enjoying every minute of it.

Blaarrrrrgggggghhhhhh blares my new muffler.

"Now all I need are some fat rims and lowering springs," I shout over the loud racket.

"Really? I'll order 'em for you," says Mika in all seriousness.

"No, don't!" I say at once and jab him in the ribs. "I was just kidding. Mika, you're my boyfriend, *not* my mechanic."

His lips curve into a thin smile. "I can be both."

We exit off the highway and my Subaru rolls to a stop at the lights. Abruptly, I hear an arrogant rev of an engine. Turning my head, I come face to face with a *real* ricer. The Honda Civic has a wing attached to the back.

I suppress a snort. The wing looks like a park bench.

Arrogantly, the young punk jerks his head at me and revs up his engine.

Mika elbows me. "I believe he wants to race you."

I regard the driver with frank amusement.

VROOOM, VROOOM, VROOOOM! He begins tapping his gas pedal.

The light turns green and the ricer screeches off, leaving skid marks all over the road.

Languidly, I gently ease off the brakes and drive like Little Miss Daisy.

"Maddy!" Mika balks. "We need to do an engine swap so we can smoke the shit out of ricers like him."

"Shut up, Mika. You're not coming near my car ever again."

He laughs and tousles my hair.

Sigh. My hair is permanently flattened, and I have a fart can muffler affixed to my car.

Twenty minutes later, I swing my car into the Lightning Speed parking lot and stall the engine. Mika tells me he'll wait for me outside. Taking a deep breath, I start for the building and feel a sudden thrill compounded by happiness, relief and trepidation.

Sailing into the office, I walk by Truong's cubicle for the very last time. He throttles me from behind and jams me in a headlock. "Hey, we're still celebrating your farewell at Phở Hoa tonight aren't we?"

"Phở-king right we are!" I laugh, breaking free from his puny grasp.

Glancing briefly to the left, I catch Ingeborg looking distressed.

"Arch and I vill be there. Maddy, ve vill miss ya so much. It vill neveh be de same here vithout you," she chokes with emotion and bursts into tears.

"Oh, Ingeborg," I soothe. "I'll miss you guys more than you'll ever know, but we'll still be in touch."

She sniffles. "Yah, ve vill. Facebook me and Twitter me, okay?"

Karsynn barges into our intimate gathering. "We're going to party it up at that Vietnamese noodle house tonight!"

"Yes we are." I link my arm with hers. "And you can come, just as long as you don't bring your porn star friends with you."

Kars pulls a face. "Humph! Just so you know, Pamela is *not* my best friend. We're already fighting over the remote. If I have to watch one more episode of *Keeping Up with the Kardashians*, I will shoot myself."

Truong snorts with laughter. "Stop pretending! We know how much you just *love* your new airhead friends. Speaking of which, let's line them up in a row and create a wind tunnel."

"Okay, Kars," I smirk. "I've changed my mind. You can bring Pamela Pornero tonight."

"I don't want to," she harrumphs. "Pamela wouldn't *get* any of the subtleties of a Vietnamese noodle house. She actually thinks the Vietnam War is still going on, *and* she thinks Vietnam is in Africa!"

Abruptly, Hilary pokes her head out of her watch tower and gives us the *look*. "What's with all this ruckus? You people have calls to take! GET BACK TO WORK NOW OR ELSE YOU WILL ALL BE WRITTEN UP!"

The fiery Führer does not make idle threats, and so the crowd quickly disperses.

"Madison!" Hillary growls and beckons me with a whip of her head. "Get over here."

Cautiously, I make my way to her desk. "Yeah?"

"I hear you're leaving us," she states with some hesitation and I give a slight nod. "Well, good luck," she mutters grudgingly.

I force a smile. "Um . . . thanks," I say stiffly.

"And if they're ever hiring managers at Ajon, I'd appreciate it if you'd let me know," she remarks in a perfunctory fashion.

I jerk my head up in surprise. "I will."

Rising ceremoniously to her feet, she looks me squarely in the eye. "Sometimes, it's not easy being a manager here."

At once, I feel a flicker of hope. Hope for Hillary the Giant Not Ready Nazi. This whole time, I'd vilified, demonized and ogre-rized her so much that I'd lost sight of the fact that she, *too,* might be suffering alongside us, that she, *too,* might be under pressure from *her* bosses at the top.

She'll always be as popular as a pork chop in a synagogue, but this is a good start.

Before her hard-won pork chop exterior cracks any further, Hillary promptly dismisses me. "You'd best get going now. I know Douglas is in his office waiting for you to sign your dismissal papers." She extends her hand and I shake it firmly.

"Don't come back to this place, Maddy."

"I don't plan on it."

Half an hour later, my dismissal papers signed, I hoist the cardboard box into my arms, ready to walk out of this place for good. For some inexplicable reason, I find myself stalling.

Spinning around, I gaze out at the infinite sea of cubicles. The ocean of calls will continue to flow and flow. And flow. The tide may ebb, but it never dissipates. For twenty-four hours a day, seven days a week, three hundred and sixty-five days a year.

I am profoundly humbled by my experience here, and I harbor a deep respect for everyone that works in this call center. They come from all walks of life: mothers who work to supplement their family income, college students who support themselves, fathers who juggle two jobs, grandparents who can't survive on social security alone, military men and women on reserve (even a couple of marines and Navy Seal officers), veterans, farmers who no longer find farming a lucrative business, an anesthesiologist who lost his license, small business owners who filed for bankruptcy. They're folks like you and me, just trying to make a living.

Oh sure, there's the occasional child molester and crazy meth addict. Pocatello *is* the meth capital of Idaho, after all. But for the most part, they're good, honest, hardworking people.

And if there's one thing I've learned during my time here is that there's humanity in this place. We're not machines. Most of us have good intentions and genuinely want to help our callers.

Despite our best efforts, all too often callers forget that we're human. They say things over the phone that I'm positive they'd *never* consider saying face to face. And if a caller said half of that crap to my face, there'd be two decks— me decking the caller, and the caller hitting the deck.

Or is it two hits? Me hitting the caller, and the caller hitting the ground.

Either way, it'd be an aftermath of blood and guts.

Out of my peripheral vision, I spot a group of new hires in 'nesting.' And I find myself smiling in spite of myself. Little do they realize what they have signed up for. They are probably just treading water at this point, but soon they will be flailing away in shark infested waters. The waters I'd swam in for over a year.

And without a doubt in my mind, I know that some of them will drown. The turnover rate here is exponentially high. This job is clearly not for everyone.

It's a dirty job, even worse than scrubbing toilets.

A toilet doesn't talk back. But the callers do. And they throw feces at you. *Okay, no more 'bodily function' metaphors.*

Metaphors aside, when callers are being verbally abusive, dropping F bombs and threats, and we're on the receiving end of a constant bombardment of complaints, rants, and negativity, it somehow affects us after a while.

Trust me, I've seen my co-workers break down in tears and suffer from nervous breakdowns. But I guess I can sort of see both sides of the equation. Oftentimes the customers' complaints and frustrations aren't without merit. They don't call us when they're happy or satisfied; they only call when there's a problem and they're pissed off. And Lightning Speed only adds more fuel to their raging fire by forcing them to go through a barrage of prompts: *If you need help with your password, press 1. If you need help getting online, press 2. If you need help with your cell phone, press 3. If it is a billing issue, press 4.* And it goes all the way up to prompt number 12.

The highly annoying automated attendant harasses the callers with a dizzying tree of numbers. Not surprisingly, some callers get confused and punch their way into oblivion. And then when you add on the interminable hold times— *Sheesh!* By the time the callers get to me, their blood pressure is skyrocketing through the roofs; they're ticking time bombs ready to explode!

The callers unleashed their rage on me when they were upset with Lightning Speed, and yes, I was forced to swallow the brunt of the blame and take the flack because I'd represented the company. But I wish I could've said, "Yes! I agree with you! This company sucks! And it's not *me*. It's *them*. I'm handcuffed by this demented system! Screw Lightning Speed. Leave. Don't give them your business!"

On top of that, management never stopped breathing down my neck to get my calls wrapped up in two minutes or less, because the shorter my calls were, the more calls I could take. And the more calls I could take, meant the more I could sell!

It's *sick.*

I was stressed and pressured from all sides—from the callers, from management and from the QA bastards. It is no wonder call center jobs rank among the most stressful in America, on par with firefighters, cops and paramedics.

Squaring my shoulders, I start for the elevator. As I turn the corner, I walk by the Quality Assurance Assholes for the very last time, the brainless KGB squad who delighted in chipping away at our humanity.

Making my way down the narrow hallway, the blinding lights from the Sales Dashboard flash at me like a neon banner at a used car dealership.

Every single call that filters through this center is treated as a sales prospect.

Sadly, I'd become a part of this ugly machine, pushing products and services that the customers didn't want or need. Forced to swear allegiance to the Sales Flag, I'd swallowed the bitter pill of dissent for fear of being arrested by the KGB and sent off to the firing squad.

For some, this job is permanent. Absurdly enough, there is a minority here who actually *like* this job. To say these folks are patient is an understatement. But they insist that they love what they do. From what I've observed, they tend to be religious and immensely forgiving. Or maybe they're just doused on a ton of alcohol and drugs to numb the pain.

And then there are others who keep on working here, some for over thirty years, despite the fact that they're miserable as hell. In my opinion, there's only one explanation for this sort of behavior: battered wife syndrome. In denial about the abuse they suffer, they have come to accept their dismal fates; they feel hopeless, trapped, like they have no other choices, no other options.

I want to seize them by the shoulders, shake them hard and say, "Leave your bastard husband. *Oops,* leave your bastard job! You're strong enough. You can do it. You can find a better job! You can leave this blasted place. At one time, I, too, considered staying. But it's not worth it. If you love yourself, leave!"

For others, this is merely an in-between job before something better comes along. For me, this experience has been a myriad of things. A stepping stone, a small but steady paycheck, a whole lot of stress and diabolically fun.

Someday, I will look back upon this experience with delirious laughter and absolute horror. Make no mistake, a call center is something to be experienced before you can truly grasp the meaning of *a living Hell*.

But it seems as if human beings form the closest bonds when faced with adversity. Call it our natural defense against painful and catastrophic situations.

Consequently, this call center holds a very special place in my heart. This slum, this bleak and dismal labor camp is where my most memorable friendships have blossomed.

Truong will always remain one of my very good friends. He's pursuing a degree in interior design and sticking around until he's done with college.

Saint Ingeborg Draganov, bless her heart. I love that girl like a sister. She's a rare bird; she actually *likes* this job and plans on working here for the rest of her life.

I tip my hat to her; she possesses patience and virtue beyond measure.

And Karsynn, my dear Kars. She and I were buddies before I even set foot in this call center, and we remain the best of friends as I step out. The friendship and bond we share has only grown stronger, not hampered in the least by Pamela Pornero and the rest of the Call Center Termites.

Kars aims to snag a supervisor position in a year and become a director in five. And I have no doubt in my mind that she'll succeed. She's ballsy and determined, plus she's a pro at playing the demented office politics games.

Idealistic and optimistic, Kars tells me that when she claws her way to the top, she'll make some changes. Changes that will help the plight of the people here. Although I hope she'll follow through, I remain realistic.

Arriving at the elevator, I jab the button with one finger.

The elevator door pings open and I step in.

Whirling around, I glance back one final time and realize that I have no regrets. Working at Lightning Speed Communications has given me the skills to prepare me for future jobs. My skin is now tougher than leather. Correction. Tougher than steel. And I am certain that I can handle anything thrown my way.

All the abuse has only served to make me stronger. I emerge from this call center a new and liberated woman, much like Tina Turner after she walked out on Ike.

In the past, whenever I'd called Bank of America, FedEx, Delta, Anthropologie or J.Crew, I'd always been the customer, and I'd never thought twice about the person on the other end of the line.

But I've now had a peek behind the Iron curtain.

I've lived in a world that we all experience but seldom bother to understand once we hang up the phone; a world that was at one time foreign to me.

It became *my* world.

I lived and breathed call center.

And now *I know*. Now I understand.

Riding down the elevator alone, all the memories come flooding back. The rare but occasional nice callers who'd brightened up my days, sweet old ladies who were so grateful and thankful for my help that they'd wanted to send me their home-baked cookies and homemade salsa, the tight-knit friendships that I'd built, the evil management that I'd tolerated, the QA bastards who I will forever despise, the calls—the good, the bad and the ghastly, and all the ones I'd tried to find humor in.

Oddly enough, even a vivid picture of my dingy six-by-six foot cubicle flashes before my eyes. It was my windowless space in this crowded place . . . and it shall always hold a special place in my heart, much like the people who work here.

Truong, Kars, Ingeborg and Mika—*they* were the best part of this job.

The elevator doors pings open.

Dazedly, I make my way toward the exit gates and Security Guard Adnan checks my box. I pass inspection.

"Bye, Missus Lee," he says jovially.

I swipe my badge for the final time and hand it to him. "Bye, Adnan. Take care."

The automatic glass doors swish open and I shuffle out.

Outside, I am relieved to see Mika leaning against the front fender of my car, James Dean style.

Just the sight of him soothes me.

Upon spotting me, a smile breaks over his face. And with long and quick strides, he is soon beside me. "You ready?" He gently pries the box from my hands.

My voice catches in my throat. "I'm ready."

"I know." He touches my hair and brushes it back from my brow. "It's like leaving a small chunk of your life behind."

I nod and swallow hard, not trusting myself to speak.

It feels as if I'm leaving my second family.

"Hey . . ." he soothes, cradling my face between his hands. "Today is an ending, but it's also a beginning."

I rest my burning cheeks against his palms.

He's right. I really should embrace both.

We walk in silence to my car.

He opens my door and I slide in, still subdued. After shutting the door behind me, he jogs over to the driver's side and deposits my box onto the back seat.

Hunched over the steering wheel, he reaches for his keys and shoots me a sidelong glance. "You sure you're okay?"

I smile warmly at him, letting him know that I am.

He switches on the ignition and fiddles with his iPod.

Seconds later, we zoom off and the music begins playing. It's *First Day of My Life,* my favorite number by Bright Eyes.

Leaning back, I close my eyes, feeling the dampness on my lashes.

As the song gathers steam, I whisper languidly, "Mika . . ."

He squeezes my knee. "Yeah, babes?"

I lapse in and out of a semi-meditative state as the car bumps along potholes in the road. "I think I'll write a book. I'll keep on working at Ajon to help pay the bills, but writing a book is something I've always wanted to do." After a thoughtful pause, I declare, "So I'm going to do it."

"Do it," he says, increasing the pressure on my knee. "Have you thought of a title?"

My lips fall into a lopsided grin. Prying one eye open, I tell him, "Confessions of a Call Center Gal."

www.ingramcontent.com/pod-product-compliance
Lightning Source LLC
Chambersburg PA
CBHW020345180626
46812CB00001B/343